The Choreography of Environments

The Choreography of Environments

How the Anna and Lawrence Halprin Home Transformed Contemporary Dance and Urban Design

JANICE ROSS

OXFORD
UNIVERSITY PRESS

Oxford University Press is a department of the University of Oxford.
It furthers the University's objective of excellence in research, scholarship,
and education by publishing worldwide. Oxford is a registered trade mark of
Oxford University Press in the UK and in certain other countries.

Published in the United States of America by Oxford University Press
198 Madison Avenue, New York, NY 10016, United States of America.

© Oxford University Press 2025

All rights reserved. No part of this publication may be reproduced, stored in a retrieval system,
transmitted, used for text and data mining, or used for training artificial intelligence, in any form or
by any means, without the prior permission in writing of Oxford University Press, or as expressly
permitted by law, by license or under terms agreed with the appropriate reprographics rights
organization. Inquiries concerning reproduction outside the scope of the above should be sent
to the Rights Department, Oxford University Press, at the address above.

You must not circulate this work in any other form
and you must impose this same condition on any acquirer

CIP data is on file at the Library of Congress

ISBN 9780197775639 (pbk.)
ISBN 9780197775622 (hbk.)

DOI: 10.1093/9780197775660.001.0001

To Maya, Hestu, Niobe and Oskie

Contents

Acknowledgments	ix
Introduction	1
1. The Floating Staircase and the Choreography of Processions	11
2. Choreographing Nature: The Dance Deck	65
3. Disappearing Chairs and Participatory Dances	130
4. The Picture Frame, Not the Picture: Windows in the Halprin House	177
5. Expanding Home: The Sea Ranch	202
Appendix: Selected List of Exhibitions and Films of Anna Halprin, 2005–2021	229
Notes	231
Bibliography	241
Index	247

Acknowledgments

The writing of this book unfolded across a long stretch of time, weaving together influences both direct and seemingly tangential. There is no direct line as to how influences feed into germinating ideas, but certainly the work of Anna and Lawrence Halprin has been the subject of much of my writing over the past three decades. Up until this book, all of that writing happened during their lifetimes, and, as my colleague the late Joan Acocella once advised me, writing about the dead is far easier than writing about the living. When I began to write about the Halprins after both of their deaths in an effort to understand more fully how the dynamic of their lives together influenced their work, I was liberated to take an unusual approach to their collaborative work. Focusing on the artifacts in their home, including select architectural features and furniture, I found that the objects of the home still seemed very much alive, radiating a vitality as if indelibly marked by the Halprins' presence.

Yet it wasn't so much the death of Anna Halprin in May 2021 (two months short of her 101st birthday) that pushed this long-gestating project forward as it was the sale of the Halprin house in Kentfield, California, in September 2022. Effectively, this marked the death of the house as the Halprin home. Daria, the Halprins' elder daughter, generously let me take a final walk through the house and its grounds with her in late June 2022 just after it had been staged and was about to be listed for sale. It was a farewell to the house and also to the seventy years of influential art innovation that flowed from this site. I wanted to understand the sources of memories the spaces of the house, furniture, and property retained: Where do the fragments of remembrance and history lodge in a building and grounds that once held such rich and vigorous lives? In performance, extraordinary care is given to shaping and designing the spaces in which dance is presented, but what about the spaces in which the lives of those creating dance are lived? How might these settings for daily living help sculpt the visions that shape the art?

Looking back, I am grateful for more than a decade of generous interlocutors and colleagues whose invitations to speak about and pursue my research on the Halprins stimulated my thinking about domestic objects and spaces in relation to dance creation. The opportunities to join colleagues internationally challenged and expanded my thinking. These include the symposium "The City Dance of Anna and Lawrence Halprin," hosted by the Halprin Landscape Conservancy in Portland, Oregon (2008); the Cantor Arts Center at Stanford University and the residency/event "Awaken: Dancing With the Rodins" (2007); the Festival d'Automne/Centre Pompidou, Paris, Anna Halprin celebration (2008); serving as Invited Dance Scholar at Emory University, Atlanta, Georgia (2011); participating in Gabriele Brandstetter's and Nanako Nakajima's conference on "The Aging Body in Dance," the Freie Universität Berlin, Germany (2012); lecturing at the California Historical Society symposium on "The Dance and Architecture Legacy of Anna and Lawrence Halprin," San Francisco (2016); delivering an invited talk at the Los Angeles A&D Museum symposium on "The Landscape Architecture of Lawrence Halprin" (2017); keynoting at the "Radical Bodies Conference" at the University of California, Santa Barbara (2017); delivering invited talks on Anna Halprin at Tamalpa Institute, California (July 2021); participating in the International Conference on Performance and Temporality at the University of Grenoble, France (2021); delivering talks at the Tamalpa Institute Korea in Seoul, South Korea (2021); and speaking at the "Three Landscapes Symposium: The Halprins and JB Blunk," at Blum & Poe Gallery, Los Angeles (2022). Thanks also to Lucia Ruprecht whose 2022 special issue of *Dance Research Journal*, "Queering Dance Studies," allowed me to theorize objects, particularly the skeleton, in relation to Anna's mentor, Margaret H'Doubler.

This book is indebted to the masterful research and editorial skills of Kathryn Dickason. Sophia Cocozza's thorough archival work and persistence were also invaluable, as was Christine Tulley's early feedback. Special thanks to my editor at Oxford University Press, Norm Hirschy, for his early vision and faith in this project and infinite patience with questions. Sue Heinemann, my former editor at the University of California Press and a photographer and living archive of Halprin facts, was a cherished resource. The anonymous readers offered valuable early feedback that helped me think through cross-disciplinary issues. Conversations across the years with Daria Halprin, Rana Halprin, Paul G. Ryan, and Norma Leistiko were foundational in bringing Anna's and Larry's work to life. Years of interviews, conversations, and lunches with Anna at the Halprin homes in Kentfield and The Sea Ranch, as well as several interviews with Larry and scores of interviews with Anna's dancers, collaborators, former students, and associates, made possible the contextual framing of this book. I am indebted to the kindness of archivists Charles Birnbaum of The Cultural Landscape Foundation, Kirsten Tanaka at the San Francisco Museum of Performance + Design, William Whitaker and Heather Isabell Schumacher at the Architectural Archives of the Stuart Weitzman School of Design at the University of Pennsylvania, Nicole Santiago at the Francis Loeb Library and Graduate School of Design at Harvard University, Holly Gore of the Wharton Esherick Museum, Laura Graziano of the Berkeley Art Museum/Pacific Film Archive, Norton Owen of Jacob's Pillow, and Meg Partridge of the Rondal Partridge Archives.

I thank the many photographers, filmmakers, and artists for the use of their beautiful images: Andrew Abrahams and Open Eye Pictures, Kim Beeson for Constance Beeson, Pierre Bal Blanc, David Birnbaum, Rick Chapman, Ruedi Gerber, Giacun Caduff and Vanja Tognola of ZAS Films, Wayne Hazzard, Matt Hagen, Susan Landor Keegin, Paul G. Ryan, Jens Wazel, John Kokoska, Paul Kozal, Sopia Wang, Leslie Williamson, and Laura Whitcomb of the Warner Jepson estate.

Finally, this book is dedicated with love to my emotional home, my family: my daughter, Maya, and my grandchildren, Hestu, Niobe, and Oskie, for their encouragement, love, and joyful presence. I extend special gratitude to my partner, Alan Ponchick, for his unwavering calm, love, and manifold forms of support.

Introduction

The Choreography of Environments: How the Anna and Lawrence Halprin Home Transformed Contemporary Dance and Urban Design explores a seemingly quirky premise: objects and the domestic spaces that movement-based artists, like dancers and urban designers, occupy seep into their aesthetic consciousness, significantly shaping their approach to movement invention and choreography. If these objects and spaces happen to have been designed by a leading modernist architect and landscape designer working with the dancer, then the aesthetic imprint is amplified. Dance innovation becomes pressed into dialogue with spatial, environmental, and urban agendas. *The Choreography of Environments* builds on this premise to consider the use of ordinary objects from a private residence as lenses into viewing dance innovation.

Specifically, this book posits the Halprins' 1950s iconic mid-century modern home and expansive outdoor dance deck as a hidden archive. It explores four objects from their house and gardens (staircase, deck, chair, and window) to trace how, despite the conservative postwar climate, this intimate domestic space became a radical template reshaping postmodern dance invention and its expansion into civic, social, and environmental engagement in the twentieth and twenty-first centuries. The work that happened in this White, middle-class, Jewish American home in a San Francisco suburb paved the way for changes that continue to resonate today across contemporary dance, performance, and urban design. These include defamiliarizing urban landscape and gardens as cloistered theaters where civic identities are rehearsed, orchestrating collective problem-solving and invention, normalizing the nude body, privileging a utilitarian and responsive rather than sentimental approach to dance in the environment, and repositioning choreography as a vital medium for urban planning.

These four representative objects of staircase, deck, chair, and window in the Halprin home are used to trace the burgeoning of dance as a forceful medium for civic engagement and its valorization of the ordinary in movement. Dance, architecture, and landscape design would have a profound

The Choreography of Environments. Janice Ross, Oxford University Press. © Oxford University Press 2025.
DOI: 10.1093/9780197775660.003.0001

2 THE CHOREOGRAPHY OF ENVIRONMENTS

confluence through these shared domestic spaces and objects of the Halprins' lives. Through cross-disciplinary movement and environmental workshops, improvisatory explorations of objects, environmentally responsive design, and group urban problem-solving, Anna collapsed boundaries between work and home, parenting and performing, and retreating into nature and advancing toward civic participation. As she juxtaposed a conservative domestic approach focused on the traditional nuclear family with precedent-shattering art making, Anna rewrote Cold War gender constraints on home life, working mothers, and the containment of sexuality. These experiments expanded categories of her choreography and the sensual body, situating dance training and choreographic invention as practices compatible with domestic and private family life. At the same time, these intersections also re-engaged nudity as a de-eroticized presence in live art and the environment, positioning it as a critical partner in urban culture. Thus, her work illuminated the aesthetic potential of the exposed body as a performance medium in the public sphere with all its sensual, ill, aged, and differently abled complexities.

For nearly seventy years, the Halprins effectively rechoreographed daily life and theatricalized the ordinary in the built and found landscapes of Cold War America using their redwood and glass home, wooded environs, found naturescapes, and expansive dance deck adjacent to Mount Tamalpais and overlooking the greater San Francisco Bay as their foundry. Together their outdoor movement workshops, events, and community-designed urban awareness projects became models for politicizing the daily performances of public spaces, linking idealism and activism in the dancer's body. Watching his wife teach and rehearse daily on the hillside studio below their home, Larry discovered how to choreograph engagement in his urban design projects. Correspondingly, dancing on a cantilevered deck in the midst of a redwood grove shifted Anna's understanding of dance as a fundamental part of nature and environmental design rather than as something removed and rarified. She recast the outdoors as a mentor for poly-attentiveness. Reframing ordinary actions as dance and immersive engagement through urban space as choreography, Anna gained from Larry a sharpened discovery of how public spaces script civic identities and how designed movement in those spaces illuminate social and political forces.

The Choreography of Environments lets individual features and objects in the Halprin house and gardens tell the remarkable story of how, from separate disciplines, Anna and Larry wielded movement. In their work it became a unique medium of twentieth-century experimentation, social power, and inclusion valorizing the prosaic body. Borrowing the concept of spatial bricolage from spatial humanities and anthropology, this project seeks to make salient the poetics and politics of space and the ethics of how the Halprins and their publics used it to mix utilitarian and natural objects from across social divisions to create new cultural identities.

Decades before live-work spaces and home office hybrids became a feature of the postpandemic world, the Halprins pioneered the unique discoveries possible when spaces of art making flowed into spaces of routine family life. Unusual among artist couples of the era in that they had two children whom they raised as participants in Anna's dance works and their joint design/movement workshops, theirs is a story of the private theater of family life and the manner in which living spaces shape the artistic mind. For the Halprins, domestic space scripted and modeled identities, proclivities, and social relations just as profoundly as more traditional public performance spaces did. Their working methods became prototypes for what would emerge decades later in the global turn to work-at-home models. That the Halprins achieved this feat in the daunting conservatism and racism-laced tensions of postwar America is an index of not only their tenacity but also the deep privacy of where they worked and the disarming subtlety with which their innovations began. This arrangement, an artifact of financial privilege the Halprins' comfortable middle-class status made possible, along with the fundamental apoliticalness of their work, allowed Anna the dual identity of a typical 1950s housewife and mother yet with a boundary-pushing art practice in the gardens that allowed her to wear both identities at once. On the dance deck she was an unbridled experimentalist, playing with emotional risk and physical nudity. However, after hours, she hewed to more traditional postwar domestic roles including raising children and maintaining a Jewish home as a priority. Over time the tensions between these two worlds evolved into her aesthetic identity and stamp. Eventually, she found her way into a dance of the practical and the possible. Ironically, it was within this pairing that she also found the radical.

Using the distinctive features of the structures and grounds of the William Wurster–designed house and Lawrence Halprin–designed gardens and dance deck as scripts, *The Choreography of Environments* traces the seventy years of dance experimentation launched from this site. The Halprin house and grounds remodeled how bodies interact with environments and fellow citizens in the public world, offering new paradigms for understanding

4 THE CHOREOGRAPHY OF ENVIRONMENTS

dance, civic spaces, and the systems that sustain them. The body that was incubated from this house and gardens, with their splendid seclusion, would challenge norms of American dance and urban design. It achieved this by being shrouded as acceptable through its honoring of an emphasis on the nuclear family.

The 1950s postwar suburban home was overwritten with Cold War gender roles, family dynamics, and political posturing and thus seems an unlikely locus for reformist innovation. The fact that it was reveals the Halprins as stealth revolutionaries. Drawing on the Halprins' personal archives and years of fieldwork, hundreds of photographs, and scores of interviews, this research leverages personal objects to explore the tensions, collaborations, missteps, and transformative art generated across decades by these two influential California artists and their impact on modernist conceptions of movement and performance. New theories from ecocriticism and environmental studies are referenced as methodologies and means to pose alternatives to what Donna Haraway has called "the ocular-centric epistemologies of art history." In its place, her concept of "tentacular thinking," an epistemology based on the model of a spider that favors touch, trying things out, and nonvisual modes of knowing through multisensory and embodied engagement, is introduced as a model for understanding how the Halprins interacted with their environments.[1]

With the death of Anna in 2021 at the age of one hundred (Larry predeceased her in 2009 at the age of ninety-three) and the sale of the Halprins' Kentfield home in 2022 (their second home at The Sea Ranch was sold the previous year), this is a timely moment to examine the role of novel and ordinary objects in the Halprin house and gardens for their influences on contemporary dance. Nested within this investigation is also the story of the Halprins' reciprocal influence on each other's work. The dual legacy of this iconic American art couple forms the background for this dance-focused exploration. Through their commingling of urban design, architecture, environmentalism, performance, and dance, the Halprins redrew the trajectories of American dance and landscape design. The work highlights how people can become active agents in negotiating the politics of space, manipulating the environment and utilitarian objects around them through everyday actions. This is a practice that Michel de Certeau has framed as *The Practice of Everyday Life*. Anna would rewrite de Certeau, often focusing on the rhetoric of walking as he did, but instead making everyday life a practice of dance.[2]

INTRODUCTION   5

Anna and Larry were both emissaries seeding early twentieth-century German modernism in the American mainstream, a thread woven across the book. It was not just that Anna and Larry were a dancer and architect who happened to come together and let their art influence each other. Rather, they were separately and significantly shaped by the two major experimentalist art streams from Europe flowing into the interwar twentieth-century United States: German dance modernism and the Bauhaus architectural radicalism, respectively. Thus, it is no surprise that they found aesthetic compatibility as they individually pushed further into new territory: each disciplinary foray demanded a rethinking of the body's connection with its environment while allowing it to be alternately compliant and rebellious. The outdoor workshops, classes, performances, and community-designed urban renewal projects the Halprins led became paradigms for politicizing public space. They did this by prioritizing the body's engagement with built and found objects and by framing this as training for social fellowship. Turning daily actions, such as descending a set of stairs, into dance, and daily ambulation through designed urban space into choreography, Anna inspired discoveries of how built spaces impact our bodies—bodies that included the Halprins' own young children as performers and other bodies historically excluded from those deemed viewable in dance. Turning traditional family life into a platform for dance innovation helped seed age, health, and racial and ability diversity broadly in postwar dance. The Halprin home presented four object lessons, each one inviting an elevation of the ordinary in a different way. It did this tacitly by removing the air of exclusivity and eliteness from dance and softening the drive toward formal performance, replacing it instead with the convergence of a movement vocabulary of functional actions, landscape, and eco-consciousness.

The first chapter begins with a close reading of the modernistic floating staircase in the entrance foyer of the Halprin home. The staircase is positioned as an introduction in broad strokes to one of the most iconic features of each artist's work and its locus from this distinct object in the home. Inspired by Arts and Crafts woodworker Wharton Esherick's first floating staircase, its inclusion in the Halprin home echoes Esherick's belief that the design of something should be part of the landscape and not dominate it. Central to this chapter is a discussion of the nature of the practical and aesthetic work the stairs perform. They are a site of transition upstairs to the private bedrooms of the home and, in the gardens, they lead down deeper into nature and ultimately to the creative privacy of the dance deck below. The modernist stairs in the house and the multiple packed earth and wood stairs that wind through the sloping levels of the gardens and hillside are read as inspiration for the lines of bodies moving up and over; steps constitute a recurring motif in Anna's choreography. Symbolically, they are also precursors to what will become Larry's signature use of waterfalls in his urban landscapes. The more varied the stairs of the Halprin property, the fuller the references to water suggest themselves with dirt paths as streams, broader steps as rivers, and steep strings of descending stairs as precipitous waterfalls and cataracts. This frames the argument that movement is one of the key constants for the work of both Halprins and that stairs, and the mini performances of negotiating balance that they elicit, are prophetic.

The many stairs in the Halprin home and gardens index several signature elements in the work of both artists. For Anna, stairs and the simple ambulation of bodies up and down were kinesthetic training, perpetual demonstrations of the marvelous mechanics of the human skeletal system. The rising and falling pace of bodies climbing vertically and descending precipitous inclines echo throughout her works via the repeated actions of dancers climbing up and down cargo nets and lighting scaffolds and across orchestra pits and the uneven terrain of meadows and beaches. This unembellished simplicity of human movement on steps carries the beauty of the ordinary as dance. This is one of the core aesthetics of Anna's embrace of task performance as dance and a way to allow the body at all stages of life to partner with the natural world. In relation to Larry's environmental designs, stairs echo the visual rhythm of waterfalls, one of his most emblematic elements, while modeling how he imported wild nature into urban centers, choreographing it for sound, motion, and tempo. The examination of the various stairs on the Halprin property illustrates how it is not just objects themselves but *how our body experiences them* that sets these discoveries in motion. Key dance works that evidence this, and which are explored, include Anna's *Procession*, *Parades and Changes*, and *Blank Placard Dance*. For Larry, the de facto dance occasioned by encounters with designed urban spaces will be referenced in regard to his *Ira Keller Forecourt Fountain* and *FDR Memorial*, major urban design projects where Anna's choreographic influence of processionals is also deeply engraved.

Chapter 2 looks at the object that is the destination point of the longest cascading set of stairs on the Halprin property: a huge redwood deck. Known internationally as "the dance deck," this is the open-air laboratory where Anna grew the dance works that defined her as a leading contemporary

INTRODUCTION 7

dance artist. The most famous feature of the Halprin property, this irregularly shaped redwood platform cantilevering off the hillside below the Halprin home is where thousands of dancers from around the world came to study, perform, observe, and learn from her. Working in the midst of nature on a dance surface punctured by the gnarled trunks of madrone and oak trees pushing through cut-out openings, Anna and her students stretched dance's boundaries. They developed tools for responding to social issues and resources for awakening emotional healing through movement that celebrated the body as an instrument, an erotic force, a part of nature, and a physical form that was rarely or primarily "just a dancer's body." The result was a radical rethinking of scale, norms, and gestural repertoires of bodies as performing mediums. Working outdoors on the dance deck, the body was rediscovered as a fleshy sensorium, an object alive to tactile discovery. The dance deck would become a literal launching pad for many of the most far-reaching evolutions in mid-twentieth-century dance and theater innovation. It was a theater situated in the heart of family space—and the lighting, staging, and scenic expertise of Arch Lauterer, a highly regarded theater wizard working with modern dancers and choreographers of the period, were behind its novelty as an open-air theatrical space. This chapter explores how the dance deck as an object prompted an investigation of the body as an object. Stages are sites where art becomes public and where bodies take on visibility and legibility and expand the expository potential of the physical. The dance deck was not merely an outdoor space used for dance; it was a radically rethought prototype of a new theater integrated deeply into the landscape and framed consciously by stunning water and flora panoramas. Gradually nature and this found environment became not just background but *context* for dance, a collaborator and partner in a living and evolving relationship.

One of the themes explored in this chapter is the implicit pedagogy of nature and how in allowing trees to puncture the deck, thus honoring the preexisting forest, a new equilibrium between people, nature, and art spaces was modeled on the Halprin property. (What other dance studio has ever had holes cut in the middle of its flooring so that trees could grow through?) Bodies reverted to an animalistically raw sensuality in this space. This chapter illustrates how the deck intersected with the postwar American cult of the body, modernist architecture, private gardens, and domestic nudity as the vanguard of natural living and sexual liberation. The seclusion of the deck fostered concealment and invited disclosure, and Larry and Anna used

8   THE CHOREOGRAPHY OF ENVIRONMENTS

these in different ways as they designed undressed exercises in their influential "Taking Part" summer workshops in 1967 and 1968, normalizing nudism in the private enclosure of the Halprin gardens. At the same time, mainstream home and garden magazines were depicting middle-class American families enjoying nude sunbathing in private enclosed patios. Anna would become a bridge between this and the German *Nachtkultur* (social nudity as a health culture practice originating in late nineteenth- and early twentieth-century Germany), which her college dance professor Margaret H'Doubler sampled, and the postwar sexual liberation and youth culture movements. Two of Anna's major works, *The Bath* and the dressing and undressing section of *Parades and Changes*, and Larry's work on the *Donnell Gardens* and dance deck are highlighted from this fresh perspective of the confluence of *Nachtkultur*, domestic nudity, Cold War suburban culture, and the newly objectified body germinated on the dance deck.

Chapter 3 focuses on the impossibly uncomfortable chairs of the Halprin home as an unusual path into exploring Anna's erasure of the spectator in her dances and Larry's animating of physical engagement from visitors to his urban landscapes. Chairs are customarily objects designed to invite repose. They provide a place on which to rest comfortably while observing and quieting the spectator's presence. This is particularly true when viewing performances, yet puzzlingly, the most prominent chairs in the Halprin house were also the most brutally uncomfortable. Modernist art objects in their own right, chairs like the rough-hewn wooden log chair by artist JB Blunk, "the throne" (as the Halprin family dubbed it), made sitting on the cement floor of the living room a more inviting option. Even the theater seating facing the dance deck refused to yield to relaxation. Instead of sinking into the soft upholstery of traditional plush theater seats, those viewing dance performances on the dance deck had to perch alertly while sitting erect on one of the few narrow, backless, wooden plank benches that were clustered in the dirt at the base of the stairs, just above the deck.

Blunk's "throne" chair is introduced as a gateway to trace this disappearance of the spectator from the Halprins' work beginning soon after the family moved into their custom-designed home in the Marin County neighborhood of Kentfield. As Anna worked on the dance deck, her pieces shifted from proscenium-framed traditional seated audience arrangements to gradually erasing the separations between spectator and performer. Larry's work too eschewed passive spectatorship. Instead of armchairs for docile contemplation, he designed urban environments that increasingly de-emphasized places to sit. "Motation" was the term he invented to describe his use of movement as a starting point to generate form in urban design, and it also references his regard for the human body in motion as a primary environmental design tool. "The environment exists for the purpose of movement," he declared. Just as bodies were pressed into action in the respective works Anna and Larry made, so too the motions of bodies in the house and in performance began to blur as increasingly the choreography of daily life and its functional gestures became the danced subjects of Anna's works and the implicit narratives of Larry's landscape designs.

Chapter 3 draws a throughline from these early beginnings in works like Anna's boundary-erasing *Five-Legged Stool* to her aggressive audience participation piece, *Ten Myths*, and the lighthearted *Seniors Rocking*. Here the spectator is recast as witness, actively receiving, and responding to, the performers' intimate disclosures from an attentive and receptive posture. The emphasis is on supporting and participating by being visually attentive rather than judging. These dances are read as fascinating parallels to Larry's evolving delegation of agency and his evolution of prompts to move spectators into participants in his urban design projects: *Ghirardelli Square* (1962–1968), *Freeway Park* (1969–1976), *Levi's Plaza* (1982), *FDR Memorial* (1997), and *Sigmund Stern Grove* (2005). These environments set visitors in motion through uneven terrain with multiple options for directional changes, prompting them to wind their way through on their own paths and also by similarly avoiding the traditional feature for passive contemplation of a landscape: the park bench. There are spots where one can perch in Larry's urban designs, but places for extended, sedentary repose are rare to nonexistent in the works of both Halprins. This anomaly is used as an entry point into exploring how Anna and Larry reshaped the role of observer into that of active contributor. Both envisioned their art doing important social work to reshape people's relationship to their bodies and the natural environment. This was an understanding that needed to be encountered physically, not just passively and visually. In their reformulation, the model spectator became someone in possession of an empathetically alert body ready to act. Like the stairs and the deck, chairs illustrate how the Halprins rechoreographed the anatomy of domiciliary physicality through a routine household object.

Chapter 4 argues that windows are a fascinating symbol for the Halprins' philosophy of living in, and with, nature and for valorizing the everyday. Windows are read as a means for framing the ordinary in the world outside.

10 THE CHOREOGRAPHY OF ENVIRONMENTS

Revealingly, the majority of the large plate glass windows in the Halprin home focus on routine views of nature. In fact, the side of the house that faces the most dramatic vista—a sweeping view of the greater San Francisco Bay—has few windows that capture this stunning panorama. Instead, throughout the house, all of nature is positioned as equally interesting without a single big focal point or heightened emphasis commanding our gaze to the environment as a spectacle. The home, like the Halprins' lives, is about transparency and the grace and fascination of that which is normally overlooked. Key pieces of evidence from Anna's dances, including her *Hangar*, *Ceremony of Us*, and *Still Dance*, and Larry's *Freeway Park* are explored as meditations drawn from lessons these windows taught about the artfulness of the ordinary and the transparency of interiors at each stage of life. Like a window, these dances can be considered subtle tutorials in seeing.

The Choreography of Environments concludes with a visit to the Halprins' second home, their weekend retreat at The Sea Ranch, the rural development on the rugged Northern California coast that Larry masterminded in the 1960s. Here in Chapter 5, the signature markers of their aesthetic—spare stairs, a wooden deck perched on a hillside overlooking the Pacific Ocean, floor-to-ceiling plate glass windows, and uncomfortable modernist seating—make another appearance, this time as more muted echoes of the original objects in the Halprins' main home. The Halprin house at The Sea Ranch was their base for two influential dance and architecture summer workshops, Experiments in Environment, where in the summers of 1966 and 1968 they prototyped communal problem-solving and creative community formation with a mix of dancers, architects, and designers as workshop participants.

The Choreography of Environments ends by tracing this legacy of domestic objects and architectural features in a home to consider the implicit choreography and pedagogy of the ordinary. Like a prop piece, a stage, an arena of spectatorship on ourselves, and a proscenium arch framing where to look, objects and architectural features of our homes and gardens expand our perception of the world. They rehearse our bodies and senses daily in how to be receptive to what we find outside our door and how to forge new, embodied, sensation-rich relationships to the world from sensory perspectives that don't always privilege just the human and the ocular. The Halprin home is an object lesson, through objects, in how the spaces in which we live exert determining forces on our capacities to navigate the world's urban, political, and environmental challenges and crises.

1

The Floating Staircase and
the Choreography of Processions

The Instinctual Dance of Stair Walking

If there is a single object that sets the body dancing, it is a set of stairs. Domestically, functionally, and theatrically, stairs allow the body to partner with itself and move through space with a rhythm. It's not clear precisely when stairs began to creep into the dance vocabulary of Anna Halprin— but for the visitor to the Halprin home an encounter with stairs is immediate and the impression lasting (Figure 1.1). Entering a home by stepping under a staircase sounds like the opening line of a fairytale. Indeed, walking through the front door into the Halprin house in Kentfield, and stepping directly under the home's floating interior staircase, was both ordinary and exceptional—ordinary because, after all, it was the front door, and exceptional because one was standing under a staircase that seemed to hover in the air. If this was indeed the front door, the mini foyer was curiously scraped of the grandeur and the ceremony of an entrance, replaced by this sly demonstration of engineering and architectural virtuosity. Instead of trumpeting arrival, one slid into a slender hallway shadowed by a levitating staircase with no supports between treads as it marched in a steep rise up the wall and out of view into the private second floor (Figure 1.2).

The sensation for a visitor to the entranceway stairs was one of being swept into an invisible stream, beginning with this plunge into unwitting participation in an architectural sleight of hand. "Trust me," the floating staircase seemed to say. "Yes, there are no supports between these wooden treads. And, did you notice, there is also no side anchor on the right, just one slender pipe handrail? But you will be safe. Just stay alert." Alertness, an openness to risk, a parking of caution at the door, and a dispensing of formalities were the tickets of entry into the home, lives, and art of Anna and Lawrence Halprin.

Passing underneath the staircase, visitors are immediately propelled into the flow of life and performance inside, toward the big island in the compact kitchen, the sunny wall of glass windows extending from the kitchen to the

The Choreography of Environments. Janice Ross, Oxford University Press. © Oxford University Press 2025.
DOI: 10.1093/9780197775660.003.0002

Figure 1.1. View of the floating staircase from the exterior entrance courtyard of the Halprin house, Kentfield, California. Photograph by Ernst Braun. Lawrence Halprin Collection, Stuart Weitzman School of Design, The Architectural Archives, University of Pennsylvania, Philadelphia.

breakfast room, and the long rectangular combined dining room and living room; wherever the gathering of people happens to be, a force impels guests inward. Upon entering, the little *pas de deux* with the staircase helps prompt participation in the flow and community of the Halprin home. Equally important as an introduction to domestic choreography, it also announces the house and its surrounding gardens as players.

The presence of this staircase and its several companion stairways crisscrossing the Halprin property sets in motion subtle yet persistent movement patterns for Anna as a dancer that rippled through her life as a choreographer. Walking on stairs presents a unique test for maintaining dynamic balance. Steps present uncertain challenges to gait because one is always actively balancing. Absorbing the gait disturbance of level changes forces a repeated shift from standing to walking to stabilizing. It involves careful placement of the individual foot in these three dimensions. Effectively the body is unstable in the static sense at all times when walking stairs as

FLOATING STAIRCASE 13

Figure 1.2. View looking down the staircase from the private second-floor bedrooms of the Halprin home, Kentfield, California, c. 1950s. Lawrence Halprin Collection, Stuart Weitzman School of Design, The Architectural Archives, University of Pennsylvania, Philadelphia.

it shifts between foot placement and actively rebalancing, and this rhythm undergirds Anna's work. Stairs demand an immediate attention to the body's position in space and a physical alertness to its proximate environment. This continual and close dynamic between the objects in our lives and ourselves parallels that between ourselves and the physical forms we inhabit—which Pierre Bourdieu theorized as a facet of *habitus*, the way the containers of our lives contour our actions in the world outside. The fact that Anna was a dancer interacting with the stairs of an architect and landscape designer so intimately intensified the impact of domestic space and its objects on her and imparted a unique legibility to the repercussions on her dance work. Like a cyclical ripple effect, the dances she would create as a consequence offered lessons and models of physical responses to designed objects that would in turn influence Larry's own methods of urban design.

In 1951, when the Halprins commissioned the architectural firm of Wurster, Bernardi, and Emmons to design a simple, compact redwood and glass home for them on a dramatic two-and-a half-acre site Larry had picked out on the bayside flank of Mount Tamalpais, floating staircases were still novel (Figure 1.3).[1] They evolved domestically from the 1930s sculpted

Figure 1.3. Front patio and exterior of the Halprin home, Kentfield, California. Photograph by Tom Fox, 2016. Courtesy of The Cultural Landscape Foundation.

wood experiments of Wharton Esherick, who not only floated but also spiraled his hand-hewn wooden treads in arabesques upward, from one level in a home to the next (Figure 1.4). Esherick's work, particularly this staircase, had been featured prominently in the 1940 New York World's Fair in Flushing Meadows. Poised between a staircase and a work of sculpture, it was a major element of the World of Tomorrow displays of futuristic homes and their furnishings. With its treads made of oak and its vertical support of a single redwood tree, this staircase presented simultaneously the rugged past of rough-hewn wood and its modernist future with its silky, smooth finish. "Make it like a puppy's ears," Esherick was known to instruct his assistants as to how smoothly polished he wanted his wood surfaces. In the Halprin home, the opening staircase marched as much as it floated. It was sparely functional and linear, dispensing with the Arts and Crafts funkiness of Esherick's staircases while retaining their quiet drama. Its boards were sleek

Figure 1.4. Wharton Esherick spiral floating staircase on display at the World of Tomorrow.
The Pennsylvania Hill House in the America at Home Pavilion, New York World's Fair, 1940. Photograph by Richard Garrison. Courtesy of the Wharton Esherick Museum.

16   THE CHOREOGRAPHY OF ENVIRONMENTS

and smooth, stained a warm golden hue. It immediately established the open airy yet controlled atmosphere of the home. One ascended or descended. One did not *make an entrance* from either the front door or the stairs. The basic forthrightness of staircase design was honored but accented with a sleek modern utility. This entranceway staircase asserted, as did the other various stairs interlacing the balcony and gardens on the Halprin property, the belief that beauty is derived from utility, not ornamentation or sentimental expression. This also aligned with the credo of Christopher Tunnard, whose book[2] on landscape design was a strong early influence on Larry.[3]

This tension between the integrity of a form and the utility and safety of its functioning as a bodily experience would at times present problems in the Halprins' domestic sphere. This was true in regard to the Halprins' floating staircase during the early years of their life in the home as a young family. Daria, the elder of the Halprins' two daughters, recalled how growing up in the Halprin home, despite numerous tumbles off the edge and slips through the open slats of the stairs by children and, later, grandchildren, the Halprins never modified the design of the staircase. Rather, they just fastened temporary netting along the outside while preserving the open floating aesthetic with the slender metal rail on one side. Rana, the younger sister, recounted matter-of-factly how a childhood friend once got her head stuck between the treads of the stairs, and yet it continued to be a favored play space for children to race up and slide down on pillows.[4] Safety aside, objects in the environment were there to be engaged with, but one also had to be attentive to using the body thoughtfully and respectfully in relation to them. This conception of how environments are performative spaces and our bodies are always in active negotiation with them was one of the key lessons of the remarkable design and art of Anna and Larry. Like the staircase, their work existed in a productive tension between the accessible and the risky, the informal, and the cool aesthetic of modernism. All of these competing tensions profoundly helped to shape the body of work Anna would make across her lifetime on this property.

The Harvard Years and Bauhaus Influence

Larry and Anna's introduction to this modernist aesthetic stemmed from the three years they spent living in Boston as newlyweds. They resided in Boston while Larry attended Harvard's Graduate School of Design (GSD), which combined architecture, urban planning, and landscape architecture. In 1941, when Larry entered Harvard after receiving a graduate degree in horticulture from the University of Wisconsin, and a year before Anna formally moved to be with him, Harvard's program was a thriving center of design innovation. It was headed by Walter Gropius and Marcel Breuer, recent émigrés who fled Germany once the Nazis ordered the closure of the Staatliches Bauhaus, the famed school of design, architecture, and applied arts in Dessau, Germany, that Gropius directed. Harvard's GSD dean, Joseph Hudnut, recruited Gropius in 1937 to chair the School's Department of Architecture. Gropius, and his students and colleagues who joined him, quickly became an important bridge between prewar German modernism, with its utopian vision of a new society where art and artisans were central, and the United States, where modernism was still more practiced within silos of traditional disciplinary divides. This thread of European modernism complemented Anna's own aesthetic lineage, which came from the other great German prewar avant-garde: the expressionist dance (*Ausdruckstanz*) of Mary Wigman. Halprin absorbed this by proxy via her college dance professor at the University of Wisconsin–Madison, Margaret H'Doubler. Although not a dancer herself, H'Doubler made prewar trips to Germany, bringing her students to interact with the German modern dancers at Wigman's school. She also hosted Harald Kreutzberg, the German Expressionist dancer who trained with Wigman, on the several occasions of his tours to the United States in the 1930s. In place of the emotional intensity of German Expressionist dance, H'Doubler's path into premodernism was through a focus on the kinesthetic integrity of the body's skeleton as a system of elemental forms that carried their own structural logic. Years later Anna reflected that this fundamentally architectural approach to movement she gleaned from studying with H'Doubler enabled her to work with the architects at Harvard. It also gave her an essential foundation from which she would launch her own experimental approach to a movement design that, like that of the Harvard designers, was interdisciplinary, empathetic to new forms, and expressive and responsive to the modern age.[5]

The Harvard School of Design was also in the midst of significant changes the year Larry entered to start his Bachelor of Liberal Arts degree. Larry's tenure at Harvard's GSD overlapped those of classmates Philip Johnson (who completed his graduate degree in architecture between 1940 and 1943), I. M. Pei, (1942–1946), Edward Larrabee Barnes (who graduated from the GSD in 1942 and, like Larry, served in the navy), and Paul Rudolph

18   THE CHOREOGRAPHY OF ENVIRONMENTS

(1940–1943). This was to be a watershed cohort literally changing the landscape of American architecture, urban design, and their public reception as well as American life. Gropius was now firmly entrenched, and his shaping of the program was apparent. This was made all the more certain by the resignation of Henry Hubbard, chairman of the Department of Regional Planning, who left in August 1941 after a lengthy tenure. What the resignation meant for Halprin was that he arrived just as Gropius and his associates were newly autonomous in the curricular changes they implemented. Gropius's presence configured Harvard's program in the utopian spirit of the Bauhaus, which under his leadership had advocated for dismantling boundaries between not only disciplines but also hierarchies between art and craft as well as fostering collaborations among artisans, architects, and artists from across art forms.[6] Interviewed decades later about the impact of this experience in the Harvard program, Larry credited it with opening a new understanding of the relationship between his and Anna's respective fields. "A whole new aspect of art was in front of us," he said. "All of a sudden, we saw that all art and all life became one and that we were involved in an art that would include dance, the art of architecture, the art of landscape architecture, the art of design in general and social problems. All of a sudden [these] were intricately linked!"[7]

In less than a decade, Anna and Larry would find their way into a West Coast model of their own mini Bauhaus, replicating and extending this interdisciplinary perspective with a distinctly California spirit. Each would achieve revolutionary breakthroughs in their respective disciplines while at the same time forging unique overlaps between dance and landscape architecture, movement, and the environment. Larry would develop an original sensitivity to form, light, ecology, and history that transcended the rationalism of this Bauhaus education.[8] The stairs on the Halprin property can be regarded as emblematic of how domestic objects in their home became prisms into the aesthetic upheavals each artist's work would generate. Michel de Certeau's theory of how cultural resistance is registered through repurposing common objects is a productive frame for regarding how designed objects in the Halprin home slid from domestic to aesthetic implements by virtue of how dancers and artists interacted with them. "Design is not a frivolous activity" would become a core of Larry's philosophy. "I do not differentiate between design and life. Life and design to me are the same thing, and you can't turn either one of them on and off."[9]

Reflecting further in his final years, Larry observed in an autobiographical essay how the stairs in the Halprins' gardens had been not just paths but literal ties binding their working and domestic lives together. He wrote:

> I decided to choreograph the entire site as a walking sequence that meandered along an ancient logging trail through a redwood grove to a dance deck that would cantilever through the woods and float twenty-five feet above the sloping ground. We felt this linkage would symbolize our life—living and working, learning, and growing together. The dance deck and rehearsal studio sited twenty feet below the house were designed to provide Anna with a personal creativity space that would be connected to the house by a set of stairs that climbed up to her office through an informal amphitheater of benches.[10]

Wurster, whom Larry had met at Harvard, designed the house with his firm and input from both Halprins. Larry designed the gardens and these linkages of stairs, including a staircase that led from the second-floor balcony of the house to a small patio-like deck outside the kitchen's sliding glass doors. In 1954, two years after they moved in, Larry would add the larger exterior dance deck for Anna so she could work on her art without having to leave their young daughters, six-year-old Daria and two-year-old Rana Ida (Figure 1.5).

This second deck was to become the defining feature of the home, rendering it a unique site of art making. The long plank stairs leading to it were a critical liminal zone across which members of the Halprin family daily traversed a work/life intersection, a life/work fusion, and, at times, a life/work friction. The main residence itself was a compact, mid-century modern prototype, but the views the property offered of the ocean, mountain, and forests were astonishing: both expansive and intimate (Figure 1.6). In addition to a panoramic vista of the upper San Francisco Bay and tidal marshes, the hillside site was surrounded by woods of redwood and madrone trees. "It was not easy to find such a dream spot and we looked for a long time before we managed to find a place that met all of our requirements," Larry said, enumerating the property's proximity to the hiking trails, lakes, and redwood forests of Mount Tamalpais; the privacy of it on a street where the children could play safely; and it being a lot large enough to permit expansion beyond the house for a dance studio. "Finally, it would have to be something reasonably priced," he concluded.[11] "It seems very odd now to think that at such a

Figure 1.5. Anna Halprin with young Daria on stairs leading down to the dance deck, Halprin home, Kentfield, California, c. 1950s. Photograph by Lawrence Halprin. Courtesy of the Halprin family.

young age we thought we could afford to build a new house, but in those days Marin County was just being discovered and land was relatively inexpensive," Larry said, reflecting decades later on his and Anna's boldness in taking on the commissioning of a new modernist home. "The bank, however, wasn't

Figure 1.6. View toward the greater San Francisco Bay from the front patio of the Halprin home, Kentfield, California, c. 1950s. Lawrence Halprin Collection, Stuart Weitzman School of Design, The Architectural Archives, University of Pennsylvania, Philadelphia.

interested in loaning money to such a young couple so Anna's father loaned us the money." Larry was referring to Isadore Schuman, a Russian Jewish immigrant who as a teenager had made his way with his brother from the Russian city of Odessa to Ellis Island over the course of a year-long journey

22   THE CHOREOGRAPHY OF ENVIRONMENTS

by foot. Like many Eastern European Jewish immigrants without money or a formal education, Isadore worked his way into retail clothing sales, one of the few labor paths open to Jewish immigrants.[12] Isadore eventually added real estate ownership to his work portfolio and thus understood the value of home ownership for the young family.[13]

In this house, Larry and Anna would find an extreme privacy in an urban setting crucial for creative thinking. "I think both of us shared a real love for being in a natural environment," Anna said. "I don't think I could have survived in New York even if I had stayed because an urban environment is not my place."[14] While Anna credited the rural seclusion and rustic beauty of the property for allowing her to move into experimental models of teaching dance and generating work, Larry found in the same environment the possibility of supporting art innovation while also living a quiet domestic life. "It was possible because of this place that we're in, essentially, to live what you might call a 'normal' life, a normal family life," he reflected in an interview he gave in 1990. "It made it possible for us to do that and carry on our careers at the same time."[15] Indeed, Anna and Larry would redefine not only their approach to art but also their approach to domestic life. Up until she married Larry at the age of nineteen, Anna had planned to become a professional dancer, and in the 1940s she understood that choice automatically entailed forgoing marriage and a family.[16] It was Larry's support of her dance practice that prompted her to revise her plans and re-envision a life on the West Coast as both a parent and an artist. For Anna, in particular, she would discover a stealth creative partner in the environment and stairs built into the natural beauty of the Halprin property. Seventy years later the home remains as secluded, remote, and secret as it had been when it was constructed at the end of a dead-end lane where it remains the only house.

Modest in scale but sweeping in its vision of a new relation between home and the nature around it, the property would become the locus of invention for pivotal approaches to art making for both Halprins. Simultaneously, as a product of the new liberalism of the postwar housing boom and a resistance to the conservative constraints of middle-class values, the house supported and challenged aspects of both. "Our site was steep and forested and its character has immeasurably affected the development of our personal and professional lives," Larry said years later.[17] It was a literal "bauhaus," or "building house"; here they assembled their experimental visions using space, the human body, and the landscape. Although Anna was never actually enrolled in the Harvard program, as soon as she completed her Bachelor of Arts in Dance at the University of Wisconsin in 1942, she joined Larry in

Cambridge. In Boston Anna taught dance at Windsor, an elite private girls' school where most of the students came from families of privilege, and also at a very different site—a settlement house for children from Boston's Black community. In the years ahead Anna would continue to work with racially and economically disparate populations, often using dance, idealistically, to try to bridge differences. She also continued to work on her own choreography, supplemented by occasionally performing for Harvard's design faculty and students. In addition, Anna attended public lectures, periodically sitting in on Larry's classes, including the general design seminar, as well as social gatherings at the GSD, absorbing the Bauhaus workshop approach to creativity and the intellectual liveliness of its Harvard community.

"It was like looking at the whole universe and seeing dance in the perspective of a much broader context," Anna said of being in the circle of Larry's classmates and teachers at Harvard. "The Bauhaus [exposure] was just the most eye opening and expanding experience for me, and the continuation actually of my education at Wisconsin," she said. "I gave classes in movement to students who wanted to do that," she recalled of how in 1943 she began offering dance classes to architecture and design students two nights a week in a studio she rented.[18]

Here she led the architecture and design students into embodied experiences, structured as problem-solving situations in which she asked the students to use the materials in the room, like chairs and tables, to build an environment and then move through it. Pedagogically she was inviting them to physicalize what they were processing conceptually by breaking down boundaries between form and function and using ordinary domestic objects from a house to do this. "Bauhaus architects and artists were so open to the other arts," she said of their receptivity to dance, noting also how much they influenced her in turn.[19]

The Harvard period offered a way for both Anna and Larry to think differently about objects in the home. "All of a sudden we saw that all art, and all life, you might say in a way, became one," Larry remarked when reflecting on Harvard's impact on them and the deep lessons this immersion in European modernism had on both of them professionally.[20] "[We saw] that we were involved in an art that would include dance because [Oskar] Schlemmer had danced at the Bauhaus. And the art of architecture, the art of landscape architecture, the art of design in general and social problems, all of a sudden were intricately linked, and that was what we spent most of our time about."

What Anna specifically embraced was a methodology of investigation and interdisciplinary collaboration—an approach far outside the norm of how she had experienced contemporary dance up until this point. She said:

24   THE CHOREOGRAPHY OF ENVIRONMENTS

> It was an approach to dance and to art that was totally new for me. Because studying at Wisconsin with H'Doubler . . . my approach to dance was on a very scientific level, because she was a biologist. She wasn't a dancer, she simply taught dance because somebody needed to do that . . . but it was purely from the point of view of the person, the person oriented it. [So] I didn't have any conception of the total scope of dance in relationship to theatre, to space, to architecture, to all the other arts, to a social concern about the role of the artist. Then when I went to the Bauhaus [referencing her exposure to the community at Harvard], it was like looking at the whole universe and seeing dance in the perspective of a much broader context. . . . It brought in a whole tradition that has affected me for the rest of my life.[21]

This introduction to disciplinary connections between architecture, movement, and landscape design that the Harvard approach provided primed Anna with a new openness to the lessons in form and function that the stairs of the Halprin home would soon deliver. As early as Larry's student years at Harvard, the Halprins had been outliers in the zeal with which they used their bodies as investigative art mediums. They were active participants in the program's many social events, and their presence at the GSD as public dancers was infamously memorialized on the occasion of a sixtieth birthday costume party given for Walter Gropius in May 1943 by the school. A pair of old black-and-white snapshots capture Anna and Larry in self-fashioned dramatic re-creations of costumes from the famous movement study of the Bauhaus, Oskar Schlemmer's *Triadic Ballet* (*Triadisches Ballett*, 1922). Reflecting decades later on how this period impacted her own art, Anna immediately recalled these social events. "I was so influenced by their parties, which were like no other party you've ever been to in your life!" she said. "They would do costume parties, and people would show up in costumes. They would do free dancing, and it was just wide open."[22] This dynamic of open possibility, coupled with a respect for how function shapes form, was exemplified in Bauhaus experimentations using choreographed movement to consider the body as a formal structure in space. *Triadic Ballet* was the most famous of these and it champions task-like movement performed by dancers and nondancers moving in elaborate geometric costumes along precise mathematical floor grids. Conceived by Schlemmer as a plot-free work performed by three dancers moving silently across three acts that evolve from colorful and playful to darkly ceremonial, it was not so much dance as a staged demonstration of the human body abstracted into its constitutive geometric forms of cones, spheres, and cylinders. The performers executed simple locomotor spatial patterns encumbered by these unforgiving costumes of wood, glass, and metallic constructions representing extreme stylizations of body parts. Their figures transformed the stage into a new formal architectural space. Simultaneously, the body was distilled into *its* architectural essence; this was an abstraction into pure form that would influence the simplification of the moving body Anna's dance would pursue in the privacy of the Halprin property.

Indeed, Larry and Anna were well aware of Schlemmer's dance and design experiments. The photographs of the two of them costumed like *Triadic Ballet* dancers are the most often reproduced images of their Harvard years. In them, Larry, who built their Bauhaus-spirited costumes, displays the awkward discomfort of a nondancing man finding himself in tights, bare-chested and with a large horn-like headpiece wrapped around his brow. Anna, however, wearing leotard and sweatpants, accented by an abbreviated skirt of strings, her face covered with a Cubistic half mask, shines. She is clearly in her element, boldly driving Larry across the dance floor with the charging energy of a machine as he gamely keeps pace. The other staid and modestly costumed pairs of dancers two-step cautiously, hugging the perimeter of the room as Gropius observes with amusement from the side. Anna and Larry comically reference *Triadic Ballet* through Anna's makeshift string tutu and splashed face paint mask and Larry's conical headpiece worn over a large paper collar. But it is the steering of their bodies through public space that really announces their ownership of their prominence on the dance floor and the depth of their citation of Schlemmer's famous movement study. Although it is a still image, there is a discernible angular abruptness to their foxtrot arm positions and the stiff-legged lurching angle of their legs as they endeavor to translate a two-dimensional design aesthetic into fully rounded three-dimensional movement slicing through space (Figure 1.7). Poised to put their own stamp on the Bauhaus aesthetic, and already the objects of attention, and perhaps some envy, the Halprins understood how corporeal engagement with physical space deepens perception. More than just an amusing souvenir from a college soiree, this early photograph reveals how each of them was able to put their body into their understanding of an art and aesthetic. They were physicalizing space and form while anointing the body as central to both.

The second photo commemorates their success. Here Anna holds aloft a champagne bottle that Gropius has just awarded her as first prize for her costume and its animation through her dancing (Figure 1.8). It too is prescient, suggesting how swiftly Anna mapped the design aesthetic of the Bauhaus

Figure 1.7. Anna Halprin dancing with Lawrence Halprin (center) at a costume ball for Walter Gropius's sixtieth birthday, Harvard University, 1943. © Anne Griswold Tyng Collection, GSD History Collection. Courtesy of the Harvard University Graduate School of Design.

onto her anatomically trained understanding of the dancing body. This discovery of dance through Anna's daring spirit will also help drive Larry's architectural innovations. It also similarly hints at how a corresponding anchoring in the ethos of cross-disciplinary and communally built work will shape Anna's explorations in dance, including how the stairs as object play a central force. Many more accolades lie ahead for both in their respective fields as they stand united in this moment through their shared homage to Schlemmer's experiments in fusing motion, space, and the human form. This quest would occupy the boundary-pushing work each would pursue within a few short years from the Halprin home and gardens. The stairs provide a "stepping off" point for how Anna and Larry each abstracted, amplified, and rendered extraordinary the ordinary.

In the postwar period, the Bauhaus legacy impacted a generation of American artists, both those like the Halprins who encountered it at Harvard and those at the Chicago Art Institute and Black Mountain College in North Carolina, influential American arts educational centers where other prominent Bauhaus artist refugees landed. However, not all of the Bauhaus artists

Figure 1.8. Anna (in costume) receiving first prize from Walter Gropius at Gropius's sixtieth birthday party, Harvard University, 1943. © Anne Griswold Tyng Collection, Stuart Weitzman School of Design, The Architectural Archives, University of Pennsylvania, Philadelphia.

who provided this influence were able to do so in person. Schlemmer, who chose to remain in Germany, living in what has been called "inner emigration," registered his defiance about the shutdown of the Bauhaus in a final art gesture from his home in Wuppertal.[23] In 1932 he made a painting of the school's staircase: the despondent and remorseful *Bauhaustreppe* (*Bauhaus Staircase*). Here, those earlier bold bodies of abstraction in *Triadic Ballet* that inspired Anna and Larry's live performance have been numbed into faceless and expressionless figures mechanically ambulating up and down the open architectural planes of the most famous feature of the shuttered Bauhaus school—the imposing open stairs.[24] Memorializing two iconic aspects of the Bauhaus legacy in this final study, Schlemmer drew attention to the grace of the human body's formal beauty set against the school's famous architectural feature that orchestrated the daily motion of its inhabitants (Figure 1.9). One might think of *Bauhaus Staircase* as an encore performance of *Triadic Ballet*, rendered covertly. This gesture would prove prospective as well as retrospective: Schlemmer's visual ode is prophetic of the staircase as an artery of change and metaphor for motion that would re-emerge within a few years,

Figure 1.9. Oskar Schlemmer, *Bauhaustreppe* (Bauhaus Stairway), German, 1932. © Museum of Modern Art, Number: 597.1942. Licensed by SCALA/Art Resource, New York.

separated by a vast geographical distance, now evolved into a visual motif in Anna's dance and Larry's landscape design.

Stepping into Nature: The "Prelude" Stairs

The most frequent destination for dance visitors to the Halprin home lay outside, directly through the kitchen and out a sliding glass door and into the gardens of the back patio on the way to Anna's dramatic outdoor dance studio: the dance deck. Arriving at the deck meant negotiating yet more stairs, but now embedded in the garden. The first of the two sets of stairs to the dance deck presented itself in the form of gently curving wood and loosely packed dirt steps down to a small soil terrace on the lower level of the Halprin home outside where Anna maintained her home office (Figure 1.10). These stairs, and their companion set placed further down the hillside, imprint deeply on Anna's choreographic work. The presence of the stairs in the gardens reflected Larry's parallel aesthetic of using nature as a model for his art and design. More specifically in this instance, these stairs borrow from those found winding through the trails in California's public parks. "The stairs were raw, rustic and raw," was how Rana described the redwood and dirt stairs of the Halprin gardens. "They were just the kind of natural redwood stairs used in the trails around Marin my father was hiking. He liked using mostly materials used in parks, and our property was more like a park."[25]

If we consider stairs as the before-and-after of a waterfall—before Larry's engineered waterfalls in his public works had water coursing through them and, years later, after drought, damage, and neglect had temporarily rendered many of the public ones dry—the stairs in the garden of the Halprin home might be regarded as silent, dry waterfalls. These steps are a prime example. Prior to Larry, water features in gardens were primarily just that, features—static ponds and reflecting pools or basins with spouting jets of water that displayed their artifice even as they wowed with their feats against nature of shooting upward before remembering gravity and falling to earth. A student of water in nature, Larry treated designed water differently, respecting its authentic properties, textures, and qualities. Beginning with his earliest landscape designs, like the Caygill Garden in Orinda, California, which he created in 1950–1951, Larry gave water a personality (Figure 1.11). A photo shoot with Anna, Larry, and local photographer Ron Partridge soon after the garden was completed captures her in dancing dialogue with the splashing water and quintessential California vistas of this hilltop garden. The discipline

Figure 1.10. "Prelude" stairs to the lower terrace of the Halprin gardens, Kentfield, California. Lawrence Halprin Collection, Stuart Weitzman School of Design, The Architectural Archives, University of Pennsylvania, Philadelphia.

Figure 1.11. Anna Halprin dancing on the edge of an early fountain designed by Lawrence Halprin, Caygill Garden, Orinda. Photograph by Ron Partridge, 1951. Lawrence Halprin Collection, Stuart Weitzman School of Design, The Architectural Archives, University of Pennsylvania, Philadelphia.

of traditional modern dance training is clearly visible in her lifted and upright carriage as she poses high on the balls of her feet, her cross-laced sandals suggesting the ribbon-tied pointe shoes of a ballerina. As she balances on the edge of Larry's softly trickling fountain, the full skirt of her blue and white dress billows around her like the rippling surface of the water and the lingering memory of a turn she has just completed (Figure 1.11). Another image that Larry took during this same staged photo shoot captures Anna posing bare-legged in a pale yellow leotard, her body a modernistic constellation of angles as she turns to the side in profile, one hip jutting out and her arms held open as if she has just alighted insect-like on the perimeter of this garden. She is the object of two cameras as she accessorizes the real focus of the photo shoot—the formal abstraction of Larry's garden. While Partridge pulls in for a close-up of Anna, the dancer, Larry remains at a distance, shooting from behind Partridge and framing Anna's spiraling form and its shadow in the water at her feet as if she were the dynamic headwaters of the tiered fountain. Her body here, like Larry's garden, bristles with taut discipline. Every angle of her limbs is as designed and carefully placed as the polished stones and poured

32   THE CHOREOGRAPHY OF ENVIRONMENTS

concrete walkways of the garden's hardscape beneath her. Like this backyard that hovers over the edge of a classic Bay Area view of distant brown hills, there is a dynamism to all the choreographed forms here—living and industrial (cover figure). In both photographs one feels the exuberance of Anna's energy already pushing at the limits of the codified contemporary dance vocabulary in which she has been trained up until this point. Like Larry, she is poised to break through these established conventions of her art form in the next few years. Gravity is something to be resisted here, but soon it will re-emerge as friend, literally grounding her with a weighted relationship to land. Designed poses like these will disappear from her dance lexicon as will sweetly Romantic images of women as naiads and sylphs. Larry too will ease his control of nature, opening his and Anna's art to more of a shared dialogue with and responsive reading to, the environment.

Exploring Larry's designed stairs as dry waterfalls helps illuminate Larry's credo of using expressive forms that evoked processes of nature to render landscape architecture a lesson in ecological sensitivity. For Anna, the stairs of the Halprin home and gardens imprinted kinesthetically as much as visually. Traversing them became a daily warm-up practice and cool-down exercise: before one even reached the deck for class or rehearsal there were scores of steps to be traversed, and afterward, they demanded an arduous ascent up again to the house. Like the influential modern dance choreographer Doris Humphrey, one of Anna's early mentors who reframed the essence of dance as the repeated arc of fall and recovery, Anna would find in the miniature fall and recovery of walking downstairs a movement refrain and patterned physical memory that would seep into many of her dances. This refrain occurs in patterns both subtle and visibly referential.

In 1965, the same year Larry was working on his *Portland Open Space Sequence* of dramatic urban waterfalls and fountains for downtown Portland, Anna premiered her evening-length piece that would become her signature work, *Parades and Changes*, in Stockholm, Sweden. Essentially a paean to stairs, *Parades and Changes* takes bodies in the motion of climbing stairs, descending and ascending scaffolds and ladders, and elongates and customizes them across the aisles of the theater and stage over the course of the hour-long work's five sections. The dancers' stair walking is not the only prosaic and repetitive action culled from daily life that is enacted here. The cascading fall of clothes being removed and dropped on the floor as they undress, dress, and undress again, three times, presents another sequence of waterfall images. So too does their tearing of huge linear rivers of butcher paper, which they repeatedly drop and gather in falling shreds of paper as they prepare to exit the stage through a trapdoor, trailing long strips of paper behind them like water flowing into a drain (Figure 1.12).

When Larry exported this energy of falling water into suburban settings, he choreographed it. He domesticated it. He made it dance. He set it in motion coursing down rough stone stairways. His most consistent movement pattern and visual metaphor for this, across his long career, would be the plummeting descent of a waterfall, the wet and natural precursor to his designed stairs of dry land. The foreshadowing of his work with waterfalls is seen in his design of stairs in the Halprin home where they served as Anna's inspiration. A student of nature's majesty in the High Sierras from the early years of his arrival in California, Larry spent sixty years exploring, refining, and defining the crashing tumble of a high mountain waterfall. He learned how to incorporate it into urban spaces with its movement integrity intact. Huge rushing torrents of water, washing over massive rough-hewn boulders, became signature features of his most acclaimed urban designs. The earliest dramatic example of this in Larry's work was the *Portland Sequence*, commissioned by the city in 1965. This is an eight-block sequence of four designed public spaces including plazas, interactive fountains, and linking

Figure 1.12. Paper-tearing section from Anna Halprin's *Parades and Changes*, Centre Pompidou, Paris, France, 2004. Photograph by Rick Chapman: http://www.rickchapman.com. Courtesy of Rick Chapman.

pathways with the three most dramatic spaces highlighted by distinctive treatments of falling water. *Lovejoy Fountain* was the first of these to be designed and completed, opening in 1966, followed by *The Source* in 1968. Next was *Pettygrove Park*, a quiet oasis of rolling mounds of grass, stonework, stairs, and trees intersected by pathways and without water features, and culminating in the final space in 1970, the dramatic *Ira Keller Fountain* (originally named *Forecourt Fountain* or *Auditorium Forecourt*), a monumental aqueous chorus of movement and sound (Figure 1.13). The larger design of the four sections of the *Portland Open Space Sequence* itself, with one feeding into the next and the next, is itself a processional of landscapes, echoing the Halprin garden in Kentfield, which Larry conceived as "a choreographed sequence of penetrations leading from the house, through the woods, down flights of steps to the Dance Deck."[26]

Like Anna capturing the texture and nuance of water flowing over bare skin in *The Bath*, Larry's *Portland Open Space Sequence* is an immersive meditation on the qualities of flowing water. Inspired by the distinctive natural landscape framing the city of Portland, it begins softly and modestly, like an ascent into the lower-level alpine landscape of the nearby Western Cascade

Figure 1.13. Lawrence Halprin at Lovejoy Fountain, Portland, Oregon. Lawrence Halprin Collection, Stuart Weitzman School of Design, The Architectural Archives, University of Pennsylvania, Philadelphia.

Mountain Range. This starting point for this quartet of spaces is the intimate public courtyard surrounding *The Source*, a small brick chimney with water trickling out of it like an artesian spring. A public pathway then leads to *Lovejoy Fountain*, a dramatic evocation of the rushing streams, foaming waterfalls, and placid pools of the higher regions of the Cascades. Stairs make a direct appearance in *Lovejoy Fountain* in the form of sequences of layered concrete platforms and stepped terraces, many with a spiraling descent that imparts a distinctive rhythm amid the visual image of the froth of falling water. The lush green glade of Pettygrove Park provides a tranquil break through its quiet pathways that lead between office buildings to the dramatic culminating space of the *Ira Keller Fountain* in a greenspace across the street. There, on a steep lot in the center of the city, Halprin built a deep and massive urban waterfall, a thundering cascade of thirteen thousand gallons of water per minute coursing over a rugged wall of jagged boulders twenty feet high (Figure 1.14).

As much an event as a waterfall when it opened in 1970, the roaring water of the *Keller Fountain* became an immediate attraction for waders,

Figure 1.14. Dedication of Forecourt Fountain (later renamed Ira Keller Fountain) in Portland, Oregon, June 23, 1970. Lawrence Halprin Collection, Stuart Weitzman School of Design, The Architectural Archives, University of Pennsylvania, Philadelphia.

36   THE CHOREOGRAPHY OF ENVIRONMENTS

climbers, and dancers, who scaled its rocks and drenched themselves in its plummeting waters. The civic transformation initiated from this *Portland Open Space Sequence* was profound and emblematic of how declining urban spaces might be reimagined and repurposed into interactive arenas. This is one of the ideals that both Halprins, working in their respective disciplines, would explore across their lifetimes. Prior to its contested demolition as part of Portland's urban renewal projects beginning in the late 1950s, the area of the *Portland Sequence* had been an ethnic enclave, home to a predominantly Jewish neighborhood with five active synagogues and also populations of Italians, Greeks, and Roma. This history and the painful legacy of American urban renewal causing the destruction of urban communities were something with which Larry had a complicated relationship as he benefited from access to these newly cleared spaces and at the same time shaped his commissions to redress the estrangement and exclusion caused by urban redevelopment through works that offered inclusion and invitations for spontaneous engagement.

With the Portland project, Larry defied the conventions of both American urban renewal and mid-century modernism, designing the kind of inviting, exhilarating public space of the grand historic plazas of European cities. At the opening ceremony for the *Ira Keller Fountain* Larry had the opportunity to model how civic engagement with his design might be performed. The occasion was particularly timely since the opening on June 23, 1970, followed by just a few days the killing of four Kent State students by the Ohio National Guard during this period of numerous campus protests against the US war in Vietnam. Addressing a group of students standing by as well as a cadre of Portland police officers keeping watch, Larry took the microphone and, gesturing toward the assembled city officials, said: "These very straight people somehow understand what cities can be all about," using the rhetoric of the time to designate the dignitaries as symbols of the status quo but also facilitators of this liberatory public space. Aligning himself with the protesting youth, he continued: "So, as you play in this garden, please try to remember that we're all in this together. . . . I hope this will help us live together as a community both here and all over this planet Earth."[27] Halprin, in his suit and tie, then promptly jumped into the fountain waters. He was followed by the students as they collectively welcomed "play" as a newly sanctioned public activity in American inner cities.

In witnessing the opening of the *Portland Open Space Sequence*, the usually restrained Ada Louise Huxtable, architecture critic of *The New York*

Times, praised it as "what may be one of the most important urban spaces since the Renaissance."[28] Celebrated for its capacity to magnetically draw people into active encounters with public parks and squares through its dynamic merging of design, nature, and social consciousness, the artistry and construction of the *Portland Open Space Sequence* has been credited with changing the history of American urban space.[29] Larry's stairs had become the prototype for a contemporary urban waterfall, an abstracted version of the nearby mountains but also a theme-and-variations play on the fundamental properties of how running, crashing, and quietly ebbing water flows downstairs. Water and stairs are the steadiest recurring motif in the three *Portland Open Space Sequence* spaces with water. Ranging from the diminutive scale of the layered red bricks of *The Source* fountain to the crescendoing drama of *Lovejoy Fountain Park*, stairs and waterfalls represent performances of curated nature as centerpieces redefining American mid-century urban renewal and public spaces in inner cities. Literal waterfalls offer this hybrid of nature as a counterpoint to Portland's cityscape of towering buildings filled with their barren "waterfalls" of stairwells (Figure 1.15).

Long before he designed the *Portland Open Space Sequence*, Larry had begun what retrospectively was the research for it; he made a tradition of taking his two young daughters on annual summer backpacking trips into California's High Sierras where he studied, sketched, and experienced some of nature's most stunning waterfalls. The *Ira Keller Fountain* recreated Larry's vision of the most violent cascading water of the backcountry vistas

Figure 1.15. Ira Keller Forecourt Fountain with high-rise office buildings visible in the distance, Portland, Oregon. Photograph by Jeremy Bittermann, 2016. Courtesy of The Cultural Landscape Foundation.

38 THE CHOREOGRAPHY OF ENVIRONMENTS

he encountered. He sketched, photographed, tamed, and sculpted this power of water for an urban environment and landscape, exporting key qualities of Oregon's Cascade Mountain Range with its hard-edged volcanic features. Like a four-act opera, with the *Ira Keller Fountain* being added last in 1970 in response to the enormous popularity of *Lovejoy*, the quartet of *Portland Open Space Sequence* spaces uses water and the motion of bodies to orchestrate changes in scale, tone, and participation. Just as Anna was exploring processions of dancers across space as an abstraction of the vertical momentum of stairs flattened and elongated, the *Portland Open Space Sequence* would be Larry's first use of processions architecturally in his landscape designs of sequential spaces—an exploration that he would continue through many of his designed spaces including very prominently his late-career *FDR Memorial* in Washington, DC. Stairs imparted a processional rhythm and structure to the works of both Halprins. They were choreographic but also musical, rhythmic, spatial, and nonhierarchic.

The *Portland Open Space Sequence* is notable for its narrative that unfolds across the spaces, beginning with the water burbling up from the ground in the first "room" of *The Source* and flowing to *Lovejoy* and then through a series of runnels traveling across an eight-block expanse of city environment before eventually spilling over into the huge concrete-block cliffs of the *Ira Keller Fountain* and into a still pool below. On a summer day, it is customary to see the public doing its own processional dances on them, down them, and through them. Children jump and splash in the fountain's waters, adults wade in at lunchtime, and marriages have even been performed framed by the cascading waterfalls. Similar to the floating staircase's invitation to curious adults and energetic children alike, for Larry the premise of this fountain is that it is a catalyst for what life in the city should be—a feast of motion, sound, and beauty, with quiet corners that also supply solace. "Participation and activity are essential factors in a city," he wrote in *Cities*, his early treatise on the choreography of public spaces. "One can be a passive spectator in the enjoyment of other arts, but the essential characteristic of the city as an art form is that it demands participation; it required movement through its spaces."[30] Indeed, with the Portland project there are many stories of random passersby, as well as dancers, who responded to the invitation to perform that the waterfalls extend. In *Cities*, Larry catalogs the essential objects and features that give cities globally their identities, and, not surprisingly, he devotes one of its most extensive sections to water, discussing how to program it, sculpt it, and shape the edges of the surfaces over which it will flow so that it will fall freely as it spills.[31] His narration about water in gardens is tinged with affection, revealing how he treats flowing currents of water as others might tend growing plants.[32] Long before public consciousness of climate change, Larry regarded water as a precious ecological resource, and one essential to how he shaped barren urban environments into sites where city dwellers would convene to experience nature and reconnect with its rejuvenating essence.

Lessons from Walking on Stairs

Anna's choreographies offer an interesting parallel to Larry's designs. They essentially explore how nature might be experienced by proxy through patterns of movement shaped by utilitarian actions in the environment and exported to and explored on the stage of the dance deck. Effectively, Larry's experimentations with falling water and ascending structures exported from what he found in the wilderness have a counterpart with how Anna was exploring movement in the backyard, taking the natural found objects and actions of daily life and recontouring and abstracting them into dance. Each was also borrowing from the other's essential medium, creating processionals that were landscaped and designed environments that were also choreographic. The result was the charting of new territory for both. With Anna, gesture amplified became an object of contemplation rather than communication, and with Larry, nature became an object of communication rather than just contemplation. The stairs in the Halprin house and gardens simultaneously prompt and symbolize these engagements and exchanges.

On a practical level it was when Larry was away with the Halprin daughters in the Sierras on their annual summer sojourns into the wilderness that Anna had the expansive solitude to do her most immersive teaching and choreographing in a series of legendary summer workshops. Intended as a break from parenting for Anna, these weeks offered her creative time and unbounded experimentation. Anna had long been drawn to the virtuosity of the ordinary and the ordinary as virtuosity. Like Larry, she was working to bring a new focus to the primacy of materials, a central modernist tenant uniting the work of both. The garden stairs have a transparency about their media of dirt, gravel, rough wood, and fallen leaves, just as Anna's dance sought the frank beauty of the unembellished body in the process of doing blunt direct actions (Figure 1.16). The natural materials of the quiet connecting stairs,

Figure 1.16. Redwood block and dirt stairs in the Halprin gardens, from the Bushell Homes real estate listing of the Kentfield house. Photograph by Jacob Elliott: https://www.jacobelliott.com/. Courtesy of Jacob Elliott.

and the choreographic virtuosity of the little controlled falls they demand, have a parallel in Larry's designs that is both functional in relating to the culture of the moment and virtuosic in how they infiltrate open space with built space, using urban design to put humans in a dynamic experience with the natural world. Anna too honored the essential medium of her art form, the human body, by liberating it from the burden to always represent something or someone. Instead, she allowed it to be, simply and naturally: a human performing responsive actions as she moves through space, an achievement that carries its own mastery of the concrete fleshiness of being in the world. She was striving to break away from what she saw as the hindrance of the conscious mind. "Movement can be a reproduction of nature and if we can break through the controlling mind then we can find our true force," she remarked in her seventies in a personal communication after speaking at a conference in Italy about her use of dance improvisation in the lives of children as a model. "The only way to break through that controlling mind is to go into chaos. That is something I'm just beginning to understand about why I've used improvisation so much," she said.[33]

While the short prelude steps of the Halprin gardens leading to Anna's basement office have none of the drama of these massive public waterfalls Larry would later design, they are important conduits in the Halprin gardens, taking one into a gentle and deeper descent into the property and closer to the pull of the dance deck (see Figure 1.10). These quiet connecting steps provide an echo for visitors, a garden version of the opening floating staircase, just as retrospectively they would provide a look backward at the origin of the momentum of falling in Larry's public environments. Each step of these stairs is a narrow dirt ledge ending in two slender redwood planks whose dimensions give the visual illusion of wooden boards floating atop the rocky soil. The unevenness of the loosely packed platform of dirt pitted with gravel and dried leaves forces the walker into a mini dance, demanding attention to the placement of each footstep. Like a prelude to the huge curling staircase leading to the dance deck just ahead, these little stairs have their own rhythm. They swing the walker in a fanning arch of steps to the right just before depositing him or her near the start of the big cascading steps curving to the left and descending down to the dance deck. Like the wind-up of a swing dancer cueing his partner that he is about to hoist her in a swooshing arc in the air, these short fanning steps signal: "Get ready! The big Lindy flip of the descending stairs to the dance deck is coming up!"

Though not initially as imposing as the entryway staircase, these two sets of garden steps echo not only Larry's fascination with the movement of water but also the stair-stepping rhythm of Anna's daily life as a dancer. Historically, other dancers have been drawn to stairs, most prominently the great tap dancers of the 1930s like Bill Bojangles Robinson and the Nicholas Brothers. Working in one of the few performance genres of the era open to Black performers, these virtuoso artists used stairs to add performable space to tiny stage sets crowded with big bands and musicians, or elaborate sets in the instance of Robinson's film work with Shirley Temple. Staircases thus became invitations to virtuosity. Using stairs as mini stages, these dancers tapped their way up and down, punctuating the visuality of their journey with an acoustic counterpoint: the sharp percussive snap of their tap shoes on polished wood. The Nicholas Brothers' most famous tap dance flash act captured in the 1943 film *Stormy Weather* showcases the two slamming themselves down into full splits as they descend a twin set of stairs. Leapfrogging, the dancers alternate jumping over the head of each other, crashing down in a full split on the step below as they descend, turning their bodies into a synecdoche for the foot. Early Hollywood musicals expanded the scale and reigned in the drama of tap dancing on stairs when White dancers, most notably Fred Astaire and Ginger Rogers, appropriated the vibrancy of the Black tappers in their tidy rhythmic tap numbers down the grand staircases of Hollywood musical films of the late 1940s. This history of stairs in dance is manifested in Anna's own particular response to their implicit rhythmic structure, but rather than try to echo it as a virtuoso feat (the Nicholas Brothers set an impossible-to-equal standard in this regard), she abstracted and peeled away the vertical motion of walking stairs. The reduction that resulted was a pure focus on process and functionality. The stairs were not an excuse but the subject, or, more accurately, the object as subject. This would become a prime lesson of Anna's approach to postmodernism and one of the most imitable and abstractable lessons of her teaching.

Larry also exported his curating of images, objects, and, influenced by Anna, rhythms and movement patterns from the wild environment back into designed urban landscapes. One example is how the implicit theater of water coursing down stair-stepping boulders takes a dramatic turn in Larry's valedictory to his work as a design environmentalist, his *FDR Memorial* in Washington, DC, completed in 1997. Larry called this twenty-year project his "apotheosis" and "the culmination of his life's work."[34] Spread across four distinct rooms, each evoking a historic period from one of Roosevelt's four-term presidencies, the *FDR Memorial* uses water and its motion aesthetically and symbolically. It manipulates different qualities of water to reference Roosevelt's love of sailing, naval leadership, and later water therapy for his paralysis from polio. Larry also uses water autobiographically here, referencing his personal romance with falling water from his treks in the Sierras, which he used to make study sketches and photograph waterfalls; his wartime service at sea in the navy; and skills developed over a lifetime of sending torrents of water tumbling down the bumping descent of massive, stacked stones, echoing the play of stairs on the Halprin property (Figures 1.17 and 1.18).

As part of the theater of water use in the *FDR Memorial*, Larry orchestrated the music of its fall, stair-stepping masses of huge, strategically placed boulders of reddish-hued carnelian granite in the War Room to generate a roar of chaos that also masks the noise of jet planes on approach at nearby Reagan airport. He manipulated the stairs deftly as a white noise musical instrument, a means of scoring the falling water for mood, narrative, and noise abatement. The most dramatic and culminating image of the memorial is that of a blasted waterfall emblematic of the waste of war and the destruction of the built and natural environment. In this penultimate room of the memorial the water crashes wildly, the structure of its conduit shattered, the stairs broken and hurled about the gardens (Figure 1.19). For Larry, visual turmoil and the broken aerated surface of water are textures to be explored and manipulated, and the dry waterfalls he experiments with in the Halprin home and grounds are precursors to this work. The influence Anna had on Larry's work and the nature of their symbiotic creative relationship is discernible in the memorial via the movement patterns through which visitors are led as they view the succession of rooms that constitute this work. In orchestrating his design narrative of FDR's presidency, Larry has implicitly choreographed visitors into a processional configuration that flows through the spaces, each one thematically shaped around a momentous event from FDR's presidency and accompanied by a different acoustic scale of falling water.

44 THE CHOREOGRAPHY OF ENVIRONMENTS

Figure 1.17. Lawrence Halprin's sketch of a waterfall from a hike into the Sierra Nevada Mountain Range, California. Lawrence Halprin Collection, Stuart Weitzman School of Design, The Architectural Archives, University of Pennsylvania, Philadelphia.

Figure 1.18. Lawrence Halprin's photograph of waterfall in the Sierras, c. 1960s. Lawrence Halprin Collection, Stuart Weitzman School of Design, The Architectural Archives, University of Pennsylvania, Philadelphia.

Figure 1.19. FDR Memorial showing "War Room" waterfalls and tumbled granite blocks. Photograph by Roger Foley, 2016. Courtesy of The Cultural Landscape Foundation.

Cascading Stairs and the Drama of Arrival

The most implicitly choreographic stairs on the Halprin property are the dramatic serpentine steps prancing down the steep hillside to the dance deck. It isn't until we encounter this set of stairs that their relationship to Larry's fascination with the movement of water becomes clear. At the same time the pulse of the momentum they animate in the body becomes palpable. Over six hundred feet in length and descending at a steep incline, they literally spill the dancer from the domestic spaces of the house and gardens onto the performance space of the stage of the dance deck (Figure 1.20). These steps echo the design cadence of the redwood boards and loosely packed dirt structure of the fanning short run of "prelude" steps leading to Anna's office, but they add in something more—a rippling series of gently sweeping curves that intensifies the drama of arrival. Like the smaller tributaries of creeks and streams leading to a crashing waterfall, this duo of the smaller stairs and the deeply descending grand stairs evokes the falling water of the High Sierras that was a lifelong design inspiration for Larry. There is no water on these

Figure 1.20. Cascading stairs from outside Anna Halprin's office to the benches above the dance deck. Photograph by Jens Wazel, from his film *An Afternoon with Daria Halprin*, 2022, https://www.jenswazelphotography.com/Series/Stories/Daria-Halprin. Courtesy of Jens Wazel.

stairs, but the inescapable visual rhythm of their descent carries its own music and sonic imprint.

Thus, the repeating sets of stairs of the Halprin property are rehearsals. They are dry waterfalls, riverbeds for the flow of human bodies down, up, and deeper into the spaces of the home and gardens. They are the tributaries that deliver bodies from one environment to another, from the domestic to the artistic. Laurie Olin, a leading architectural historian of Larry's work, lauded his gardens for the Halprin home as part of the canon of mid-century American landscape design and works pivotal to Larry's development out of the more than three hundred residential gardens he designed in the San Francisco Bay Area during this 1949–1961 period.[35] Olin names "the nonrectangular platform" of the dance deck as a fundamental element of the landscape's innovative significance. While he does not call out the stairs leading to it specifically, Olin does note the significance of Larry's masterful work with water as a defining characteristic of his renown. Although no designed water ever flowed down the garden stairs of the Halprin home,

48 THE CHOREOGRAPHY OF ENVIRONMENTS

dancers, spectators, and the thousands of students who studied with Anna over the seventy years of her teaching and performing on the deck most certainly did.

Stairs exercise a ghostly presence in their impact on Anna's choreographic work. Anna took the movement of the descent and began experimenting with the impact dancers moving in linear sequences might produce if they were stretched laterally in movement processions or set on paths ascending and descending obstacles vertically. One can imagine the impact of her watching dancers and students arrive day after day, threading their way down the curving steps to the dance deck, shedding potential dance images with each descending footstep. A graceful descent down rippling stairs sets the body in motion with a unique dynamism. As it descends, the body is essentially moving through a succession of controlled falls with each footstep. Maintaining a graceful upright carriage adds a beautiful tension to this daily feat, a pull through the spine of suspension against gravity, while the foot reaches downward, allowing the architectural structure of the stairs to choreograph each person who steps down it. The artist Marcel Duchamp famously, and ironically, captured this in his precedent-shattering 1912 modernist oil painting, *Nude Descending a Staircase, No. 2*. Here an abstracted figure, represented by a series of nested cylinders and cones stacked so that they suggest the dynamic cadence of a body in motion, is depicted as if in a time-lapse image of descent downstairs. Presciently, Duchamp later commented in an interview that the huge scandal this painting initially provoked when it was presented at the 1913 Armory show in New York stemmed from the fact that his nude was in motion. "One just doesn't do a nude woman coming down the stairs.... It seemed scandalous," he remarked.[36] In fact, in 1887, several years before Duchamp painted his *Nude Descending*, the photographer Eadweard Muybridge had created a series of motion studies, chronophotographs of forms in motion, and these included a nude woman walking downstairs. Duchamp, who was aware of Muybridge's motion studies, noted that while he knew Muybridge's work, it was the idea of depicting the movement of a nude coming downstairs using "static visual means," that is, paint on canvas, to do this that really interested him.[37] Anna's translation of the motion of bodies descending stairs pulled in the opposite direction—toward an amplification of the action of a controlled fall into fuller movement. Eventually she would also find her way to the nude body as a subject in her workshops and dances, playing with it in repetitive structures that echoed the processionals of the stairs.

The outside stairs on the Halprin property intensified the challenges presented by the interior staircase because outside a stunning vista of what lies just ahead teases the walker—the tiered gardens, the dance deck, and the sparkling blue waters of the greater San Francisco Bay beyond. "Look quickly, but watch out," they tease. "Yes, it's a great view, but remember your body." Like waterfalls, staircases are themselves reminders of the captivating sight of the pulse of steady motion, only instead of water, now it is through the controlled falling and recovery of the body. Larry, in fact, once briefly addressed the distinctions between interior and exterior stairs specifically according to the nature of the pace of the kinesthetic experience they demand of the walker. "The point to remember is that outdoor steps require a different proportion than those indoors, largely because the scale of striding and walking is different," he wrote, specifying that indoor stairs need to be proportionally shorter and thus more comfortable, and safer, than their outdoor counterparts.[38] All stairs on the Halprin property then held the potential of danger and injury as in the floating staircase without protection that the young Halprin children negotiated. This epiphany as to how a shift in attention can allow one to harvest the exceptional from the ordinary, to repurpose risk as revelation, is one of several modernist trademarks the Halprins' work advances.

Larry had his own fascination with how topography and space choreographed human movement, and he would develop his personal systems, which he dubbed "motation," for graphically recording, studying, and scripting this on grand scales in urban centers and pedestrian hubs. Stairs have their own topography and motion imperative; they effectively choreograph human movement so that a body descending stairs to take a dance class in this respect is always already engaged in a little dance of descent. The about-to-happen needs to be regarded as already underway by shifting one's viewing frame for where choreographed human movement occurs. Viewed choreographically, the long staircase to the dance deck incorporated an implicit sensation of controlled falling followed by swift recovery as one navigated the narrow tread, each step angling just slightly toward the final destination of the deck below. Offering an experience evocative of stepping down the dry bed of a waterfall, Larry had taken the airborne metaphor of the floating staircase, set it in nature, and transformed it, through the cascading stairs to the dance deck, into an earthy, noiseless, waterless waterfall streaming with people. These various sets of stairs on the Halprin property in a sense all wend a path from the spaces of domestic life

50 THE CHOREOGRAPHY OF ENVIRONMENTS

to the threshold of where the art life begins. Larry crafted a delivery system for dancers arriving to work with Anna and also for Anna and the Halprin daughters, who danced with her, to traverse a footpath that delivers them from home to art and back up again as they transition the consciousness of their body from prosaic to poetic, utilitarian to aesthetic, across the length of the ninety-one-step decline.

The Steep Functional Stairs

In 1975, as the numbers of people attending Anna's classes, workshops, and performances grew, a set of plain, steep wooden stairs was added at the far western border of the Halprin property to shunt students and spectators away from the Halprins' private residence and directly from the parking pad to the dance deck or companion indoor dance studio Larry added for Anna in the 1970s. On occasion, Anna would place signs along these efficient stairs, turning the act of descending them into a miniature exercise in engagement. Even though this staircase was quite ordinary compared to the others, Anna orchestrated it into an experience through this series of do-it-yourself stage directions for every person who walked down the stairs. It began with a hand-lettered poster at the street-level entrance instructing arrivals to recast their descent into an intimate "sensory walk." Sue Heinemann, a participant in several of these beginning in the early 1970s, remembered how instead of a hurried inattentive rush to get downstairs for the start of a workshop, the path of arrival down the steps was suddenly reframed and slowed into a sensual feast as each entrant was cued to transform the passage into a sensory experience filled with the sounds, smells, textures, temperatures, and colors of nature. "Stop. Look. Listen," a hand-lettered directive would suggest. "Pause periodically to just listen to the music of nearby wildlife and distant urban transit; notice Mount Tamalpais off in the distance," the functional stairs themselves seemed to advise. "You have already begun your workshop. It is happening now."

Once a workshop had formally begun and moved deeper into the Halprin grounds, participants encountered other more hidden loamy paths of packed earth steps meandering up and down through moist redwood groves on shaded hillsides (Figure 1.21).

These legacies of what walking on stairs did to groups of bodies, slowing them into deliberate, linear, processional configurations of evenly moving

Figure 1.21. Daria Halprin walking on the loamy stairs through the redwood grove on the Halprins' Kentfield property. Photograph by Jens Wazel, from his film *An Afternoon with Daria Halprin*, 2022, https://www.jenswazelphotography.com/Series/Stories/Daria-Halprin. Courtesy of Jens Wazel.

figures, recur as a motif in many of Anna's most significant dances stemming from these initial years of working on the dance deck. Among the most notable works in which a virtual staircase of linearly moving bodies occurs are *Procession* (1965), *Parades and Changes* (1965–1967), and *Planetary Dance* (1981). *Procession* takes the momentum of the staircase and levels it, presenting the dancers as a successive line of people advancing across the stage. As they walk, they collide with clumps of costumes and props, which they try on and discard, progressing through each article of clothing or wearable prop. The act of self-adornment is presented as a wild and freeing event in itself (a distant, messy homage to those Bauhaus costume parties of the Harvard years, perhaps). Stairs also made an acoustic appearance in *Procession* by way of composer La Monte Young's score, in which he repeatedly hurled empty trashcans down the concrete stairwells just outside the theater at the University of California, Los Angeles as Halprin and her dancers performed inside on stage. Like a sonic analog, the audience heard the thundering crash of metal cans bouncing down the exit stairs just outside the theater while watching the procession of dancers through, up, and over the various encumbrances of props Anna had created for them on stage.

The following year, Anna exported the stairs to Italy. Invited to present a commissioned work with her company at the 1963 Venice Biennale, she shipped a massive cargo net from California to Venice. This mesh rope grid was to be used as the central prop in *Esposizione*, the commissioned work Halprin and her dancers presented at Teatro La Fenice, the famed nineteenth-century jewel box opera house in Venice. The net was draped across the front of the stage, and the dancers used the open loops of the netting as a pliable rope ladder, climbing up, over, across, and through this ropey staircase to the shock and chagrin of the formal Italian audiences who were unprepared for what seemed an undisciplined desecration of their beloved opera house. The cargo net as portable aerial stairs subsequently became a frequent prop in workshops in the woods on the Halprin property. On tour elsewhere, when carting along a cargo net wasn't practical and theater restrictions prevented hanging it, Anna repurposed the backstage scaffolds in theaters, used for changing lights and suspending props, as rolling staircases for dancers to ascend and descend. This moment is captured as a historic image in a historic photograph of the 1964 Swedish premiere of *Parades and Changes* in which the dancers scamper up three stories of ladders angled within the cubist frame of a looming scaffold (Figure 1.22). Scaffolds were also used in subsequent performances in New York where Anna added the challenge of carrying a goat up the scaffold stairs with her as she ascended to a second-story platform (1965–1968). In all instances she and her dancers climb the scaffold ladders with the matter-of-fact directness of students ambulating to or from the dance deck. The staircase is something to be encountered, climbed, and descended with a utilitarian economy while being regarded with the close attention reserved for a choreographic wonder.

As the floating stairs of the Halprin home and gardens were thus exported onto the mainstages of Western theater, the incidental dance they occasioned gained new choreographic legibility. Even when ladders or scaffolds were not literally on stage for the dancers to climb, the stairs as important generative objects in the Halprin home resonated throughout Anna's work and teaching for the duration of her career. As with Schlemmer's painting of the *Bauhaus Staircase*, the attention she directed to the raw labor of climbing and descending stairs and her respect for staircases as objects with their own implicit narrative would be foundational to Anna's aesthetic play with linearity and inexhaustible in the interest it held for her as an artistic and pedagogic

FLOATING STAIRCASE 53

Figure 1.22. Anna Halprin's *Parades and Changes* performed by Charles Ross, John Graham, Daria Halprin, A. A. Leath, Kim Hahn, and Yani Novak at the Moderna Museet, Stockholm, Sweden, 1965. Photograph by Ove Alström. Anna Halprin Archives, Museum of Performance + Design, San Francisco. Courtesy of Katrin Ahlström.

device. What began with the stairs would extend into her incorporation of other routine objects from the Halprin property, presented as new artifacts to be experienced by exploring them physically. Yvonne Rainer, who came from New York to study with Anna on the dance deck during her summer 1960 dance workshop and who would go on to become one of the foundational postmodern dancers, still recalled decades later this novelty of Anna's use of objects in the workshop. "It was where I was first exposed to movement in relation to objects," Rainer said, praising Anna as a great educator.[39]

In addition to working with objects literally in her teaching, Anna explored the de facto choreography that resulted from the flattened staircase: the processional line. Often, she would take a long column of students, distribute blindfolds to everyone, and instruct the group to form a line and negotiate their way collectively across the uneven, root-filled terrain of the woods surrounding the Halprin home in a "trust walk," as Anna dubbed them (Figure 1.23). When the sensory work dipped into deprivation in exercises, as with this adding of blindfolds, participants had to cluster tightly together,

Figure 1.23. Blindfolded walk with Experiments in Environment workshop students on hillside of Halprin gardens, 1968. Photograph by Paul G. Ryan. Lawrence Halprin Collection, Stuart Weitzman School of Design, The Architectural Archives, University of Pennsylvania, Philadelphia.

and forming a blind processional they tentatively negotiated earthen steps that could now only be felt tactilely, not seen.

In removing vision as a tool for negotiating steps, Anna was endeavoring to open students' awareness to the proprioceptive negotiation necessary to ambulate up and down from one part of the sloping terrain of the property to another. Immediately, the students' awareness shifted from their eyes to their feet, and their attention intensified and tuned into the sounds, air temperature, smells, and textures of the ground, anything they could fasten on to assist in their maneuvering safely on the uneven terrain on which they were walking. These trust walks became a standard tool of her teaching, a way of de facto herding students into a snaking procession, binding them together by necessity as they reached out to rest their arms on the shoulder of the person in front of them. The dancers thus extended the reach of their awareness like a human centipede negotiating rocky earth. Processions are aesthetic but when participants link together, they also become configurations of safety and support, particularly on rocky terrain, where each step requires stabilizing oneself and the loss and recovery of balance—just like walking on stairs. Soon Larry too imported this processional use of blindfolds into his design workshops with architects and designers (Figure 1.24). By forcing

Figure 1.24. Lawrence Halprin leading blindfold trust walk in Japan. Courtesy of The Cultural Landscape Foundation.

56   THE CHOREOGRAPHY OF ENVIRONMENTS

awareness of space and environment back into the body, he revealed to walkers how the urban environment is filled with sensate data and qualities well in excess of the visual. At the same time he was also awakening them to how the world is experienced by those who cannot rely on sight and the design considerations this knowledge necessitated. The result was to intensify the experience of design as an exciting encounter with the environment and bodily realities. "I did not want to copy nature," Larry reflected late in life in recounting how sketching on backcountry hikes allowed him to become ever more deeply involved with discovering ways to include natural forces in his design process. Just as Anna was doing, Larry used design to broker a freshly intensive experience with life: "In those studies and sketches I relinquished any romantic notions of nature in favor of a firm belief in its process of growth and change—the evolution of natural form-making, the movement of water. I did not want to copy nature, but I wanted to design an experiential equivalent that would be appropriate for each situation."[40]

Eventually Anna used levity as well as gravity in her treatment of the processional march that chains of walking bodies invited. Her most ironic processional was *Blank Placard Dance*, a dance sited in public space that is a direct commentary on the marching line as a vehicle of civic protest (Figure 1.25). Staged as an outdoor event in San Francisco's Civic Center during 1970, a period of frequent antiwar political demonstrations by sign-carrying protesters, Anna erased the cause and staged her event as a protest for, by, and about protests by having each dancer carry a large white picket sign that was intentionally blank on both sides. The performers' somber demeanor was at intentional odds with the humor of their nonmessage, and what gave it impact was the tight physical efficiency of their march as they walked purposefully while neither advocating nor resisting anything. Anna made this work following her own arrest for staging an improvisatory event on the street outside her Divisadero Street studio with a group of her San Francisco Dancers' Workshop dancers. Her handcuffing and transport to jail via a San Francisco Police Department van happened to be documented by a cameraman Anna had hired to film the group improvisation. The resulting film, *The Bust*, chronicles this unscripted dance of random and chaotic actions colliding with laws of public assembly once the dancers are on the street. In the midst of the chaos Anna steps forward to claim responsibility and is handcuffed and briefly arrested until the $500 bail is posted. *Blank Placard Dance* is her danced response to San Francisco authorities. Having discovered that city guidelines specified that as long as a ten-foot distance

Figure 1.25. Anna Halprin's *Blank Placard Dance*, Market Street, San Francisco, c. 1970. Anna Halprin Digital Collection, Museum of Performance + Design, San Francisco.

was maintained between marching individuals they were not considered a parade or protest and in need of permission to assemble, Anna returned to a public sidewalk and decided to use San Francisco's Civic Center as a site of borderline disobedient civic play, just as Larry did in Portland with his impromptu dip in the *Ira Keller Fountain*. For Anna, just as for Larry, stairs were the precursor on which this processional in public space was built, only now with marching bodies rather than a sequence of landscaped environments as the repeating element.

Throughout her career Anna returned repeatedly to this processional line of bodies as her movement leitmotif. In 1981, when she premiered what would become her annual *Planetary Dance*, she revisited this again, now as a ritualistic configuration (Figure 1.26). Here the line has transfigured into spirals of ritually pulsing participants in this large-scale outdoor work open to public participation. The procession from the staircase has closed into itself, becoming a series of snaking curves and concentric circles, each

Figure 1.26. Drone photograph of the "Earth Run" from Anna Halprin's *Planetary Dance*, in Santos Meadow, Marin County, California. Photograph by Tom Rosencrantz, featured in the film *The Planetary Dance* (2016), directed by Andrew Abrahams. Courtesy of Andrew Abrahams/Open Eye Pictures.

absorbing and expelling participants who walk, jog, or run to the pulsing beat of a drum, flowing like rivulets of water rushing downhill and into larger and larger streams. The performers begin at the peak of Mount Tamalpais at sunrise and then gather together in a meadow downhill at Mount Tamalpais State Park, Mill Valley, California. As the participants mingle, they begin to coalesce as a community in preparation for the tightly rhythmic mass of processional lines and walking, jogging, and running circles of the "Earth Run."

In 2017, Anna was invited to the fifty-seventh Venice Biennale, fifty-four years after her first visit, and it was this *Planetary Dance*, her grandest processional, that curator Christine Macel specifically requested as the work to represent Anna in the main exhibition of this distinguished international art exhibition.[41] A participatory public staging of *Planetary Dance* was also offered for all who wanted to join in. That distant line of dancers single-stepping their way down the stairs onto the dance deck at the Halprin home beginning in the 1950s had long been internationalized as a ritual in scores of nations around the world and was now being memorialized, sixty years later, as an elegant score, a map of the processional line's global art reach. The score for the dance, literally the graphic blueprint for the precise spiraling, arcing, and snaking lines the dancers are to trace on the ground with their bodies, was reproduced on a massive scale, covering an entire wall in the Venetian Arsenale, like an oversized public "how to" manual (Figure 1.27).

Amanda Levey, a dancer who saw the installation and who had performed in a community event of this participatory dance with Anna elsewhere previously, noted the emotional impact this kinetic impulse of crowd movement in lines had on the participants: "How many times in your life do you get to do the exactly same thing as everyone one else, to feel yourself move as part of a larger organism?" she recalled Anna asking rhetorically as she taught the work to a group of dancers including Levey. "I felt the group relax and surrender the need to stand out and be noticed, able to experience the power of the collective," Levey said of the effect of Anna's words and instruction on the crowd. "I distinctly remember the feeling of running in those concentric circles with such a large group. It was as though there was a forcefield created so that my feet did not touch the ground—I felt as though I was flying,"[42]

Figure 1.27. Score for *Planetary Dance*, Fifty-Seventh Biennale, Venice, Italy. Graphic design of the score by Stephen Grossberg; photograph by Sue Heinemann, 2017. Courtesy of Sue Heinemann.

60 THE CHOREOGRAPHY OF ENVIRONMENTS

Levey noted of the circling momentum Anna's score had captured. It was like speeding down a steep endlessly spiraling staircase.

The Afterlife of Stairs in the Halprins' Dance and Landscape Design

In 2014, five years after Larry's death, Anna closed her final personal circle after a lifetime of literal and metaphoric collaboration with him. She led an international farewell performance processional on the pathway of *The Haas Promenade*, his iconic stone walkway and itself an architectural procession, overlooking the old city of Jerusalem, Israel. With scores of Jewish, Arab, Christian, and Druze women on the broad avenue of the promenade, or *Tayelet* (the Hebrew word for promenade), Anna headed a mass participatory peace walk with Israeli local Elana Rosenbaum and her interfaith group, bringing together groups of women from as many disparate religious traditions as responded to an open call for participants (Figure 1.28). Standing shoulder to shoulder about six abreast, the women advanced with the slow pace of an old broad river winding its way through sedimented streambeds. The stairs were now flattened and the poetry of the walk slowed; those youthful sprints up and down the long stairs to the dance deck were softened into a gentle slope and quieted here into a trudging peace march intended to signal compassion, commonality, and the weight of sorrow decades of conflict have deposited on these mothers, sisters, wives, and friends of its victims.

Nostalgically, Anna was reaching back to the inspiration of her earliest walking experience on one of Larry's landscapes, those of his stairs of the Halprin house and gardens, as a way of bringing forward what that discovery of each other's art through the domestic objects and spaces they shared had meant to them as artists and partners with a common Jewish heritage. In a sense she was commemorating, amplifying, and distilling the capacity for a staircase to choreograph those who trod on it through this *Peace Walk*. By honing the afterlife of the stairs into a living line of slowly ambulating bodies, Anna had come full circle through the literal to the metaphoric, the symbolic, and back. She was retrieving the resonance of the Halprin house stairs on a lifetime of her work and her collaborations with Larry and the objects of their home. Practically, walking a level path is one of the final choreographies an aged body can do. It is also one of the simplest and most

Figure 1.28. Anna Halprin holding hands with Susie Goldman Gelman, leading the *Women's Peace Walk* (2014) on Lawrence Halprin's Richard and Rhoda Goldman Promenade, an extension of the Haas Promenade, Jerusalem, Israel. Photograph by Sue Heinemann. Courtesy of Sue Heinemann.

ritualistic. Photographs documenting the Israel *Peace Walk* show Anna, her curly gray hair in a soft cloud about her head, smiling and stepping crisply at the helm of the broad stream of marching women. She is glamorous, as always, wearing a flowing turquoise scarf and loose pants and tunic. The impression she gives is that of a surge of water rushing down the dry and dusty path of Larry's promenade in the midst of the parched physical and emotional landscape overlooking the ancient sites of Jerusalem, including the City of David, the Dome of the Rock, the Mount of Olives, and the rebuilt Hurva Synagogue.

The Yosemite Falls Corridor

A similar gesture of remembrance and summation can be felt from Larry in his last major work, his redesign of the approach to the *Yosemite Falls*

Corridor. Having narrated history through the waterfall, Larry now found himself with the penultimate commission of his career: the National Park Service wanted him to redesign the walking approach to Yosemite Falls, one of the most breathtaking waterfalls in America and a lifelong inspiration for Larry. With the Bauhaus spirit of fusing technologies of production with beauty and functionality long embedded in his own aesthetic and design process, Larry once again took nature as his partner. His ambition was to highlight the awe-inspiring falls so that "the design would feel as if it had emerged organically . . . like it had evolved through the forces of nature."[43] Effectively, he was framing the waterfall as a celebrity, making it the star performer, and creating sites of spectatorship for the public as they came to gaze upon it (Figure 1.29). Subtlety manipulating the found environment of boulders and trees into his design, he enhanced nature, selectively clearing vegetation and orchestrating, like a three-act performance, how the three sections of Yosemite Falls—the Upper Yosemite Fall, the middle cascades, and the Lower Yosemite Fall—gradually disclose themselves to viewers as they approach. Larry also worked to improve visitor circulation, rehabilitating

Figure 1.29. Lawrence Halprin's redesign of the pedestrian approach to Lower Yosemite Falls, Yosemite National Park, California, 2005. Photograph by Phillip Bond, 2016. Courtesy of The Cultural Landscape Foundation.

surrounding habitats by bringing in additional boulders to slow erosion and planting more native plants to protect fragile downstream areas.

Larry completed the Yosemite project in 2005, at the age of eighty-nine, four years before he died. He was gifting the public, where his love of falling water had begun for him, a vista, a theater of awe before a waterfall. His art so evolved that it had now become invisible, indistinguishable from the California landscape that had inspired it those many summers ago spent backpacking in the Sierras. Careful to incorporate wheelchair-friendly viewing sites along the approach to the falls, Larry was making space for bodies of different abilities, bodies slowed by health issues, including advancing age. Two years earlier, in 2003, he had suffered the loss of vision in one eye due to an ulcer on his cornea. From that point forward, he wore a black eye patch over his right eye, but his larger vision remained undiminished as he continued drawing, designing, and seeing the world as it *should be* ever more clearly. As his valedictory to falling water, he offered the experience of a beloved waterfall contemplated from the comfort of a home. Poetically, he had redesigned an approach to the majestic Yosemite Falls that echoed that first view of the private gardens of the Halprin home, glimpsed through the sliding glass doors of the kitchen and just past the floating staircase entrance (Figure 1.30). Having begun as an architectural and practical feature of the Halprin home, the stairs were now settled deeply into the aesthetic life of both Halprins. As each shaped their late-in-life works, the residue of the stairs was present for both: each artist took the stairs as object and metaphor and used them to dig into new territory in their respective disciplines. For Anna the stairs had distilled into the purity of the danced processional and a succession of repeated actions. For Larry the stairs of his gardens returned him to the procession of falling water and the paths through nature that brought people to witness this majesty of nature that had never ceased to inspire him.

In the final years of her life, Anna continued teaching up until the COVID-19 pandemic, a few months before her one hundredth birthday. The stairs of the Halprin home continued to inspire her despite her gradual inability to walk them as accidents, injury, and age limited her stability. To facilitate her access to the dance deck, groups of her dedicated students would band together and, interlacing their hands, form a small human sling chair and gently carry her down the long cascading stairs to the deck. When class ended, they gathered together and hoisted her back up again. Undaunted,

Figure 1.30. View of the back deck of the Halprin home from the kitchen, Kentfield, California. Photograph by David Birnbaum, 2022. Courtesy of David Birnbaum.

she had never once complained about the labor of the trek down and up the stairs across nearly three-quarters of a century. Even as the challenges of old age claimed her balance, stamina, and, finally, mobility, she never gave up her desire to traverse Larry's stairs to her space for making dance.

2

Choreographing Nature

The Dance Deck

If someone had to pick the one object on the property of Anna and Lawrence Halprin that has attained the most celebrity, "the dance deck" is the easy winner. At first glance, the leaf-strewn wooden platform on the edge of a steep hillside seems an unlikely candidate to be an internationally renowned dance space. Yet since the 1950s, this space has been a destination for generations of dancers and hundreds of international students and the launch pad for a series of transformative experiments with dance, architecture, and the environment. No object in the Halprin home and grounds has been more photographed than the dance deck, garnered more coverage in the popular media, or received more accolades in articles in art, landscape design, and architecture magazines, and museum exhibitions (Figure 2.1). As an architectural feature that evolved into one of the most internationally known dance spaces in America and a laboratory for groundbreaking transdisciplinary experimentation, this wooden platform occupies a distinct status as object, symbol, and agent. On the surface, the dance deck might seem merely a trendy backyard feature born in the postwar era of mid-century modernist homes, simply appropriated for use by a dancer. Yet viewed from the intersecting perspectives of theater, social history, and the architecture of domestic space, it is a transformative object. It represents a radical fracture for sites of performance; an opening for a new regard of the body in urban, rural, and domestic environments; and a rethinking of how artists and their families interact with the suburban outdoors in their places of residence. The deck was a catalyst, setting in motion new models for the relation of the body to public and private space and introducing new modes of versatility for outdoor decks as spaces of performance and the negotiation of modernism and the American body.[1] The deck carried this force because it was the product of a collaboration between three iconoclastic artists of the mid-twentieth century, each from a different discipline but united in their fascination with the motion of the human form and the implicit imperatives

The Choreography of Environments. Janice Ross, Oxford University Press. © Oxford University Press 2025.
DOI: 10.1093/9780197775660.003.0003

Figure 2.1. The dance deck soon after completion in 1954. The Halprin house, Kentfield, California. Lawrence Halprin Collection, Stuart Weitzman School of Design, The Architectural Archives, University of Pennsylvania, Philadelphia.

of natural and architectural spaces: Anna (dance), Larry (landscape architecture), and Arch Lauterer (lighting and theater design).

"The dance deck" is always formally referenced with those three words: the word "dance" affixed to "deck" as tightly as the smooth Douglas fir planks composing the deck are nestled side by side and hammered snugly onto supporting braces as they wing off the Marin hillside, and the word "the" because of its singularity. At first glance, the dance deck looks like a level platform of wood, but as we draw closer, subtle elevation shifts become evident, contributing to its unique character as a dance space. The dance deck is sharply angular and irregular in form, and bordering the main deck are two smaller elevated decks at its margins; the one to the left is a rectangular platform three inches above the main deck, and the other, a larger irregular rectangle at the furthermost point of the deck, is also elevated just slightly and shaped like the broad prow of a ship (an unintended ironic nod, perhaps, to the origins of wooden decks before they migrated from ships to backyards).

Figure 2.2. Dance deck with view of greater San Francisco Bay. Anna Halprin Digital Archives, Museum of Performance + Design, San Francisco.

This trio of deck surfaces is framed by a low wooden railing with a wire mesh interior that allows unimpeded views of the redwood grove that hugs the deck on three sides and, at the furthermost point, invites a glimpse outward, toward the faint blue of the San Francisco Bay in the distance (Figure 2.2). As with the staircase, the emphasis is on the object's aesthetic beauty, with the wire mesh functioning as a gesture toward safety that is effectively invisible.

The Dance Deck: The Stage in a Suburban Backyard

Part of the novelty of the dance deck for performers was that it combined at the same time a theatrical area situated in a domestic space and a domestic object reoriented as an art-making platform. The theatrical expertise of Mills College Professor Arch Lauterer (1905–1957), a highly regarded theater artist doing lighting, staging, décor, and *mise-en-scène* designs for early modern dancers, was behind its radical novelty as both an outdoor deck and an arena of artistic invention. Early in May of 1954 Larry began soliciting bids from contractors for the building of the deck, scripting very carefully its placement and proviso that no trees were to be cleared, with the exception of two small ones less than four inches in diameter. He further specified that the surface of the deck was to have nails set below the top of the floor and the wood was to be sanded and coated with boiled linseed oil, preparations that would make for a smooth, weather-resistant, and nonslippery dance floor. Within a few weeks Larry was also finalizing Lauterer's involvement in the project. In a June 2, 1954, letter to Larry confirming his participation, Lauterer's excitement is evident as he writes with anticipation of what he already predicts will be the importance of the deck to dance: "You are well underway on the construction of the dance deck, according to Ann who I saw for a few moments at the Harry Partch recording rehearsal," he writes, referencing a musical event at Mills and using Anna's name before she added the "a" in 1972 after surviving cancer. "I am so glad that it is actually a fact—for I am sure it's going to be like a 'shot in the arm' to the dance world with all its problems of economics and art." Lauterer concludes this letter by agreeing to his own relatively modest compensation, suggesting how strongly the opportunity to be part of the deck's design is the prime motivator: "I consider $75.00 a proper fee for the services," he writes. "These included two trips to consult with you; one at your home and one at Berkeley and two examinations of plans for comments and suggestions."[2]

Long before he was commissioned to design the dance deck, Lauterer already had his own developed relationship with nature as a mentor. In the mid-1930s, when Lauterer was working at Bennington College in Vermont, he used to walk a gravel road that crossed over a small bridge near a grove of pines. As Catherine Osgood Foster, a fellow faculty member at Bennington, recounted, Lauterer announced one evening at a party that he had given himself the assignment of walking to the bridge every day after lunch for six months to observe a three-foot-square piece of ground beside the bridge in minute detail. Foster remembered his enthusiasm at how much it was possible to observe and remember in such an unremarkable slip of ground. She noted:

> He gleefully claimed he had learned by heart every pebble, every blade of grass, every stick, every wisp of moss, every crumble of clay. And not only that, he had seen how the light has struck these objects differently in different seasons, and how the shadows and relationships of line and color had changed as the sun moved south through the fall and then as it moved back after Christmas. He had seen how textures looked on cloudy days and how new forms seemed to appear, or new surfaces or lines, when the snow

CHOREOGRAPHING NATURE AND THE DANCE DECK   69

melted away and revealed again some of the objects he had gotten to know so well before the snows came.[3]

This anecdote speaks to Lauterer's capacity to turn himself into a student of the natural world, but with the sharpened senses of a theater artist practiced at building evocative environments rather than uncovering them. Yet in this instance he was viewing the dirt patch with its tiny surface of growing and dried plants as a lighting designer might consider the props on a miniscule stage while determining the best quality and angle of lighting to use to evoke the desired dramatic effect. These were prime skills he would bring to his collaboration on the dance deck. This anecdote suggests the care not just the Halprins but also Lauterer exercised in choosing where to place the deck so that it could capture the play of sunlight and shadows throughout the day as it was engineered to achieve its ends of functionality, inspiration, and beauty.

Foster reported that Lauterer said he was thrilled he had seen something new every day in observing the microcosm of the Bennington landscape. Lauterer suggested his experience would be a "marvelous exercise for a designer to discover relationships between shapes, colors, directions and lighted surfaces." As he enthusiastically recounted his discoveries, Lauterer was challenged by another guest at the event, the composer Otto Luening. Luening asked quietly if he had also *heard* something different every day? Lauterer reportedly laughed with pleasure and responded that now he would have to go back and do it all again the following winter so that he could add an attention to sounds as part of his nature observation. Foster recounted this story in a posthumous tribute to Lauterer to demonstrate how he was "always pushing forward the edges of his awareness." More than that, though, it also reveals an acute sensory attentiveness to nature as a mentor in design and, equally importantly, in perception.[4] Foster's story also demonstrates how modest Lauterer was about his expertise and how readily he accepted correction and a request to "do it over" if a respected artist told him he had missed something—a good skill for his future collaboration with a pair of artists like Anna and Larry.

Lauterer located his own initial inspiration in rethinking stage space, scenery, and especially light as expressive materials in theater productions as dating from his research into the theoretical writings and work of the Swiss architect and theorist of stage lighting and décor Adolphe Appia. Lauterer too operated in the spirit of the Bauhaus, by proxy, through this study and emulation of Appia. Appia's work, in turn, had served as early inspiration for the Bauhaus artists, especially Oskar Schlemmer, who, inspired by Appia's concept of theater as "rhythmical spaces," shaped his 1925 idea of a theater where a rhythmically moving human body is used to explore the connection between space and flat surfaces—precisely the kind of movement study featured in Schlemmer's *Triadic Ballet*.[5] Appia was no stranger to movement (he had collaborated with the French movement teacher Émile Jaques-Dalcroze on several experimental theater and dance productions), and he had argued for a revised hierarchy in theater design so that production elements would cluster around displaying the movement of living performers, highlighting their actions rather than static elements. Lauterer seems to have been particularly inspired by Appia's approach to making human movement the focal point of theater production. Reminiscing about her interactions with Lauterer decades later, it was this quality of a new regard for space in relation to dance that Anna identified as a major insight she learned from Lauterer directly and implicitly through his work on the deck. "I learned a lot about how to keep a focus on the whole stage space when I am dancing from Arch," she said. "He used to always talk about the implied space. His use of space was a much broader idea than dance usually considered," she explained while demonstrating how one could shift focus by pulling back and sensing as fully as possible the entire space surrounding one on stage. "Arch was a great teacher," she continued. "He had such a broad understanding of space."[6]

Achieving this focus on the movement of dancers on the dance deck, without the drama of surrounding nature overshadowing them, would be a delicate calibration for both Lauterer and Larry. To guide attention to the volumetric space of the deck itself rather than glancing past it as simply an empty platform, the irregular contours of its angles helped direct awareness to its interior space instead of toward a vanishing point at its borders in the distance. In addition, the seemingly quirky inclusion of trees puncturing the floor of the deck further pulled attention to the spaces between the trees— the actual open-air volume where dancing bodies move in three dimensions as they play with gravity, stasis, motion, and elevation.

Placed too far from the house to function as a backyard terrace for socializing, and devoid of any of the usual outdoor patio furniture, there is no mistaking that the dance deck, from its very conception, was designed as a unique and exclusive space with specific intentions for a use beyond routine backyard relaxation (Figure 2.3). Its distance from the Halprin house and its setting amid a shaded redwood grove immediately contradict the

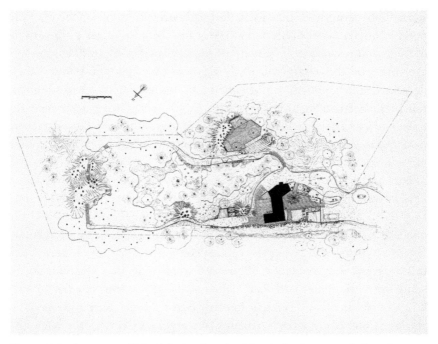

Figure 2.3. Lawrence Halprin's site sketch of the deck placement below the Halprin house, Kentfield, California. Lawrence Halprin Collection, Stuart Weitzman School of Design, The Architectural Archives, University of Pennsylvania, Philadelphia.

usual placement of domesticated decks of the 1950s typically used for outdoor meals, sunbathing, barbecuing, and socializing (see Figure 1.21).

At the time the dance deck was built, the majority of domestic decks were affixed directly to the back of suburban houses as reoriented porches. This use of decks as an architectural feature in mid-century modern homes first came into use a few years earlier, in the late 1940s. A privatizing of the nineteenth century's ubiquitous front porch—which was traditionally a small-scaled platform for neighborly socializing adorned with rocking chairs or porch swings for comfortable spectatorship—decks signaled the opposite. Initially decks were part of a popularization of private social spaces for the new homeowning White middle classes in the immediate postwar years. They offered functionality and suburban seclusion. Decks also signified a new multipurpose use of individual gardens as sites of recreation, leisure, daily domestic chores, childrearing, and personal socializing, all removed from public scrutiny. In contrast to the neighborly points of connection front porches offered, decks reflected a retreat inward into homes as the advent of radio and television shifted end-of-the-day socializing from community exchanges on the veranda to nuclear family time indoors. Into the early decades of the twentieth century, the main rooms of homes had been customarily placed on the front street side of houses since streets were generally quiet and safe arteries where the daily life of neighborhoods flowed past enjoyably. However, by the mid-twentieth century, as streets became noisier, more noxious from gasoline fumes, and less safe, suburban backyards offered a retreat from all of this, especially for White suburban homeowners.

However, if Whiteness is not the presumed standard, a more complex and multifaceted view of the suburban modernist backyard is possible and one that has particular relevance for the Halprins. Architectural historian Kristina Wilson offers what she calls a "counter-history" of modernism to this progressive reorientation of homes toward backyards. She does this by using the work of architect Paul Williams, the sole author of color to publish a book about mid-century modern home design during the postwar era, as a contrasting frame. Williams, she argues, celebrates the backyard, and the increased space of suburban life, as offering freedom and privacy of a different sort: "freedom from prying eyes and privacy from the judgement of White eyes," she posits, introducing a racialized perspective on mid-century modern homes and their backyard spaces.[7] The Halprin backyard was conceptualized in such a way that it could be argued to occupy a midpoint on this continuum between mainstream White and the racialized non-Whiteness of Jews in mid-century America. Add to this the fact that in addition to being Jewish both Halprins were artists, and the dialogue between freedom, privacy, design, behavior, and the backyard environment of their Marin home becomes more complicated. Unsettling Whiteness in this way as the presumed standard for reading modernism, Wilson foregrounds Williams's viewpoint as an African American architect to offer alternative values and focal points. This allows modernism to be read as "a style that is less invested in establishing boundaries against something and more committed to promoting the agency of those living within it."[8] Following the lead of Frank Lloyd Wright, whose mid-century designs popularized decks as a way to maintain privacy but also preserve a connection to the outdoors, decks were used to enhance interior living spaces by merging inside with outside. They often gestured toward this by literally making the deck contiguous with the house, separated by the clear panes of a floor-to-ceiling sliding glass door. In its placement as well as function, the dance deck signaled a radical break from this tradition.

Larry himself was in a career transition in the period prior to the construction of the Halprin house and gardens, prompted by a concern over the elite (White) client base. He was moving from his first professional work as an associate landscape architect in the offices of the nationally acclaimed landscape architect Thomas Church to striking out on his own after being with Church's firm from 1945 to 1949. Larry's last major project with Church was the *Donnell Garden* in 1948, for which he served as project designer. Set on 5,500 acres of cattle ranchland in the Sonoma Hills of Northern California, land owned by Dewey Donnell, heir to the Marathon Oil Company, the *Donnell Garden* is considered one of the most significant gardens of the twentieth century and an icon of California postwar modernist living and design. Described by architectural historian Laurie Olin as "the opening salvo of modern design on the West Coast, [a work] that changed the way we live,"[9] the *Donnell Garden* also rapidly entered the cultural mainstream, appearing on the April 1948 cover of *House Beautiful* magazine. Its status as an icon of modern landscape architecture derives from its quality of curvilinear abstraction echoing images from surrealist painting and sculpture, and what University of California at Berkeley College of Environmental Design Professor Marc Treib described as its presentation of "a new sense of space—modernist space—in which movement of eye and body produced sets of discovered experiences, always new."[10]

The freeform pool, with an abstract sculpture by Adaline Kent rising out of its midst, echoes the curvilinear forms of the bay wetlands in the distance (Figure 2.4). The sweeping expansiveness of the site gestures toward spatial freedom and an effortless flow between proximate and distant landscapes, designed and natural environments. Most significantly for the Halprin house, in addition to the kidney-shaped pool, the garden features an irregularly shaped wood deck, designed by Larry and lined by benches and a railing on one side and set away from the house. In the *Donnell Garden* this deck is placed on the edge of a freeform concrete terrace and pool, and it seems to stretch toward the distant view with its edge suspended twenty feet off the ground and punctured by an open cluster of live oak Live Oak trees that reach up through it (Figure 2.5). The hushed beauty and calm the garden projects derive from the purity and simplicity of its biomorphic forms and the soft abstraction of the pool, stone terrace, deck, paved walkways, and curving lawn. They quietly and gracefully echo the vernacular California

Figure 2.4. Thomas Church–designed freeform pool in the Donnell Gardens, Sonoma, California. Photograph by Millicent Harvey, 2016. Courtesy of The Cultural Landscape Foundation.

Figure 2.5. Donnell Gardens, deck pierced by oak trees. Photograph by Charles Birnbaum, 2005. Courtesy of The Cultural Landscape Foundation.

landscape of the San Pablo Bay wetlands in the distance. Although the dance deck was still six years in the future, with his work on the deck in the *Donnell Garden*—its complex shape, its location perched on a hillside twenty feet up from the ground at some corners, removed from the house, and with edges that rachet out toward a distant view and a surface perforated by the live trees he found growing there—Larry had created a prototype for the dance deck.

While certain features of the deck in the *Donnell Garden* and the Halprin dance deck may be similar, the domestic culture surrounding each was very different. If the *Donnell Garden* presented the California landscape as an expansive visual spectacle, the Halprin dance deck proffered it as an intimate, tactile, and kinesthetic experience. In exporting this exemplar of a deck from an open hilltop on a huge cattle ranch in Sonoma to a small, wooded hillside in Marin, Larry would bridge purpose, class, and politics. Years later, in reflecting on his departure from Church and Associates soon after completing the *Donnell Garden* project, Larry spoke about his motivations as stemming from a growing discomfort he felt with the Church office's focus on "clients who were primarily well-to-do socialite types wanting large gardens designed as places to entertain out-of-doors."[11] "Tommy was apolitical and his gardens were terribly elitist," Larry said.[12] The Donnell family with their extraordinary inherited wealth was an extreme example. "What I was lacking was a true interest in designing for a socially elite client base," Larry explained, noting that he identified himself with "labor movements, Zionism, and efforts to change the political power structure in the world. . . . I wanted to expand my design potential into a broader-scale community work. I wanted to break out of the 'garden box' and work on large-scale projects. I wanted to expand the ideas of landscape design into new realms of social importance including architecture and art." Once he opened his own office in San Francisco in September 1949, Larry said he "immediately felt a great sense of liberation and energy."[13]

Larry's move to his own practice marked the beginning of his infusion of these ideals and politics into his design process. The San Francisco Bay area and especially Marin County were particularly hospitable to Larry's interest in discovering how to yoke urban design to issues of social importance. This was a quest that Anna would parallel with her own explorations into crucial social problems through dance. When the Halprins arrived in Marin County in the late 1940s, this North Bay suburb of San Francisco was already taking on its identity as hospitable to iconoclastic artists and political liberals. For Jewish artists like the Halprins, there was an additional point

76   THE CHOREOGRAPHY OF ENVIRONMENTS

of intersection—liberal Judaism. Jewish Studies historian Marc Dollinger summarized Marin of the late 1940s and early 1950s as a region where "a leftist Jewish couple could find a happy place. You are not keeping Kosher, but you are living in nature."[14] Geographically, Marin had only recently been physically linked to San Francisco with the completion of the Golden Gate Bridge in 1937; previously this North Bay suburb of San Francisco was an outpost without easy travel access. However, in the eight years the bridge had been open by the time the Halprins arrived, Marin was on its way to establishing a reputation as a locale uniquely hospitable to artists and where spirituality rather than organized religion was embraced. Leaving the more traditional observant religious practices of their families behind, Anna and Larry had landed in a San Francisco suburban community where Jewish identity was worn as a cultural rather than religious affiliation.

Anna had been preceded in her move to Marin by her Uncle Jack, who had been exiled from the tight-knit Orthodox Schuman family in Chicago after marrying a non-Jewish woman. Jack and his wife fled the Midwest for the far West, ending up in Mill Valley, where an interfaith marriage was not an issue.[15] "We visited him, fell in love with the area, and found a tiny house nearby on the edge of the bay, looking south to the skyline of San Francisco," Larry recounted in describing how their visit to Uncle Jack provided their introduction to Marin County. "There, from the comfort of our first house, I could feel that the war was truly over, the heaviness of the past years transformed into a great outpouring of energy and excitement," he said, referencing his wartime duties on a naval destroyer.[16] The Halprins had joined an influx of Jewish veterans and their families who were benefiting from Cold War policies that enabled homebuying and the opening of new businesses. Across the United States, between 1945 and 1965, one out of every three Jewish Americans left urban centers for the quiet and affluence of the new suburbs.

The Bay Area Jewish community the Halprins encountered had been shaped by an overwhelmingly German Jewish leadership in San Francisco whose politics were assimilationist, favoring the reform side of Jewish religious affiliation. This stance had led to conflict during World War II when, in the face of rising threats to European Jewry, San Francisco's Jewish leaders had rejected Zionism and responded timidly to the Holocaust, refusing to join rising calls of alarm. Yet this accommodation also may have helped lead to a comparatively low degree of antisemitism locally since it allowed the religious community to elide much of the politics associated with accusations

CHOREOGRAPHING NATURE AND THE DANCE DECK   77

of "Jewish tribalism."[17] "They actually downplayed the Jewish dimension of the Holocaust for fear that it would look unseemly if Jews dwelt on the suffering of their own. Also, they staunchly opposed Zionism, afraid that Jews would be accused of dual loyalties," is how Bay Area Jewish history writer Fred Rosenbaum explains it.[18] Rosenbaum uses the label "cosmopolitan" to describe the postwar Bay Area Jewish community's emphasis on social justice and the arts paired with their more secular approach to Judaism.[19] "The Bay Area welcomed iconoclasm," he said, noting that "a lot of the artists in literature and the visual arts were going against the grain like The Beats. The Bay Area is a fertile area for radical works and iconoclasm would have been embraced."[20]

For both Halprins, the philanthropy of the established Jewish families in the Bay Area, many of whom traced their presence back to the Gold Rush, would also become an important support network, funding and commissioning several of Anna's and Larry's works and adding to the resources they cultivated. Nationally, Larry was part of a Cold War–era migration of Jews to places where men could be identified as White and male and not stand out for their foreignness. The draw of places with economic privilege and newness, like the Bay Area, was part of this global phenomenon underlying the Halprins' move to Marin County, and the affordances of being there resulted in their never leaving.[21] In time, with the expansion of their family, the Halprins would affiliate with the conservative Congregation Beth Sholom in San Francisco's Richmond District, drawn by its charismatic Rabbi, Saul White. In White's congregation the Halprins would have found a marked contrast to the ultra-reform stance of San Francisco's Jews of German origin. Writing in wartime editorials, White had been outspoken in battling San Francisco's Jewish aristocracy, echoing Larry's Zionist stance in his argument for the need for a Jewish state and sounding the first alarms in the Bay Area during World War II about the extermination of European Jewry.

In subtle ways, the dance deck would become a pulpit for Anna and Larry's own fellowship focused on reforming Bay Area arts and expanding disciplinary connections between dance and landscape design into new levels of social importance. Within less than a decade, Larry would essentially cease working on private gardens completely, focusing instead on community life and ways of incorporating democratic social living patterns into large public spaces where people came together. The dance deck was ready-made for just this credo of incorporating democratic living patterns into public space since so many aspects of this already govern its functioning: it

78 THE CHOREOGRAPHY OF ENVIRONMENTS

is a public space where people come together; social living patterns are the foundation of much contemporary dance content; and each time a dance work is made or performed for an audience, a community is constituted and a dialogue initiated. In addition to being a space of art making, the dance deck also presented a hybridizing and liberalizing of the functions of a dance studio and stage. Traditionally dance studios and stages have been places where hierarchies of order and power are reinforced, signaled by performers' locations on the stage, their relationships to each other and audiences, and their indexing of where the power of decision-making resides. Much of the dance work Anna would undertake on the deck played directly with challenges to hierarchical authority through her embrace of improvisatory methods. While she customarily reserved veto power over what was ultimately included in the finished piece, her process allowed for a cultivation of individual voices that was rare at the time in group works, a process that would evolve into a leading postmodern compositional method by the following decade of the 1960s.[22]

The scales of intimacy and expansiveness Anna's work toggled between in response to the immediate and proximate environments of work and home deepened her interest in individualized movement stories. This is reflected in her use of privatized behaviors and actions, like dressing and undressing or bathing, as material for choreographic investigations of domestic situations. Effectively, she took a newly private object, the deck, and re-engineered it, keeping its potential for drama intact while making it a site for amplifying usually hidden homelife activities into artworks for outside consumption. This very act of repurposing suburban homelife as art material implicitly pushed back against modernist boundaries and divides. The public world of the front porch, the hidden world of the indoor dance studio, and the curated design of classical gardens were now merged within the modern idiom of a deck set in the midst of a secretive garden.[23]

Seemingly intuitively, the probing physical intimacies that Anna would unfold on the dance deck leveraged this quality of deep seclusion and a breeching of social boundaries as gateways into new depths of psychological, emotional, and physical discovery. For centuries, porches had functioned as unique semi-public outdoor sites where communities met informally through interactions that fostered social cohesion but which also permitted a consciously curated sense of what dimensions of oneself and one's life were private and which were public. The deck fractured this separation, switching after-work and weekend family time from house fronts to backyards; they

CHOREOGRAPHING NATURE AND THE DANCE DECK 79

expanded what was private and shrunk what was public. Architecturally, the placement of decks as appendages immediately behind the house was also used to maintain a seamless effect between indoor and outdoor living as one moved from the interior of the home, through a sliding glass door, and directly onto a small deck and into the backyard and garden. It was a succession of spaces that offered concealment and invited new disclosures. It was in this larger context of the deck as an architectural object that Anna came to explore the possibilities of her own custom-designed dance deck as a generative aesthetic object.

In 1945, a few years before the Halprin family moved to their custom modernist house on Ravine Way in Kentfield, they purchased their first home, a small tract house in Mill Valley, very close to where they had first visited Anna's Uncle Jack in his home. Originally built to house wartime workers from the nearby shipyards of Sausalito, the Halprin house was a simple nine-hundred-square-foot bungalow on a tiny one-eighth acre lot with an undeveloped backyard Larry described as "just waiting to be designed."[24] *Sunset Magazine* gave Larry a small stipend and asked him to show how he might improve the site, displaying the before-and-after gardens in a subsequent feature in the magazine. Larry remodeled the house and arranged the garage to be a makeshift studio for Anna, and the small garden he created became his first working-class backyard domestic retreat (Figure 2.6). It would become an early exemplar of the emerging Bay Area landscape design approach to utilizing the full exterior of small lots as work, play, and living-in-the-outdoors spaces and a prototype for Larry's nascent philosophy about how design, and particularly garden design, can enhance lives.[25] This tiny garden did not have any decks; instead, it enacts Larry's ideas of extending living space to the outdoors through a curving paved asphalt terrace and hedges of privets and evergreens to be used as living privacy fences.[26] It's a modest beginning, but through a subsequent series of articles published in prominent architectural journals about this Mill Valley house, he clearly positions it as the launch of his vision for a radical reconsideration of livable and creatively inspirational backyard design. He lauds it as sharing paradigms with "good theatre in the garden," to borrow the title of his July 1947 feature about this house and backyard in *Sunset Magazine*. Suggesting that landscaping problems might productively be thought of as creating an engaging performance, with qualities including variation, drama, and points of emphasis, Larry advocates the use of plants "in a dramatic manner," spotlighting those with exceptional features. He continues that music can be introduced

Figure 2.6. Young Daria playing in the backyard patio of the first Halprin home, with Hardoy butterfly chairs visible on the patio, Mill Valley, California. Lawrence Halprin Collection, Stuart Weitzman School of Design, The Architectural Archives, University of Pennsylvania, Philadelphia.

through "the trickle of water, bird songs. You can bring action with fountains, the flight of birds, or an open fire at night," he said. His comments are prophetic about just the kind of layering of sensory stimulation the dance deck at the Halprins' future home in Kentfield will invite. Larry's philosophy being modeled here, that "the backyard is America's most mis-used natural resource" and that "the great challenge for the garden designer is not to make the garden look natural but to make the garden so the people in it will *feel* [emphasis added] natural,"[27] presages what, within a few years, will become the credo of working on the dance deck with its transformative capacity for inspiring investigations in contemporary movement.[28]

A Duet with Nature: Theater in the Garden

Traditionally, dance studios have been places where the body is trained out of innate naturalness through a repetition of exercises and movement phrases that drill dancers in technique and canons of repertory as a means of transforming them. This methodology is premised on shaping dancers to be expressive in communicating the pre-scripted narratives and gestures of set choreography. In contrast, under Anna's direction, the dance deck became a place where her approach to dance was to make the people doing it feel, look, and be as relatively unfettered and open to discovery as possible. The dance deck would become instrumental in facilitating the recovery of this presumed naturalness in contemporary dance.

The dance deck adamantly resisted being an everyday object and space in the sense of the typical backyard deck of the 1950s. It was both more and less: a stage, but positioned on a remote edge of a suburban backyard; a garden object, but one which generated theatrical invention and deflected traditional domestic use. One descends to it as an important final destination. It is not something to be traversed or stepped down from; indeed, there is nothing beyond it at its final elevation but treetops and open sky. Like the Halprin house itself, the dance deck carries the aesthetic imprimatur of its makers: in this instance, Lauterer and the Halprins. Prefiguring and literally setting the stage for the rich exchanges between dance and landscape design that will unfold on the deck across the next seventy years, here is where the three disciplinary skills of these collaborators will intersect: Lauterer's expertise in theater production, staging, lighting, and directing; Larry's landscape design acumen in siting and shaping the deck; and Anna's physical response to its surface, environment, and space as a dancer. These three outlooks position the deck reflexively as the first cross-disciplinary experimental object that this platform for creative invention will inspire. "My whole approach to design from early on reached out into nature," Larry said, reflecting years later on the aesthetic lens he brought to his collaborative role in designing the dance deck. "The deck then was not an object, [it] did not become an object in the landscape, it became part of the landscape and that is very different," he said, positioning it as deeply integral to the environment (which for him constituted not-an-object status). At the same time Larry noted specifically the way the freeform of the deck was contoured in response to the trees, the mountain views, and other natural elements of its setting.[29] "This has been a premise of mine ever since," Larry said of his redefinition of the deck as part of the landscape, "and so it was a place that affected her [Anna's] work and affected mine also as a role model for the future."[30]

Larry once teasingly observed that the dance deck marked the first time that Anna was his client. Indeed, it was she who requested Lauterer be

82 THE CHOREOGRAPHY OF ENVIRONMENTS

involved in the planning as well. "She wanted him to collaborate with me," Larry recalled, "because she knew that I could handle the architectural aspects of it and the design, but Arch could give it a flair of what it was like to make a deck that a dancer could use. He loosened the whole thing up."[31] Over time these practical modifications would resonate deeply as major aesthetic shifts for both Halprins. "Actually, I think left to my own devices I probably would have made it square and more classical in its forms and so forth," Larry reflected afterward. "But he [Lauterer] devised the idea of moving around amongst the trees and getting walkways at different levels and those had a tremendous influence on what she was able to finally achieve," Larry said of the dances Anna would make on the deck. "And it was because he [Lauterer] was part of the design team."[32] Larry's comments here suggest that while he had designed a deck for the *Donnell Garden* that had trees puncturing it, when it came to designing a deck for dance, he likely would have retreated to a more traditional model if not for Lauterer influencing him to radicalize that space as boldly as he had the *Donnell Garden* poolside deck. The collaboration proved transformative for everyone involved. In a series of lectures Larry gave soon after the completion of the dance deck, he advocated for a paradigm shift from regarding gardens as decoration around the outside of the house to a broadened consideration of the house and property as a whole where gardens are considered a place to live in as much as the buildings themselves.[33] Nowhere was this shift more evident on the Halprin property than how Anna, and eventually Larry, would use the dance deck as a laboratory for extensive art experimentation.

For Lauterer, the collaboration on the dance deck brought him the closest he would ever get to his longtime creative ambition—that of designing a theater just for dance. By 1954 the fifty-year-old Lauterer was well established as the preeminent design innovator for the emerging field of contemporary dance, having created the celebrated spare sets and lighting designs for major works by Martha Graham, Hanya Holm, Merce Cunningham, and Doris Humphrey, among other leading New York choreographers with whom he collaborated (Figure 2.7).[34]

At the time he consulted on the dance deck with the Halprins, Lauterer was a member of the dance and theater faculty at Mills College in Oakland, California, having been recruited to Mills after years as production director at Bennington School of the Dance and Sarah Lawrence College, as well as other leading East Coast centers for modern dance. At Bennington Lauterer had been on faculty from 1934 to 1942, during which time he had adapted

Figure 2.7. Arch Lauterer reviews script with student Laura Howard (class of 1956), Mills College, California. Detail from Mills College yearbook, *The Crest* (vol. 40, 1955). Marian van Tuyl Papers, Special Collections, F. W. Olin Library, Northeastern University (formerly Mills College, Oakland, California).

the Bennington Armory into a theater before America's entry into World War II resulted in the military reclaiming it a few years later.[35] Lauterer was tireless in advocating for productions where the movement of performers and the stage lighting and décor were unified in support of the human body in motion. "Every theatre house should be a home for the specific activity taking place within it," he argued. "Yet the most forward-looking art of our day, the modern dance, has no home. In every age except our own, theatres have developed structurally in relation to what went on inside them," he continued, lamenting the omission of dance from equal architectural respect.[36] The commission to design the dance deck with the Halprins would give Lauterer his longed-for opportunity to redress this by designing from scratch an entirely new theatrical space tailored for contemporary dance and one which would in turn foster new models of movement training, spatial and dance invention, and environmental responsiveness.

Outspoken in his dislike of traditional theatrical embellishments— like black velvet curtains and busy sets—Lauterer complained that these features ruined the possibility of seeing the body in unencumbered space. He envisioned instead a new forum for theater, "a space in which the actions and qualities of human life can come into being, can maintain a life of their own."[37] This sounds prescient of the dance deck and what would become Anna's use of it as a platform on which to manipulate ordinary objects, including the human body, as a means of highlighting their inherent performable realities. In an interview he gave in 1945 advocating for a new model of theater for dance, Lauterer praised the potential impact of such a space as affecting more than just the field of dance. He anticipated it would be impactful for theatrical performance in general: "Dance could revolutionize our current theater practice and ideology by restoring drama and movement to their rightful and fruitful station of organic independence," he said shortly before the Halprins commissioned him to codesign the deck with Larry. This suggests the depth of Lauterer's belief in just how profoundly a separate dedicated space for each performing art could inspire investigations into the basic quality of each one.[38] Certainly a deeper investigation into the essence of dance would become Anna's driving mission. "I don't focus on just my personal body but on my holistic body," she observed years later in discussing the impact of the dance deck on her aesthetic philosophy. "I collaborate with my environments because I have a strong attitude about the body not being an object. It is part of a total environment in space. That is influenced by Larry's work. You can see that in how our house is in and out of space. . . . My

CHOREOGRAPHING NATURE AND THE DANCE DECK 85

physical body is what I relate to on one level. But what I am most concerned about is relating beyond—to the environment—that is my holistic body."[39] Anna's comments reveal how the deck, by virtue of expanding the concept of a dance space, also expanded for her the conceptual scale and boundaries of her own and others' bodies working on it.

A Choreographic Vision

Coming from an opposite approach—the design of space—Lauterer embraced a companion vision: he once described theaters broadly as "a progression of becomings and releases," with the designer's function being "the discoverer of the patterns which would move the audience."[40] Although he was speaking of drama in this instance, his vision is choreographic, with its honed focus on motion and physical impulse—dynamics he found missing in traditional theaters. In describing theater buildings as such, Lauterer blames the dominant nineteenth-century model of these structures as being "originally constructed for hearing rather than for seeing . . . they were conversation-conscious rather than action-conscious." The presence of these buildings as essentially the only available spaces where dance was viewed thus "distorted" the art form as he saw it. He protested that theaters were impossible places in which to see dance since they so privileged sound over sight and were designed to project the spoken word.[41] "Actually, the best area for seeing movement is the area *between* the orchestra and the mezzanine," Lauterer once observed, referring to the empty space between the stage and the first row of seats for the audience. "But, of course our theatres leave that space blank," he lamented in an interview he gave in 1945.[42] In sum, Lauterer decried the stage as an inherited convention that distorts dance, flattening a three-dimensional art into a two-dimensional perspective "at war with the purpose of movement. . . . The picture-box stage is not only an outmoded form which does not suit the dance; it is a form, a convention if you will, which is completely at odds with movement and constantly destroys movement," he complained.[43]

With this comment deriding "the picture-box stage" as ill-suited for dance, Lauterer may have been not so subtlety referring to a theater at another prominent summer dance center just fifty miles away from Bennington College in Vermont where he lived and taught from 1937 to 1942. That theater, located in the Berkshire Hills of Massachusetts, belonged to modern dance pioneer

86 THE CHOREOGRAPHY OF ENVIRONMENTS

Ted Shawn, who had erected a space he called the "first theatre designed for dance in North America," a rustic barn-like structure on his dance retreat of Jacob's Pillow. Set on a former mountaintop farm, Jacob's Pillow had been established by Shawn in 1931 as a modern dance summer center where throughout the 1930s Shawn presented summer demonstrations of his men dancers. Early in July of 1942, Lauterer's last summer at Bennington, Shawn debuted his theater, a standard proscenium-arched structure with 154 folding chairs for seating, designed by Joseph Franz, a German immigrant who relocated to Stockbridge in the Berkshires. Frantz had been introduced to Jacob's Pillow through a cousin, Caroline Fetzer, whom Shawn had engaged to teach the women students when The Pillow started admitting women in 1934.[44] As soon as The Pillow was incorporated in 1941, Shawn, ever the pragmatist, recruited Franz to join the newly forming board of directors, and within weeks Shawn named Franz the architect of the new dance theater. Four years prior to designing Shawn's dance theater, Franz had designed his first, and only other, performance space through a similar circumstance of convenience when, as a board member of the Boston Symphony Orchestra, he stepped in and scaled back costly plans for a new music theater at Tanglewood that had been designed by renowned architect Eero Saarinen.

Streamlining Saarinen's plans to trim costs, Franz reshaped the Tanglewood plans to be a more compact open theater, the Serge Koussevitzky Music Shed, with high beams like those of the Ted Shawn Theatre while preserving Saarinen's wonderful acoustics. Trained as an engineer, Franz designed from practicality rather than architectural expertise, building his own home and a few local mercantile stores in the Berkshires, and installing underground wiring for the main street of his hometown of Stockbridge, Massachusetts. At Tanglewood, Franz had proudly noted that he trimmed costs by omitting features focused on sight in favor of hearing—essentially those features customarily needed in a theater for dance. Writing about the Music Shed, as it was affectionately known, local journalist M. D. Morris noted of Franz's adjustments: "Since there would be no need for scenery in a purely musical enterprise, he omitted the scenery storage space in the roof. . . . Feeling that to hear was far more important than the actual need to see the players, the slope of the floor was reduced from twelve feet to three feet of pitch, thus omitting an expensive grading operation. The floor cover material itself was eliminated in favor of tamping the earth in place. . . . [W]ings were cut out and the last row of seats was moved back several feet.[45] Just how Franz engineered going from one sensory emphasis to its extreme other is not reported, nor are the architectural details of how he chose to emphasize dance in his only other performance space commission, the Ted Shawn Theatre at Jacob's Pillow. The stage of the Ted Shawn Theatre at Jacob's Pillow featured a large barn-like rear door that was used for moving in set pieces or occasionally as a backdrop for filming, but The Pillow archivist Norton Owen reports that the lush green of the woodlands behind the theater was only rarely used as a nature-scape backdrop for live performances.[46] Otherwise, it was a fairly traditional theater with a high, open-beam ceiling and a raised stage that made for good sightlines from the bank of 154 folding chairs that constituted the original seating.

On the West Coast, the Halprin dance deck pushed the idea of performing in a rural setting to very different and new extremes. Unburdened by New England worries about summer downpours and excessive heat and humidity, the deck dispensed with the formal structures of indoor theaters in favor of a different kind of vulnerability to the elements and nature. Built twelve years after the Ted Shawn Theatre, the dance deck also differed significantly from Shawn's East Coast stage in that it was conceived in the context of a mid-century modern house and garden setting, and as a teaching space primarily and an informal performance space secondarily. In time, however, the dance deck would evolve into hosting increasing numbers of Anna's performances. On occasion, informal events by fellow visiting artists also happened on the deck. One of the earliest of these, and the most often referenced, was a one-time lecture demonstration by Merce Cunningham, who, on a summer evening in July 1957, presented a one-hour talk and demonstration about his approach to dance.[47] For decades afterward, the only surviving copy of the hand-typed text of his talk languished in Anna's basement storage boxes along with her own materials until 2004, when this author came upon the faded onionskin copy of it in doing research about Anna's early years. This document offers an interesting and inadvertent snapshot of the contemporary East Coast dance world's response to the phenomenon of the dance deck: unaccustomed to the foggy chill of summer evenings in the San Francisco Bay Area, Cunningham prefaced his talk by joking about the weather, later asking Anna earnestly: "But where do you live in the winter?" assuming that working on the dance deck could only be seasonal.[48] Even into the twenty-first century, the dance deck never lost its status as an oddity in the dance world and a site that elided the essential comforts of indoor dance studios.

88 THE CHOREOGRAPHY OF ENVIRONMENTS

It wasn't until 1981 that the East Coast gained a major outdoor dance stage in a rustic setting, when Jacob's Pillow built a simple platform in the woods to accommodate overflow student rehearsals. Initially the platform, which had been placed on a pile of rocks, was bordered by a dense forest of trees. Many years later, when this rear bank of trees was cut down to make room for a new septic field, a stunning vista of the Berkshire Hills behind the stage was revealed.[49] Eventually in 2021, this led to the platform's formal expansion into the Henry J. Leir Outdoor Stage, set on a hillside and framed by a sweeping panoramic view of nature.[50] Lauterer's vision had at last implicitly migrated back to the neighborhood of his own first attempts to model an ideal and dedicated space for dance.

In Lauterer the Halprins had found the perfect fellow renegade, an esteemed theater designer who, propelled by his dislike of traditional theaters, created the ideal space to support the classes, workshops, performances, and investigations into bodies in motion that would be foundational for the work of both Anna and Larry. Collaborating with Larry on the design of the dance deck gave Lauterer his fullest opportunity to prototype his aspiration of designing a space uniquely suited for dance. Lauterer once described his goal as that of creating a structure where the movement of the body was so vital that spectators themselves felt physically transformed just by the visual stimulation. Several years earlier, while coteaching a seminar on Experimental Production with Martha Hill at Bennington, Lauterer had played with movement of bodies in space by experimenting with the effects of lighting on a moving body. Choreographer Alwin Nikolais, who was a student in that class, still recalled vividly decades later one exercise in particular that Lauterer introduced as having profoundly altered his own vision of the potential of dance, prompting him to spend the rest of his career rethinking lighting as possessing its own kinetic force. Nikolais, marveling at how convincing just manipulating the lighting had been in reshaping the impression of a body in motion, said:

> He had set up a lighting circumstance in which a spotlight came through the stage from upstage to downstage. I remember his asking, "What did you see? What did you see?" And we looked and looked, and he had it done over and over and over again. Then he said, "You must look at it very carefully and give me a reaction to what you saw." None of us came up with the expected reaction. Then he pointed out what we had failed to see. We were so engrossed, I guess, in just watching the figure, that we didn't see

CHOREOGRAPHING NATURE AND THE DANCE DECK   89

the figure in relation to the light. What happened was that the trajectory of the light was such that the dancer walked into the light slowly and went out quickly. But it was an illusion. The dancer did not actually change his physical speed.[51]

Lauterer, who tragically succumbed to a lengthy illness just three years after completing the dance deck, never realized his total dance theater building.[52] Correspondence between Lauterer and Larry during the time the deck was under construction reveals that Lauterer was also designing an extensive exterior lighting system with the capacity to not just light the dance deck but also spotlight, dim, color wash, and otherwise play with the illumination of the dancers as they moved in the outdoors.[53] This feature of the dance deck was never completed and there is no information as to what happened, whether the Halprins ran into zoning restrictions on exterior illumination or it proved too costly. But for the life of the deck all events there relied on the natural illumination of daylight. Larry, writing in posthumous tribute to Lauterer, noted with remorse that the innovations with space and light that Lauterer had begun in these designs for the deck project were as close as he would ever get to actualizing his dream of the first theater built exclusively for dance.[54]

In eulogizing Lauterer and his contributions to the dance deck soon after his death, Larry credited him as authoring its most novel features: "The dance deck was our mutual product—but Arch gave it its specific spatial impetus in terms of dance. He kept it free in shape and multileveled and this will always strongly influence the dances which are made on it. The wonderful spatial qualities of dance which the deck helps generate will always owe much to his influence."[55]

It is impossible to overestimate how significant a role these deeply worked details of space, light, and elevation nuances in the flooring and shape of the deck played in the innovativeness of the work Anna and Larry would develop there. Judging from the Halprins' own reflections, just a few years after the completion of the project, and in their retrospective oral histories recorded decades later, the object of the deck transfigured the direction of both of their artistic lives. Seventy years later, the dance deck remains one of the most singular dance spaces in the world. It is emblematic of the fusing of the disciplines of dance, theater architecture, and environmental design. For Anna, the space would prove cathartic with a presence that generated its own improvisatory movement possibilities. "It has a sense of just floating in the woods all by itself," she remarked years later in reflecting on how radically it

Figure 2.8. Anna Halprin standing on the dance deck soon after its completion. Anna Halprin Digital Archives, Museum of Performance + Design, San Francisco.

transfigured her approach to movement and how it offered the seclusion of a professional dance studio in the midst of a domestic garden (Figure 2.8). "You can't even see the house from the deck," she said happily. "It was the most marvelous space and shocking because I had never danced in a space that wasn't rectangular ... no ceilings, no boundaries. And it just meandered in and out of the trees," she continued, awed still at the memory of its novelty.[56] "The space itself is alive and kinetic—it is changeable _ it invites movement—challenging it by its own sense of movement," Larry agreed, writing enthusiastically about the deck soon after its completion. "Since it is non-rectangular it generates a different influence on dance than does a space based on right angles."[57]

Over the next few years, due in large measure to Larry's own writing about the deck and its status as a landscape architecture benchmark, word of the dance deck continued to circulate nationally in architectural arenas and increasingly feature articles and praise followed. Other architects sometimes even became advocates themselves. One such example was in 1957 when Kenneth W. Brooks, a prominent architect from Spokane, Washington, wrote to the editor of the leading architectural journal, *Progressive Architecture*, extolling the experience of having visited the Halprin property on a late summer evening to witness a performance by Anna and her dancers on the dance deck. Praising the dance deck as a "truly classic experience showing the potential of Landscape Architecture particularly when combined with the talent of Ann Halprin and her co-workers," Brooks urged *Progressive Architecture* to do a feature about the deck, arguing that watching dance on the dance deck was "an experience comparable to a first visit to Copenhagen's Tivoli or your first walk around St. Marco's Square,"[58] effectively ranking the deck as one of the great public art spaces in the world.

An Unlikely Collaboration between Architecture, Dance, and Nature

The dance deck was arguably the first and most transformative professional collaboration between Larry and Anna—a gateway into the aesthetic each would pursue separately and together for the rest of their careers. They merged their art fields and sensibilities into the construction of an object that *itself* was an aesthetic object but which also generated art. Historically stages have been distinctive sites where bodies are transformed and acquire legibility and visibility as they communicate scripted meanings. Although the deck was a nontraditional stage, like a stage it was a space where bodies could transfigure and content could be displayed to a public.

When it was built in 1954, soon after the Halprins' second child was born, the dance deck was placed in the Halprin yard in a location far downhill from the house and situated in an intimate *pas de deux* with nature, an innovation Lauterer advocated for. A pair of towering madrone trees punctured it in the foreground, their limbs intertwining overhead to form a thirty-five-foot-high vaulted arch framing the center of the deck. Upstage, two other trees reached through the deck, their twisted trunks suggesting the torque of a living force that had just wound its way through the floorboards (see Figure 2.8). In the 1958 feature article in *Progressive Architecture*, a consequence of Brooks's letter about the Halprin home, gardens, and deck, Larry describes the entire property as "a hillside transformed into a living environment." He remarks on what he calls "the dominance" of the whole natural environment and his respect for that in situating the dance deck fifty feet below the house and in a form that echoes the irregular angularity of the glassed-in living room far

92 THE CHOREOGRAPHY OF ENVIRONMENTS

above it. "I attempted to put on the land what would enhance it, and in that way to enrich the living environment of my family," he explained.[59]

In his writings about the dance deck, Larry described this arching of the madrone trees as a de facto proscenium arch, the picture frame–like border of drapery at the front of a traditional stage, but in this instance the frame was rendered with living elements of nature. "The deck floats above the ground but the trees anchor it in its space. Along the East face it is closed by a grove of redwoods which form backdrop and sound reflector," Larry wrote, using theatrical terms to note how things like the small level and angular changes of the deck seem to already be orchestrating the dancing bodies who will fill it: "The form of the deck responds to the site—it meanders to avoid tree clumps, it reaches out to open spaces—it elongates to include trees as anchor points and finally it returns to the hill. The deck is a level platform floating above the ground. Where it almost touches earth, it is half a foot from ground level—at its highest point it stands thirty feet above the sloping ground."[60] For Anna, it took some time to adjust to working on the deck due to the oddness of the form and the interruption of the madrone trees. A more conservative dancer might have labeled these features inconveniences and disruptions to uninterrupted space on which to dance, but Anna never did. Taking the oddness of the space as a challenge and mandate, Anna worked with it, allowing it to change her expectations, methods, and, ultimately, vision of how dance might respond to the world.

Larry, in turn, marveled at the structural details of the deck, exulting, "The construction is reminiscent of bridges, the live load with groups of dancers is enormous and since the platform is free standing, great attention to methods of sway bracing had to be given The surface could have been solid in which case it would have had to be built like a boat—tongue and groove—caulked and slightly cambered to shed water. It was finally decided to let the rain go through—space the boards and round their edges. The boards are oiled several times a year to keep the surface filmy"[61] (Figure 2.9). He saw a structural marvel where Anna saw an inspiring collaborator.

Writing in the same essay, Anna offers her own contrastingly physical response to the deck, describing in sensory-rich terms what it's like to be dancing outdoors in the woods with "walls replaced by trees" and where "confining ceilings are non-existent, and the sky is a long way up." She notes acoustic differences as well, saying, "Sounds are different." These observations reflect the enhanced sensitivity to nature that this platform already inspired in her within the first few months of its use. "There is a

Figure 2.9. The dance deck under construction, Halprin house, Kentfield, California, 1954. Lawrence Halprin Collection, Stuart Weitzman School of Design, The Architectural Archives, University of Pennsylvania, Philadelphia.

basic envelope of deep silence—punctuated by soft wind noises, bird calls, fluttering of leaves, and the hum and crackle of insects," she continued with her sensate description of smells like foliage and the "deep sweetness of leaf-mold." "How does this out-of-doorness affect dancing?" she asks rhetorically. On a practical level, she notes that there is less need for musical accompaniment, while on an emotional level she describes a bolder sensibility and embrace of risk and exposure: "one becomes less introverted and more receptive to environmental change," she writes. "The spatial structure of the deck forces a complete reorientation of the dancer as the space explodes and becomes mobile."[62] Her description here suggests how the deck itself and its setting bring their own imperative of change and expansion for her and the dancers working on it.

Anna was so overwhelmed by the abundance of possibilities the dance deck presented that initially she spent several weeks just absorbing its presence and potential. "I would go every day for the first month and try and settle, you know like a dog trying to find their place, trying to find my power spot in that space and trying to find 'is there a center here?'" she recalled of its enticing strangeness. "Well, does there have to be a center?" she asked herself, tracing further the conundrum an irregular stage space presented. Eventually she came to a resolution. "Well, the center is in me. I can take my center wherever I want and choose to be," she said. Anna elaborated on her thought processes during those initial weeks of just sensing the possibilities the dance deck offered. "So, the sense of place and being present would depend on where the light was, where the wind was coming from, where the sounds were. And whether I wanted to feel cozy in a corner, whether I wanted to be exposed. It changed my whole sense of my body presence; it gave me a totally new attitude about how to relate to space in movement. Not only did it loosen Larry up in terms of his architecture, but it also had a profound effect on my sense of movement."[63]

An Invitation to a New Regard of Objects

Working at home and on a deck seems to have inspired Anna to keep the body's actions on the scale and directness of what bodies in homes did naturally—prosaic, functional things, often with ordinary objects. Like a parent setting up exploratory play environments for a child, Anna began to introduce domestic objects with which her students and dancers could interact. Often these were routine household and garden items—water poured into bowls and buckets, fallen branches from the yard, lengths of wrapping paper, items of ordinary clothing. In her works these were never just static props or objects with fixed meanings and uses; instead, they were puzzles to be manipulated, repurposed, poured, torn, worn, stepped upon. These encounters were much more like those people have in their home with the objects around them than the representational use of "props" as symbolic forms in traditional dance and theater. In Anna's dances, objects, like the dancers, did not necessarily signify or stand in for something or someone else. They just were, bluntly and transparently. The physical configuration of the deck in the outdoors and its proximity to the home were instrumental in prompting this. As she worked, Halprin slowed, stretched, and expanded, digging deeper into the basic functionality of the body in a spirit similar to that with which she examined the objects she brought to the deck. Rather than elaborating or complexifying, she began working human bodies more like a landscape architect situating and tending plants: she planted, nurtured, fed, pruned, positioned, and then watched how they grew.

Nature, the passage of time, and a retreat to convenience modified several of these more nuanced details of the dance deck. Eventually all of the perforating madrone trees died, broken boards needed replacing, and the deck became essentially one large, extended, flat surface with raised corners. However, the imprint of nature, and the deeply respectful initial relationship between the built and the found environment that the dance deck finessed, remained a permanent legacy. It stood between two worlds: the utilitarian simplicity of architectural design and the private intimacy of domestic and art-making spaces. When Larry commented retrospectively that had the dance deck not been so influenced by Lauterer's innovations it would likely have emerged as a traditional classical stage, he also noted that this would have resulted in Anna's innovations being far more muted.[64] Anna agreed, recalling how she read the space choreographically: "Because it has no boundaries there was nothing to prevent me from making trails and going out. We had acres of wonderful, wooded areas with all kinds of magical spots. There was nothing to prevent me from extending the deck all the way out to the mountain if I wanted to go there and so my whole idea of where you dance changed completely.... [T]ime changed; the idea of space changed. It simply exploded every barrier of theatre that I had ever known"[65] (Figure 2.10).

This sense of multiple threads of twentieth-century art innovation intersecting at the crossroads of the dance deck is in part what gave it its force as such a generative space for twentieth-century art innovators. It was not just the performance of dance but the pedagogy of how Anna approached dance training and how Larry approached landscape design that underwent significant revision when her work shifted to the dance deck. Anna once remarked that she became "almost animal-like" in response to the influence working outdoors on the deck. "I could adapt my body temperature to work in all kinds of weather. Sometimes I would be dancing with mittens on or with shoes on. I got so that even when it rained, I would accept rain as being part of the environment and it was the beginning for me of redefining movement," she said.[66] One of the first methodological changes this inspired was a loosening of the links between cause and effect in dance composition. She was fond of observing that one never objected to the layering of randomized sounds in nature with disparate visual stimulation. Leaves and berries fell on the deck while the laughter of children playing in the woods was muted by the foghorns from distant ships in the bay, yet one simply took this all in as it occurred with no thought of wishing that the berries fell in time to the

Figure 2.10. The dance deck from underneath, Kentfield, California. Photograph by Ernst Braun, c. 1950s. Lawrence Halprin Collection, Stuart Weitzman School of Design, The Architectural Archives, University of Pennsylvania, Philadelphia.

foghorns or that the children's voices were synchronized with the steps of the dancers traipsing on the fallen leaves on the deck. The lesson was that in nature nothing was an intrusion; everything could go with anything was the mantra of the natural world. Eventually it was the tidiness of the ABA form of classical modern dance choreography with its deliberate cause-and-effect sequencing, arc to a climax, and predictable logic that appeared impossibly artificial to Anna. Working on the irregular form of the deck, with its open invitation for disruptions from the surrounding environment, shifted both Anna's and Larry's approach to working from carefully controlled production to open-ended research, discovery, and development. "This place just seemed to draw people as being a very concentrated non-judgmental, non-pressured place to just research and experiment, because a lot of people, a lot of artists, were simultaneously breaking barriers," Anna said of the allure of the deck.[67]

The Dance Deck as a Parenting and Workspace

Domestically, the most important growth happening in the Halprin household during the initial years of the dance deck was that of the two little Halprin daughters, Daria, who was six years old when it was completed, and Rana, who was two years old. A major reason the dance deck was built initially was to facilitate Anna juggling being both a stay-at-home mother to the girls and a working artist. Prior to the construction of the dance deck, Anna had a frightening experience leaving the children with a caregiver who became inebriated and passed out while babysitting. In the process, the woman also accidentally started a small fire with her lit cigarette. Fortunately, a neighbor noticed and called Anna and the fire department. Anna, who was teaching in the San Francisco dance studio she shared with dancer Welland Lathrop at the time, recounts that she raced home upon hearing the news. She dates her decision that she needed to work closer to home to this experience. Plans to construct the dance deck began soon after. At the same time the deck was being built as a site to emancipate her body, the decision to work at home also meant Anna was conforming to stereotypes of White postwar suburbia where, as historian Kristina Wilson has noted, popular books and magazines of the era relentlessly portrayed women as ultimately always responsible for the domestic sphere, even if they had professional success outside the home.[68]

Very quickly, the blend of Anna's working on the deck, while her two daughters played under her supervision nearby, became normalized—— at least for the Halprin family. "I used to do all my practicing on the dance deck," Anna recounted. "And I remember the kids used to have their friends over and there was a gravel area just in front of the dance deck and their little friends would come to the edge of that and look over and watch me dancing," she said, noting that this annoyed her daughters, who could not understand the other children's amazement at having a mother who danced, and on an outside deck! "The girls [Daria and Rana] would be so upset," Anna recalled with a hint of pride at how effectively she straddled the two spheres of traditional suburban motherhood and art making. "They would say 'what are you watching that for? Doesn't your mother dance like that all day long too?'" she recounted, knowing very well how unique her situation was.[69]

The dance deck was an object that afforded Anna multiple opportunities to code-switch between not only between being a parent and a professional dancer but also, within those identities, between being a traditional

98 THE CHOREOGRAPHY OF ENVIRONMENTS

postwar suburban housewife whose responsibility to the domestic sphere circumscribed her daily existence and an adventuresome dance experimentalist. An example of Anna's identity as the former was memorialized in a 1954 photo of her, Larry, Daria, and Rana posed in their living room as part of a professional photo shoot for an article about Larry (Figure 2.11). Anna and the two girls all wear the identical, girlie, Lanz of Salzberg Tyrolean print dress with puffed sleeves, a full skirt, and a prim white collar that was trendy

Figure 2.11. Lawrence and Anna and daughters in "Mommy and Me" dresses, c. 1955. Courtesy of the Halprin family and Lawrence Halprin Collection, Stuart Weitzman School of Design, The Architectural Archives, University of Pennsylvania, Philadelphia.

CHOREOGRAPHING NATURE AND THE DANCE DECK   99

in the 1950s. The family is standing in their spare, modernist living room with its bare concrete flooring underfoot while behind them the metal and canvas form of a Hardoy butterfly sling chair can be glimpsed, a status symbol of modernist abstraction, and discomfort. Larry wears loose corduroy trousers, a sports shirt, and casual loafers as he pauses in a relaxed pose, holding Rana on one hip. In contrast, Anna and Daria stand stiffly in their tight-bodice, full-skirted party dresses and patent leather shoes, locked in the same conformity and fashion-over-comfort rules as the chair behind them. Anna and Rana wear their hair gathered in matching tidy updos, following the unwritten code of twinning couture proscribing that mothers twin with their youngest daughter. Pointedly girlish (actually bordering on infantilizing for an adult woman), these outfits are emblematic of the "mommy and me" fashion trend of the 1940s and 1950s when there was an emphasis on family and mother-daughter sewing as civilian support of the war effort and later as a symbol of suburban affluence. These matching outfits were favored in particular by White middle-class mothers with the stay-at-home leisure time and money to shop for, or sew, mirror-image outfits for themselves and their daughters.[70] Blowing up a little girl's dress to her adult mother's dimensions, while ostensibly intended to emphasize the mother's girlish youthfulness, was also a not-too-subtle postwar fashion symbol of insularity in the family, a demonstration of the woman's reproductive fertility, and a middle-class status marker of the limited world they were confined to when they moved to the suburbs.

Outside, downhill, and beyond the magazine photo shoot, a different world of mother-daughter relations in the Halprin household unfolded. This is documented in the many photographs Larry took of Anna and the girls joyfully dancing on the deck (Figure 2.12). Rather than signaling containment of "the woman of the house" (a demeaning phrase used in popular media of the time to reference a wife who managed the household while her husband earned the family income), this is play for the girls and research for Anna. The photo of Anna playing with lengths of fabric with Daria and Rana attests to how she was able to fold the easy innocence of childhood games with her daughters into opportunities to develop methods for eliciting the same casual movements in adults as the girls' little and unfettered bodies displayed. This photo captures Anna immersed in a moment of the simple beauty of play with her two free-spirited daughters. One can imagine her harvesting impulses for dance from this leisure recreation, noting, for example, how, in dashing under strips of fabric held aloft by upstretched arms, a small body

Figure 2.12. Anna Halprin dancing with daughters Daria and Rana on the deck with long ribbons of fabric. Photograph by Lawrence Halprin, 1959. Courtesy of the Halprin family.

instinctively crouches down while stepping under the roof formed by the two lofting ribbons. These are moments that arise easily and spontaneously from doing simple tasks that Anna would later revisit in the context of raw material for choreography and game-like structures with her adult dancers. This is not artificial domesticity or imitative art, but rather the beginnings of a path into a rediscovered naturalism that would shape much of Anna's work on the deck in the decades ahead.

Anna's playing with her children by setting their bodies dancing, on the very space in which she worked professionally with her dancers with *their* bodies, at times led to a seepage of actions and approaches from one realm to the other. Before she began working on the deck, Anna, like the majority of dancers working in Western theatrical dance, knew dance studios as deliberately bare, sequestered spaces, and empty interior rooms—the norm for a professional dance studio. In these indoor spaces the intention was to remove as many of the interruptions of daily life as possible and to make them places where attention was honed inward rather than outward to the world outside with its interruptions. This is traditionally accomplished by shutting doors and windows to prevent anyone from looking in from the outside.

These spaces are illuminated by bright artificial lights even in the daytime; street shoes are forbidden on the floors and eating food in the room is prohibited, as are observers, unless limited numbers are specially permitted to watch silently from the margins of the room. Sounds, other than specifically chosen music tailored as accompaniment, the dancers' footfalls, and occasional exclamations, are the only noises permitted. One wall is customarily dedicated to floor-to-ceiling mirrors reflecting the entire population of the room back onto itself continuously.

Most of these traditions and artifacts of dance studios were intentionally left behind when Anna moved to the deck. As her working methods evolved, she was beginning to see these customs as bracketing out the pleasures and richness of subjective experiences in dance, particularly those of the impingement of the natural environment in all its dimensions. Influenced by Larry, who had little interest in decorative ornamentation in gardens and cared much more about how people moved through the spaces he built, Anna used the dance deck as a way to give dancers as broad a range of movement options and experiences as the space and its location made possible. In time, the music she would include as accompaniment on the dance deck would grow to be as improvisatory as the dancing.

One of the first traditional features of a dance studio Anna jettisoned to facilitate open movement discovery when she moved to the dance deck was the mirror, a feature of dance training since the eighteenth century. Throughout the entirety of her life, Anna essentially never used mirrors on the outdoor deck.[71] Following the lead of her college mentor, Margaret H'Doubler, Anna instead prompted dancers to *sense* the physical presence of their interior bodies. She did this by honing their proprioceptive attentiveness as to where their bodies were in space, prompting the discovery of alignment and dynamics through sensation rather than an external reflection.[72] Her prop for doing this was a human skeleton, a standard feature of her teaching, just as it had been for H'Doubler (Figure 2.13). In fact, H'Doubler was infamous for always having a human skeleton suspended by her side wherever she taught dance. Anna adopted this, using a real full-sized human skeleton suspended on a portable stand on the deck as a means of demonstrating to her students how voluntary movement was made possible by the moveable joints of the body that allowed hinging, rotating, twisting, or ball-and-socket hip and shoulder mobility. This visual directed dancers' attention to their kinesthetic awareness of their own bodies in space and the position and movement of their muscles and joints. This was the opposite of the dominance of an

Figure 2.13. Anna Halprin teaching with a skeleton on the dance deck. Photograph by Sophia Wang, 2017. Courtesy of Sophia Wang.

exterior, surface approach focused on how the body *looks*—an emphasis that dance studio mirrors often foster.

As her daughters grew older, Anna invited other children onto the dance deck for regular children's classes. Using the deck in this respect like the playroom in a family home, she grew these movement sessions into a large children's dance program, the Marin Dance Children's Dance Cooperative, which lasted for twenty-five years and included a children's performing troupe. Over time it became a source of revenue and eventually a feeder school of a few select dancers into her company, the San Francisco Dancers' Workshop. When she began touring her work in the 1960s, the two Halprin daughters, now young teens and experienced performers, were also folded into the cast of two of Anna's major works, *Birds of America* and *Parades and Changes*. In keeping with the Halprins' efforts to separate their private family life from the public, Rana and Daria were assigned different surnames in programs to mask their relation as the Halprin children. But in performance, their presence as little Halprin-trained dancers was celebrated and explored sensitively. "I was very used to relating to children," Anna explained of their

CHOREOGRAPHING NATURE AND THE DANCE DECK   103

inclusion in her troupe as well as the children's dance group she formed. "Rana was 10 and Daria was 14 and they were part of the children's troupe. In those days children weren't taken seriously in dance as members of a cast. But I was building a family at that same time [as I was building dances]," she said in explaining the natural flow from one life space to another.[73]

Birds of America or *Gardens without Walls* is a 1960 dance Anna made on the deck that memorializes the presence of her children in her work while also incorporating a de facto movement score of a family bedtime ritual the Halprins used to prepare their young daughters to go to sleep in the house up the hill. On evenings when the girls were especially charged up before bedtime, Anna would lead them through what she called "the floppy, floppy dance" on the living room area rug. Here she would coax each child into relaxation by having them stretch out on the floor. Taking hold of both arms of each girl, one by one, she talked them into deep relaxation. Once she sensed their total release of their weight, she would swing them gently from side to side and back and forth while they hung limply like soft dolls. In *Birds of America*, she exports this exercise from the Halprin living room to the dance deck, now pairing the tallest adult dancer in her troupe, the six-and-a-half-foot-tall John Graham, with little Daria. A film documenting a performance of *Birds of America* or *Gardens Without Walls* shows how this family play was distilled and incorporated into a tender dance passage on the deck. Dressed in leotard and tights, the tall and lanky Graham stands over the small, languid body of Daria (later replaced by her younger sister, Rana, when Daria aged out of the role) (Figure 2.14). Graham gently swishes the relaxed child along the floor repeatedly while holding her first by one arm and then the other. He then cradles her leotard-clad, balled-up form, and, standing hunched over, his legs spread wide, he swings her gently in his arms as if she were a tiny primate offspring. Again and again, Graham tenderly pulls the reclining Daria toward him, finally curving forward as he grasps her arms, as her head and chest arch backward in a swooning gesture of release while he holds her arms to steady her. In these explorations of the basic physics of a body in deep relaxation, the floppy, floppy dance reveals a blurring as much as a borrowing of the identities Anna wore at 15 Ravine Way, those of suburban mother with a responsibility to prepare the bodies of her young children for bedtime and those of a choreographer entrusted with the care of dancers' bodies in preparation for making work.

Anna's approach to shaping the bodies in *Birds of America* is structural; they are being deployed as levers, fulcrums for demonstrating how weight

Figure 2.14. Performance photo of John Graham with Daria Halprin performing counterbalancing pull in *Birds of America* or *Gardens Without Walls*. Photograph by Chester Kessler, c. 1960s. Anna Halprin Digital Archives, Museum of Performance + Design, San Francisco.

transfer and balance between two objects of very different size, weight, and mass can be made to offset one another and achieve stasis. However, if one adds a dramatic and gendered lens, other narratives emerge. Daria's posture of relaxation is so complete here that it borders on erotic submission and Graham's steering of her can be read as dominating control of her body. This is an interpretation that Anna at the time seemed unaware of, but one that is impossible to escape when viewing the film within the context of twenty-first-century concerns. Daria allows herself to be manipulated like a rag doll in Graham's arms, and he maneuvers her with gentle but insistent forcefulness. Remarkable for its single-minded investigation of what a big and little person can do together, both on and off balance, this section of *Birds* is also notable retrospectively for its naïveté. There is no deliberate eroticism here, only frank physical facts about the performers' size difference and the physical reality of the adjustments one body has to make to lift and counterbalance another.[74] But if one allows gender, sex, and sensuality to creep in along with contemporary knowledge of sexual exploitation of minors, then other much more distressing possible narratives emerge in tandem with an edge of discomfort at this duet of an adult male exercising such total control over a submissive female child. Once she ventured off the dance deck, Anna would have an abrupt awakening to these kinds of disparities between what she saw as simple explorations of the human form and its functions and what others in the outside world might read differently and with alarm. The most dramatic instance of this would occur with Anna's use of nudity in *Parades and Changes*. Here what she intended as a demonstration of candor some critics and funders denounced as scandalous. In both instances she was treading the tensions between modernism and the sexualized body.

Larry too included the Halprin daughters in his research work. For him, this took the form of bringing them on the summer backpacking treks into California's High Sierras where he journeyed annually, studying the untamed violence of nature, her cascading waterfalls, rushing rivers, and tumbled boulders. He began these trips in 1954, first with Daria and later with Rana as well. Anna, excited by this release from parenting, shed her domestic duties and for four weeks in July became a full-time artist. Almost immediately, she began convening two-week summer workshops on the dance deck, beginning by inviting a small group of dancers in 1954 to work with her "improvising to find out what our bodies could do, not learning somebody else's pattern or technique."[75] A. A. Leath, who had joined Anna from the University of Wisconsin–Madison, where he had been one of H'Doubler's dance students as well as an athlete and botany major, was part of this early cohort doing workshops on the deck. He found the space transformative and actively recruited other dancers to join by extolling the novelty of the experience: "One of the fascinating things about being out there on the deck," Leath recalled in an interview years later, "was that we were separated from everything that was going on in New York. Much of what we did and how we did it was due to being out in nature. We were only one step from wilderness on the dance deck. We had Mount Tamalpais's main peak rising up before us. Everything we did evolved out of what happened in improvisation."[76] By the 1960s, word of what was happening on the deck had spread to New York and soon dancers including Yvonne Rainer, Trisha Brown, and Meredith Monk; the visual artist Robert Morris; and Simone Forti, who returned after having danced with Anna in the 1950s, joined Anna's summer workshops on the deck along with musicians LaMonte Young and Terry

106 THE CHOREOGRAPHY OF ENVIRONMENTS

Figure 2.15. Summer workshop on the dance deck, Kentfield, California, 1960. Participants: Sunni Bloland, Trisha Brown, June Ekman, Ruth Emerson, Simone Forti, Jerrie Glover, John Graham, Anna Halprin, A. A. Leath, Paul Pera, Yvonne Rainer, Shirley Ririe, Lisa Strauss, Willis Ward. Photo by Lawrence Halprin. Anna Halprin Papers, Elyse Eng Dance Collection, Museum of Performance + Design, San Francisco.

Riley (Figure 2.15). Engaging in morning-to-night movement explorations, often with objects the dancers found in the woods or on the deck and moving in open improvisations to Young and Riley's minimalist experimentations and the group's invented rituals, the workshop participants shared meals and discoveries, softening separations between workshop activities and routine life.

Monk, who would earn her own renown as a musician and dancer, was twenty-two in the summer of 1965 when she went west to study with Anna.

CHOREOGRAPHING NATURE AND THE DANCE DECK   107

She was drawn by reports she was hearing in New York from other dancers who had been in the 1960 workshop about Anna's improvisational work—that it was being done outdoors in the California sunshine and offered an alluring antidote to the more formal, indoor East Coast dance training. "I felt I needed to get away in nature," Monk said of her motivation to go west and enroll. "All that working outside and not being in a studio was wonderful. It made me think a lot about artistic identity."[77] Years later, Monk reflected that actually what had impressed her most about studying with Anna on the deck was a lesson Anna probably was not even aware she was teaching: "how she was striving to be so many things. To be true as a mother, artist, wife. There were no other women then doing that," Monk said, commenting on the rarity of Anna's juggling a hyphenated identity as a mid-century woman who had a family and also a full career as a dance teacher and dancemaker.[78] The dance deck was the essential object that made this possible.

Indeed, one of the most generative features of the deck as a creative workspace was how it facilitated slippage between identities and relations of the objects, roles, and lives in the Halprin home and garden. As she began to reframe domestic objects as art objects, Anna explored how the same actions performed fifty feet uphill in the Halprin kitchen, bedrooms, and bathrooms—things like preparing and eating food; dressing and undressing; bathing and washing hair, faces, and bodies; carrying children and objects—could be exported downhill and mined for startlingly new aesthetic potentials. The starting point was defamiliarization, an approach to art theorized by the Russian critic Viktor Shklovsky, who, writing in the early twentieth century, described the goal of art as taking something familiar or mundane and making it strange.[79] This impulse of separating objects and activities from their routine functionality and becoming reacquainted with them through the lens of art saturates the kinds of activities the permissive site of the dance deck inspired. In time, numerous dances, workshop situations, and prompts would emerge out of Anna's methodology here of invigorating perception by dissociating and attenuating objects and choreographies of the ordinary.

One example was a ritual around food sharing among workshop students. Turning the routine of a lunch break into an extension of this re-examination of the ordinary, Anna invited her workshop students to recontextualize taking midday nourishment as an occasion for prolonging perception about eating through the development of a set of actions for serving, anticipating, and eating a potluck meal with food supplied by the students. These soon evolved into routine features of Anna's workshops when the hours of a workshop spanned mealtimes. It was then a natural progression from taking meal breaks on the dance deck as sustenance to regarding the act of eating itself as an implicit choreography and worthy of the regard one brings to a performance. The result of this attention was the performance work *Lunch*, a dance Anna and three of her dancers performed in response to a 1968 commission for a performance from the Associated Council of the Arts at the Hilton Hotel in San Francisco. Invited to perform as lunchtime entertainment for the conference attendees, Anna requested an elevated table in the center of the dining room. Confronting the convening of arts presenters and administrators with a mirror held up to their elitist regard of a dance performance as little more than a mealtime diversion, Anna framed the dancers' lunchtime actions as politicized minimalist art. She positioned herself and her dancers seated at the table at the center of the room on a raised platform, and their choreography became the dissection of the act of eating the identical meal as the attendees ringing the room. The crucial difference was that the dancers proceeded in excruciatingly slow motion, squeezing out the art potential rather than the nutrition by so retarding and abstracting the routine that it became an intense ritual of lifting a fork, spearing a bite of food, and then, several minutes later, lifting it slowly to one's mouth and, more minutes later, finally chewing and swallowing in slow motion. There could be a bite, metaphorically and literally, to Anna's play with abstracting the domestic objects and practices of home life begun on the dance deck. With *Lunch*, she had effectively exported the spirit of a dance deck investigation into the public arena of the San Francisco Hilton's catered lunch.

Nudity and the Dance Deck

Far more than her work with children and food consumption, the most legendary innovation fostered by the dance deck was Anna's use of nudity. The seclusion of the deck allowed for a unique atmosphere of concealment and disclosure. It offered a rustic setting in nature but situated on a property where house and gardens were shaped by a state-of-the-art modern aesthetic. Modernist architecture already had its own uneasy relations with nudity, the sexualized body, and nostalgia for primitivism dating from the 1920s and 1930s. The intersection of these with a dancing body had resulted in a complicated and racialized legacy on the commercial stages of Europe

CHOREOGRAPHING NATURE AND THE DANCE DECK   109

through the performances of Josephine Baker during these early decades. As Anne Cheng has written, Baker, "celebrated as an icon and decried as a fetish," deftly tapped into a modernist melancholy for the naked and exposed, primitivism and the racialized, sexualized body, with her nude dancing.[80] Wielding her nakedness in performances as an act of concealment, Baker bared her skin "without conceding herself, using her flesh as style and an act of concealment."[81] When Anna turned to nude dancing on the dance deck in the 1960s, she stepped into a similar modernist frame with corresponding tensions between concealment and self-revelation, becoming present or receding emotionally. A significant difference was that she was a White Jewish woman without as obvious tensions of race and objectification, and she was not playing to mainstream commercial audiences. "Dancing outdoors and dancing with the sun and the wind and the freshness and being so close to nature. It was a very natural impulse to bare yourself, to take your clothes off," she said in describing her transition to dancing without clothes. In this statement she links the sensuous experience of feeling the textures and sensations of nature and experiencing its sounds and smells as an inducement to strip her body back to an unveiled state as well. "And there was something absolutely sacred about dancing naked," she said, betraying a romanticist nostalgia. "There's really a tradition that there is something really blessed about being naked when you dance," she continued, situating her use of nudity as enacting a primitivist fantasy and being part of a forgotten dance lineage in the West, a return to the roots of movement. "We're going back to the roots of dance, we're surrounded by a naturalness, a kind of innocence," she said of the visual pleasure of dancing on the deck outdoors. "So, it was not unnatural to dance with our clothes off," she continued.[82]

There is no exact date recording when Anna and her dancers first began shedding their clothes as part of working on the dance deck. But it is easy to imagine the progression of working with the body in quiet isolation, surrounded by redwoods, and reclining on the inviting smoothness of a wooden platform suspended off the hillside, like a giant platform bed under a warm sun, and the lure this provided for the shedding of conventions and, gradually, clothing. Just as it had with Baker, the politics of the visual shadowed Anna's actions as she played with tensions of concealment, exposure, and visual pleasure but without the extreme racialized objectification that attended Baker. Not only the dancers but also the architects and designers who took the series of collaborative Experiments in Environment workshops that Anna and Larry cotaught in 1966 and 1968 were particularly enthusiastic about embracing the opportunity to strip down to swim trunks, shorts, and, eventually, nothing (Figure 2.16).

Depending on how it is used, nudity can also be seen as a means of reobjectifying the body, of representing it as a thing to be seen, touched, explored—an object. It becomes something neutral and unadorned, something that might be examined anew like a rock, a broom, water, stairs, or a deck. Having rendered the body as this newly objective form by undressing it on the deck, Anna began to explore its prosaic existence through a series of workshop investigations with her dancers, focusing on the routine care of the body. This is particularly evident in the dressing and undressing and paper-tearing sections of *Parades and Changes* (1965) and the washing sections of the work that followed it, *The Bath* (1966). Together these two works chart a re-engagement with a new theatricality of the ordinary. The body is represented as a material thing ready to be discovered by the senses. The different bodies of the Halprin property—the person in the house and the representation on the deck—were coming closer together, and the fashionable bareness of modern design was helping to shape both.[83]

Figure 2.16. Experiments in the Environment workshop participants doing a workshop exercise in the nude, 1968. Lawrence Halprin Collection, Stuart Weitzman School of Design, The Architectural Archives, University of Pennsylvania, Philadelphia.

The summer 1965 workshop in which Anna was building *Parades and Changes* was the same workshop Meredith Monk took. Recalling that experience years later, Monk praised the originality and beauty of many of the warmup and physical exercises Anna led. Monk's description of Anna's approach to movement training and the body suggests how it was one that tenderly, but intentionally, held it up for regard as one might a cherished object. "She was doing something very ahead of its time. She really looked at what it was to be a human being who moved," Monk said while also confiding that she found an implicit, and at times uncomfortably elitist, California body-beautiful ethos underlying much of the nude work on the deck that Anna was exploring with the summer workshop students.[84] This is an interesting observation and one that is a reminder of how the act of nudity itself is always historically located in the time and place of its usage. The nudity that the dance deck loosened, and which would in turn ripple through mid-twentieth century theater and dance performance, was indeed distinctly 1960s Californian in its links to the sexual liberation, hippie, and Human Potential Movements that flourished there during this decade, and which also dipped into nudity as part of the ethos of the time. Each of these social movements in their respective ways valorized the toned, tanned, beautiful, and naked body of counterculture youth.[85] The sanctioning of this body as a medium of art and theatrical daring in dance was facilitated by its having been engineered in a suburban backyard.

Anna's use of the unclothed body in performance, while aspiring to an idealized, innocent nudity, slipped between modes that have been classically theorized as the candor of nakedness and the concealment of nudity.[86] Cheng complicates this, arguing that higher and lower forms of visual pleasures, the distinction between the nude and the naked, blur in performance because one is a precondition for the other; nakedness is always a stage on the way to nudity, and nudity cloaks the naked body once it starts to perform.[87] Anna first wielded her own nakedness in a performative way early in 1964 as a politicized weapon in a group workshop with the Gestalt psychotherapist Fritz Perls, with whom she would work for several years at Esalen, an oceanfront retreat on the central California coast and the epicenter of the Human Potential Movement.[88] While waiting for the workshop to begin that day, she started stripping off her clothes out of rage at the conservative appearance of one of the other participants; she was shamed in turn when Perls called her out for primly sitting down and crossing her legs to shield her nakedness. Awakened thus to unintended meanings the bare body could carry,

112 THE CHOREOGRAPHY OF ENVIRONMENTS

Anna returned to the deck to probe nudity for its theatrical uses as she built *Parades and Changes* from 1964 to 1965. This work's premiere in Stockholm in September 1965 marked the first use of nudity in contemporary American theater and its first use in dance by an American dance troupe. Over the next fifty years, Anna returned to the use of nudity in several works, including a final time personally as an old woman in her eighties in *Still Dance* when she enacted a series of outdoor solo performances in nature, in collaboration with visual artist Eeo Stubblefield, while costumed only with body paint and coated with mud, bark, and dry leaves.[89]

Parades and Changes highlights the process of *becoming* naked as arguably the most theatrical stage of nudity. The dance deck ghosts this choice through the manner in which it presents whatever happens on it as being of potential interest theatrically. (Not until several years later, when an indoor dance space was built adjacent to it, would there be a dedicated space for more private dressing and undressing in preparation for class or rehearsal.) The seven-minute dance passage of undressing and dressing that would result from this exploration on the deck would become the most legendary part of the ninety-minute-long *Parades and Changes*. In it the full cast of three adults and six adolescents, including seventeen-year-old Daria and fourteen-year-old Rana, coolly lock eyes with the audience and serenely remove their unisex clothes of military surplus pants, white shirts, shoes, socks, and undergarments and then dress and undress again for a total of three times. "There is a way of removing your clothes and appearing totally vulnerable—open and vulnerable—without attitude," Anna said in explaining how she shaped her use of nudity in *Parades and Changes*.[90] She had absorbed and incorporated Perls's admonition from her own failed first attempt at nudity by stripping away any intentional emotion in its delivery.[91] The act of repeating this arrival at nudity while intending to further neutralize it also retheatricalized it by making it irrefutable that this was an act, not a functional undressing.[92]

In *Parades and Changes* Anna exercised her directorial authority in editing the raw material of the deck explorations into the finished work. She and Larry were both viewed as champions of counterculture causes and collaborative group creation and at the same critiqued as authoritarian presences who retained final control over the creative process. Rather than resolving the flaws in this assertion, I am more interested in this use of *Parades and Changes* as a purity test for the Halprins.[93] It encapsulates the tensions for them as a middle-class Jewish couple committed to liberalism

CHOREOGRAPHING NATURE AND THE DANCE DECK   113

and leftist causes but living in Marin County and enjoying a bifurcated life of suburban comforts and sponsored commissions and grants from those in power. Jewish Studies scholar Marc Dollinger uses the term "allyship" to describe how American Jews of the postwar generation, like the Halprins, adapted to the political culture of the community around them. In response to being asked to contextualize a radical act like exploring nudity on the deck with a Marin address, Dollinger explains:

> White Jews are liminal figures. You are liminal if you can be in multiple social groups simultaneously, i.e., nude on the dance deck and conservative at home—they are moving through different social groups even in a single day—they can talk to powerful and powerless in the same day and that is the good news. The bad news is that they are embraced by none of them—the rich people know that they are artists living out in Marin so they are never embraced, and all of their friends know that Larry will go into San Francisco to meet with the millionaires so they will never have full endorsement because of the connection to wealth. So, it's lonely because you have no real friends.[94]

Thus, the Halprins discovered how to wield allyship with people of power as ultimately a positive force to move their social justice agendas forward. Neither Anna nor Larry had inherited wealth; rather, grants and commissions, many from foundations started by the Gold Rush–era Jewish families of San Francisco, made much of their work possible.

Parades and Changes was a product of these resources and collaborative explorations. While it began on the dance deck, it was refined at 321 Divisadero Street in San Francisco, where Anna began renting two large studios in 1963 in an old Victorian building. She had been invited by Ramon Sender, cofounder with Morton Subotnick, the musician who wrote the score for *Parades and Changes*, to share the building housing the Tape Music Center, a loose coalition of Bay Area New Music composers who had taken a lease on the three-story building on the edge of Haight-Ashbury, the center of youth activism in the 1960s. It was in this setting that Anna brought her initial explorations with nudity on the deck into sharpened theatrical focus. Carla Blank, a dancer that summer in the July workshop Anna taught several weeks prior to the premiere of *Parades and Changes* in Stockholm on September 5, remembered how in one workshop exercise Anna incorporated nudity indirectly. Dividing the dancers into two groups, she asked

114 THE CHOREOGRAPHY OF ENVIRONMENTS

one to travel around the circumference of the room on a small ledge three or four feet off the ground. The other group, which Blank performed with, walked parallel lines on an imaginary grid on the floor of the studio, with instructions to change lanes only at the beginning or end of each imaginary parallel line. As the dancers traveled, they could pick up or discard objects or clothing that were within their reach. In the process, Blank said, they went through moments of total nudity. "It was the first time I was performing nude in public, and I suddenly realized I was inches away from Robert Morris, who had come to watch the dance," she said, recalling the sense of surprise she felt at finding herself without clothes (and directly in front of the prominent visual artist) almost by accident because she was focused so intently on following Anna's choreographic instructions.[95] This arrival at nudity as a by-product something else produced was just the quality of incidental undress that Anna was endeavoring to bring to the stage in *Parades and Changes*.

Anna described her use of nudity as purely sculptural and design focused, as if one were making an abstract art assemblage out of objects that happened to be bodies rather than metal. "We really had to remove our clothes for this particular dance because of the nature of the dance," she explained of the continued nudity in the section that immediately followed the undressing, known as "the paper-tearing" section. "We were tearing paper, and the paper was the same color as our skin and as we were tearing the paper, we were making music . . . so we wanted the bodies and the paper and the environment—we wanted that imagery of its all being integrated as one song, one image and one act," Anna said.[96] Apparently she did not consider the racialized differences of skin tones in the work, and the fact that she used brown butcher paper and an all-White cast, with the exception of one Korean American dancer, Kim Hahn. Everyone was folded into an assumed uniformity of flesh as a generic skin tone. The dancers' nudity in the undressing/dressing sequence and paper-tearing section that followed it in *Parades and Changes* was deliberately demystified and delivered with the same blunt practicality that the dancers used when preparing to shower or change clothes to go to bed. This was simply a task one did in taking care of this object called the body.

Anna further objectified the body and the act of uncovering it in *Parades and Changes* by carefully rehearsing with the dancers how to undress in as slow, smooth, and uninflected a manner as possible (Figure 2.17). They stood in a line facing the audience (the processional again) while maintaining eye contact with a random member of the audience as they began to methodically

Figure 2.17. Dancers in the undressing sequence from Anna Halprin's *Parades and Changes*, Centre Pompidou, Paris, France, 2004. Photograph by Rick Chapman: http://www.rickchapman.com. Courtesy of Rick Chapman.

remove their clothes. "We wanted there to be an extraordinarily smooth rhythm throughout the line, so that your eye was constantly going to objects, seeing the bodies as interesting shapes rather than only men and women," Jo Landor, the designer who assisted Anna on the production, recalled.[97] Then, just as slowly, the performers put their clothes back on. Each time they undressed they stacked their clothes neatly in front of themselves, following their own pace. When finally the last dancer had undressed and dressed, they all simply walked around the room, paused, and began a second disrobing and so on for a total of three times. The effect of each repetition was to allow the body to be viewed with the bluntness of an object being unwrapped and rewrapped repeatedly.

The years of work on the dance deck led Anna to view the body with a certain dispassion; it became another thing that needed tending, like the human skeleton she kept by her side while teaching.[98] Anna's turn toward nudity as a performance medium on the dance deck, while often reflexively linked with the sexual liberation of the 1960s and the hippie movement, also exists at the convergence of two older lineages: the social movements of the late nineteenth- and early twentieth-century German *Nachtkultur* (nudism as part of a return-to-nature movement) and "domestic nudity," the practice of naked backyard sunbathing and gardening by suburban families that boomed during the mid-twentieth century. Halprin's college dance instructor, Margaret H'Doubler, herself had a comfort with nudity rare for professional women in the early twentieth century. H'Doubler's students reported that she joined them for occasional nude swims, and, in the early decades of the twentieth century, an album of photographs surfaced depicting a few of her women students posing nude outdoors in dance postures. During the 1930s H'Doubler also traveled to Germany with a group of students to introduce them to German modern dance, which had its own links with *Nachtkultur*. In her early training, H'Doubler had intersected with the physical culture movement in the United States where fitness buffs like Bernarr Macfadden often posed nude (in discreet profile) to demonstrate their fitness as exemplary physical specimens.[99]

Back home in the United States it was actually the landscape architecture community rather than the dance world that initially helped normalize backyard nudity in the mid-century period. These decades saw the American relationship with the body and nudism being reshaped and de-eroticized through the practice of "suburban nudism." Bolstered by a belief that a free and natural lifestyle and naked living would promote a healthier society, advocates of suburban nudism sought to recover lives removed from the pressures of modern commercial society by using the naked body in harmony with nature, social improvement, and spiritual fulfillment.[100] A sociology professor from this early period, Maurice Parmelee, author of *Nudism in Modern Life*, wrote extensively as a leading exponent of the social benefits of nudism. He espoused a connection between modernism and nudism, arguing for homes to provide a "seamless interface between human civilization and the outdoors."[101] Modernist architecture magazines, and even the mainstream publication *House Beautiful*, encouraged domestic nudity as well, depicting White middle-class families sunbathing nude in enclosed patios and beside swimming pools. The circulation of these images helped to normalize nudity in domestic spaces and reflected the postwar period's approach to nudism as family oriented through this demonstration of the naked body's restrained and controlled eroticism. California was in the vanguard nationally as a site of this domestic flourishing of nudism in natural outdoor settings. As the practice spread, it deepened emerging models connecting environmentalism and nudity.[102]

It was this already active circulation of nudity as a signifier of openness and naturalness that Anna intuitively aligned with when she brought nude dancing to the deck. In the future when the Halprins would build a second weekend home in The Sea Ranch development Larry helped design on the Northern California coast, this second home would also include a smaller outside dance space. Perched atop a massive redwood burl imported for the back patio area, Anna would work in the nude on this "deck" as well, framed by the Halprin property's dramatic overlook of the Pacific Ocean (Figure 2.18). Through these actions she would bridge the streams of European *Nachtkultur*, America's suburban nudism of the 1950s, the West Coast's sexual liberation of the 1960s, and architectural modernism.

Having rendered the body as a visible, tangible, and newly stable form by rediscovering it through undress, Anna next proceeded to explore its daily maintenance.[103] The next year, in the summer of 1966, owing in part to the notoriety of *Parades and Changes*, Anna was invited to create a work at the Wadsworth Atheneum Museum of Art in Hartford, Connecticut. Initially, she was shown the theater space at the museum but, conditioned by her time on the dance deck, she declined, telling the museum staff that instead she wanted to present the performance of this commissioned work, *The Bath*, in the fountain courtyard of the large interior atrium of the museum, the closest thing to an outdoor space she could find in the museum. She praised this courtyard space as "an environment we can extend, enliven, and make relevant by performing a simple task, bathing."[104] Here was a routine task of the daily care of the body as object exported from the house to the deck and into the world. For the next several months, in preparation for the Hartford performance, Anna and her dancers met weekly, exploring the routine act of bathing, washing faces, hair, hands, and torsos for themselves and then, branching out, with a partner (Figure 2.19). The whole repertoire of physical actions they utilized, while commonplace in the bathrooms in the house up the hill, was thrown into novel relief when exported down to the dance deck. Her intention was to heighten dancers' and spectators' awareness of the tactile and sensual quality of liquid on skin as a metaphorical stripping away of deception. "I start by bringing bowls of water and having us wash our hands," Anna said in describing how she eased the dancers into a deepened focus with the task. "The effect is terrorizing. Each performer pours into the simple act his whole essence. There it comes out in the way he bathes, and he is super-conscious of it because it is a performance.... The performance of the simple action, the natural action, objectifies what is really

118 THE CHOREOGRAPHY OF ENVIRONMENTS

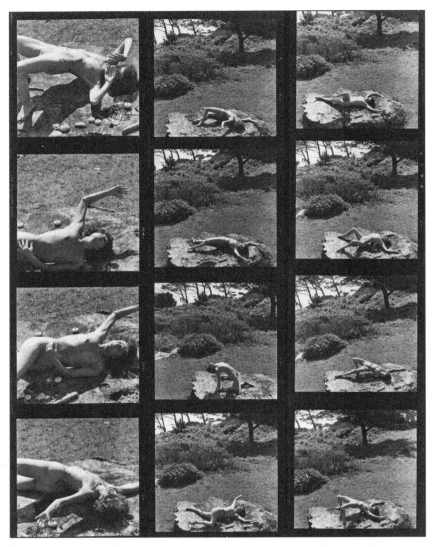

Figure 2.18. Anna Halprin doing outdoor improvisation at The Sea Ranch, California. Filmmaker/photographer: Constance Beeson, 1971. Digital transfer of original 16 mm print. 4 minutes. Anna Halprin Papers, Museum of Performance + Design, San Francisco. Courtesy of Kim Beeson.

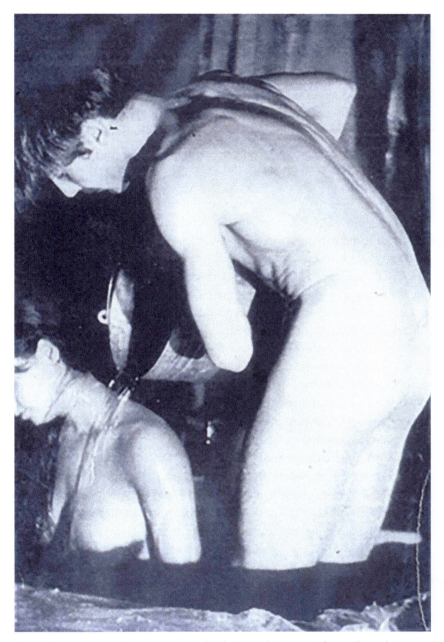

Figure 2.19. Daria Halprin and Michael Katz rehearsing *The Bath* on the dance deck, Kentfield, California, 1966. Museum of Performance + Design, San Francisco. Courtesy of the Halprin family.

120 THE CHOREOGRAPHY OF ENVIRONMENTS

going on inside the performer's self."[105] The unstated assumption was that the performer's self was White. Indeed, what would persist unexplored were racial agendas associating cleanliness in the postwar suburban American home with Whiteness. In contrast, the congestion and dirtiness of cities were then linked with those excluded from the suburbs through racial covenants, in particular, African Americans. Not just bathrooms but modernist interiors were dominated stylistically with these pairings of cleanliness and Whiteness signaled in advertisements through open expanses of floors, simple furniture forms, and an emphasis on purity and freshness with White women cleaning the house.[106]

Reasoning that the most logical costume for bathing was nudity, Anna asked museum officials for permission. Vladimir Hubernack, the museum employee responsible for the visit, gave her an immediate "no," explaining that he would lose his job if the dancers took off their clothes.[107] So she adjusted by having the dancers wear flesh-colored leotards and tights (all implicitly White as signaled through the pale cream tint of their dancewear) as a compromise. Deciding to extend this by emphasizing the opposite of undress, dressing, Anna structured the dancers' entrance into the courtyard fountain area as a processional in which they wound their way through a path of clothes and various objects that she had arranged throughout the galleries of the atheneum. The performers were instructed to advance by putting on and taking off three different items, wearing each one for a minute as they kept moving forward in a linear progression to the fountain. Anna was reconciled to not using nudity in Hartford because the performances at the Wadsworth Atheneum immediately preceded the dancers' next stop, Hunter College in New York, where they were giving the first US performance of *Parades and Changes*, with its full undressing and dressing sequence. Anna was discovering that off the deck, nudity could be much more problematic.

Ironically, the most successful exporting of the quality of ease and innocence that nudity on the dance deck had encoded happened not in a performance specifically but in a photo shoot for a special issue of *Look Magazine* made by the fashion photographer Irving Penn. Penn had been commissioned to shoot a series of photographic portraits of the most emblematic figures of West Coast counterculture for a special issue of *Look*, the first one dedicated to the arts. On September 14, 1967, the day of the shoot, Penn had rented a photographer's studio in Sausalito where one by one emblematic figures of West Coast counterculture, including the Grateful Dead, Big Brother, the Holding Company, and the Hell's Angels motorcycle gang,

CHOREOGRAPHING NATURE AND THE DANCE DECK   121

appeared before Penn's camera. Finally, it was time for Anna's San Francisco Dancers' Workshop to be photographed. Penn had never met Anna or the dancers and initially asked them to apply paint to each other in couples. Anna, who did not like that idea, persuaded Penn to let the dances begin with a warmup instead, dividing into couples, and using the act of giving each other a bath to begin moving. So, the dancers undressed and began to perform *The Bath* for Penn. He watched and then, ingeniously, he suggested first the water bowls, then the towels, then the pitchers of water—eventually all of the props—be removed. "We were left with the absolute purity of a boy and girl relating to each other in the most magical, mysterious way and yet it seemed real," Anna said years later, still recalling her awe at how Penn captured just the quality of chasteness she had been trying to achieve. "What [the dancers] were left with was creating the essence of the bath, but it had nothing to do with actual bathing anymore," she marveled.[108] The vehicle for transporting the dancers into nudity, the task of bathing the body, had been erased and what remained were just the gestures of care for each other as physical objects. Interviewed decades later, Penn still vividly recalled that afternoon, detailing through a master photographer's eyes the unique nature of the nudity marking the Halprin dancers: "Here they are without clothes, there's love, the gestures are tenderly erotic but certainly not pornographic. And there's a serenity that as a photographer I'm not used to. I didn't know Ann Halprin at all, but I know from these pictures, I tell you, I like her very much."[109] Penn's editors at *Look*, however, refused to publish the photographs because of the frank naturalness of the nudity. These photos of the Halprin dancers were the only photographs from all of the people Penn photographed that day that they would not allow. This rejection confirmed that the quality of undress the dancers projected lacked the veneer of a theatricalized show and instead revealed the confessional frankness of people paring back to that righteous body born of the dance deck.

The most comic image of nudity that grew out of work the dance deck fostered is a "before and after" diptych set of photographs taken during the 1968 Experiments in Environment workshop that Anna and Larry, along with psychologist Paul Baum, taught to forty participants drawn from performance, design, teaching, psychology, sociology, planning, dance, and personal growth training. Day seventeen of this three-and-a-half-week-long workshop was given over to what Larry's book documenting it describes as "Nakedness: cultivation of awareness and appreciation of the body" as a means to "get people into many forms of body movement and discovery of

122 THE CHOREOGRAPHY OF ENVIRONMENTS

what their bodies could do through an immediate sensory contact with the environment." Ultimately, through touching each other's bodies, the workshop leaders hoped participants would "adopt nudity as a natural state."[110] The "score," or map of activities each participant was given for the day, took as its focus "not how naked people can get, but how confident they can feel with their own bodies and how trusting and non-uptight they can become with the group." The schedule for the day cajoled: "The operative question concerning nudity was 'What are your objections to removing your clothes for a massage?'"

One week later, on the final day of the workshop, it was clear that the lesson of nudity had been absorbed by the participants and recirculated as a joking testament to just how artificial using nudity self-consciously as naturalness can be. As a final gesture of closure to the workshop the participants decided to take a pair of group photos, one clothed and one naked, and both staged on and around a wooden ladder leading from the lower to the upper small deck of the Halprins' private residence (Figures 2.20 and 2.21). The first photo in which everyone wears clothes depicts folks as goofy and relaxed, like a classic end-of-a-fun-workshop photo. The one without clothes looks markedly different. There is a quality of anxious laughter that is palpable, even from the still image, as many of the participants look up or away from the camera as if directing the photographer's attention to someone else. Larry sits at the top of a ladder glancing upward where his two daughters, Daria and Rana, stand on a second-story balcony, and they too glance off to the side. Anna is completely hidden, seated on the ground in the midst of a dense cluster of people. "Everyone stayed naked for most of the rest of the afternoon," Larry wrote in his diaristic entry for the day, suggesting a comfort with undress that is not evident from this documentation. The impression is that being naked is an edgy counterculture act, and for this population it may also have been arrived at through some group coercion.

During that same workshop Anna, Larry, Paul Baum, and the composer Charles Amerkanian had a planning meeting inside the Halprin house. A photo captures all of them clustered around the Halprins' dining table, chatting and gesturing while completely nude (Figure 2.22). As with the photos on the backyard stairs and upstairs balcony, importing nudity up into the domestic space of the home from the dance deck, and positioning it on ordinary bodies untrained in how to project controlled neutrality, resulted in an awkward tension of exposure for the participant and the imposition of the discomfort of a voyeuristic gaze for the viewer. Anna confirmed this decades

CHOREOGRAPHING NATURE AND THE DANCE DECK 123

Figure 2.20. Experiments in Environment workshop (1968), with Lawrence, Anna, Daria, and Rana Halpin, in addition to all workshop participants in the last-day group photo on the second-story deck of the Halprin home, clothed. Photograph by Paul G. Ryan. Lawrence Halprin Collection, Stuart Weitzman School of Design, The Architectural Archives, University of Pennsylvania, Philadelphia.

124　THE CHOREOGRAPHY OF ENVIRONMENTS

Figure 2.21. Second photo taken after decision to pose again, nude, 1968. Photograph by Paul G. Ryan. Lawrence Halprin Collection, Stuart Weitzman School of Design, The Architectural Archives, University of Pennsylvania, Philadelphia.

Figure 2.22. Anna and Lawrence Halprin, Paul Baum, and Charles Amerkanian, Experiments in Environment workshop, Halprin home, Kentfield, California, 1968. Photograph by Paul G. Ryan. Courtesy of Paul G. Ryan.

later when, shown this photo of the nude meeting and asked about the circumstances, she started laughing. "Oh, that's so funny!" she exclaimed, amused by the absurd earnestness of the effort to look cool while standing stark naked in a leadership meeting in the house.[111]

Larry too thought differently about the afternoon of workshop nudity years later when he expressed reservations about the photo of the nude participants being used to accompany writing about this period. He was concerned that it could perpetuate the wrong image about the workshop as a casual hippie gathering. The Halprin daughters also sensed a dissonance around nudity when the flow between the house and the dance deck was reversed and activities from the art life they were participating in with their parents tried to spread into the private domestic space uphill. "On the dance deck I was workshopping and performing nude as a teenager," Daria said many years later as a middle-aged adult, "but when I went back upstairs to my life with my boyfriend, being sexually intimate was forbidden. It was very confusing that there were such extremely different rules between the deck and the house."[112] Over time divisions between the two also became challenging for Larry. Anna tried to make a conscious effort to keep participants

126 THE CHOREOGRAPHY OF ENVIRONMENTS

and activities in both spheres separate, but there were occasions when the exuberance of the dancers on the deck burst upward into the house and family space. One of the more distressing instances occurred when Larry, who had been away on business travel, returned early to find Anna's whole workshop crew crowded into the private Halprin house with the family living spaces overflowing with wild dancing and partying. Larry exploded and stormed out, demanding that the dancers leave, while young Daria and Rana sat at the top of the staircase crying and Anna raced out and punctured the tires of Larry's car to prevent him from departing. "We just wanted our father and calm home back," they said in remembering this event. Clearly there was a limit as to just how contiguous family life could be with the art happening on the deck.

The Dance Deck and Museum Exhibitions

Using nature to expand the borders of one's awareness would become prophetic of the impact working on the dance deck would have on the thousands of students, artists, and collaborators who stepped onto its wooden surface across the nearly three-quarters of a century of Anna's teaching and choreographing there. Its influence extended beyond that of just a site of dance innovation into its being regarded as a model of structural rethinking, an architectural prototype of a new space for movement invention. Performance Studies scholar Adrian Heathfield, writing in a catalog essay for the 2018 New York Museum of Modern Art tribute to the Judson Dance Theater, lauded the dance deck as "ghost architecture" for Judson Memorial Church, thus referencing this legendary New York center for 1960s dance experimentalism as taking its ideological inspiration from the Halprins' deck as much as Anna's pedagogy.[113] This major Museum of Modern Art exhibition commemorating the innovators of postmodern dance featured in its opening gallery a massive floor-to-ceiling image of the dance deck (Figure 2.23). Superimposed on top if it were smaller photos of some of the works Anna did there. These include her signature *Branch Dance*, referenced in a dramatic black-and-white photograph from the 1950s of Anna lying on the deck, her torso arced in a dramatic spiral as her arms reach upward, echoing the curve of a madrone tree branch, while her fellow dancer, A. A. Leath, holds the actual branch, thrusting it up vertically from his own reclining posture on the stage (Figure 2.24). A group photograph of the famed 1960 summer dance

Figure 2.23. Installation view of the exhibition "Judson Dance Theater: The Work Is Never Done," curated by Ana Janevski and Thomas J. Lax, Museum of Modern Art. Photograph by Peter Butler, 2019, IN2404.8. Licensed by SCALA/Art Resource, New York.

workshop Anna taught on the dance deck was also featured as a representative of these generative two-week July dance intensives Anna offered every summer for years (see Figure 2.15).

The dance deck had also been featured internationally the previous year, in 2017, on the occasion of the once-every-five-year convening of the major international contemporary art exhibition, "documenta 14: documenta Halle" in Kassel, Germany. In this instance, the dance deck was referenced via gallery space organized around scores, images, and other archival documents pertaining to works Anna made on the deck. Curator Pierre Bal-Blanc in his exhibition notes lauds the deck specifically for its generative force in presenting "a landscape score." "The kinesthetic experience and collectivity that this interstitial space offers can be traced back to the beginnings of modern dance," he writes as an abbreviated nod to the layers of dance history Anna brought forward and from which she parted ways through her work on the dance deck.[114] Accompanying Bal-Blanc's personal view of dance history is a photograph of the dance deck, not with Anna but instead with Merce Cunningham on the one occasion when he offered that single

128 THE CHOREOGRAPHY OF ENVIRONMENTS

Figure 2.24. Branch Dance installation of the exhibition "Judson Dance Theater: The Work Is Never Done," curated by Ana Janevski and Thomas J. Lax, Museum of Modern Art. Photograph by Peter Buler, 2019, IN2404.12. Licensed by SCALA/Art Resource, New York. (The exhibited photographs belong to Anna Halprin Archives, Museum of Performance + Design, San Francisco, photographed by Warner Jepson. Courtesy Warner Jepson family.)

lecture demonstration there on a July evening in 1957. It is late summer, and the borders of the stage are crusted with dry fallen leaves, offering a vivid sense of how permissive the dance deck was of intrusions from the natural world onto this platform for art (Figure 3.23). Bal-Blanc expanded on this in a May 29, 2020, reference in an online column, *Dance Office*, dedicated to contemporary dance and performance art, praising Anna's dance deck as an "architectonic arrangement that transformed dance practice, just as the free plan and the Dom-Ino house designed by Le Corbusier revolutionized architecture."[115] The Dom-Ino house reference here gestures to the open floor plan modular structure designed by the innovative French architect Le Corbusier, which allowed for enormous freedom in designing the interior configuration of the building. In a parallel fashion the Halprin-Lauterer deck similarly cracked open how theaters configure the live body.

As an object, the dance deck would over time cement its status as existing at the crossroads of momentous occasions in American art and design environmentalism via the Halprin household. It was where multiple disciplines (dance, landscape design, and modernist architecture) were conjoined, melding Larry's architectural design and Anna's modernist dance innovations, and where two social structures (parenting and collaborative art making) fused. The impact this deck in the woods had in shaping strategies and paths of investigation for twentieth- and twenty-first-century art and artists would extend well beyond its borders on that hillside in Kentfield.

3

Disappearing Chairs and Participatory Dances

Sit Down and Make Yourself Uncomfortable: JB Blunk Seating and the Halprin Home

Visitors arriving on formal occasions to the Halprin home would have ducked under the floating staircase, turned right, and immediately stepped into the bright, window-lined living room. For the initial few years of the house in the early 1950s, a tailored, upholstered, and slim-profile sectional sofa bordered two of the plate glass windows of the living room. A pair of small, armless, thinly upholstered modern chairs stood opposite, angled toward the huge open space in the center of the room (Figure 3.1). All seating pivoted away from the inviting beauty outdoors, instead tipping inward to a large fireplace with a façade of smooth, polished river stones. The placement and slim profile of the furniture set up an air of expectant energy in the room as the open space in the center beckoned like a stage before a performance. The sparseness of the furnishings in the room simultaneously gestured toward the dominance of architecture in the house, reminding gently that in this aesthetic the formal beauty of the built environment governed. Space was something to be framed, not filled.

Beginning in 1965, and over the course of the next two years, the anticipatory vitality of the room increased and the dynamic between bodies and design intensified. The dominance of the architecture expanded as the upholstered seating disappeared, replaced instead by a series of three massive carved wooden objects intended as benches and seating (Figure 3.2). Commissioned by Larry from the Marin County woodworker and ceramicist JB Blunk, the seating was fashioned from salvaged cypress trees, material distinctive to Northern California artisans. The chair and benches had the mass of huge fallen trees, their surfaces gashed by chainsaws and then burnished to a sensuous smoothness, imparting to the honey-hued wood a warm sheen. Not fully sculpture and too uncomfortable to use as routine furniture, this seating was poised in the liminal design space between material

The Choreography of Environments. Janice Ross, Oxford University Press. © Oxford University Press 2025.
DOI: 10.1093/9780197775660.003.0004

Figure 3.1. Halprin house in Kentfield, California, c. 1950s. Lawrence Halprin Collection, Stuart Weitzman School of Design, The Architectural Archives, University of Pennsylvania, Philadelphia.

found in nature and forms engineered to echo nature as they intruded into domestic space.

Blunk's fascination with embedding process in the final work, an opposition to stasis, and a repurposing of the found elements of nature resonated strongly with the aesthetic approaches of both Halprins. As noted with Larry's redesign of the approach to Yosemite Falls, an essential aspect of his design was his valuing of the sensory experience of process and physical movement in the planning of environments and his strong opposition to stasis and symmetry. In Larry's urban designs, this would take the form of his avoidance of traditional public furniture and vista points (with occasional exceptions) and his suggestion that people sit on ledges, walls, rocks, logs, or even the ground. Anna too was actively moving toward increasing the sensory alertness of her audiences and guiding them into actively participating in her dances. Like Anna and Larry, JB Blunk found the sensuous in the essence of his medium—in his instance this was wood (discarded nature), and he

Figure 3.2. JB Blunk "throne" chair and cone bench in the Halprin house in Kentfield, California. Photograph by Leslie Williamson: © lesliewilliamson.com. Courtesy of Leslie Williamson.

revealed how each material yields its own forms, meanings, and stories. With its wily ambiguities, Blunk's works invited and repelled. His seating pieces teased visually by appearing to be sensuously undulating chairs and benches, but they jolted any user with an unyielding cold platform (Figure 3.3).

Architectural historian Kristina Wilson calls this quality in seating that *appears* appealing "visual empathy." She uses this phrase to describe objects that "present a form that looks accommodating to the user and invites the prospect of a comfortable interaction as viewers imagine what using them might be like."[1] Visually empathetic designs coax a human figure to anticipate sinking into its curves and indentations that echo the human body and invite interaction with a user. However, Blunk's designs tease just as readily as they summon. Larry's landscape designs too would alternate between inviting human users and then unsettling them with seating that was abstract and part of the landscape but not ideal for perching or reclining on—thus prompting the visitor to move along. In this way the uncomfortable seating of the Halprin home prefigured what would become the implicit pedagogy in Larry's landscape architecture and Anna's choreography: that of increasing

Figure 3.3. Installation view of JB Blunk *Throne and Bench* from the Halprin home (c. 1967), on display during "Three Landscapes: JB Blunk, Anna, and Lawrence Halprin," Blum & Poe Gallery, Los Angeles, 2022. Photograph by Josh Schaedel. Courtesy of the artists and BLUM Los Angeles, Tokyo, New York.

spectators' awareness, active engagement, and participatory commerce with their surroundings. A hard wooden bench was an odd choice for living room furniture for a family. Indeed, the spare utility of Blunk's benches looked (and felt!) more like something that belonged alongside a trail in the woods than in the most formal room of a home (Figure 3.4).

In his outdoor designs, Larry pushed this elimination of comfortable seating even further. The monumental fountains Larry included in his works of the 1960s and 1970s—the *Portland Open Space Sequence* and Seattle's *Freeway Park*—effectively imported the tumbling streams and jagged rock ledges of the Cascade Mountains into the heart of an urban city. It also imported the kind of massive hunks of stone and logs one would plop down on for a rest while hiking in the Sierras and backcountry (Figure 3.5). There are no park benches in the wilderness, and effectively this absence is also true of Larry's urban designs. There is also no plush theater seating in Anna's performance spaces. She, like Larry, was manipulating seating as a way to induce people to undergo an experience, to participate viscerally with their senses in the outdoors. Environmental immersion for Larry was never about

134 THE CHOREOGRAPHY OF ENVIRONMENTS

Figure 3.4. Installation view of JB Blunk cone bench from the Halprin living room (c. 1967), on display during "Three Landscapes: JB Blunk, Anna, and Lawrence Halprin," Blum & Poe Gallery, Los Angeles, 2022. Photograph by Josh Schaedel. Courtesy of the artists and BLUM Los Angeles, Tokyo, New York.

Figure 3.5. Detail of Freeway Park, Seattle, designed by Lawrence Halprin. Photograph by Matt Hagen. Courtesy of Matt Hagen.

passively sitting and gazing at nature; rather, it was a lesson in learning to see through feeling with the senses while engaging with surroundings through his designs. Architectural historian John Beardsley has noted that this push for participation in Larry's works inaugurated in the central decades of his career marked a dramatic departure from traditional landscape architecture. "Halprin represented rather than recreated nature," Beardsley explained about the fundamental radicalness of his innovations. "He sought to bring the experience of the rock and water of the mountain landscape for those dwelling within the brick and stucco of cities—so that they could share the experience of nature, even if in a fabricated form."[2] At the same time Larry was conscious that his innovations allowing the lightly mediated pleasures of nature to be freshly discovered in an urban setting were being taken up nationally, and eventually internationally, and his reimagining of what he called "street furniture," places for the public to repose in his environments, became a significant part of this. "Larry did not design for comfort, he designed for the ecology of it," his youngest daughter, Rana, noted about what guided his priorities in acquiring, and designing, seating.[3]

Another method for thinking about how aesthetics was prioritized over passive comfort in Larry's, Anna's, and Blunk's work is to trace the way

136 THE CHOREOGRAPHY OF ENVIRONMENTS

they tilted toward being more visually empathetic than physically empathetic. "Physical empathy" in design is a phrase Wilson uses to denote the emotional pull that objects of furniture exert on us through their promise and actual fulfillment of being enjoyable to touch and use. However, here she cautions that even physically empathetic furniture objects can harbor hidden agendas. "Ultimately such empathetic forms are also tools of control because their biomorphic shapes constrain the body that sits on them," she warns.[4] This dynamic of how design invites and then controls is an important frame for considering the subtle yet forceful quality of bodily control the uncomfortable seating in the Halprin home delivered. While it enticed with a biomorphic elegance that appeared to anticipate the bodily form and needs of the user, in practice the seating in the Halprin home could be cruel to bodies.[5] This had the consequence of jolting one into an alert posture and, soon, to rise up and move on. Thinking about how physical engagement can also be a form of control allows a different perspective on distinctions between the participatory theater of Anna's dance and Larry's designs. It offers insights as to why dance audiences accustomed to being seated were more resistant than users of urban environments to join in. Rising out of your chair at a dance performance meant you de facto became a performer; moving through one of Larry's urban spaces meant you were engaging with design ecology and urban art, not becoming the show itself. It all started with the uncomfortable chairs.

Once touched, Blunk's biomorphic seating rebuffed the sitter with irregular surfaces too stiffly vertical for reclining. Dubbed *Throne and Benches*, by the family, Daria and Rana both remember the trio of Blunk seating in the living room as being so uncomfortable that sitting on the cement floor was the more inviting option. "It's no secret that the JB Blunk furniture was not comfortable to sit on," Rana said, reflecting decades later about life in the Halprin house for the two young daughters. "We never sat on that furniture. It was art that was in the living room. Only my father loved sitting on that big throne chair, but we sat on the floor around the fireplace. Not everybody loved the furniture—we used to joke about it all the time."[6] Daria agreed, remembering how Larry's affection for the Blunk chair somehow allowed him to imagine it as a regal frame that was actually comfortable for him. "That was Larry's chair and he found it comfortable. He did. I mean, we added pillows to it when he got old. But he loved sitting in the throne chair and having the whole family gathering around," she said. "Our family joke was that Anna and Larry never actually had a piece of furniture that was comfortable to sit on," Daria laughed. "You know, it may have looked good, but it was *never* comfortable to sit on."[7]

Despite their uncomfortable nature, from the time of their arrival, the Blunk objects would remain the only major seating in the Halprins' living room for the life of the household. Viewed independently of anyone actually using them, the Blunk pieces projected a sense of inhabiting the room fully on their own, as if in conversation with one another. This was facilitated by the manner in which their biomorphic forms echoed the contours of an abstracted human body. More sculpture than chair, more relic of a massive tree than a bench, and an artifact bearing traces of Blunk's sanding, grinding, and chainsaw labors, these seats were invocations to move rather than rest and at the same time they documented the process of their making. Eventually, a set of four sleek metal-framed chairs with slung leather seats joined the Blunk seating, increasing the presence of physically awkward, but artful, seating in the room. As with the Blunk chair and benches, these were choreographic objects. The chairs forced users to cautiously drop into their slide-like interior and then struggle to decorously eject themselves from its leather recesses or risk being poured onto the floor. These mid-century modern sling chairs were enticing with their sensuousness and their visual echoing of a body touching them. In this regard the uncomfortableness of Blunk's seating and the sling chairs was aligned with the mid-century modernist chair style of spare fashion over comfort. Placing this seating in the Halprin home complemented the lean aesthetic of the architecture and landscape. As objects they supported the house in displaying itself as a modernist experience and disciplined its inhabitants into an obedience to environments and art.

Several years after the sofa and chairs disappeared, the cozy and intimate Danish teak dining table in the adjacent open dining room was replaced by a dramatic table fashioned from a rough ten-foot slab of polished burl harvested from a discarded old-growth coastal redwood, another JB Blunk work that was originally commissioned as a desk for Larry's San Francisco office and brought to the house after he closed his larger offices (Figure 3.6). The colossal weight of this tabletop was balanced on a pair of spindly redwood sawhorses. If the slyness of this repurposing of a tool of wood demolition into a structure of support went unnoticed initially, then the prank of its surface with a large open knothole was inescapable. As with the *Throne and Benches*, the table carried its history, in this instance in the form of this hole at one end where a former cavity in the trunk might have housed an owl

Figure 3.6. JB Blunk dining table, c. 1978, from the Halprin home. Displayed in the Blum & Poe Gallery, Los Angeles, 2022. Photograph by Josh Schaedel. Courtesy of the artists and BLUM Los Angeles, Tokyo, New York.

family. Daria recalled the lessons in attentiveness the table imparted every time a family meal commenced and a tablecloth was spread. "Anna didn't want the Blunk pieces to get stained with anything," Daria recalled. "So, she'd cover up with a huge tablecloth, but she'd often forget to put something over the burl hole. And so, inevitably, something would fall right through the burl hole, like a vase of flowers or a wine glass, as we were eating."[8] Daria remembered the seating around the Blunk table as being equally problematic. "Just figuring where to sit was a challenge because the table was neither round nor square, one had to tuck into a crevasse along its thick irregular edge," she said. The challenges of seating also extended to the dining chairs (Figure 3.7). "There were these wonderful chairs that went around that table," Daria said, recalling the family's set of modernist metal and leather sling chairs. "But if you sat in them, you discovered that you pretty much just slid off right onto the floor. The Halprin aesthetics were groundbreaking and

Figure 3.7. Dining room with leather and metal sling dining chairs in the Halprin home, Kentfield, California. From Bushell Homes' staged photos of the home with some original Halprin furniture used for its 2022 sale. Photograph by Jacob Elliott: https://www.jacobelliott.com/. Courtesy of Jacob Elliott.

impeccable, but they also inclined toward the artistic integrity of things over comfort."[9] Nature always had the last word in the Halprin household.

An eco-modernist aesthetic saturated the Halprin home with a mantra of design over lifestyle, or perhaps it's more appropriate to say design *as* lifestyle. It's not that the house was a showplace for streams of visitors. Quite the contrary—its secluded location meant that primarily the immediate family and very close friends were regular visitors. Rather, Anna and Larry enjoyed surrounding themselves with carefully curated artifacts signaling a deliberately contemporary life and a streamlined existence where the idea of a stage and performance was never far away. For Anna, the stakes had the additional complication of having to work within the constraints of being a traditional postwar wife in her domestic life and a boundary-pushing activist in her art life. These paradoxes resolved in a radical aesthetic as she took apart many of those givens from domestic life as fodder for her choreography, and it was in this arena where her rebellion unfolded. At home, the family honored traditional conservative Jewish observances of weekly Shabbat dinners and major

140   THE CHOREOGRAPHY OF ENVIRONMENTS

Jewish holidays, and Larry was generally the one who made the home furniture purchasing decisions. Concessions to comfort and convenience were negotiable, but the one constant was a heightened awareness of the body and a deep respect for the seductive beauty of well-crafted art. Years later, when the family would build a second home at The Sea Ranch, the modernist coastal development that Larry master-planned, Anna would quietly slip away to a local hardware store and pick up a few inexpensive plastic stacking patio chairs to be used as comfortable places to sit for family dining, mixing them in with the beautiful, but brutal, modernist seating.[10] Discomfort in these early years of invention for both Halprins was enormously generative, but in their final decades it would become just as unpleasant as it was for every other aging body.

As objects in the Halprin home, the Blunk chairs occupy a dual status as iconic mid-century modern furniture pieces in their abstraction and economy while also borrowing elements from regional California funk art—a visual art genre of sophisticated casualness that played with everyday objects, audience engagement, and subject matter that was often autobiographical. In this way, they also anticipated an emerging hybrid funk/modernist quality in Anna's dancing. Funk art often lacked a clear meaning as part of its resistance to consumer culture and preference for using found objects. In turn sensuous and ironic, several of these attributes of funk had clear counterparts in Anna's works like *The Four-Legged Stool* and *The Five-Legged Stool* and, to a lesser degree, Larry's 1960s redevelopment projects like *Ghirardelli Square*, where he "recovered" a discarded confectionary factory. The funk art movement of the 1960s was concentrated in the Bay Area, and while neither Anna nor Larry self-identified as funk artists, the Blunk objects certainly imported its aesthetic into their home.

Viewed from a design perspective, the amorphous forms of the Blunk pieces—with their hovering between organic matter, abstractions of a functional piece of furniture, and the hominess of a handcrafted object— embody the range of aesthetic qualities defining modernist furniture of the mid-century. They also highlight the linkage between human movement and nature. Their surface texture suggesting the flowing of living tissue was also pointedly evocative of the work of sculptor Isamu Noguchi, one of Blunk's major mentors. Noguchi was also an important mid-century designer of abstract biomorphic furniture as well as set pieces for nearly two dozen works by the dancer Martha Graham. Graham's signature Greek

Figure 3.8. Isamu Noguchi, male and female form on maquette for Jocasta's bed for Martha Graham's *Night Journey* (1947), paint, canvas, wood, and plaster. Photograph by Kevin Noble. © 2024 The Isamu Noguchi Foundation and Garden Museum, New York/Artists Rights Society (ARS), New York.

myth dances in particular featured sets by Noguchi, including *Cave of the Heart* (1946), *Errand into the Maze* (1947), *Night Journey* (1947), and *Clytemnestra* (1958), and, as with the Blunk objects, Noguchi's set pieces were notorious among Graham's dancers for being decorative yet often brutal to actually pose or stand on in performance (Figure 3.8). Blunk's seating, like Noguchi's set pieces, propelled action rather than repose and also built on Jungian archetypical forms sensed in the raw material, but more abstractly than the work of Noguchi. It was one thing to do this on stage as a deliberate impetus for dance, as in the tortuous bed of male and female symbols Noguchi designed for *Night Journey*. However, a very different dynamic resulted when this approach was transplanted into the domestic space of the Halprin home and guests were treated to the cruel trick of a chair on which you can't sit.

142 THE CHOREOGRAPHY OF ENVIRONMENTS

The Chair as Stage

Chairs are arguably the most choreographic items of furniture in a modernist home because each one imposes its own distinctive little dance of lowering, resting, and rising on the user. As a case in point, Anna's personal encounters with the Blunk seating in the Halprin household could appear at times more like negotiations with stage sets than family furnishings. In 2014, *The New York Times* interviewed Anna for a feature on the occasion of an exhibition at the Graham Foundation in Chicago, "Experiments in Environment: The Halprin Workshops, 1966–1971," exploring the Halprins' interdisciplinary creative process through photographs, films, drawings, and scores. Larry had died five years earlier, and so perhaps reaching intuitively as a way to include his presence, Anna chose the Blunk throne and bench on which to pose (Figure 3.9).[11] Wearing a lacy white dress draped elegantly about her, she perches on the throne, hugging her knees to her chest, her bare feet resting on the edge of the adjacent bench as she gazes out to the viewer with the quizzical ease of a forest sprite who has just briefly alighted on this old log as the dappled sunlight of oak and madrone branches through the window add to the illusion that this is a scene captured in nature, not a house. The curve of the back of the throne chair frames her perfectly; its hardness is visible but at the same time so is her ease in finding just how to position herself so that any perilousness of her positioning is masked. The previous year, when the *San Francisco Chronicle* published a feature on her in tandem with the 2013 revival of *Parades and Changes*, she had also chosen the Blunk seating as her prop.[12] In these images Anna drapes herself across the *Throne and Bench* with the deceptive ease of a ninety-three-year-old odalisque reclining on a soft chaise. However, now her stiff smile at the viewer brings an edge of anxiousness into the whole scene and redirects one's attention to what is actually her tenuous pose on the slippery surface of Blunk's *Throne and Bench*. The unease of her expression hints at her silent struggle against the chair's slick surface (Figure 3.10). In choosing repeatedly to pose on the Blunk furniture, Anna has made the modernist décor of the Halprin home as much the focus as her own body. In a single gesture and image, she timestamps herself as a mid-century modernist while projecting a parallel aesthetic statement about her enduring advocacy for participation and resistance to reclining into a cushioned old age.

Anna's pose also links her with Daria, who, fifty years earlier, was photographed in a casual moment, on this same Blunk chair, during

Figure 3.9. Anna Halprin on JB Blunk "throne" in the Halprin home, Kentfield, California, 2014. Photograph by Drew Kelly for *The New York Times*. Courtesy of Drew Kelly.

the Halprins' Experiments in Environment 1968 summer workshop (Figure 3.11). Paul G. Ryan, the young photographer whom the Halprins hired to document the workshop, captured one of the most iconic images of both Daria and that era in this single photograph. Gazing evenly at the camera without the hint of a smile or unease, Daria's manner is simultaneously defiant and seductive. She sits on the throne wearing a two-piece swimsuit covered with a sleeveless tank top, knees tucked up tightly to her chest, her bare feet on the edge of the seat as she gazes out evenly at the photographer, one bare arm draped across her chest and the other relaxed by her side. The sensuous arabesques of Blunk's forms are echoed in the fleshy

Figure 3.10. Anna Halprin on JB Blunk seating at the Halprin home, Kentfield, California, 2013. Photograph by Liz Hafalia/*San Francisco Chronicle*/Polaris.

curves of her slim bare legs and arms. Daria's spontaneous pose uncannily echoes Sandro Botticelli's *Birth of Venus*, the famous fifteenth-century portrait of Venus, born of sea spray and just arriving on land on her scallop shell as she gestures to cover her nudity with her bare arm draped across her chest (Figure 3.12). Daria is an updated hippie version of this classic early Renaissance portrait of femininity. In this image she represents the quintessential Halprin body—sensual without being overtly sexual, open, present, intensely focused, and immensely comfortable in her skin. This is the performing presence that Anna spent her career honing and animating. Like Blunk's work, the easy beauty of Daria's body is an idealization of Northern California's natural world. These images of both Anna and Daria on the Blunk furniture highlight an unremarked-on dimension of the furniture; they in fact are far more like objects of a stage set than domestic furnishings. There are very few artists who can sit on a chair and already be performing and very few objects of furniture that can sustain this impression.

As household objects free from orthodoxy and theory, Blunk's chair and benches are readily transparent about the history of their own making. A native of Kansas, Blunk discovered art while a student at UCLA. After serving in the military during the Korean War, he returned to California

DISAPPEARING CHAIRS AND PARTICIPATORY DANCES 145

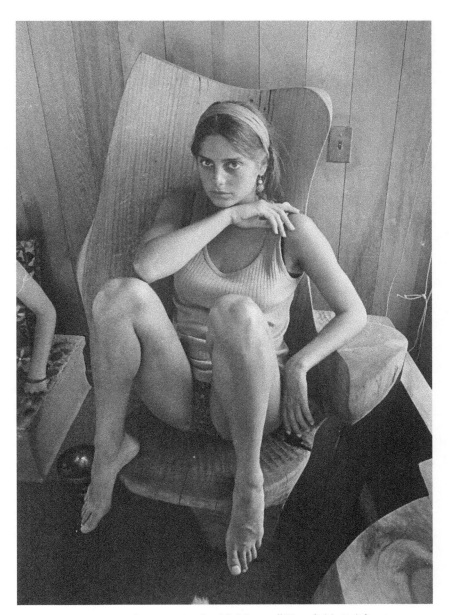

Figure 3.11. Daria Halprin on JB Blunk's "throne," Kentfield, California. Photograph by Paul G. Ryan, 1968. Courtesy of Paul G. Ryan.

Figure 3.12. Sandro Botticelli, *Nascita di Venere* (The Birth of Venus), Italian, c. 1484–1486. Le Gallerie degli Uffizi (Florence), 1890. n. 878. Courtesy of Wikimedia Commons.

in 1954 as part of the same postwar wave of veterans who, like Larry, were migrating to the west and creating new suburban lives. Blunk built his own home and studio in Inverness, Northern California, and began working in wood and clay in a style that left much of the natural form of his found wood pieces intact. It is easy to see how Larry would have been drawn to Blunk's furnishings, which, like Larry's work, were the consequence of the artist intuitively memorializing his time in nature communing with its giants. After days, and often weeks, of studying the natural forms of the dead trees, Blunk took chainsaws and hand tools to the enormous old-growth redwood burls and cypress trees, and by leaving much of the natural form intact, he highlighted the inherent qualities of the organic materials.

The Blunk benches and chairs triggered curious resonances: they looked like logs one came upon in a forest, yet they were domesticated by virtue of being placed indoors. In a curious loop they then aestheticized the outdoors, inviting a shift in perspective that made nature rather than furniture or architecture the model for constructed seating surfaces outdoors. Larry's urban designs would play with this further. Similarly, he looked to nature rather than domestic furniture as his inspiration for how to design seating where visitors to his urban spaces might pause and take in the experience

Figure 3.13. People sitting on poured concrete rounds in the midst of the landscaped glade at Levi's Plaza, designed in 1982 by Lawrence Halprin. Photograph by Alexis Woods, 2011. Courtesy of The Cultural Landscape Foundation.

before moving on. Often using found driftwood, rustic slabs of granite, or poured concrete, he effectively exported a Blunk-like sensibility to seating, moving it from his house back into nature (Figure 3.13).

Larry's work too eschewed passive spectatorship. Instead of armchairs for docile contemplation, his designed urban environments increasingly de-emphasized places to sit. "Motation" was the term he invented to describe his use of movement as a starting point to generate form in urban design, and it also references his regard of the human body in motion as a primary environmental design tool. "The environment exists for the purpose of movement," was a central dictum of his work. In a work like his *FDR Memorial* there are no park benches; instead, large, rough-edged slabs of the same carnelian granite that compose the memorial are placed thematically throughout the five "rooms" of the memorial as seating that also ties the viewer thematically to the focus of each space. In the War Room, for example, the huge blocks of red granite lie in a chaotic jumble, some resting on their sides, edges, or corners or tipped into one another like children's blocks carelessly tossed about. Their haphazardness is, of course, deceptive, as is their wily spilling

148 THE CHOREOGRAPHY OF ENVIRONMENTS

from symbolic objects in the memorial into seating cunningly recruiting us as participants in this recounting of history. The cold, hard surfaces of the granite slabs are invitations to pause and reflect, and they serve as reminders that history has already engaged us (see Figure 1.19).

Modernist Seating

After centuries of padded, cushioned, deep-seated, upholstered, armrest-heavy, contoured seating shaped to support and ease the body at rest, the humble chair met the clean modernist impulse in this postwar period. Suddenly, chairs became glamorous objects that issued their own directives to the bodies they confronted. Encountering these designed objects required an impromptu dance of adjustment where bodies were contorted into unnatural positions. Seats like Hardoy's butterfly chair with its sack-like canvas seat stretched over a metal frame that was a feature of the garden in the Halprins' first home in Mill Valley (and would later reappear in the living room of their Kentfield home and the garden of their second home at The Sea Ranch), as well as the leather and metal sling chairs in the Kentfield home, epitomized the cool geometry of modernist furniture design (see Figure 2.6, depicting Hardoy's butterfly chairs in the garden of the first Halprin home, and Figure 2.11, in the Kentfield home). The importance of the chair to modernism reflects the impulse of the era to design more toward visual impact than physical pleasure. It also demonstrates how to scale modernist design to be widely accessible. There may have been more than a bit of nostalgia in Larry's inclusion of the metal sling chairs in the Kentfield home. Designed as a tubular steel frame that served as a scaffold across which a rectangular length of leather was stretched, the chairs blended a machine-made form with the trim functionality and warm texture of natural leather. These sling chairs, therefore, could have served as a daily visual link for Larry to his years at Harvard and the Bauhaus aesthetic of the beauty of utilitarian lean design and the transparency of materials.

A chair is unique as a household object because it anticipates the body's corporeality and materiality by taking the place of certain muscles needed to hold the body in a seated posture. George Nelson, design director for the Herman Miller furniture company, in noting the great range of uses different designs of chairs address, from working and dining to reading and reclining, argued for well-designed chairs as tools to "reduce wear and tear on spine,

DISAPPEARING CHAIRS AND PARTICIPATORY DANCES   149

neck, arms, legs, and eyes."[13] As a consequence of this versatility and the small scale and affordability of chairs as furniture (and because nearly all the great designers and architects of the era experimented with designing chairs), seating functioned as a major instrument for the introduction of modernism in mid-century homes. (Even Frank Lloyd Wright, who grumbled about sitting in an ungraceful and undignified posture, designed his own range of modernist seating pieces.[14]) Nelson wrote in his 1953 book, *Chairs*, "Which objects will be selected by posterity as most typical of Western culture in the first half of the twentieth century is anybody's guess, but I suspect that the contemporary chair will be somewhere on the list."[15] The chair was on that list, but what few realized then was that this seemingly innocent piece of furniture carried with it covert politics as well. Wilson suggests that Nelson's and other modernist chair designs were "alienating or bodily uncomfortable" and that "In their abstraction—in their lack of visual empathy, their lack of figuration—they presume a level of authority over the lives of those who use them."[16] It's interesting to think about this issue of seating imposing authority in regard to seating in both Anna's and Larry's works. They both were very intentional in negotiating a politics of control through chairs by removing comfortable seating from the environments and performances they constructed as they orchestrated how to induce audiences into fuller participation.

Seating, Its Discontents, and the Move toward Audience Participation

One furnishing that was a trophy piece for the majority of postwar American homes by 1955, and proudly displayed in most living rooms, was the new commercially available television set. Yet despite 85% of homes having one, a television would never appear in the Halprin living room. Extending the reach of the chairs, the noticeable absence of a television belonged to that class of objects in the Halprin home that either by their use or placement further supported the valuing of motion over inertia. Instead of making the consumption of electronically mediated and physically detached entertainment the locus of family gatherings as a television did, the seating in the Halprins' living room signaled the opposite: this was a home that primed bodies to move. By 1968, a small television eventually appeared in the narrow hallway between the kitchen and dining area of the Halprin home, but it was never

150   THE CHOREOGRAPHY OF ENVIRONMENTS

a featured object (see Figure 2.22). Just as comfortable chairs invite repose, televisions impose passive spectatorship on still bodies, and these behaviors were not favored in the Halprin home. Feeling uncomfortable means noticing the body. Stiffness, pain, a body part cramping because of an inhospitable seating surface—these are all circumstances that redirect attention to our physical reality. Noticing the body then forces attention into the present moment—an essential precondition for dancing but also for becoming alert to one's environment and the natural world.

Uncomfortable seating prompts body adjustments; this discomfort brings physical awareness, which in turn primes the body to move. This little chain reaction of cause and effect between a body and uncomfortable seating usually transpires on a kinesthetic level; language is not necessary. However, once one's attention is drawn to the state of their own body, they bring a different receptiveness to the regard of other bodies. Anna and Larry furnished and designed their home in a way that implicitly shaped it as a laboratory environment where bodies were ever present and increased physical awareness the objective. Space was always being negotiated and activity in itself was the response. One of the productive tensions of the Halprins' art is that it was from such a deliberately domestic and modernist postwar setting that they launched innovation through movement as a prime medium in their respective work. Larry made public space a domestically scaled experience and Anna took domestic space and made it a public exploration.

While there is an inherent logic to this dynamic of discomfort, unrest, and motion that bodies encountering objects negotiate all the time, it doesn't necessarily make for compelling theater. This was the lesson Anna learned when, energized at the conclusion of the 1960 summer workshop where she had been working with a group of dancers on task performance—their unmediated responses to a range of objects and physical situations—she applied this method of "finding" movement into an evening-length work to be presented to the public. The result was *The Four-Legged Stool* (1961). This was the first of what would become a trilogy of dances drawing from domestic objects that Anna would create using chairs as props, symbols, and titles as she worked to move audiences into deeper emotional participation. Her approach would be two-pronged as initially she streamlined the work to be closer to life by redefining virtuosity as delivering the unexpected rather than the pre-rehearsed. If the live event was more immediate and shaped in the instant for the performers, as the improvisatory structure of *The Four-Legged Stool* demanded, then it should have a similar immediacy for the audience, she reasoned. When this proved not to be the case and early audiences and critics rebelled against the haphazardness of the whole evening, she worked harder to balance choice with structure in her subsequent audience participation works: *The Five-Legged Stool* (1962) and *Apartment 6* (1965).

The Four-Legged Stool was Anna's first dance made up entirely of open-ended task performance. For ninety minutes, she and her fellow collaborators, A. A. Leath, John Graham, and Lynn Palmer, performed a series of disconnected and improvisatory tasks on the stage of the small Playhouse Repertory Theater in San Francisco's North Beach, such as rolling an old tire or carefully combing a long wig extension clipped onto one's hair. Deliberately intended as a sensory immersion without clear narrative or continuity, Anna assumed audiences would feel a visceral connection as they watched these skilled dancers execute tasks like those that filled their own daily lives. In the process, choreography could be presented as a uniquely legible medium for participatory social engagement and collaborative problem-solving. Instead, the inverse happened, and the audience was left adrift without direction, or even programs, trying futilely to make whatever connections they could. "I want a partnership of the audience and the performer," Anna wrote idealistically of her evolving credo of audience participation in an unpublished collection of statements about her work from this period. "I want to participate in events of supreme authenticity, to involve people with their environment so that life is lived whole."[17] Her lofty aspirations here aligned closely with what Larry was doing environmentally, and with much more success, in his urban landscape projects. In the *Portland Open Space Sequence* he imported the rocks and water of mountain terrains into the brick and cement world of cities so that people could share the experience of nature in their urban neighborhoods[18] (see Figure 1.14). Spectators needed little encouragement to walk on the grass, wade in the water, and sit on rocks in his landscapes; for dance audiences, participation was far less natural.

Working within the frame of a theater presented distinct problems for dance since audiences were accustomed to remaining seated anonymously in a darkened theater while watching representations of reality with narrative maps and meanings. This isn't what *The Four-Legged Stool* delivered. Like snapshots from the Halprin home, *The Four-Legged Stool* was a collage of splashes of tense relations, skewed communications, and tediously repetitive gestures with household objects that Anna, Graham, and Leath performed. The most exaggerated of these involved one hundred empty wine bottles that Anna methodically collected individually from the wings and took with her as she climbed onto the four-legged stool of the title and stealthily handed them up, one by one, to a hand that reached down from the rafters (Figure 3.14).

Figure 3.14. Anna Halprin and A. A. Leath moving wine bottles in *The Four-Legged Stool*, San Francisco Playhouse, c. 1960s. Photograph by Warner Jepson. Anna Halprin Digital Archive, Museum of Performance + Design, San Francisco. Courtesy of the Warner Jepson family.

DISAPPEARING CHAIRS AND PARTICIPATORY DANCES   153

A few empty bottles might have been a prelude to the ordinary accumulation of wine bottles from wine occasionally enjoyed with meals, but the one hundred bottles Anna manipulated in *The Four-Legged Stool* was so outside the domestic sphere that it made even plain actions like these dramatic. Repetition to the point of monotony is also a trademark of minimalist art, of which Anna's work was a progenitor. "I am interested in a theater where everything is experienced as if for the first time, a theater of risk, spontaneity, exposure, and intensity," she wrote about her aspirations as she sampled ways to engage her audiences in fuller, and more emotionally exposed, participation.[19] A series of rehearsal photographs reveal the dancers sampling different roles and arrangements of the bottle-passing and tire-rolling sequences with a clear eye toward the visual impact and design that suggests a certain tension around just how much and in what way audiences were expected to be drawn in through their senses. In one sly bit of surreptitious audience participation, Morton Subotnick, the composer who wrote the commissioned score for *The Four-Legged Stool*, seems to have found a way to involve audiences by secretly recording the sounds of the audience as they entered the theater each night on the way to their seats. A short while later, Subotnick replayed what he had recorded as part of the performance so that the audience became an audience to their own ordinary actions. It was a clever and light-hearted acoustic counterpart to Anna's more labored efforts at getting audience participation. Subotnick diligently omitted any noises the audience made intentionally on evenings when they realized they were being recorded. "If they started to cough on purpose, I'd turn it off!"[20] Subotnick said of his ongoing taping of the ambient sound in the theater. He, like Anna and Larry, was working to increase participants' sensory awareness of their surroundings and one another, and this was serious business. The audience was left to shape their own meanings and content—it was expanding their capacity to having their senses stimulated that was the more important focus for the composer and dancers.

Like an abstraction of the inadvertent little *pas de deux* each body performed when they encountered the uncomfortable seating in the Halprin home, Anna intended the events in *The Four-Legged Stool* as a way to bypass dialogue and plunge audiences into an "immediate sensory conversation" with her performers' bodies. "This theater is meant to appeal directly to the senses and primarily the kinesthetic sense," she wrote in production notes to herself about the 1961 work. "Anything stirring up the mind would only serve to build up walls of preconceived ideas, of habits of perception. The point of reference here is in the tensions of muscles, nerves, and the total human responsive intelligence."[21] At the work's September 1961 premiere at the San Francisco Playhouse, audiences did respond kinesthetically, but not in the way Anna had intended. People jeered and walked out, and at some performances, the hostility and anger rose to the point where objects and verbal insults were hurled at the performers. For Anna and Larry, this was a transformative experience. They realized they would need to proceed with more preparation and explanation for audiences, and for Anna more control over which parts of the score were open and which were closed, in order to bring audiences along. It would take the next several years of trial-and-error development to arrive at works that more naturally eased audiences into engagement. In the process, the strategies of Anna and Larry changed significantly.

Anna returned to the playhouse in April of the following year with a revised approach to fostering audience participation, *The Five-Legged Stool* (1962), and this time Larry assisted in preparing audiences for the work. While sensory engagement was still an objective, the loose, improvisatory openness of *The Four-Legged Stool* was replaced by dreamscape decors and a carefully time-bound set of situations assigned to specific members of the cast, now expanded to five performers. Endeavoring to educate audiences (and critics) on how to receive Anna's work, Larry wrote a long and carefully crafted article for the city's major daily newspaper, the *San Francisco Chronicle*, which was published the weekend *The Five-Legged Stool* opened. Larry's article was an impassioned defense of Anna's efforts toward audience participation. He noted that it was a new impulse for artists to make art that "wants profoundly to be a partnership which will involve audience as much as performers" by speaking to people "in a language they can understand through their senses . . . freeing them from habit and preconceptions."[22] In language that also describes his ambitions for his own work, Larry praises Anna's art for its immediacy;"[23] "She is making theater out of physical images in ordinary life, of simple occurrences and the most deeply rooted relationships between people . . . she wants most, I think, to create an environment—a landscape, if you will, within which both audience and performers are part of the cast and the events are common to them both." he writes.[24] This goal of unleashing the theatrical in ordinary life speaks to a fundamental dynamic of the Halprin home and the force of the objects within it. Stairs, ladders, stages on stages, chairs, and windows fill the performing space in *The Five-Legged Stool*, presenting an emotional landscape that was at once highly theatrical and symbolic of the ordinary (Figure 3.15).

Figure 3.15. Staged performance photograph of Anna Halprin's *Five-Legged Stool*, on the set for the dance, San Francisco Playhouse, 1962. Photograph by Chester Kessler. Anna Halprin Digital Archives, Museum of Performance + Design, San Francisco.

A series of hip publicity images were also prepared as part of priming audiences to be receptive to the revised *Stool*. Photographed outdoors in stark black-and-white contrast, the cast posed amid a mountain of splintered boards and shattered walls—the wreckage of a demolished building (home?) in a not-so-subtle metaphor for the show's intention to do just that to the house of dance traditions. Balanced on this mound of ruin, Anna, John Graham, A. A. Leath, and Lynn Palmer stare out impassively at the camera, the slight curl of a smile of satisfaction on their lips suggesting that perhaps it was the hot intensity of their domestic squabbling that shattered this house into ruins (Figure 3.16).

What was common to Anna in the domestic environment she referenced on stage was the edgy instability of relationships and the charged symbolism of domestic objects. Chairs were also plentiful in both versions of the *Stool* dances. While common props in theater productions, the inclusion of a chair or stool in a dance is an oddity and immediately imparts an element of theater, and usually realism, to whatever will unfold. Using strategies she played with in rehearsal with her dancers, Anna was approaching her audience in the same way, nudging them to step forward emotionally and explore the

Figure 3.16. Publicity photo for Anna Halprin's *Five-Legged Stool*, San Francisco, 1962. Photograph by Chester Kessler. Anna Halprin Digital Archives, Museum of Performance + Design, San Francisco.

situation before them conceptually. However, rather than artificially imposing tensions, as traditional dance and theater did, she was trying to ignite real friction between objects and the members of her cast. She hoped that living through the reality of this with the performers nightly would turn her audiences into fuller participants in art—and ultimately for the rest of their lives. When asked about the title of her revised work, Anna responded that any number of legs would be fine for the stool—as long as it wasn't three. A three-legged stool is the most solid basic seating there is, but add one or two more legs and the lengths have to become uneven to keep the seat level. This worked as a metaphor for the power struggles within families as well as being a sly nod to all those years of uncomfortable seating in the Halprin home. Anna's use of this reference to unstable seating in her title served as a portal into the discomforts of "body consciousness" and "active awareness" she wanted audiences to feel as they sat watching discomfort on display.[25] She once said that she thought it was the absence of the traditional performance, anchors of a clear story, and accompanying actions that distressed the audiences for her *Stool* dances, but shoving them toward physical participation must certainly have been part of their increasing discomfort as well.

Three years later, in 1965, Anna again turned to her core collaborators from *The Four- Legged Stool* and *The Five-Legged Stool*, A. A. Leath and John Graham, to premiere *Apartment 6*, the final work in what had become her trilogy of the home (Figure 3.17). Everything about this two-hour-long work was hyperrealistic from the set—which was outfitted as fully as a real apartment—to the highly structured improvisations between the dancers who listened to the radio, cooked, and ate food and argued, all in real time. In expanding the works' titles from furniture for seating to the address of a residence (Apartment 6 was the made-up name the dancers gave when they ordered food during rehearsals), *Apartment 6* reached for audience participation in a new way by presenting daily life as theater and inviting audiences to witness what happens when objects, actions, and emotions unfold in the close quarters of a small apartment and under the magnification of live performance. Alternately tentative and bold, Anna was exporting her Kentfield

Figure 3.17. *Apartment 6* (1965) performance photo of Anna Halprin, A. A. Leath, and John Graham, San Francisco Playhouse. Photograph by Hank Kranzler. Anna Halprin Digital Archives, Museum of Performance + Design, San Francisco.

life into the San Francisco Playhouse in an intensified effort to push her audiences out of step with the everyday and into an awareness that seeing art is about a shift in one's state of attention. By swinging from tense to comic portrayals of gender roles and depicting them with exaggerated physicality, Anna hoped her audiences would be stimulated into sensory alertness and a heightened awareness of their links to the collective social body.

"We're not acting or dancing but rather we are being ourselves and experiencing our present relationships which have evolved over a period of 14 years we have worked together," Anna wrote by way of program notes explaining her goals in the work. "The subject of *Apartment 6* is ourselves," she continued.[26] "John Graham will have as his prime action, the use of household props ... [l]amps, radio, chairs, typewriter and so on. Leath will concentrate on externalizing his feelings, and I will primarily concentrate on compulsive tasks"[27] (Figure 3.18).

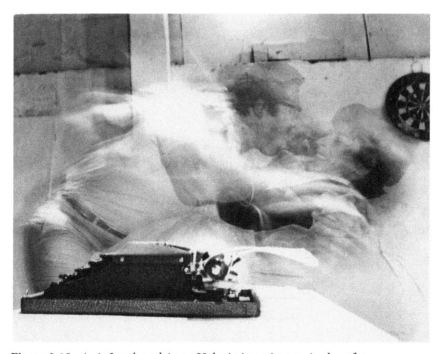

Figure 3.18. A. A. Leath and Anna Halprin in an improvised performance moment from *Apartment 6* (1965). Photograph by Warner Jepson. Anna Halprin Digital Archives, Museum of Performance + Design, San Francisco. Courtesy of the Warner Jepson family.

It's easy to read a psychoanalytic dimension into these assigned roles for the three performers as Anna comfortably played the cringe-inducing part of a servile wife whose identity turns on her ability to cook the perfect pancake for the demanding Graham. In her program notes, she assigns a domestic role for everyone, including the audience, writing, "The audience participates in our reality by being there intimately like guests for dinner. Personal responses to each other are evident, thus bringing the audience into a communal situation with us."[28] Anna's increasing push toward more participation from her audiences paralleled Larry's own evolving use of materials and forms from nature to deliver sensory experiences for spectators to his environments. In works like his *Portland Open Space Sequence* (1971), Seattle's *Freeway Park* (1976), and *Levi's Plaza* (1982), he progressively refined his techniques for creating the sensory equivalents to nature in urban centers by replicating natural phenomena like waterfalls, streams, and fallen log and rock benches. The Halprins were sharing what they loved about their adoptive state. Larry was evoking the distinct ecosystems, microclimates, and physical particulars of his favorite sites in California's ecology, and Anna was tapping deeper into the West Coast's burgeoning Human Potential Movement and Gestalt therapy.[29] Changed by her time working outdoors on the deck, Anna was similarly drawing from the realistic settings of her California environs, including the lives and objects within the Halprin home. She was working to lead audiences into engagement through the processes of choreography and integrating lessons from outdoors. While participatory democracy was a buzzword during this decade, for Anna and Larry it was not social politics that were at the forefront of their concerns so much as *cultural politics* as they each repositioned their discipline to be a medium ripe for urban problem-solving and physicalized public engagement.

In 1962, the same year *The Five-Legged Stool* premiered, Larry was approached by San Francisco developer William Roth about designing the outdoor spaces of his recently purchased complex of the old brick structures of the former Ghirardelli chocolate factory on the edge of the San Francisco Bay. Roth, who was interested in preserving and recycling these nineteenth-century buildings, asked Larry, along with architects Wurster, Bernardi & Emmons, for their ideas about how this large site might be developed using a new model for redevelopment that didn't simply raze everything to the ground and start over. With Larry as the designer for the outdoor spaces, the team evolved a plan that balanced historic preservation paired with renovation—an arrangement that would become a framework for a

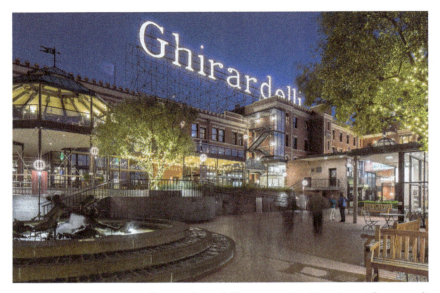

Figure 3.19. Lawrence Halprin, Ghirardelli Square, San Francisco. Photograph by David Lloyd, courtesy of SWA Group. Courtesy of the The Cultural Landscape Foundation.

new approach to urban renewal. Across the next several years as Anna was building *Apartment 6*, Larry refined his plans for *Ghirardelli Square*, designing a tiered series of brick courtyards and walkways with water features that idealized natural environments, urbanizing the experience of nature (Figure 3.19). He too was bringing a new focus on process and memory into American urban centers—in this instance the journey of meandering through an interlaced series of terraced plazas, arcades, and narrow brick paths reminiscent of his time wandering old European cities. As part of invoking these environments, Larry played choreographically in *Ghirardelli Square*, discreetly contouring visitors' motions through ramped and winding staircases, across brick courtyards, past fountains, and onto tiered balconies that beckoned with expansive views of the San Francisco Bay, Alcatraz Island, and Aquatic Park. This was a vista like that which had first captivated Larry and Anna on Victory in Japan Day, August 14, 1945, when on survivor's leave at Hunters Point Naval Shipyard at the end of the war, Larry and Anna had climbed a hilltop and watched the city and bay explode in massive, spontaneous celebrations of the end of World War II. It was a demonstration of the natural beauty and energy that solidified their resolve to relocate to the

Bay Area. When it was completed in 1968, *Ghirardelli Square* was lauded in the San Francisco Museum of Modern Art's 1986 retrospective catalog on Halprin as one of the "finest examples of creating space as theater," a metaphor he also used to describe the "theatre of movement going on all around us" when he walked through Ghirardelli Square crowded with visitors.[30] The theater of Ghirardelli resides in both the visual drama of its exterior spaces and the way in which it elicits sensory engagement and active performance from visitors. It was a prototype for turning shopping into an aesthetic experience. For decades it remained one of San Francisco's most popular tourist destinations, drawing crowds as much for its views and shops as for the way it slyly delivered the participatory experience of wandering through the narrow winding public spaces of old metropolises.

Larry's writings from this period about Anna's *Five-Legged Stool* offer a glimpse of his own evolving understanding of the theatrical possibilities of space that he was testing out in *Ghirardelli Square* and, soon after, in Seattle's *Freeway Park* and *Levi's Plaza*. He writes from the position of an urban designer as he describes a new approach to theater as a "natural habitat" with its own demands, including "first of all an eagerness to participate not just sit back and be passively entertained." This embargo on being passively entertained is reinforced by the absence of customary seating in the Halprins' works as well as by how they each deliberately masterminded spectators' participation in their disciplines. Larry writes about Anna's new conception of theater as "an activity of the senses" and "a space orchestrated to demand and require an eagerness to participate."[31] He expounds on the space of theater through the lens of an urban designer and at the same time views public space with the movement-forward focus of a choreographer. He assigns energy and even agency to ideal theatrical space, describing it as "alive and useful and all-pervasive," "demanding," and "requiring an eagerness to participate."[32] It's one thing for a dancer to do this and appropriate an already designed space, but it's radically different and on a whole different scale for an urban designer to create space with this in mind. Effectively Larry's work on *Ghirardelli Square* was beginning to turn all who were present into players and witnesses of their own performances. In so doing, he forced a pause in the consumerism of shopping, redirecting focus instead to feeling, seeing, and experiencing as the adventure of encountering the dramatic space of the waterfront square assumes its own prominence.

Initially Larry's participatory environments found an easier path to acceptance than Anna's dance did since one could enjoy his environments on a

162 THE CHOREOGRAPHY OF ENVIRONMENTS

range of levels and in one's own time while being gently led into a discovery of how environmental and social goals converge through urban design. His landscapes departed from a traditional park experience by offering more than was expected, whereas Anna's tweaking with audience expectations felt to many like they were being given decidedly less. Rather than being conciliatory, Anna responded combatively, rebounding with what would be her most aggressive forcing of audience participation of her career with the premiere in 1967–1968 of her *Ten Myths*. Now seating for spectators had effectively disappeared and everyone was expected to participate. Up until this point, Anna and Larry had just sampled methodologies of Jungian and Gestalt psychology in their work, as individually they explored relationships between individuals, organisms, and their environments. *Ten Myths* took this to a new extreme, forcing the physical involvement of the audience through instructions to slap one another, as happened on the first night, or stand still while enduring an hour of deafening drumming and blinding light, as was the script for the second night's *Myth Two: Atonement*. Specific physical challenges for the spectators were proscribed on a different scale each of the ten evenings on which the dance took place, scattered over several months from October 1967 into the winter of 1968.

All of the performances were held in the studios of 321 Divisadero Street, an old Victorian San Francisco building that Anna maintained for many years as rehearsal and performance space at the boundary of the city's Haight-Ashbury neighborhood. "*Myths* are your myths. They are an experiment in mutual creation," her distributed notes to the opening night audience invited, promising a ride of participation into a primal state "meant to evoke our long buried and half-forgotten selves."[33] The prompts across the evenings varied from instructions for all the audience members and performers to engage in group touching to carrying one another across the studio, telling stories, and putting on and removing costumes.

Irritation seems to have been felt on both sides and the tone of Anna's injunctions to her audiences read more like intellectual daring than gentle guidance: "The audience works to receive as the artists work to give," she wrote of her philosophy of participatory theater as it was evolving during the 1960s. "It is from everyday life that we find and develop our material . . . nothing is 'pretend,' everything is real—but a real on more than one level . . . and it is here that the precise meaning is an open form for the audience. . . . It is here at the multiple levels that each audience member projects his own personal life and background into what he is experiencing."[34] This is participation that carries with it the risk of exposure and emotional vulnerability—a lot to drop on a group of strangers who have gathered together for an evening of casual dance entertainment. Photographs documenting the *Ten Myths* performances, the scores for each evening, and candid accounts by Anna's dancers of what transpired reveal a series of events that breached numerous boundaries of emotional, physical, and sexual safety for performers and audience. The first hint spectators were given as to the degree of their participation was on the initial evening of *Myth One: Creation*, when they entered the performance space and searched where to sit. Patric Hickey, Anna's collaborator for scenic design, and here listed as her "environmentalist," had arranged all of the space's sixty folding chairs as invitingly open but impossible to access because they were suspended from the ceiling at eight- and twelve-foot heights above the floor. The audience was left having to negotiate sitting either on the floor bathed in pools of light or on one of several bare platforms elevated from two to eight feet off the ground and which filled the center of the space. No written or verbal instructions were given to help transition the audience into how to participate; the cueing proceeded simply by virtue of the odd things being done with chairs. From this initial moment of displacement, Anna pushed further into tactile engagement as the dancers of her Dancers' Workshop company entered the space and, lining up, began to slap each other's backs, shoulders, arms, hips, and legs until eventually the entire environment resonated with the sounds of bodies being sensorially awakened. "A dance began with audience becoming performers, the original performers acting as catalysts," Anna said afterward, tracing this transition into action from the initial tease of chairs that could not be sat upon. "The physical environment, originally meant for seating, became the stage," she said with the satisfaction of finally breaching the audience-performer divide that she had been wrangling with since the start of the decade.[35]

Each evening the audience discovered their participation was scripted in a different way—cued by seating. For example, *Myth Seven: Carry* presented entering audiences with two long rows of chairs in close proximity facing one another. The audience was instructed to take a seat and then navigate the space by carrying or being carried randomly by someone (Figure 3.20). The most combative and memorable evening for many was *Myth Two: Atonement*. Performed a few weeks after the series opened, *Atonement* was arranged as an unpleasant ordeal the audience had to undergo in an environment deliberately constructed to be emotionally and physically distressing. Normally one would think of participation in a

Figure 3.20. Performance photograph from Anna Halprin's *Ten Myths*, *Myth Seven: Carry*. Photograph by Jim Wilson, c. 1967/1968. Anna Halprin Papers, Museum of Performance + Design, San Francisco.

performance as being enjoyable for audiences—an extension of the entertainment focus of much live performance. However, pleasure is something more subjective to deliver and, in the instance of Anna's work of this era, also more elusive than discomfort. In *Myth Two: Atonement* (the title itself is a giveaway that penance and redemption will be part of the bargain), all of the walls and floors were covered with taped-up pages of the same page from that morning's daily newspaper (Figure 3.21). The lighting at head level was a bank of blindingly bright lights and the accompaniment came from a lone snare drum on which Casey Sonnabend had been instructed to play the loudest and most sustained drum roll he could for the full hour of the performance.[36] In one explanation for the evening, Anna tellingly referred to what she was doing as "research." "The whole reason for doing these *Myths*," she said, "[was] that I wanted to find out what people ... what ordinary people would do, and how they would react. I was doing it to study audiences."[37] In this instance, her referring to a scored evening dance event as "research" effectively elides any judgment about it as successful art and releases her from aesthetic valuation. In contrast, the marketing materials for *Ten Myths*

Figure 3.21. San Francisco Dancers' Workshop and audience members performing Anna Halprin's *Ten Myths, Myth 2: Atonement*, at the San Francisco Dancers' Workshop Studio, 321 Divisadero Street, San Francisco, in 1967. Courtesy of Sue Heinemann and the Halprin family.

refer to the series as "a spontaneous exploration of theatre ideas" and "an experiment in mutual creation." This language aligns more with Larry's own evolving approaches to landscape design as the product of fostering public engagement from process through to the carefully mediated final results of urban projects. As soon as she began working with audiences specifically to foster engagement, however, Anna's work could assume more of an air of impatience, conflating preparation and display with the same hasty blur that collapsed spectators into participants. Throughout its duration, *Ten Myths* continued the theater tradition of charging admission at the door for "seats" even though there were none provided for a public who showed up and were drafted to participate.

Turning the tables so that the watchers become the ones who are studied was a dynamic facilitated through the work of both Halprins as they forced people onto their feet. The one piece of furniture that facilitated this more than any other was the simple bench, and its origins extend back to that fundamental performance platform in the Halprins' lives, the dance deck (Figure 3.22).

Figure 3.22. Anna Halprin standing by a tree on the dance deck with Daria and Rana seated on the benches at the Halprin house, Kentfield, California. Photograph by Lawrence Halprin, 1955. Courtesy of the Halprin family.

Benches

While the novelty of the dance deck has been noted extensively, the seating that Larry designed in tandem with it—six tiered rows of wooden benches tucked into the rocky hillside just above the deck—was equally and profoundly influential. When Anna abandoned the traditional indoor theater, she also left behind customary upholstered plush theater seats. Instead, the dance deck featured hard, backless wooden planks, seating that required good posture and a strong spine from students and audience members alike. Rana remembers the deck seating as echoing the kind of rustic benches Larry would have come upon in hiking park trails. "Larry would never have put backs on those benches facing the dance deck, because they would have impeded the line and view from up on the hill down to the deck and gardens beyond," Rana explained about the hard, uninviting seating above the deck. Like the deck, the benches honor the unwritten credo of the Halprin home: to build *with* nature not *on it*, suggesting how her parents also enjoyed the benches' implicit command to visitors to sit up and pay attention. "We also used them as a stage," Rana added, "like a Greek Theatre where you can use it to step up and down."[38] Asked if Anna might have requested different seating from Larry for the dance deck, Rana replied, "My parents respected each other's process and Anna would never have interfered in that way."[39] As with the deck, she nested her art within the environment she was given and invited the epiphanies and challenges it brought.

Gesturing simultaneously to bleacher seating and stadiums for athletic events and the modernist penchant for stylish benches, the dance deck seating was one of the most intimate architectural collaborations between Larry and Anna and where their shared unsettling of the passive spectator commenced. Contrary to theater seating, the arrangement for spectators at the dance deck refused to yield to relaxation. Instead of sinking into the soft upholstery and easy anonymity of traditional plush theater seats, those viewing dance performances on the deck always had to perch alertly, spine erect, on these six narrow, long, wooden planks clustered on the rocks and soil at the base of the cascading stairs just above the deck. This was practical as well as symbolic. The use of simple bleachers for seating radicalized even further the break with tradition the deck initiated. The benches were made of the same Douglas fir as the deck and were spaced so closely that to sit on them one had to tuck up their feet tightly underneath, knees bent deeply as if already poised to stand. Backless and armless, these benches were cousin to the high-fashion mid-century slatted bench made famous by designer George Nelson.

Benches have a modernist history. The Blunk benches belong to a certain cachet for this form of seating in the postwar era. In particular, with the Herman Miller Company's iconic seating, Nelson introduced his model of a spare, simple platform for sitting in his company's first furniture collection in 1946, in a design that featured the allure of abstraction over comfort. There was also an implicit elitism to the bench. The widely read postwar shelter magazine, *House Beautiful*, described the slat bench as "the bench with the high I.Q.," an observation, it has been noted, that essentially branded it as "intellectual furniture."[40]

Nelson reportedly once said that his design for this bench was motivated, at least partially, by the intention to make the sitter move on: "The reason slats were used rather than a solid plank was partly to save lumber, but mostly to create a seating surface sufficiently *un*comfortable to induce visitors to leave in twenty minutes or less," he once quipped.[41] Nelson was not alone in

168 THE CHOREOGRAPHY OF ENVIRONMENTS

this era in playing with the design of seating with the deliberate intention of creating discomfort as an inducement to rising and departing. A few years earlier, in 1945, the Italian artist Bruno Munari had debuted an even more blunt art variant on seating you don't want to sit on, his "Chair for Very Brief Visits." This was a slender inlaid walnut and aluminum chair with a hard seat that was sloped at a perilous forty-five-degree-angle, and which continually threatened to dump the user off and onto the floor. It's one thing to be ejected from a chair as an intentional failure of the chair, but another to struggle to stay seated. For Anna and Larry, they reimagined and played with displacement as a successful launch into dancing or moving through a designed environment.

One of the earliest photographs showing an audience seated on the benches at the dance deck comes from the July 1957 guest lecture demonstration Merce Cunningham presented there (Figure 3.23). In a photograph Larry took from the stairs high above the deck during Cunningham's performance, a well-dressed crowd sits pressed shoulder to shoulder on the six narrow rows of benches. The men wear suits and several of the women have sweaters wrapped tightly around their shoulders against a late afternoon chill. Those in the back row lean backward uncomfortably in the vain hope that the piled dry leaves behind them might provide some support. The audience as a whole looks like they dressed for a different event than the one they have found themselves in. As if voicing their sentiments, Cunningham had asked Anna earlier while rehearsing on the deck for the demonstration, "But where do you live in the winter?" hinting that this outside dancing arrangement could only be frolicsome play in a child's summer treehouse. Yet it is the overdressed audience on the benches that registers the most discomfort in this image. In a curious reversal, their cramped physical state is more palpable than that of Cunningham's as they nestle crouched down among the trees and leaves, bereft of comfortable seating as they behold this puckish individual dancing before them in a clearing in the woods.

It's also the unremarked-on presence of these hillside benches in the iconic photo taken of Anna's 1960 summer workshop participants that gives the image its distinctly summer camp playfulness and conveys the exploratory tenor of this crowd (see Figure 2.14). Some stand, some sit, one has a parasol, another a cape of paper clutched around them, and Trisha Brown hides her face entirely behind her hair brushed over her face. Bleachers as much as benches, this deck seating is cousin to the tiered row of stadium seats at sporting events—the bleachers for spectators dating back to the nineteenth

DISAPPEARING CHAIRS AND PARTICIPATORY DANCES 169

Figure 3.23. Merce Cunningham in lecture demonstration on the dance deck, July 20, 1957. Lawrence Halprin Collection, Stuart Weitzman School of Design, The Architectural Archives, University of Pennsylvania, Philadelphia.

170 THE CHOREOGRAPHY OF ENVIRONMENTS

century and far earlier if one includes the stone benches of classical Greek theater. As seating for contemporary dance, however, these bleachers at the dance deck gesture forward to the gymnasium bleachers of postmodern dance venues that will unfold in the years ahead, led by some of the Halprin workshop participants pictured here.

A critical dimension of Larry's environments is also this discarding of the seating staple of landscape design—the park bench. Literally and metaphorically, there are no park benches in almost all of Larry's environments. One does not repose; one engages. The parks Larry referenced were national parks and here a well-placed rock or a strategically positioned log provided sufficient seating to situate one to take in the landscape. As University of California, Berkeley Landscape Architecture Professor Randolph T. Hester has aptly noted of Halprin, "He laid the foundation of legitimacy for participatory landscape architecture in ways no one else could. . . . [H]e wanted people to learn experientially, not secondarily. Feelings and images were more important to him than words."[42] While in dance this is not a novel hierarchy to privilege feeling and seeing over words, it most certainly was in urban design when Larry began using environmental planning processes to create shared experiences for participants. "He wanted people to learn their feelings, not intellectualize them," Hester said in regard to how Larry made landscape design a participatory experience beginning from the early stages of community statements of needs through to group problem-solving by the individuals whose lives would be most impacted by his design projects.[43] As the fruits of these shared planning sessions went out into the world with the completion of the project, new communities of participants joined in learning through the experiences it offered.

By exporting the artifacts of seating from their home and woodsy environs—slabs of wood and hunks of stone as benches—into their public art, the Halprins worked to dislodge the passive spectator in the construction and reception of dance and urban design. Backless benches and rocky platforms would become the norm in their art and ultimately in the fields of dance and urban design that they both trailblazed. Instead of audience comfort, invisibility, and anonymity, the spectator in both Anna's and Larry's works became a physically present participant. Far more than just a design accommodation, the benches Larry created to overlook the dance deck also instilled a mandate of bodily awareness in all who sat on them.

The uncomfortable chairs and benches of the Halprin home and gardens offer an important path into Anna's erasure of the spectator in her dances and Larry's focus on animating physical engagement from visitors to his urban landscapes. As Anna worked on the dance deck, her pieces shifted from proscenium-framed and traditionally seated audience arrangements to erasing ever more fully the separations between spectator and performer. Tracing how the life of chairs in the Halprin home had their own material existence and an anatomy that rivaled that of the flesh-and-bone body allows new understandings of the force of objects in our homes. New materialist theorists, including dancer Alison D'Amato, have argued for a decentering of human cognition as the epitome of evolutionary achievement, advocating instead for an elevation of things, "objects," and environments, particularly those our bodies encounter through movement, as having their own force and agency.[44] The little movement responses these encounters engender, according to D'Amato, take on their own materiality, almost as a thing or object created by the body dancing. For Anna and Larry, daily encounters with unwelcoming chairs can be argued to have set in motion, literally, their own art approaches to seating strategies that effectively mobilized collaborators and visitors to their artworks. The history of the Halprins' own repeated physical encounters with odd seating effectively preconditioned them to discovering through uncomfortable seating how they might literally move others.

The Last Chair Dances

In the final decades of their lives, Anna and Larry would both return to chairs or seating as subjects and objects in their work. In 1999, in response to Larry's hospitalization in intensive care the previous year (due to complications following a surgical procedure), Anna built an entire dance, *Intensive Care: Reflections on Death and Dying*, for dancers seated on rolling office chairs. Drawing her movement vocabulary from the grimacing, clawing, and thrashing gestures she witnessed among patients tethered to life support machines in the intensive care unit, she used wheeled desk chairs draped with bed linens as mobile platforms for each dancer. Giving the performers the gliding ease of celestial skaters while also referencing the rolling means by which the ill are transported in medical facilities, Anna used chairs in *Intensive Care* to shape tableaux of bodies resisting, struggling, and, finally, yielding to death. Costumed in lengths of gauze-colored bed linens suggesting both hospital gowns and death shrouds, the dancers skimmed across the floor while seated in chairs that referenced

Figure 3.24. Anna Halprin in *Intensive Care: Reflections on Death and Dying*, Centre Pompidou, Paris, France 2004. Photograph by Rick Chapman: http://www.rickchapman.com. Courtesy of Rick Chapman.

hospital wheelchairs, gurneys, and floating platforms of clouds in heaven. "Art is my way to cope with what happens in life," she said of her turn toward this dance on rolling chairs as her way to come to terms with Larry's brush with death and her own mortality (Figure 3.24). "In dance you have an opportunity to bypass romanticism if you go directly to the body, it may not be pretty but it's real," she said, explaining that she referenced her own fear of death and experience with cancer in creating *Intensive Care*. "All your experiences are housed in the body. Looking at death is a way of looking at life."[45] The paradoxical situation of dancing while seated on a chair that keeps skidding across the floor adds an unusual tension to the bodies in *Intensive Care*, who must repose on, and at the same time power and steer, their restless chairs. As the dance progresses and she approaches more closely the hour of her death, Anna's gestures become more violent and frenzied. Kicking her feet in the air and throwing the sheet covering her from side to side, her mouth open in a grimacing silent scream, she veers wildly around the stage on her chair, its erratic motion amplifying the quality of panic and desperation her gestures convey as this chair becomes a base one cannot exit.

In 2005, soon after her eighty-fifth birthday, Anna shifted tone. Pointedly focusing on the stories that chairs themselves can tell about old age, she began collecting rocking chairs and recruiting participants from several senior retirement centers in Marin County. Wanting to reflect further on her own growing concern with death and dying in a community of peers, but this time with a sense of levity rather than fear, she convened a group of fellow seniors and invited them to find movement that began with what their bodies could do safely and comfortably. Now, instead of removing or disguising chairs, she featured them, providing each of the participants, who ranged in age from their sixties to their nineties, with a large rocking chair. Over weekly workshops at the retirement homes, she and her assistants culled a repertoire of simple arm gestures and easy rocking motions from observing the kinds of movements the residents did in their rocking chairs. Now, the chairs added rather than subtracted movement for the participants, shielding and amplifying routine smaller actions like tipping to and fro into an easy dance of momentum set in motion by the push-and-pull recovery of rocking with heels and toes on the ground. When showtime arrived several weeks later on a warm afternoon in early October, the seniors were transported to their rocking chairs, which had been arranged in a series of rows on an island in the middle of a small lagoon at the Marin Civic Center, and *Seniors Rocking* commenced. Process and performance simultaneously, part community development and part inventive participatory dance, Anna's re-engagement with seating, now in old age, shows just how durable the chair as impetus, object, and metaphor remained across her life as an artist (Figure 3.25).

The same year *Seniors Rocking* premiered, Larry's redesign of Sigmund Stern Grove, one of the final projects of his career, opened, prior to his ninetieth birthday. An iconic outdoor space in San Francisco built by the Works Progress Administration as a sloped meadow set among giant eucalyptus, redwood, and fir trees during the 1930s, it was overdue for a redesign of its landscaping, audience, and concert spaces. Sigmund Stern Grove would be the only other outdoor theater space Larry had worked on since code signing the dance deck fifty years earlier. Stern Grove was also part of the legacy of cultural philanthropy of one of San Francisco's leading Jewish families. Rosalie M. Stern purchased Stern Grove and gave it as a gift to the city of San Francisco in 1931, in memory of her husband, Sigmund, a prominent civic leader, stipulating that it was to host free music and dance concerts for the city. Although it was already a partially built outdoor

Figure 3.25. *Seniors Rocking* (2005) by Anna Halprin, Marin Civic Center, California. Performance footage from *Breath Made Visible: Anna Halprin*, a documentary film by Ruedi Gerber, ZAS Film AG, 2009. Courtesy of Ruedi Gerber.

environment, Larry brought his honed skills for sensing what he called "the spirit of the place" from his decades of working in nature to this new project of redesigning Stern Grove to bring it into a new balance of public access and environmental preservation. Across six years and through participatory procedures that were a summation of his lifetime of doing what architectural historian Randolph Hester has called "scoring collective creativity and legitimating participatory design," Larry and fellow architect Andrew Sullivan convened public outreach workshops with community stakeholders to assess needs, threading them through the design process and into the final product in what was by now his signature participatory landscape architecture planning process.[46] Inspired by the site's topography and ancient models of great Greek amphitheaters, Larry designed grass terraces and stone retaining walls that blended into the site's sloping topography and Works Progress Administration–era stonework. Terracing the slope upward toward the front and fashioning rows of low grassy benches bordered by stepped granite toward the back, with layers of fallen logs further uphill,

Figure 3.26. *Spirit of Place* (2009) dance performance, choreographed by Anna Halprin as a tribute to Lawrence Halprin, at Sigmund Stern Grove, San Francisco, redesigned in 2005 by Lawrence Halprin. Photograph by John Kokoska. Courtesy of John Kokoska.

Larry's redesign provided seating and good sightlines for upwards of twelve thousand viewers and picnickers while also allowing wheelchair access (Figure 3.26). In describing his aspirations for the Stern Grove redesign, Larry invoked Anna's dance aesthetic as a model. "My intention was to create a mystical place where one would be inspired to reach into oneself. I wanted to design a living theater for everyone to use, a place where people can walk their dogs, picnic, meditate," Larry said of his ambitions in redesigning Stern Grove. "I wanted a place where lovers could meet and children could play," he said with an inclusive nod toward the influence on him of all those years of Anna's work with children and adults on the Halprin deck in Kentfield and shoreline at The Sea Ranch. "Such everyday activities are incorporated in the dance choreographed by my wife, Anna."[47]

In a reciprocal gesture, Anna found herself so inspired by the ritual of expansive and inviting theatricality Larry's redesign imparted to Stern Grove that she created one of her final site-specific dances, *Spirit of Place*, for the new space in May 2009, a few months before Larry died. Pulled by what she called the generous and ancient quality of the terraced benches of grass and

176 THE CHOREOGRAPHY OF ENVIRONMENTS

stone for the audience, "like the Delphi," she said of its Grecian formality, Anna built a ritualistic work for a cast of seventeen dancers. Now, instead of making spectators participants, she flipped locations. "I want the audience to be sitting on the stage, and I want the dancers to be where the audience is. Because that's where the excitement is and the inspiration," she explained of her decision to scatter her performers far into the banks of stone and grass benches on the hillside as their performing sites.[48] Some wore white animal masks and all moved with the tense alertness of frightened deer; later performers played the benches as if they were welcoming props, draping themselves over the stone bleachers, falling, and then improbably rolling uphill against the rows of empty benches with the equanimity of those who can defy gravity. Periodically, people out for a walk with their dogs strolled by. Meanwhile, across the amphitheater, an attentive audience sat quietly on stage, absorbing the reversed beauty of seeing seating as a backdrop for performance.

4

The Picture Frame, Not the Picture

Windows in the Halprin House

"The Picture Frame, Not the Picture"

If there is one architectural feature of the Halprin home that distills the philosophy of its leading architect, William Wurster, and links its aesthetic to the work of both Halprins, it is the walls of huge redwood-framed glass windows throughout the house. Far more than designed ornamentation, these expanses of glass are a signature aspect of Wurster's "soft modernist" approach to residential architecture and reflective of his core belief about design. "Architecture is not a goal. . . . Architecture is for life and pleasure and work and for people," he declared in 1956, soon after completing the Halprin home. "[Architecture is] [t]he picture frame, not the picture."[1]

The picture frame of the house Wurster designed for Anna and Larry would inspire two long careers of generating remarkable portraits of life. The frames of the windows would become tutorials in how to direct attention and notice the overlooked, as well as the importance of bringing sustained focus to the world (Figure 4.1). Over time these tutorials would foster the Halprins' self-fashioning of their personal choreographic and urban design frames as vital dimensions of their work, workshops, and legacies. The windows would allow Anna and Larry to see themselves *seeing* and to regard the found environments of nature and cities with close attention as they constantly sought out how to find something new within the familiar. Beginning every morning and ending every day in Wurster's frame, with its modest and modernist virtuosity, was transformative for both Halprins. Wurster's interior and exterior ornamentation was minimal, directing focus to the walls of windows. These expansive sheets of glass offered unimpeded views of the outdoors with its natural light, warming sun, and shadows of the late afternoon, all of which made the visual and tactile rhythms of nature an inescapable part of daily existence in the home (Figure 4.2). "Bill Wurster and I sited the house so that it captured both bay and mountain views in almost every direction," Larry wrote of their close collaboration in shaping the sightlines

The Choreography of Environments. Janice Ross, Oxford University Press. © Oxford University Press 2025.
DOI: 10.1093/9780197775660.003.0005

178 THE CHOREOGRAPHY OF ENVIRONMENTS

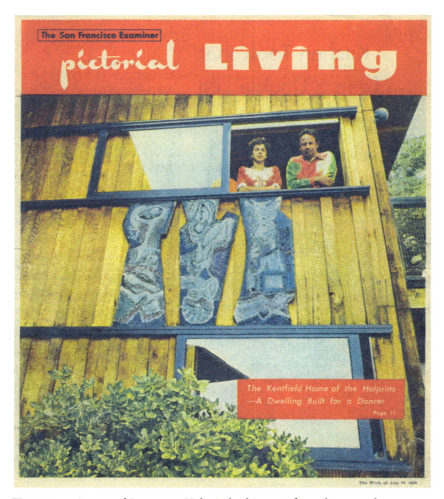

Figure 4.1. Anna and Lawrence Halprin looking out from the second-story window of their Kentfield, California, home in 1959. Photograph by Ted Needham. Lawrence Halprin Collection, Stuart Weitzman School of Design, The Architectural Archives, University of Pennsylvania, Philadelphia.

through each window.[2] Wurster's soft modernist aesthetic was exemplified by his skill at smoothly blending the newest technological materials and construction techniques—which included novel support and weight-bearing methods that made possible plate glass windows—while retaining a feeling of simplicity and cozy intimacy. This has a direct correlation to the soft modernist aesthetic of Larry's and Anna's art. The cutting edge rubbing against

Figure 4.2. Windows looking (east) from the breakfast room to the living room of the Halprin home, Kentfield, California. From Bushell Homes listing in 2022. Photograph by Jacob Elliott: https://www.jacobelliott.com/. Courtesy of Jacob Elliott.

the comfortably inhabitable united the work of all three. Like the chairs, the windows helped infuse modernist simplicity into the daily life of the house while simultaneously heightening spatial awareness.

Wurster's achievement highlighted what Bay Area architect and coauthor of a biography of Wurster, Caitlin Lempres Brostom, called his "incredible sense of scale." "He was very good at building a very small house that had a sense of graciousness," she said, praising the sense of quiet in his spaces, the lack of trim on most doors so they blended into the adjacent walls, and his oversized windows that gave the sensation of expansiveness to relatively small living spaces.[3] These qualities would also become defining trademarks of the Bay Regional Style. This was the influential architectural movement Wurster helped define through natural wood staircases and other attributes like these in the Halprin home, and it was the spirit of this movement that Anna and Larry would absorb and export into dance and landscape design. Wurster masterfully blended the essence of contemporary design with traditions of the Bay Area's relaxed indoor/outdoor lifestyle, dematerializing walls to feature the environmental beauty and access to gardens as sites to be used rather than for visual display alone.

Architecture, landscape, and dance already had an early intertwined history with design innovation and nature in the Bay Area, most notably through one of Oakland native Isadora Duncan's childhood friends, Florence Treadwell Boynton. In 1912, the Boynton family had purchased acreage on a steep hill above the University of California (UC), Berkeley campus. They engaged a neighbor, Bernard Maybeck, who also happened to be the leading Bay Area architect of the time and one of Wurster's future mentors, to design a pair of circular outdoor porches, defined by a snaking line of thirty-four 20-foot-high cast concrete Corinthian columns. This twentieth-century classical Greek edifice, the Temple of Wings as it became known, was left as an open-air structure, with canvas awnings that could be lowered when it rained. The porches, or "wings," each of them capped by a huge dome, were bordered on one side by a hill. A grove of eucalyptus trees in front served as a windbreak. Overhead, on the underside of the domes, blue fresco–decorated surfaces met the blue of the sky through center skylights, accentuating the impression that the home was disappearing into the landscape. The flagstone floor was heated by means of hollow earthenware tubes, and a central concrete fireplace with four openings provided additional light and warmth in the winter. Matching this rustic neo-Grecian architectural style with corresponding dance and lifestyle choices that foreshadow a similar intertwining of architecture and lifestyle in the Halprin household, the Boynton family subsisted on a raw vegan diet, dressed in Greek togas and sandals year-round, and performed and taught Duncanesque interpretive dance to students who traveled to their outdoor temple platform to study with them.[4]

Climatically and socially, the San Francisco Bay Area was welcoming to the unusual lifestyles of its artists; however, the presence of the Boynton family with its habitation and food choices earned their neighborhood the sobriquet "nut hill". In the same way, a few local Kentfield parents forbade their children from going to the Halprin home because of Anna's community of dancers experimenting on the deck. That which some saw as idiosyncratic, Larry and Anna grabbed as opportunities. In reflecting back on the specific quality of the San Francisco Bay Area that drew him to it when he first visited, Larry remarked on the feeling that it seemed unfinished, especially compared to New York and European cities. "What I found was the incompleteness of San Francisco, that it had a feeling like a forest with young seedlings growing up beneath in the underbrush and that there was a lot of change about to happen," he said. "I always think of cities as organic phenomena anyway. They're ecologically in a certain kind of niche . . . and San Francisco just seemed ripe for growth. Ripe for opportunity."[5] For Larry this aura of freshness and an energetic embrace of change also played out in the distinctive use of materials in the Bay Area architectural tradition. "There was a California attitude about the use of wood, the use of humility in architecture, the use of simplicity and plainness," he said, noting that it had a strong effect on him aesthetically. "I also had a profound feeling that architecture and the design of the environment could affect social behavior," he said of his early intuition about a linkage between design and inner emotional life.[6]

The Windows of the Halprin Home

As elements of the Bay Area Regional Style, the windows of the Halprin home can be viewed as tidy architectural counterparts to Larry's and Anna's own art and honoring of nature and raw environments as partners and mentors. With their warm translucence and undivided expanses of clear glass, these windows dominate the few redwood walls in the main rooms of the house. Bordered by narrow wood beams, the windows also echo the slender branches of the coastal oak and madrone trees just outside, which in turn offer a second frame around nature outdoors. These layered frames further blur the distinction between indoors and outdoors, found and preselected, open and closed, a theme already found in the stairs and chairs of the home. In situating the Halprin house to allow magnificent, and magnificently ordinary, views of the property equally, Wurster's windows permitted the immediate landscape and site of the home, as much as the proximate views of Mount Tamalpais and distant views of the San Francisco Bay, to orchestrate attention rather than the building itself. For two artists looking to nature and the found environment as models for structuring encounters between spectators and experience, the windows of the Halprin home became perpetual lessons in seeing. Every room in the house had visual access to the outside through floor-to-ceiling windows and glass or sliding glass doors. In the process, the windows effectively tutored residents of the home on how to sustain attention and the importance of calibrating it across different perspectives. "He was simplifying to allow attention to be directed to the view instead of the detail of the house, and that required a lot of sophistication," architecture

182   THE CHOREOGRAPHY OF ENVIRONMENTS

professor R. Thomas Hille observed of Wurster's approach to residential design honed during this postwar period. "It's hard to talk architects into doing that these days," he noted of the humility of Wurster's design. "They want people to be gawking at their houses instead of other things, like the view."[7]

So artfully do the windows and architecture of the Halprin home modestly deflect attention from the sleek engineering of industrial materials of modernism and instead frame the natural beauty of the property that Wurster's artistry virtually disappears. Instead, residents and visitors become attuned to topography, season, time of day, and a seamless visual and physical flow from indoors to outdoors. Wurster's houses have been praised for their livability and for being dwellings that are far more intentional and artful than they initially appear because of the ways their easy comfort unfolds over time.[8] One of Wurster's defining qualities was his attentiveness to the California landscape and native materials. In addition to designing scores of homes throughout the Bay Area for elite clients, Wurster also did several projects with Halprin's first employer, the leading landscape architect Thomas Church, including designing Church's summer home in Santa Cruz, California. An innovative educator as well as an architect, Wurster, together with his wife, Catherine Bauer Wurster, a public housing advocate, developed the concept of environmental design, combining the disciplines of architecture, landscape architecture, and planning under the College of Environmental Design, which Wurster founded and led at UC Berkeley beginning in 1959, prophetically defining the field in which Larry would spend his career.

Collaborating closely with both Halprins as he designed their house, Wurster was the ideal partner. He used materials and spaces to enhance and expand the domestic lives of his clients rather than imposing a way of life on them, an approach that was essential in working with two artist clients like Anna and Larry. As architectural historian Margaret Crawford has noted of Wurster: "He had the ability to design houses that fit into their environment so perfectly that they hardly seem authored. . . . Free of stylistic insistence, they appear to be generated solely by the circumstances of site, climate, and the client's needs and budget."[9] The fit was so good that over time the Halprins only made one major adjustment to Wurster's windows in the home—and that was on the single-pane clear-glass front door. One afternoon in the early years of living in the house, while engaged in a wild chase indoors with her sister, little Rana ran headlong into the glass front door, shattering it and slicing her face and cheek on the cut glass. "I was very fast, and I got to the door first," she recalled triumphantly. "But Anna was horrified at all the blood and raced me to the local emergency room."[10] After that, Wurster's original front door was replaced with a custom-designed wood and glass Dutch door that, while stylistically anomalous, safely reduced the surface area and risk of open glass. Going forward, the top half of the front door would often be left open, a signal that someone was home and an invitation to reach over and unlatch the bottom door to admit oneself to the house.

Viewing Race

While the windows of the Halprin home offered continual lessons in attention to visual, tactile, and sensual qualities, this pedagogy through architecture and landscape design also had racial resonances. Due to the remote rural setting of the home in a wealthy enclave, the family never felt the need for the protection and shielding that could have been provided by more walls and fewer windows and which would have been necessary in a more urban and less exclusive setting. For years the Halprins never had any curtains in the house until concern about sun damage to the Blunk seating prompted them to install a few bamboo shades in the living room that could be lowered during the sunniest time of day on select windows. This kind of confidence and seclusion in the 1950s carries with it the implicit racial privilege of an upscale White suburban neighborhood existence, defended through racial covenants of the same kind that had initially made it problematic for the Jewish Halprin family to become property owners in Kentfield. Only in a residential neighborhood of extreme privacy, and policed exclusion, could a family of four live so transparently to the outside.

From the late nineteenth to the early twentieth centuries, landscape design in America had been wielded politically by pioneers like Frederick Law Olmsted as a way to guide settlement and expansion by inducing people to settle down through the development of gardens, private estate grounds, and municipal and metropolitan park systems that brought nature into the controlled proximity of cities. This curating of nature as a political force was also used as a stealthier means of shaping development. Historically, landscape had been used as a means to stimulate and direct urban and economic growth, often by the displacement of Indigenous and Black people. Even the dichotomy in the profession between landscape designers, like Halprin, and those who implemented the designs, the gardeners and laborers, has a

184 THE CHOREOGRAPHY OF ENVIRONMENTS

troubled history of exclusion in America, with White students admitted to the schools of landscape architecture and Historically Black Colleges and Universities (HBCUs) offering more training in the labor to implement those designs.[11] As children of first-generation Jewish immigrants whose parents had fled persecution in Eastern Europe, Anna and Larry both selectively addressed tensions of social and racial inequities through deliberately inclusive practices at different stages of their work, but it was never the sustained central focus for either of them. Rather, their role as activists focused on how to reconstruct society through subtly shaped encounters and spatial proximity between people and environments.

On the broadest scale, their work was about what art historian Jenny Odell calls the critical precursor to taking action, which is "teaching people how to sustain attention and how to move it back and forth between different registers."[12] The views that the windows of the Halprin home framed, although appearing wild and rural, were in fact consciously controlled lessons in this kind of "granularity of perception," Odell's phrase to describe her own lessons in seeing gleaned from years spent in nature.[13] This was not accidental. "My father's work was always about the site first," Rana said of Larry's emphasis on allowing a chosen piece of land to direct where and how his landscape design and development, and the framing of views on it, proceeded. This attention started with his own home. "Larry left specific directions as to how trees were always to be trimmed to maintain the views," Rana explained of the personality of the Kentfield gardens. "We could not see the city, but we had a view of the Bay. My father's design nurtured the creative spirit of the house. We were enclosed in a safety space. The woods surrounded us like a compound."[14]

Through their repeating duets with the outdoors, Wurster's windows charted the passage of time daily and seasonally as nature came into view; foliage bloomed and wilted; the sun warmed the rooms and then, as shadows lengthened, the air cooled; and the outside faded into darkness and life moved back inside each evening. As a continual background experience, everyone in the family became connected to time, light, and climate in a way usually encountered only if living outdoors. The kitchen, living room, bedrooms, and even bathrooms had glass doors that opened to the front and back gardens, allowing an easy step outside to a ground-level patio, brick terrace, or decking (Figure 4.3). Since it was not just the view but the actual possibility of walking outdoors that continually beckoned, one had the sensation of being already in nature at all times. With a foundation of only 2,200 square feet and no garage, the footprint of the two-level, three-bedroom, two-bathroom

Figure 4.3. Master bathroom with sliding glass door to the outdoors, Halprin house, Kentfield, California. From the Bushell Homes listing in 2022. Photograph by Jacob Elliott: https://www.jacobelliott.com/. Courtesy of Jacob Elliott.

Halprin home itself was modest—but the windows and sliding glass doors amplified the sense of scale it projected. This showcased another defining feature of Wurster's architecture: its artful pairing of opposites so that seemingly contradictory qualities and sensations became complementary. Examples are the feeling of expanse projected by what were actually small to modestly sized rooms through the use of extensive windows, and the illusion of architecture that was spare and simple but which was actually undergirded by a complex and nuanced elegance of expensive materials and tightly edited details. The coexistence of these dualities also had correspondences in Anna's and Larry's process and works with their sophisticated embrace of modernist strategies to illuminate the simple elegance of the found environment. What has been called "soft modernism" in Wurster's architecture because of how he mixed elements of mid-century architecture—sleek, clean lines; natural materials; and transparent barriers—with modern accents of luxury to soften things and make spaces more livable inspired what could be called the Halprins' own version of "soft modernism" in dance and landscape design. It was Wurster's windows in the Halprin home, as much as any other element, that facilitated this seamless flux.

186 THE CHOREOGRAPHY OF ENVIRONMENTS

In writing about Wurster's design for their home, Larry described it as "a series of pavilions," highlighting its intentionally airy and open quality where, as is characteristic of traditional Japanese pavilion buildings, space exists as a continuum with only a sheer layer of rice paper separating inside and outside. Architectural modernism facilitated this interconnection of a building's internal spaces with the environment outside by engineering that made possible the replacement of a bearing wall with a structural frame, recasting the wall as a screen.[15] While Larry did not write much about windows directly, one well-worn book from his personal library, Sibyl Moholy-Nagy's *Native Genius in Anonymous Architecture*, contains an interesting argument as to how the design of windows in homes determines the capacity of those spaces to speak to us. Moholy-Nagy, an influential design professor and writer and the widow of one of Larry's Bauhaus-trained mentors, Lázló Moholy-Nagy, presents a transhistorical and transglobal compendium of brief descriptions of 150 kinds of houses in a format that seems a direct model for what Larry would do six years later in his *Cities* book. In her entry about the function of windows, Moholy-Nagy writes, "After site, the shape and placement of openings is the second most decisive characteristic of a home's architecture."[16] She argues that "the simplest and the most sophisticated designs exert their esthetic influence on the environment through the balance of wall enclosure and wall opening. . . . A house exterior can invite or reject simply by the indication of its windows."[17] The plentiful and wide-open windows of the Kentfield house, then, may explain the remarkably inviting warmth the Halprin home exuded, sometimes against the wishes of its inhabitants. The sheer number of windows in the Halprin house, and the preponderance of wall space given to them, imparted an easy and generous welcoming spirit to the house. This invitation from the windows is a quality that also may have contributed to the appearance in the house of students from Anna's classes and workshops who wandered up from the deck and, uninvited, into the private spaces of the house, to the great annoyance of others in the family.

Window Lessons for Dance

The most immediate positive lesson of Wurster's "picture frame" was its capacity to model for Anna and Larry how each could wield their art discipline as a frame and use it as a means to enhance one's capacities for reflection. Larry made urban design a portable frame that others could take into the environment, nature, and the world. He used landscape as a way to construct a communal vision that moved people from individual reflection into an increased awareness of how to effectively engage with their surroundings and each other. Anna created models of dance training and dance creation that would become frames for social relations—and simultaneously for the emotions and psychological states conditioning them. These models subsequently became one of the most transportable of her innovations because leading dancers who studied with her made their own frames and took these east, back to New York, as roadmaps into postmodernism. For better but also at times for worse, the bare windows of the Halprin home accustomed its residents to living on display, which, especially for Anna, would be an element from daily life she would in turn fold back into the dance she developed. Through Wurster's windows the place of the Halprin home assumed its own life, linking the human life inside to the nonhuman life outside with an invitation to find the enjoyable in this tension of urban life.

In her earliest works playing with these ideas, Anna explored how this integration of the physical inside and environmental outside that architectural modernism fostered also had psychological dimensions. Within a year of moving into their Wurster-designed house Anna premiered her first site-specific urban outdoor dance, *People on a Slant* (1953). Like a city street scene glimpsed from an apartment window, *People on a Slant* is a snapshot of the angled walks of two women and a man as they negotiate the steep sidewalk outside the Union Street studio in San Francisco where Anna taught and rehearsed before the dance deck was completed. An improvisation performed by Anna and her fellow dancers, A. A. Leath and Jenny Hunter Groat, and with costumes designed by Larry, *People on a Slant* features all three performers comically struggling to remain vertical and resist gravity while walking on a steep sidewalk in an array of silly costumes. As a dance it is a slight work; its interest lies in how it reveals Anna starting to train her choreographic eye to roam outside and reframe an *un*exceptional urban site, and the functional actions it prompts, as holding aesthetic interest. She would rapidly learn to trust increasingly whatever her frame captured and allow that to be the starting point for sustaining her attention as she collected new reasons and ways for herself and her dancers to move.

Within four years she would experiment with making the frame itself an indelible part of the performance when she staged *Hangar* in 1957, a group improvisation on an airplane hangar under construction at San Francisco Airport. In this work, Anna instructed her cast of seven dancers, which included herself, to respond through improvisation to the space and architecture of the construction site. Dashing barefoot across a debris-strewn field leading up to the three-story-tall structure, the dancers scrambled up the looming unfinished behemoth of the hangar. Wearing the modern dance uniform of the era of black leotards and tights and scurrying like a swarm of small insects, the dancers scaled the mountain of orange I-beams, stretching their bodies against the hard geometry of its lattice of window-like openings. Norma Leistiko, one of the dancers, had noticed the airport construction site several days earlier and suggested it to Anna as a possible setting in which to improvise. Working in the inverse of Larry during this period, Anna was seeking out established and unusual urban landscapes as found environments that she then allowed to dictate to herself and her dancers the nature and quality of movement that should happen within them. *Hangar* was a dramatic example and the only environmental improvisation of this scale ever captured on film. Once Anna saw the structure, she was immediately drawn to its huge open grid of steel beams—like a three-story-high wall of window frames without the glass (Figure 4.4). The film, which includes footage shot by William Heick of the site from an airplane, and the still images documenting *Hangar* are spectacular. There is a spare simplicity to

Figure 4.4. Detail of *Hangar*, improvisation with Anna Halprin and filmed by William Heick, with the San Francisco Bay visible in the distance, 1957. Film still from *Breath Made Visible: Anna Halprin*, a documentary film by Ruedi Gerber, ZAS Film AG, 2009. Courtesy of Ruedi Gerber.

THE PICTURE FRAME, NOT THE PICTURE   189

the way the architectural grid frames the dancers' bodies hovering in the air. In the distance, the ports lining San Francisco Bay shimmer like an industrial equivalent of the bay view from the Halprin home. The hard abstraction of these images, however, conceals a different story of the personal experience of the dancers. Simone Forti, one of the original performers, responded sharply upon being reminded about dancing in *Hangar* decades later: "I hated being there! I was so uncomfortable on those I-beams," she said. "I remember feeling it was dangerous."[18] Like layers of stacked picture frames, the setting and documentation convey visual images, not the physical reality of the dancers, and it is this newly affective territory of the interior experience of the dancer that Anna would soon begin focusing on in her work.

Framing Lived Experiences

No aspect of Anna's work reveals her evolution from a concentration on the visuals within a frame to the lived experience of the performers working inside it more vividly than how she addressed race. Her signature work in this regard, *Ceremony of Us*, commissioned by Studio Watts in Los Angeles in 1968, sought to explore racial divides between a group of eleven Black actors and her San Francisco Dancers' Workshop group of eleven White and Asian dancers in the wake of the assassination of Dr. Martin Luther King Jr. and the ensuing race riots. Anna had already been developing compositional strategies to replace dance's traditional focus on uniform technical training in favor of movement-generating systems that, like the empty frame of a window, could capture a range of emotional, physical, and autobiographical content. "I have stripped away all ties with conventional dance forms," she wrote in an unpublished manifesto-like document about this new approach to dance theater. "The lives of the individual performers, the training, rehearsals, and the performances form a process in itself, the experience," she declared.[19] In describing the fluid exchange between her performers' lives and the process of assembling a dance occasion, Anna is also highlighting how, just as with a window, simply bringing attention to the ongoing changes of living forms illuminates what is beautiful in them.

Initially working with these two populations separately in their respective cities, Anna pushed to "feed life into a new art form," generating material through weekly encounters where the participants were led through simple game-like tasks such as lining up against the wall and falling to the floor in succession like dominos one after the other or moving through the room in a tightly linked serpentine line. These activities demanded careful attention to the group and thus made it easier to participate without individuals feeling they were performing.[20] Yet the subject matter she was edging them toward was anything but playful. "The Dancers' Workshop faces major societal issues through creative, innovative theatre which aims to merge societal and aesthetic confrontations," she stated. "I am interested in a theatre where everything is experienced as if for the first time, a theatre of risk, spontaneity, exposure and intensity."[21] In the final two weeks leading up to the *Ceremony of Us* performance, the two groups came together in San Francisco for the first time, and the intensity and risk threatened to spiral out of control. Under Anna's direction, the performers probed their layers of difference in encounters ranging from describing each other's facial differences like skin color and physical features reflected in handheld mirrors to simulated birthing rituals using psychotherapeutic techniques Anna adapted from her Gestalt therapy study with Dr. Fritz Perls. This fascination with the surface differences of skin color is epitomized in the most reproduced photograph from this work, a black-and-white image of the entire group of dancers resting on their backs on the floor of the 321 Divisadero Street studio as they coyly stare up at the photographer, having been posed by Anna in tangled web of White and Black flesh. There is a palpable and easy familiarity to the performers' casual touching as the women's bare arms intertwine around the arms and legs of fellow dancers of both sexes in contact that ranges from soft touching to firm gripping. The atmosphere is both consciously sexual and teasing as the performers regard the photographer with a level gaze, hinting at physical intimacies that may have preceded and may also follow this moment (Figure 4.5). Larry Reed, one of the men in the San Francisco group, recalled the climate in the studio as being one of intense experimentation with an emphasis on emotional and physical sensations. "I think this was one of the transition projects for Ann, where she went from being performance oriented to being therapy oriented," Reed said of the multiple frames around *Ceremony of Us.* "She really went from wanting to be an avant-garde theatre person to wanting to be a therapeutic dance person. And this was on the way to that."[22] A therapeutic focus is generally concerned with the unseen interior, while performance depends on a legible exterior. These paired approaches play in another way with private-public tensions that windows also separate and link.

Figure 4.5. San Francisco Dancers' Workshop and Studio Watts performers group photo for *Ceremony of Us*, 321 Divisadero Street Studio, San Francisco, 1968. Photograph by Susan Landor Keegin. Anna Halprin Collection, Museum of Performance + Design, San Francisco. Courtesy of Susan Landon Keegin.

Environments of Conflict

In an effort to get at underlying social tensions within the Watts and San Francisco groups, and by extension their inner-city communities, Anna was reaching for the resource most familiar to her for addressing interpersonal conflict, the *au courant* tool of White hip suburbia: psychotherapy. Adapting Perls's "hot seat" techniques, she developed exercises ranging from detailed verbal descriptions the performers gave of one another's bodies to partner touching, massage, carrying and washing each other, and enacting lead-and-follow games. She was breaching social frames of separation dividing Black and White individuals by using performers' bodies and movements tactically to address racial tensions rocking the nation. Soon after the completion of *Ceremony of Us*, Anna received a $50,000 grant to turn her choreographic techniques into models for "addressing multiracial confrontations through

192 THE CHOREOGRAPHY OF ENVIRONMENTS

artistic expression." At a press luncheon Anna hosted with her dancers to announce the award, a *San Francisco Chronicle* reporter described a media event awkward in its simplistic and essentialist approach to racism. "We have discovered that there are racial differences, even in the way people move," Anna told the assembled press, who themselves had been filtered through a space divided by multiple frames of cultural and racial differences signified through offerings of food and the positioning of dancers divided by race. "To avoid or deny this is false. One has to learn to respect those differences through a humanistic theatre.... Verbal expression is so easily misunderstood that a single statement can be both positive and negative, depending on who hears it. We don't really communicate very well with words. But movement is much more basic," she asserted.[23]

Years later in reflecting on this short-lived phase of pitching her work to foundations as research, Anna said, "I was trying to get at something more basic, more humanistic. . . . To use my experience with Gestalt therapy to integrate emotional responses through an art process instead of therapy. I wanted the dancer to be a whole person," she said of her shifting goals.[24] The psychological nakedness she sampled as a result was replete with possibility but also more risk since it takes special skills to caretake people after they open themselves up emotionally without leaving them too vulnerable, and this would uncover more than Anna, or the performers, anticipated. "We saw this as a real opportunity," the poet Wanda Coleman, one of the women in the Watts group, remembered years later. "All the Black members of that troupe felt this was a beginning, that this was going to take us to great heights."[25] Anna was continuing to metaphorically remove the glass from the window, collapsing outside and inside within the frame she was turning on racial relations in America by throwing together the two worlds of Black and under-resourced South Central Los Angeles young adults and the White and socially advantaged new age youth of San Francisco's Haight-Ashbury. In an effort to meet a prearranged performance deadline for the opening of *Ceremony of Us* at the Mark Taper Forum, a major theater in Los Angeles, preparations lurched between using dance to probe race relations collaboratively and autobiographically and hastily packaging what was emerging from these experiments into an event for a ticket-buying audience.

The public event fell short in several respects. (When night falls outside, uncovered windows become mirrors, and they don't always reflect back what one expects.) In trying to force audience engagement, Anna had set up race as an identity window frame to mirror the audience back to themselves. This

THE PICTURE FRAME, NOT THE PICTURE   193

began by forcing the audience to choose a doorway lined by Black dancers or one lined by White dancers in order to enter the theater. The price of entry to the show for the puzzled spectators was de facto the tacit declaration of one's racial allegiance revealed by which doorway people chose to enter. Anna professed surprise when each member of the audience self-selected through the row of dancers who shared their skin color. By foregrounding each spectator's awareness of their identity between the categories of Black or White and Asian before they entered the theater, Anna had implicitly imposed a frame for viewing the entire performance through the lens of race. Given how combative things had become in rehearsal for the dancers in preparing the show using similar material highlighting surface markers of race, the decision to turn a frame of race back onto the unsuspecting audience seems an odd choice. In the lead-up to the premiere of *Ceremony of Us* in February 1969, several of the performers from Watts had voiced their discomfort about the absence of real salaries, and others noted the troubling gender hierarchies and sexual tensions playing out along racial lines. In the same way that modern design has been argued by critical race theorists to carry its own counterhistories of race in this postwar period, *Ceremony of Us* too revealed power structures, biases, and racialized agendas still lurking within choreographed dance shaped to specifically begin to redress these social issues.[26]

The public and critical response to *Ceremony of Us* was mixed. After these initial performances in Los Angeles, it was performed only a few more times before being memorialized in a thirty-minute black-and-white film compiled from rehearsal footage made by KQED, San Francisco's local PBS station. The frame of the camera sensationalizes the dynamic of Black and White flesh in close contact through a series of fragmented clips of the dancers touching and exploring one another in candid footage shot on one of the final rehearsal days leading up to the performance. Effectively, Anna was working in the reverse of Larry, using choreographic structures to explore how urban environments become interiorized and then shifting and externalizing their accompanying belief systems through movement games.

As Anna's methodology transitioned from public performance to an emphasis on private action, and as she tried to summon her performers and audiences into an orchestrated community in *Ceremony of Us*, Larry was extending his resources for fostering kinesthetic and sensory participation in the design of public environments. "I had long felt that citizen involvement was vitally important for public projects because in a democracy we all need

194   THE CHOREOGRAPHY OF ENVIRONMENTS

to have a sense of ownership in our communities," he wrote, describing his efforts as trying to reach beyond the limits of his own creativity in addressing social challenges.[27] In 1968, the year *Ceremony of Us* was being built, Larry completed a lengthy commissioned study, *New York, New York*, for the City of New York in which he prototyped a process for developing proposals for six urban renewal projects in the city that could effectively redefine the meaning of open space in the urban environment. From its jaunty reference to the title song of the 1940s Broadway musical celebrating the metropolis, *On the Town*, Larry's study was a template for citizens taking ownership in shaping and navigating their cities. Heralded as the first major proposal stressing the importance of citizens participating in their own environment, *New York, New York* revealed to Larry that rather than creating buildings, "the architect's job is basically to create spaces for people to be in."[28] Just as the large, single-pane plate glass windows of mid-century modern homes had replaced the multiple small, divided panels of Victorian windows, the Halprins were expanding the scale through which they viewed and addressed urban problems of revitalization, striving for an ever bigger picture. While the 1960s and 1970s were the years of the most dynamic practice for Larry as well as for Anna, the pressures of this era on addressing immediate social ills and injustices were finally a less felicitous match for Larry's interests and skills, as architecture historian Alison Hirsch has noted.[29] He was more interested in creating urban nature and then stepping back and letting the civic experiences this fostered engender new types of social participation, revitalization, and eco-literacy. Throughout his life he retained an idealist belief in a common humanity and bond that these experience-based processes of his work could stimulate.

The boldest and largest-scaled example of this was Larry's *Freeway Park*, a massive concrete abstraction of nature spanning Interstate Five in Seattle, Washington. Officials from the Seattle Park Commission had originally contacted Larry after having read *Freeways*, his 1966 report to the secretary of transportation in which he argues for a reconceptualization of freeways as part of the cityscape. The Seattle officials' initial request was modest; they solicited Larry's ideas for how to develop a small urban park adjacent to the freeway, which, having been developed to speed people from the airport to downtown, had sliced through the heart of the city. Larry promptly expanded the scope of their vision. "I was determined to show that it was feasible to handle freeways in such an elegant manner that they would improve, rather than destroy, the cities they served," he stated.[30] Like a worker in a high-rise office building looking through his windows and observing the freeway severing the financial district from a residential neighborhood and medical districts, he reconceptualized this wound as an opportunity. "The trick," he said, "is to perceive the old freeway as a part of the cityscape and tame it, rather than complain about it."[31] Responding to the huge gulch created by the freeway as if it were a found environment, Larry proffered an innovative solution: reunite its two split halves with a giant park arcing over the freeway. He imported the nature of the nearby Olympic Mountains with their tree and shrub species and water features to heal an urban catastrophe created by the short-sighted transportation decision to accelerate access from the Seattle Tacoma Airport to Seattle by building the freeway. Larry conjured usable urban space literally from the airspace above the roadway. Taking inspiration from the vistas, sounds, and textures of nature, he enlarged the original small park site that had been proposed, making it spill onto the roof of a planned parking garage and into the airspace above the speeding traffic. He had created a lush, waterfall-filled park in midair. Structuring it as a multilayered series of brutalist gigantic cement blocks and planters filled with mature trees and plants, waterfalls, fountains, stairways, and ledges for sitting and viewing, Larry, together with project director Angelica Danadjieva Tzvetin, achieved a conceptual as well as engineering and design feat (Figure 4.6).

Figure 4.6. Lawrence Halprin's *Freeway Park*, Seattle, spanning the Interstate 5 freeway. Photograph by Matt Hagen. Courtesy of Matt Hagen.

196   THE CHOREOGRAPHY OF ENVIRONMENTS

One of the grandest examples of his dictum to "not copy nature but to design an experiential equivalent appropriate to the situation," *Freeway Park* enacted a civic repair comparable to the social healing Anna aspired to with *Ceremony of Us*. Both works were conceived on a grand scale and were profoundly urban and participatory in the experiences they offered and the tutelage in social and eco-environmentalism and aesthetic mindfulness they pioneered.

Over time the tacit lessons of the Halprin house windows, with their implicit tutorials in how to direct attention and focus to the world and notice the overlooked, were increasingly visible in Anna's and Larry's works. They were honing their capacities to take California modernism from the domestic space of the garden and house to public spaces. Exporting the familiar into unexpected places and using it to face threatening difficulties, they revealed a model for how humanity might creatively manipulate and remain engaged with neglected aspects of urban life and ecology, including the scars of racism and unsightly freeways. Just as Larry's work was evocative of distinct ecosystems, Anna too began building dances that indexed the texture of eco (and social) micro-climates and their imprint on bodies, beginning with her own. Across the decades of the 1970s and 1980s, just as Larry was doing, she too expanded the scale of her work into urbanscapes, modeling how they might be stretched to offer possibilities for more comfortable and mindful habitation.

As the grand processionals of stairs and echoes of waterfalls that rippled through Anna and Larry's home and earlier works now softened into a quiet intimacy, the Halprins framed the role of memory in their gaze outward. In 1978, Larry debuted his poetic processional homage to the Gold Rush–era history of Levi Strauss jeans, his *Levi's Plaza* park outside the company's San Francisco headquarters. In this built campus of grass, streams, and waterfalls at the edge of the city's waterfront, Larry's history met the history of the Levi Strauss Company through the form of a narrative told through water. In front of the Levi headquarters building he designed a dramatic cluster of cement stairs and huge granite boulders washed with a roaring torrent of water (Figure 4.7). Here the stairs of the Halprin home converge with the waterfalls that were their inspiration in a wild dance. It begins in the plaza immediately in front of the Levi headquarters where water thunders over a huge granite block (from the *FDR Memorial* stone), Larry's rendition of the headwaters of the California Sierras. The water then slows as it crosses under Battery Street and re-emerges as a gently meandering pebble-lined brook wending

Figure 4.7. The stair waterfalls of Lawrence Halprin's *Levi's Plaza* (1978), San Francisco. Photograph by Marion Brenner, 2016. Courtesy of The Cultural Landscape Foundation.

its way through the adjacent green space he designed to be evocative of the Sierra meadows sliced by steams where Levi's first customers, the miners of the California Gold Rush, panned for nuggets. Wandering through the landscape like a slowly wending procession, this stream that began in *Levi's Plaza* is simultaneously a memory piece about the Levi company's history and a snapshot of the Sierras where Larry began his own eco-literacy discoveries a century later. The Halprins were refining the sensory travels that their art proffered. Their work, like the proscenium frame of a stage, or a window, offers temporary insulation from a disordered outside. They usher the public into the focused hush of a designed experience and a journey across California's landscape, refracted through a window of distance and time.

The experiential equivalent of nature that Larry forged through abstraction in *Freeway Park* and *Levi's Plaza*, by asking people to experience deeply what they are habituated to ignore, has an interesting counterpart in a series of solitary dance works deep in nature that Anna turned to in collaboration with artist Eeo Stubblefield on the cusp of her eighth decade, the *Still Dance* series of 1998–2002 (Figure 4.8). Working with Stubblefield and

Figure 4.8. Anna Halprin performing *Still Dance* from *Tree Series*, The Sea Ranch, California, 1997. Concept, makeup, and photograph by Eeo Stubblefield. Courtesy of Eeo Stubblefield.

performing nude, outdoors, and alone, her body covered with the varied debris of landscape—mud, the mulch of rotting ferns and redwoods, wet sand, brittle and dry straw—Anna allowed her body to be painted and buried in found environments in the woods and at the seashore, with environments and costuming selected by Stubblefield. Moving with the slow heaviness of an aged animal, an organism in nature being buffeted by wind, water, or the tides, she allowed the forces of nature to configure her body as if it were an eroding landscape, a living object in decay. The result is a stunning compendium of ecosystems, a *Still Dance* that epitomizes Anna's transition from her initial approach to dance as movement in the service of predesigned choreography to that of movement in response to the deep bodily awareness of being in nature. She was reading nature through dance with the same immersion that had propelled Larry's lifelong search for what he described as "perceiving deeply rooted subconscious needs as the basis of design and finding the essential characteristics of nature to use as vocabulary in the design processes."[32]

As Larry aestheticized freeways, she honed the beauty of old age, layering on it the discomforts, and dangers, of being nude in frigid, wet, and windy sites in the raw ground. Rather than a show of designed movement for an audience, here stillness and the visceral textures of a body enduring dampness, stickiness, and itching flesh while half-buried in a decaying log outdoors are being performed in *Still Dance* (see Figure 4.8). "California is a very emotional environment to live in," Anna once said of the emotive connection she felt with nature in the west.[33] In a series of photographs documenting these improvisations with the environment, the eighty-year-old Anna is shown placing herself in the center of a framed slice of nature, a scene glimpsed through a camera lens instead of a window. "I think an aged body in its own way is like an old rock," Anna said soon after completing *Still Dance* as she reflected on how she was using nakedness as a metaphor and "a way to allow nature to stir up old feelings that are in the body."[34] "It makes me feel that I am being true to the natural world around. The dances touch deep places in me like little treasures so that I always come back feeling reborn in some way," she continued. "Something spontaneous happens in that moment of being naked in the ground."[35] Rather than dance as movement, this is dance as the before and after of movement—actions so slowed down that Anna's body has settled into a living stasis like that of plants or water in nature. Stubblefield and her camera are the only witnesses, documenting these improvised duets of woman and earth. The dancer has become the environment.

In this final series of solos of *Still Dance*, Anna effectively planted her body in the nature she had observed for so long through the windows of her home. More than twenty years later, on the occasion of her one hundredth birthday on July 13, 2020, Anna would find herself in a forced still dance, confined to a wheelchair, having lost the use of her legs from a series of fractures in her hips and back. Now, due to the COVID-19 pandemic, the windows of her bedroom became the portals of her contact with the outside world as her elder daughter, Daria, visited her daily, conversing with her outside as Anna sat on the second-story balcony just beyond the sliding glass doors of her bedroom. "I climb an extension ladder placed in the patio below my mother's balcony, while she sits in her wheelchair looking down at me," Daria wrote in a group message she shared on the occasion of Anna's one hundredth birthday.[36] "This is how I have to visit her every day. COVID-19 makes it too risky for both of us to be in close physical contact. When Anna first lost the use of her legs three months ago, she turned a corner into stillness and quiet, a kind of peaceful calm that I had never before experienced in or around or with her," Daria wrote of her mother's sudden forced stillness. "My mother had always been a mover, a doer, a go-out-and-grab-life-by-the-horns creator. My mother has always loved life, loved dancing, loved creating, loved witnessing people in the studio dancing the real stuff of their lives."[37] These truths Daria poetically describes of her ailing mother are also the truths revealed by the windows of the Halprin home in their function as literal and metaphoric portals to "the real stuff" of nature and the lives of the family.

Windows were an equally potent presence in Larry's final days. As his agility and mobility too became curtailed by the impediments of an aging body, increasingly he regarded his beloved California landscape from inside, positioned in front of the picture windows in the Halprin Sea Ranch and Kentfield homes. With his easel, watercolors, and sheets of paper at the ready, he translated what he saw through the windows before him into ebullient, freeform watercolors. No longer robust enough for a vigorous hike, he immersed himself in nature visually, through the windows, painting what he saw as if the glass of the window had disappeared. Daria recalled that in his final days, confined to the Kentfield home, Larry began and ended each day positioned in front of the sliding glass doors of the living room (Figure 4.9).

Figure 4.9. Lawrence Halprin painting a watercolor in the window of his home in The Sea Ranch, California. Photograph by Charles Birnbaum. Courtesy of The Cultural Landscape Foundation.

THE PICTURE FRAME, NOT THE PICTURE   201

"We set up his table for him right in front of those big glass doors, so he could look out at the garden," she said.[38] The windows of the Halprin home, it turned out, offered views in two directions: looking out always carried with it the possibility of someone looking in, of being regarded from the outside as spectacle and spectator, the surveyed and the surveyor. Training in looking thus was also training in being seen. Those windows were effectively a proscenium frame onto the theaters of the natural world. They served as a constant reminder to Anna and Larry to integrate the experiential equivalencies of nature into the work of their public and creative lives.

5

Expanding Home

The Sea Ranch

A black-and-white photograph documents a moment of layered activities on a driftwood-littered beach. In the foreground, Anna, barefoot and chicly attired in fitted houndstooth plaid slacks, a black turtleneck sweater, and a shell necklace, reclines on a large log, her body angled in a curve echoing that of the gnarled wood. Her eyes are closed, her brow furrowed in a manner suggesting focused concentration rather than relaxation. Sand spills down the front of her sweater, overflow from an improvisatory ritual she has just completed of chewing and swallowing sand (Figure 5.1).[1] At the far end of the log her daughter Daria pounds a drum, and behind her a cluster of men and women drive big lengths of driftwood logs into the sand as one woman ceremoniously holds aloft a twisted hunk of wood.

Welcome to Driftwood Village. It's day five of Anna and Larry's second twenty-four-day-long Experiments in Environment workshop for dancers and architects at the remote Northern California vacation home community of The Sea Ranch.

On the surface, this image seems to capture too easily the risible aspects of the 1960s in the San Francisco Bay Area—the disorder, invented ritual, and trendy irreverence of the White middle class as they pushed the boundaries of social conventions, so much so that it might almost have been staged ironically. However, Anna and the other participants are working in earnest, enacting, with determined literalness, Larry's credo that good urban design begins with a deep bodily response to the environment. "I think she just wanted to go further than anyone else," said Paul Ryan, who photographed Anna's theatricalized sand eating that day as part of his documentation of the workshop (Figure 5.2). As he photographed the workshop (he also documented the first one in 1966), Ryan became a de facto participant, and decades later he still remembered the mix of skills of the participants as one of its most radical features. "I think the workshop cross-pollination was a big, big, deal. The young architects were studying to be architects and the dancers

The Choreography of Environments. Janice Ross, Oxford University Press. © Oxford University Press 2025.
DOI: 10.1093/9780197775660.003.0006

EXPANDING HOME: THE SEA RANCH 203

Figure 5.1. Anna Halprin, Driftwood Village—Community, The Sea Ranch, California. Experiments in Environment workshop (July 1968). Photograph by Paul G. Ryan. Courtesy of Paul G. Ryan.

204 THE CHOREOGRAPHY OF ENVIRONMENTS

Figure 5.2. Anna Halprin eating sand as part of an improvisation, Driftwood Village, The Sea Ranch, part of the Experiments in Environment workshop, July 1968. Photograph by Paul G. Ryan. Courtesy of Paul G. Ryan.

EXPANDING HOME: THE SEA RANCH   205

were Anna's dancers and were open to things to get the architects to be more physically expressive. Most were between twenty-two and thirty years old," he said, still marveling decades later at the novelty of seeing dancers building physical structures on the beach and the architects becoming dancer-like as they began to think about the movements of stacking logs on the beach as having their own choreography.[2]

In literally taking the environment inside herself, Anna was pushing intimate sensorial engagement with nature to an absurd extreme. Discarding concern with her own comfort, despite her fashionable 1960s suburban attire, she is deep into the task she has assigned herself. Her actions are illustrative of the deliberateness with which she and Larry mined California's liberal eco-consciousness culture of the 1960s and 1970s as they searched for pathways to harness groups into collective and creative alliances. Focusing on cultivating individuals' relationships with nature, they bracketed off the era's activist politics as they embraced its spacious aesthetic possibilities, honoring the grounding principle of The Sea Ranch that "the landscape would be the dominant influence."[3] Something else was operating here as well. The structures being built were essentially domestic spaces, many of them skeletal shelters with a few temples and other places of ritual observance. Oblivious to the cold, dampness, and grit, the participants happily nested inside their constructions (Figure 5.3). Viewed decades later, a more immediate association Driftwood Village suggests is that of a homeless encampment, the initial innocence of the era in which it was made having faded into the fractured social politics of the twenty-first century. Inside Larry's recipe for that day in 1968 (the same project had been assigned in the previous workshop in 1966) was an invitation to reimagine home as the starting point for connecting with the environment. Viewed this way, Anna's focused eating of sand becomes a performance of domestic life inside a world whose material resources are worn wood, saltwater, the sound of crashing waves, and sand.

As Larry looked toward the found landscape, Anna was retreating further from trained dance techniques and deeper into a definition of dance as an exploration of human nature told through the physical vernacular of everyday tasks. She was seeking what she called a vocabulary *any* body could do. "I want to make dances in which the movement itself is so real and direct that it will create an experience in the present that does not need to be mediated by an act of interpretation. It is not so much a matter of inventing interesting, clever, or evocative movements to access the body's inner wisdom," she wrote

Figure 5.3. Driftwood Village, The Sea Ranch, California. Experiments in Environment workshop, July 4, 1966. Lawrence Halprin Collection, Stuart Weitzman School of Design, The Architectural Archives, University of Pennsylvania, Philadelphia.

in a distillation of her quest for the most essential *un*mediated actions. "It is more a process of finding an ordinary movement that is essential, one that serves the intention of the dance," she said of her belief that using "a common language of the body" would make for more intense and meaningful engagement with audiences.[4] The Halprins' joint approach to eco-performance at The Sea Ranch took kinesthetic experience as a basis for new techniques of collaborating with others and for increasing interactions with the natural environment through tasks that used the found materials on a beach for real-world projects—like this pop-up commune of human habitats.

The first two days of the workshop focused on gradually immersing the dancers and architects, who made up the majority of workshop participants, into experiences in the urban environment to heighten their perceptual skills. This began with individual "urban awareness walks" in San Francisco where participants were given suggested behaviors to assume and instructed to "pay attention to the drama of the environment" in locales as varied as the upscale shopping district of Union Square and a parking lot. The next day included exercises in slowing attention to take in more of the sensate data of the world through group blindfolded walks in nature at the Halprins' Kentfield property. Here the forty participants held hands in a long line to heighten their nonvisual sensory awareness of the textures, smells, sounds, and temperatures of the environment (see Figure 1.23). Now, for six days, they were camping out and communally sharing a rented house at The Sea Ranch. "Both of our art forms were influenced by and arose from natural processes, and Anna and I recognized that The Sea Ranch provided another powerful place for such studies," Larry explained of the impetus for relocating the summer workshop for several days to this secluded site of their own second home.[5] This was a somewhat surprising choice, since more typically second homes are designed specifically to be places where a family goes to get away from work and the demands of others. From its inception, however, the Halprins had intended their Sea Ranch home as a working laboratory and teaching space where family time and their lives as artists would coexist even more fluidly than they already did at their Kentfield home (Figure 5.4). "I thought it contained opportunities that fit all of my family's dreams,"

Figure 5.4. The first Halprin home at The Sea Ranch. Charles Moore, William Turnbull, and Lawrence Halprin house, 1966, destroyed by fire 2001. Photograph by Lawrence Halprin, 1982. Lawrence Halprin Collection, Stuart Weitzman School of Design, The Architectural Archives, University of Pennsylvania, Philadelphia.

208   THE CHOREOGRAPHY OF ENVIRONMENTS

Larry said of The Sea Ranch house as he enumerated the virtues of placing this second home in a private rocky cove overlooking the sea. In this way, it echoed the earlier architectural features of the Halprins' Kentfield home on the edge of a mountain and with distant views of the waters of the greater San Francisco Bay. Both Halprin homes were isolated from other houses; marked by ladders, stairs, and uncomfortable seating; and positioned with unimpeded views stretching far away into an offshore distance. They also shared a fluidity of space and movement with their abundant windows and sliding glass doors that minimized the separation between interior space and nature as a summoning force outside. "The cove was accessible down a series of natural rock steps, and I could imagine us fishing among the rocks below," Larry said of The Sea Ranch house's location on a rocky ledge above rich beds of abalone. "On the cliff's edge we could easily locate a cabin that would make us feel as if we were riding the waves on the bow of a ship," he said, noting that in fact the ship it reminded him of was the naval destroyer on which he served during World War II. "There was plenty of space for an art studio for me, an outdoor dance space for Anna, and lots of room for the kids and their friends."[6]

Well into their final years, the Halprins continued to spend weekends, holidays, and long summers at The Sea Ranch, using it as a place of retreat from the outside world but also a lab to advance their ideas for re-examining the elements of design in their respective fields. "Larry loved going up to The Sea Ranch so, so often," Daria said. "He felt a little bit more distinction between private and public space there because there was no dance studio and dance staff."[7] This suggested how, despite having the same walls of welcoming windows, without the dance deck, the spillage of Anna's dance world into the private Halprin family world was much more limited.

Infused equally with 1960s counterculture idealism and mainstream pragmatism in its search for group design solutions to civic problems, the Experiments in Environment workshop relocated to The Sea Ranch for several days so that participants could explore with abandon a rural coastal environment as they built architectural spaces. The seclusion gave them freedom to play with the essentials of creativity, allowing many perspectives to converge as they simultaneously conceptualized and moved through design problems while attending to the environment as a collaborator. Hoping to develop repeatable structures for creative group work and collective problem-solving, Anna and Larry made the centerpiece of The Sea Ranch visit an excursion to Gualala State Beach, a public site just north of The Sea

Figure 5.5. Driftwood tower, Driftwood City, The Sea Ranch, California, 1966. Anna Halprin in distance in jeans and hat with Charles Moore. Photograph by Lawrence Halprin. Lawrence Halprin Collection, Stuart Weitzman School of Design, The Architectural Archives, University of Pennsylvania, Philadelphia.

Ranch, known locally as Driftwood Beach. Here, where the Gualala River meets the Pacific Ocean, piles of driftwood logs, like the Pacific Ocean's lumberyard, were readily available (Figure 5.5).

The participants were instructed to build a fantasy city in nature, sanctify it, inhabit it, and then destroy it on the final day. The score, or guiding rules, was deliberately spare, allowing participants to discover what conservationist Aldo Leopold once called "the land ethic"—how the relationship between people and the land is intertwined in an expanded definition of community. In his influential *A Sand County Almanac*, Leopold cautioned that rather than being approached solely as an economic problem, land use needed to be thought about in terms of what was "ethically and esthetically right . . . [what] tends to preserve the integrity, stability and beauty of the biotic community."[8] These were attitudes the Halprins were already developing in their own work, and the workshops were experiments in how to make this emotional and sensual relationship to environment compelling for others, especially those developing and performing in it.

210   THE CHOREOGRAPHY OF ENVIRONMENTS

The most documented event of the 1968 summer workshop was the construction of a driftwood village. Presented by Anna and Larry as "an ideal way to get people to make direct use of the resources of the environment to produce expressions of collective creativity," the assignment was spread across two days with a deliberately spare written score serving as the performable recipe for each day.[9]

> Driftwood Village Score:
> (Day 5) Driftwood 1
> I would like you to contact the environment of this beach. It is made up of sound, water, cliffs, and driftwood.
> Using this environment and these materials build an environment according to this place and your own interests and needs.
> (Day 6) Driftwood 2
> Move into the environment. Take down the structure that was built yesterday. Use this as the motivation to build an environment as a community. i.e., whatever choice you make must include your awareness of its impact on the whole group. Giving up old structures is part of the way of finding new structures.[10]

The second morning on site had gotten off to a rough start when participants arrived late and lingered at breakfast, resulting in the cancellation of Anna's movement session on "identification with the sea." The dancers in the workshop seemed to have been more accustomed to trusting messy play to yield useful material than the architects, who displayed a divorce between their enthusiasm to trust in the Halprins' unusual processes and their skepticism that it would result in usable tools back in their professional lives.

In fact, the collective collaboration among stakeholders evolving here would become an important model in the years ahead for Larry's eco-environmentalism projects like the redesign of the *Yosemite Falls Corridor* and the *FDR Memorial*, and it would extend as well to the larger field of urban design. For Anna it would also mark a shift into an increasing use of participants' personal stories ("myths") as a starting point for building large collective group works to tap into her Jungian-inspired model of "a group myth expressing a common human need."[11] Larry too was looking for new ways to elicit group input into the design process while still retaining control over the final outcome. "I think what drove me was a desire to inspire my own office and expand our creativity," Larry said of his motivation in creating the

EXPANDING HOME: THE SEA RANCH   211

workshops with Anna. "I was frustrated by the roadblocks I encountered in the office whenever I presented new and different approaches to thinking and designing," he confided.[12] Architectural historian Alison Hirsch affirms the enduring influence of the Halprins' processes on the fields of urban renewal and ecological planning, extolling Larry as a pivotal figure who brought nature into the city as a powerful force in environmental planning. "It is important to recognize that Halprin's work has a richer dimensionality than much of today's theoretical discourse within landscape architecture, since he was not only interested in the urban organizational scale, but also made significant and meaningful physical interventions at the human scale," she noted.[13] "He focused less on formal products than on the process that generated them, as well as how those forms invited human interaction and enhanced public life in cities undergoing urban renewal."[14] In describing the genesis of his focus on process, in both the planning of his designs and the experience for those who used them, Larry dated it from his early days trekking in the Sierras and his discovery of how in nature beautiful things arose and were formed by torrents of waterfalls and the erosion of rocks. "I said to myself let me design in the same way that erosion forms arise in nature or that glaciers form things. Let me find the essence of how as a principle I can go at designing and then it will have the same brightness that stuff up there has," he said, explaining that it was a way of thinking about design as a process that gave him "a vernacular and a language that I then have used ever since. It has to do not so much with natural form but natural process and the way of discovering it."[15]

The Sea Ranch

In 1964, a decade of lessons from the Halprins' suburban San Francisco home had expanded onto the 5,200-acre stage of rugged Northern California coast that would become known as The Sea Ranch. A unique vacation development of 1,500 homes spanning ten miles of jagged coastline that Larry helped mastermind, planting more than a half-million trees, The Sea Ranch formally opened in May 1965, the product of a vision that melded architecture, environment, history, and an ethos of collectivity and individualism to create a second-home community. The marketing campaign announced it as "the most unusual second home colony ever conceived by nature and man," rightly assigning nature as much credit as the designers for its attractions.[16]

The governing ideal was that nature should predominate and that housing should sit lightly, and almost invisibly, upon the land. Initially the Halprin family had camped on the land in the style of Larry's process of embedding himself in nature to feel the essence of a site. Although neither camping nor cooking was ever Anna's forte, she gamely prepared family meals outdoors on a camp stove in a coastal meadow. She was trying to maintain the semblance of a routine family life in a site that was whipped by winds so fierce she said she had to struggle not to be knocked over (Figure 5.6).

Eventually the Halprins built a small weekend cabin on five acres of astonishing coastline, a site Larry chose as recompense in part for his work as one of the master planners of The Sea Ranch development. (This was an irony not lost to subsequent critics who noted his development plans prohibited any building on the coastline.) Within a couple of years, in 1966, the Halprin cabin was replaced by a larger but still compact redwood and glass openbeamed house with plentiful windows onto nature, an angled plank roof positioned on the coastal bluff above steep wave-splashed cliffs and framed by a separate studio for Larry, and a huge old redwood burl placed over a rock where at times Anna did her daily warmup movement ritual (Figure 5.7).

Designed by Charles Moore, William Turnbull, and Larry to conform to the barn-like vernacular simplicity of The Sea Ranch architectural guidelines, the Halprin Sea Ranch house had a small footprint, an air of social informality, Bohemian naturalness, and breathtaking ocean-front views. As with the floating staircase in the family's Marin home, Daria and Rana both recalled the treacherousness of the open deck on the oceanside of the house, which reached to the edge of the cliff and was absent railing, allowing an unobstructed, if perilous, view. In The Sea Ranch home, just as with the Kentfield home, as much of daily life as possible took place outside. "Their creativity was in the outside in nature and nature was left very raw and used as a creative theatre space," Rana said of her parents' lives there. "The Sea Ranch was not about sitting around in the house. They were always outside, and we were always eating outside," she said. "There was a second kitchen outside at The Sea Ranch and we would prep and eat our meals out there."[17] The effect was to maximize the experience in nature but adapted with a few essential domestic comforts.

In 2001, the Halprin home at The Sea Ranch burned to the ground in a freak electrical fire and was replaced by a redesign as close to the original as possible. Although both Anna and Larry were in their eighties at the time, they immediately rebuilt the house with an urgency as if the family had lost

Figure 5.6. Anna Halprin preparing breakfast during a Halprin family work trip to The Sea Ranch, California, in 1965. They are camping on the site where they would eventually build their home. Courtesy of the Halprin family.

Figure 5.7. Anna Halprin doing movement ritual on a redwood burl on the back patio of the Halprin house in The Sea Ranch, California. Photo still by Ruedi Gerber, from his documentary film *Breath Made Visible: Anna Halprin*, ZAS Film AG, 2009. Courtesy of Ruedi Gerber.

a cherished member (Figure 5.8). Filmmaker Andrew Abrahams recorded a tearful Anna walking amid the burned ruins of the old house, examining shards of burnt pottery and caressing the huge blackened and charred beams like a lover touching the limbs of her dead beloved.

Now for the third time, the trademark features of the Halprin home were inscribed in the architectural elements and furnishings of their new house: a dramatic staircase in the entryway, a small deck, an amphitheater with log seating a short distance from the house, large unobstructed picture windows, and seating Daria remembers as being even more uncomfortable than that in the Kentfield home (Figures 5.9 and 5.10). By now the influences of Anna and Larry's daily exchanges with these objects from the original Halprin home in Kentfield had settled so deeply into their existence that it's not surprising their Sea Ranch homes included them as well. The rebuilt Halprin vacation house was nested in the midst of an epic Northern California environment. It was shaped by Larry's and Anna's absorption of the tacit lessons of their Kentfield home with its archives of stairs, decks, chairs, and windows

EXPANDING HOME: THE SEA RANCH   215

Figure 5.8. Photo still of Anna Halprin in the burned ruins of the Halprin house at The Sea Ranch, California. From *Returning Home* (2003), a documentary film by Andrew Abrahams, Open Eye Pictures. Courtesy of Andrew Abrahams.

shaping the world they found and providing an aesthetic impetus for using their art to shape the world they wanted.

The vision of The Sea Ranch had begun in the early 1960s when Larry was engaged by Al Boeke, a representative of the development company Castle & Cook, to assemble a team with the initial objective of assessing the feasibility of turning a huge sheep farm into a new town three hours north of San Francisco. When that was deemed impractical, the plan shifted to developing the wind-swept site into a vacation community for second homes but one that would, in Boeke's words, "respect the land. We would put people on the land in a way that they were inconspicuous," he said. "And we weren't going to build a recreational community for destination and play, but a meditative—a quiet, meditative community for 'just folks,' ... not special folks, just folks."[18] Gathering the architectural firms of Joseph Esherick & Associates and Moore, Lyndon, Turnbull & Whitaker, as well as geographer and soil engineer Richard Reynolds, Larry immersed himself in the landscape, hiking its length, camping for weeks, and sketching as he charted wind directions, paths of sunlight, and the climatic effect of daily temperatures on

Figure 5.9. Main living room and sunroom/dining room from the Halprin home at The Sea Ranch, California (rebuilt in 2003 after a 2001 house fire). Staged for sale after the death of Anna and Lawrence Halprin, from Liisberg and Company listing, 2021. Photograph by Paul Kozal. Courtesy of Paul Kozal.

his body. With perceptual skills honed through years of having witnessed Anna's play with the dynamics of environment and space on bodies as essential partners in her work on the dance deck, he responded to the windswept and overgrazed meadows, craggy cliffs dropping to the sea, and clusters of

Figure 5.10. The rebuilt Halprin house at The Sea Ranch, Boeke, Moore Lyndon Turnbull Whitaker, Esherick & Associates. Photograph by Saxon Holt. Courtesy of The Cultural Landscape Foundation.

second-growth trees on the hillsides as empirical scores, movement texts with stories of the land's Pomo Indian and more immediate logging, grazing, and farming histories. The result was what *Progressive Architecture* in a feature on Halprin and The Sea Ranch dubbed "ecological architecture" on a "planned organic environment" with a vision so profound that it required a rethinking of land ownership, use, stewardship, and suburban lifestyles.[19] This fusion of modernist architecture with dance anchored in ordinary movement, and responsive to land management, environmental planning, landscaping, and real estate sales, resulted in a model of development based on *un*development.

Experiments in Environment Workshops at The Sea Ranch

By the summer of 1968, The Sea Ranch was already garnering national attention in architectural publications as well as mainstream media as what *Sports Illustrated* called "a remarkable new resort community." Larry was championed as "a new breed of landscape architect, an environmental planner," and "the man behind the magnificent use of the land at The Sea Ranch" in part for his and The Sea Ranch team's skill at balancing developer-driven financial objectives with the preservation of nature and a liberal lifestyle.[20] He was successfully wedding conservationism with pragmatism at The Sea Ranch through his philosophy "to plan environments that let people live on the land without destroying it."[21] The visuals of The Sea Ranch were controlled like a carefully scripted stage set. Houses were tucked up into clusters away from the shoreline and open meadows, maximizing views of the cliffs and ocean. Cars were to be hidden behind fences, manicured gardens and lawns prohibited, and the modernist/Bay Regional Style buildings muted with a design code specifying that all structures remain unpainted, allowing their unfinished siding of wood native to the locale to weather naturally.

In the same way that Anna's summer dance workshops on the dance deck had drawn dancers and artists from the east as word of their radical openness and experimentation with nature circulated, so too Larry's environmental planning at The Sea Ranch pulled architects and designers west. Chip Lord had just graduated from Tulane University's School of Architecture in 1968 when he left for San Francisco to take the Halprins' Experiments in Environment summer workshop. "It was a new way to think about design and the environment, something that had barely been touched on in the school of architecture," Lord said, noting that, although middle-aged, the Halprins represented role models with values far from the mainstream cultural establishment of the time. "I subscribed to the feeling that our parents had screwed everything up and we had to reinvent—start from scratch and essentially restructure all institutions," Lord said.[22] It was the rub of the two ways of processing the world between architects and dancers that presented a radical opening of possibilities for Lord. "The architects had, for the most part, no sense of their own bodies. And the dancers were all about sensing their bodies and moving in space," he marveled.[23]

Curt Schreier, who with Lord would go on to found Ant Farm, the influential, alternative architecture and environmental design collective in San Francisco later in 1968, also came west that summer. Schreier too remarked on the novelty of what he called the cross-flow between the dancers' sense of movement, space, and action and the architects' focus on the "environment-centric organization of space." "The idea of having an entire group with an environmental awareness doing movement that related to the space is what turned it from just being an analysis for architects to actually being a dance form," he said.[24] He recalled with amusement how one local resident observing the construction of the Driftwood Village stepped forward after watching a group struggling to move a large hunk of driftwood and offered to bring his hauler to do it quickly. "But of course the whole point was to actually explore the movement and the heft of this thing," Schreier said, suggesting how profoundly the workshop had shifted his perception to the degree that he could appreciate the physics of maneuvering the log as a choreographic event.[25] Using this platform of the Experiments in Environment workshops, Anna and Larry were both drawing on the first years of their own breakthrough work in their respective fields and marrying them with the environmental mandate of The Sea Ranch to enhance the character of the land and its enjoyment without destroying it. The paradigms that emerged would reshape their own work to include an increased focus on process, a search for the vernacular in both movement and urban design, and a deepened regard for movement as a catalyst for experiencing nature.

In the same way that Anna's new approach to movement discarded the technical training of technique in favor of what she called intrinsic movement drawn from the efficient actions of everyday life, Larry's vision of land stewardship at The Sea Ranch similarly respected the found features of the site itself and took them as templates for design and development. "At The Sea Ranch there was no way to use what the sea was, no natural harbors, except to just enjoy nature's largest picture window," Schreier succinctly observed of the dramatic coastline. "That was always the cliff of the design questions, why not leave it the way it was?"[26] For Lord it was the novel experiment in communally clustered housing, the Condominium One development at The Sea Ranch, that stood out for him. "California seemed interesting because of The Sea Ranch,"[27] he said.

The qualities that defined these Experiments in Environment workshops, and those that Schreier and Lord both identified as reasons motivating them to come west, were also among the signature features of the Halprin home in Marin. These included a recalibration of perception as a movable frame on the natural and urban world, a fresh negotiation between interior and exterior new models for participatory creation, and an emphasis on art and design as arising out of a group's communal response to site. Although serious issues, all of these reworkings had a sense of play and whimsy underpinning their radical positioning, and this was an aesthetic the workshops and The Sea Ranch echoed. As architecture historian Simon Sadler noted, The Sea Ranch had "a lightness to the gravitas" and a perspective on development

220 THE CHOREOGRAPHY OF ENVIRONMENTS

that was effectively a "self-deprecating riposte to formal ideas about how much control over a site a designer could and should bring," he wrote.[28] He also noted its separation from politics. "Civil rights and the escalation of the war in Vietnam felt a long way away indeed," he continued. "The Sea Ranch was, if anything, an escape from the national strife as it erupted in the social and political unrest. . . . [I]t offered a slow time refuge from a historically charged moment. . . . Any revolution being enacted here was going to be 'soft,'" he concluded.[29] Indeed, the workshops, for all their daring, left the next step of where and how to use these skills and insight in the larger world up to individual participants.

In an impassioned rationale he wrote at the conclusion of the 1968 workshop, Larry argued for the urgency of unified group approaches to problemsolving as the antidote to the dangers of alienation—a popular catch-all term of the time to describe social and personal estrangement in the 1960s and 1970s. "The results of this feeling of alienation can lead either to apathy and cynicism or to revolution and the demand for change," he wrote. "These in turn can lead to dictatorship or chaos unless we can find methods to reinstate real involvement in what happens to our lives. . . . [W]e must do this as collections of individuals working together toward achieving our objectives."[30] This assumption that there is a common set of values shared by all the participants reflects a certain idealistic and race- and class-blind innocence to Larry's aspirations.

To prototype a unified group approach to problem-solving, the Halprins assembled a group of forty people for their Experiments in Environment workshops drawn from a range of professions including dance, architecture, theater, design, psychology, and sociology for an immersive experiment. The charge was finding a way to work together as a group while allowing individual views and differences to be aired and then melded together through creative consensus, achieving the goal of "collective creativity." Enlisting the assistance of the psychologist Dr. Paul Baum, who had helped Anna defuse *Ceremony of Us* tensions in the group, the Halprins structured a series of "intense experiences to experiment with and open up new concepts of the idea of community."[31] In the announcement he circulated to schools of architecture and design across the country soliciting participants, Larry described the goals of this summer workshop as progressing from individual awareness through personal interactions with the environment and culminating with interpersonal and large group environmental constructions contrived through collective problem-solving.[32] He and Anna were distilling workshop

EXPANDING HOME: THE SEA RANCH   221

techniques as part of their legacies, and The Sea Ranch workshops were the site of what was finally their most profound collaboration, a focus on the process of making work rather than the finished work itself. The processes of attuning to an awareness of one's own body and becoming sensitized to the dynamics of working physically with others outdoors were presented as precursors to how social groups coalesce, how rituals are enacted that bind them, and then how these resolve into the creation of enduring social structures of families and communities living and working together.

When it was completed, Driftwood Village was comprised of a variety of structures including "temples, homes, ritualistic and totemic devices, places for relaxation and contemplation," all revealing what Larry called "an instinctual sense of community formation" that recalled how structures and communities have historically begun. For Anna, communities announced their presence through communal play and rituals, and so for her the spontaneous rites of drumming, chanting, and dance processions the architects and dancers created to consecrate these built spaces prior to ritually destroying them were confirmation of participants' full investment. Having the workshop focus on building a small village on a beach adjacent to The Sea Ranch—the very site on which Larry was in the midst of collectively designing a huge village of second homes—folded play and work tightly together.

Before returning to San Francisco and the Halprin home in Kentfield where this Experiments in Environment workshop concluded, Anna led participants in a processional departure ritual at The Sea Ranch beginning with the unfurling of a huge roll of white paper that the group first inscribed with memories of workshop events and then carried in a winding processional line and placed in a meadow (Figure 5.11; see also Figure 1.12). The prop was familiar from the paper-tearing section of *Parades and Changes*, and Anna was now repurposing it as a banner of memories. After memorializing their Driftwood Village experience, participants returned the following day and concluded by shredding and burning the paper and flinging its remnants into the ocean. In her summary about this final day at The Sea Ranch, Anna noted that at least one participant responded with tears at this violation of the spectacular natural environment, a reaction that Anna dismissed, saying: "Others felt it as a very moving ritual at the end of important experiences together, that the paper was of natural elements that would be absorbed and recycled as part of ongoing natural processes."[33]

222   THE CHOREOGRAPHY OF ENVIRONMENTS

Figure 5.11. Experiments in Environment workshop participants unfurling one hundred yards of paper memorializing the workshop en route to shredding it into the sea, The Sea Ranch, California. Photograph by Paul G. Ryan, 1968. Courtesy of Paul G. Ryan.

Figure 5.12. Terre Parker in Anna Halprin's *Awaken* at The Sea Ranch, California. Photo still from *Journey in Sensuality: Anna Halprin and Rodin*, a documentary film by Ruedi Gerber, ZAS Film AG, 2016. Courtesy of Ruedi Gerber.

EXPANDING HOME: THE SEA RANCH   223

The workshop instructions for this final day at The Sea Ranch specified that the long scroll of paper with notations from all the participants was to be "ritually offered to the sea" by being cast into the ocean. This is reminiscent of the Jewish ceremony of Tashlich, a ritual using water that would have been familiar to both Anna and Larry from their Jewish upbringing. Tashlich is performed on the first day of Rosh Hashanah and is a time when Jews proceed to a body of running water, preferably one containing fish, and symbolically cast off their sins by writing them on small slips of paper that they then toss into the water. Anna tended to adopt aspects of Jewish religious observance more freely as ritual than did Larry, who had a more religiously conservative upbringing. Nature may have been first as a source of inspiration, but art and design agendas were generally the ends toward which both were ultimately aiming. Anna paralleled Larry's working approach to nature in the sites of his projects where he drew not just inspiration from nature but also its actual materials as he excavated granite, rock, and stones to bring back and represent nature in urban settings and make more accessible its experiences. She did this by using movement as a messenger for the body's interactions with the environment, leading her students and dancers to respond sensorially to ecosystems and then utilize what they harvested as raw material for dance.

The Experiments in Environment workshops, and a subsequent handbook Larry published called *Taking Part*, were his attempts to distill and share with the field of environmental planning and urban design these fruitful years of absorbing the influences of living and coteaching with Anna. They both deployed the moving body as a gateway to engagement with environments from the rural to the urban by using a common body language of functional movement discovered through tasks like moving and stacking logs. The architects and designers in the summer workshops certainly noticed how their play at collectively making a Driftwood Village on the beach was a tiny version of the grand-scale coastal community Larry and his professional Sea Ranch collaborators were building out of local wood on the California coastline. The Sea Ranch rendered the concept of a collective group as architecture, debuting the novel structure of clustered homes called Condominium One, a prototype for what would become the globally ubiquitous form of townhouses and condos, buildings containing multiple individually owned homes. Architect Donlyn Lyndon, one of Larry's collaborators, noted how the structure of a condominium neatly echoed the collective group ethos Anna and Larry were aiming for with the workshops. "There

224 THE CHOREOGRAPHY OF ENVIRONMENTS

weren't many people who had done condominiums at that point, it was an exotic new thing and marvelous way of thinking about collective things," Lyndon said of Condominium One, built in 1965 as the first unit at The Sea Ranch. "It was the individual and the collective together."[34]

The Sea Ranch Legacy

Well into the twenty-first century, The Sea Ranch development continues to enjoy idolization by architecture and ecology enthusiasts. Writing in *The New York Times* in 2008, architecture critic Patricia Leigh Brown noted: "The Sea Ranch has achieved a sort of a cult status among architecture mavens, who house-gawk rather than bird-watch.... They come to see a style forged by A-list architects (shed roofs to deflect the wind, windows punched through redwood boards) but perhaps more than that, to pay tribute to a big idea: Then-radical notion, influenced by Mr. Halprin's experience on a kibbutz, of open land held in common and houses designed in deference to nature."[35]

While the unique communal situation of living and working on a kibbutz was a utopian experience for Larry as a young man in Israel, its ideals of voluntary socialism and collective living had been tempered by years of an upscale suburban life in the Halprin house in Kentfield by the time he began The Sea Ranch project. What The Sea Ranch revealed more readily was the communal settlement aspect of a kibbutz blended with an environmentalist Northern California spirit of shared stewardship and protection of the land meets traditional capitalist private ownership of property. In many ways, The Sea Ranch experiment succeeded beyond its founders' expectations— the one major exception being the unintended exclusivity it acquired over time as property values escalated and the almost entirely White middle-class residents remained. By the standards of most coastal second homes, the Halprin Sea Ranch house was modest in size and design (the family referred to it as a "cabin"), but the home's location on the edge of the continent was so astounding, as well as its cachet as the Halprin home, that when it was listed for sale by the family at $8 million in late 2021, after the death of Anna earlier that year, it sold in a matter of weeks for $12 million, by far the highest price ever paid for a Sea Ranch property.

The days of radicalism that Experiments in Environment inaugurated at The Sea Ranch also continue to be revisited as history and prototype by dance and performance historians and architectural and environmental activists. In 2023–2024, the Museum of Modern Art in New York hosted *Emerging Ecologies: Architecture and the Rise of Environmentalism*, the first major museum exhibition to survey the relationship between architecture and the environmental crisis of the 1960s and 1970s in the United States. The Sea Ranch and the summer workshops were featured among the exemplary projects exhibited. A slide loop of images included photographs of dancers and architects building Driftwood Village, the sensory walk, and nude work on the dance deck from the Kentfield days of the workshop. As was true in the era in which they debuted, these were still the only prototypes using dance and performing bodies in conjunction with ecological awareness. Of all the examples in the exhibition, the Halprin display drew the largest clusters of curious museum patrons. The Experiments in Environment workshop, now more than fifty years old, remained in the vanguard for putting dance in relationship with environment and scaling community development to be minimally invasive to native ecologies.

Long after the summer 1968 workshop ended, Anna continued to return to The Sea Ranch as a site for her dance workshops and performances. The spirit of those summers of experimentation with dance in the environment with Larry had never really ended for her. After Larry predeceased her in 2009, she began a series of posthumous collaborations, using The Sea Ranch summer Experiments in Environment workshops as a template. "Our lives are so intertwined," she once said. "Larry had a different kind of mind than I did. I thought of improvisations, and he had a way of systematizing process. That helped me deepen and develop my work. So, it was a system we had with a very different mindset but a similar goal."[36]

Among the most intimate of Anna's posthumous collaborations with Larry was *Awaken*, a set of movement studies based on Auguste Rodin's sculptures of lovers she began during what turned out to be the final period of Larry's life. Larry would sketch the dancers working with her as they improvised in the redwood grove behind the Kentfield house, making watercolors that showed the dancers' forms melting into the tree trunks and branches of the forest—a final lyrical fusing of their two domains. After Larry's death, Anna continued reflecting on Rodin's figures, working on the beach at Sea Ranch as she shaped a series of nude tableaux with her Sea Ranch Collective dancers. A meditation on love, the erotic body, aging, and loss, Anna contoured *Awaken* as a tribute to those decades of discoveries about dance and environment that she had developed with Larry on these sands. Using dancers

226 THE CHOREOGRAPHY OF ENVIRONMENTS

skilled in her anatomically based approach to movement sited in nature, she shaped and edited a series of choreographic enactments of Rodin's wax, bronze, and stone sculptures.

Several threads cross through the achievement of the dancers in *Awaken*, as witnessed by a photograph of Terre Parker, captured in a rapturous moment of performing on the desolate Sea Ranch beach (Figure 5.12). Nude, she swoons back in a deep reverie, arching her back against a wave-splashed rock on the shoreline, her chest and neck thrust open to the sky. Her surrender is so complete she seems to be returning to the land; or rather, like a being the sea washed up on the beach, she is engaged in a slow, sensuous yielding of her flesh back to rock and sand. The quality of completeness between body and nature that Anna often said was at the heart of her quest in working in the environment—especially Larry's environments—is viscerally evident here. Deeply at home with the body, Anna emphasized its magnificence just as Larry presented the glories of his medium, nature, for a new regard.

The Sea Ranch was Larry's greatest environmental address. Here he came closest to achieving his animating drive—that of bringing attention to nature, to how people move through created space, with a heightened perception to the form, balance, and innate choreography of an environment etched with layers of overuse. In fusing dance, landscape architecture, and urban design, the Halprins had effectively pioneered what decades later would be named by cognitive neuroscientists as embodied cognition, denoting the symbiotic relationship between the human motor system and our sensory faculties. Architecture critics would eventually follow; among the first of these was Harvard Professor Sarah Williams Goldhagen, who correlated cognitive neuroscience to urban design, designating buildings and their interiors and landscapes "action settings," places defined by objects and designed spaces that help mold what people do and think and how they engage with one another. These information cues are critical to our lives with others, she asserts, because they shape how we absorb and perform normative standards of behavior.[37]

Effectively The Sea Ranch workshops were prescient rehearsals in these awarenesses, priming us to attend to how the built environment and its designs animate and socialize the body into action. Decades after those 1960s summers, neurobiological research into canonical neurons (neurons that respond to the presentation of an object) and mirror neurons (neurons that respond to the performance of an action) would confirm on cognitive and physiological levels the deep interrelationship between the human body, its sensory and cognitive faculties, and the environs of the built and natural worlds. These encounters help shape our sense of self, identity, well-being, and efficacy in the world.

In many ways, Anna's and Larry's art, conjoined, primed a generation to be attentive to ecosystem crises of the twenty-first century—environmental devastation and climate catastrophe—and to respond to these viscerally as much as intellectually. Larry once commented that he learned not to copy the forms of nature but to understand the processes by which natural forms arise.[38] Anna too learned not to copy set forms of dance but to work from the processes by which movement and expression arise in each body and the collective body. Those lessons the stairs, decks, chairs, and windows the Halprin home in Kentfield taught, and which their home in The Sea Ranch replicated so closely, revealed how bodies are always in a duet with the environment and that there is an imperative to notice, participate, and respond. Both Halprin homes were object lessons, tutoring their inhabitants, through objects, in how the spaces in which we live exert determining forces on our capacities to navigate the world's urban, political, environmental, and climate challenges. These were the revelations their workshops, works, and lives disseminated into the world. That duet between dance and landscape architecture begun at the Halprin home was in fact a trio, a continual dance of awareness between embodied human cognition, the physical environment, and the concomitant meanings we make of the world.

APPENDIX

Selected List of Exhibitions and Films of Anna Halprin, 2005–2021

(Listed in Chronological Order)

Part I: Exhibitions

Anna Halprin: At the Origin of Performance, Musée d'Art Contemporain de Lyon, France, 2006; Yerba Buena Center for the Arts, San Francisco, 2008. Included in *Looking for Mushrooms* (Cologne: Museum Ludwig, 2009); *100 Years: A History of Performance Art* (New York: Museum of Modern Art and PS1, 2010); *West of Center* (Denver: Museum of Contemporary Art Denver, 2011), *Danser sa Vie* (Paris: Centre Pompidou, 2011), *Moments* (Karlsruhe: ZKM, 2012), *57th International Art Exhibition of La Biennale di Venezia* (2017), *documenta 14* (2017), *We Is Future: Visions of New Communities* (Essen: Museum Folkwang, 2023; Dohee Lee led a *Planetary Dance* there).

Anna Halprin: Parades and Changes, MATRIX, Berkeley Art Museum, 2013.

Ally: Janine Antoni, Anna Halprin, Stephen Petronio, Fabric Workshop and Museum, Philadelphia, 2014.

Experiments in Environment: The Halprin Workshops, Graham Foundation, Chicago, 2014.

Radical Bodies: Anna Halprin, Simone Forti, and Yvonne Rainer in California and New York, 1955–1972, University of California, Santa Barbara, and the New York Public Library for the Performing Arts, 2017.

Anna Halprin: Body Radical, de Young Museum, San Francisco, 2018.

Janine Antoni and Anna Halprin: Paper Dance, The Contemporary Austin (offshoot of earlier exhibition, *Ally*), 2019.

Part II: Films

Breath Made Visible: Anna Halprin, filmed by Ruedi Gerber, ZAS Film AG, 2009.

Seniors Rocking, filmed by Ruedi Gerber, ZAS Film AG, 2010.

Journey in Sensuality: Anna Halprin and Rodin (featuring *Awaken*), filmed by Ruedi Gerber, ZAS Film AG, 2016.

Videos by Jens Wazel: *A Morning with Anna*; *In the Kitchen with Anna*; *Anna Halprin/ Dancing at 96*; *Conversations with Anna Halprin*; *In the Studio with Anna Halprin*; *Planetary Dance for Ukraine*, 2016.

Healing Power of Dance, Russian TV documentary, 2017.

230 APPENDIX

Part III: Performances

Planetary Dance, thirty-five-year annual participatory event in San Francisco Bay Area and other venues, ongoing since 1987.

Intensive Care: Reflections on Death and Dying, Cowell Theater, San Francisco, 2000; Jewish Community Center, San Francisco, 2006; Centre Pompidou, Paris, 2007.

Seniors Rocking, with seventy performers ages seventy and up, Marin Civic Center, California, 2005.

Awaken, Halprin garden, Kentfield, California; Cantor Art Center, Stanford, California; The Sea Ranch, California, 2009.

Spirit of Place, part of trilogy as tribute to Lawrence Halprin in Stern Grove, San Francisco, 2009.

Song of Songs, part of trilogy entitled *Remembering Lawrence*, performed by Shinichi, Dana Iova-Koga, and Jim Cave on the Halprins' dance deck in Kentfield, California, 2011.

The Courtesan and the Crone (premiered in 1999), performed on the Halprins' dance deck in Kentfield, California, 2013.

Parades and Changes, with music by Morton Subotnik (premiered in 1965). This piece changes with each new cast. Revivals include Bay Area cast for Berkeley Art Museum, 2013; Vertigo Dance Company in Israel, November 2014; dressing and undressing sequence at de Young Museum, San Francisco, 2018.

Peace Walk, part of trilogy entitled *Remembering Lawrence*, Jerusalem, 2014.

Remembering, performed for Anna Halprin's ninety-fifth birthday celebration with Jahan Khalighi, on the Halprins' dance deck in Kentfield, California, 2015.

Notes

Introduction

1. Donna J. Haraway, "Tentacular Thinking: Anthropocene, Capitalocene, Chthulucene," in *Staying with the Trouble: Making Kin in the Chthulucene* (Durham, NC: Duke University Press, 2016), 32.
2. Michel de Certeau, *The Practice of Everyday Life*, 3rd ed., trans. Steven Rendall (Berkeley: University of California Press, 2011).

Chapter 1

1. The initial parcel was two and a half acres and then the Halprins purchased two additional parcels of land adjacent to theirs that had been owned by friends, expanding the lot to five acres. "I didn't want to be hemmed in by the size of a property," Larry explained. Unpublished interview with Lawrence Halprin, conducted by Janice Ross, San Francisco, October 16, 2000. Private collection of Janice Ross.
2. Christopher Tunnard, *Gardens in the Modern Landscape* (London: Architectural Press, 1938).
3. Alison Bick Hirsch, *City Choreographer: Lawrence Halprin in Urban Renewal America* (Minneapolis: University of Minnesota Press, 2014), 29.
4. Interview with Rana Halprin, conducted by Janice Ross, Mill Valley, California, September 9, 2022.
5. Stephen Steinberg, Anna and Lawrence Halprin interview, reel 15:28, Museum of Performance + Design, San Francisco, Janice Ross Papers.
6. Ibid.
7. Steinberg, Anna and Lawrence Halprin interview, reel 15:28.
8. I thank an anonymous reader for this insight.
9. Anon., "Cities Don't Have to Be Ugly," *Engineering News-Record*, November 7, 1968, 53, Lawrence Halprin and Associates, Collected Articles and Photocopies.
10. Lawrence Halprin, *A Life Spent Changing Places* (Philadelphia: University of Pennsylvania Press, 2011), 75.
11. Ibid.
12. Janice Ross, *Anna Halprin: Experience as Dance* (Berkeley: University of California Press, 2007), 4.
13. Larry's parents were similarly first-generation Jewish immigrants and his father too had been successful in the clothing business. Initially retiring at thirty-five, he subsequently lost everything in the stock market crash of 1929 and never succeeded in rebuilding his former level of wealth. Neither family was a beneficiary of inherited wealth, despite Olive McKeon's incorrect assertion to the contrary. The phrase "inherited wealth" used in conjunction with first-generation Jewish Americans in this instance echoes rhetorically the exclusionary bias of antisemitism; see McKeon, "Rethinking Anna Halprin's *Parades and Changes*: Postmodern Dance, Racialized Urban Restructuring, and Mid-1960s San Francisco," *TDR: The Drama Review* 64, no. 2, T264 (2020): 118.
14. Anna and Larry Halprin, unpublished interview by Stephen Steinberg, for KQED documentary *Inner Landscapes*, 1991, 43, author's personal collection.
15. Ibid., 43, 49.
16. Ibid., transcript 7:43, 48.
17. Halprin, *A Life Spent Changing Places*, 75.
18. Steinberg, Anna and Larry Halprin interview, reel 15:21.
19. Ibid.
20. Ibid., 28.
21. Ibid., 22.

232 NOTES

22. Ibid., transcript 7:58.
23. Schlemmer lived in essential seclusion in Wuppertal until his death in 1942.
24. Schlemmer, 1932, Publication excerpt from MoMA Highlights: 375 Works from The Museum of Modern Art, New York (New York: The Museum of Modern Art, 2019) https://www.moma.org/collection/works/80049.
25. Interview with Rana Halprin, conducted by Janice Ross, Mill Valley, California, September 1, 2022.
26. *Lawrence Halprin: Changing Places*, San Francisco Museum of Modern Art exhibition catalog, 1986, see 1952 entry in anonymous Chronology.
27. Anon., "Protests Then and Now: Keller Fountain at 50," Portland Parks Foundation, June 17, 2020, accessed February 8, 2024, https://www.portlandpf.org/news/2020/6/17/cn5ny46k9yogw5npg1tkt1lubv36r9.
28. Ada Louise Huxtable, "Coast Fountain Melds Art and Environment," *The New York Times*, June 21, 1970, 53.
29. American Society of Landscape Architects, Landscape Award citation, accessed February 8, 2023, https://www.asla.org/2021awards/2805.html.
30. Lawrence Halprin, *Cities* (New York: Reinhold Publishing Corporation, 1963), 193.
31. Ibid., 148–49, 158, 160.
32. Ibid., 142.
33. Personal conversation with the author, December 3, 1993, Kentfield, California.
34. Reuben M. Rainey, "The Choreography of Memory: Lawrence Halprin's Franklin Delano Roosevelt Memorial," *Landscape Journal: Design, Planning and Management of the Land* 31, nos. 1–2 (2012): 161–82.
35. Halprin, *A Life Spent Changing Places*, ix.
36. Piere Cabanne, *Dialogues with Marcel Duchamp* (Boston: Da Capo Press, 1987), 44.
37. Katherine Kuh, ed., *The Artist's Voice: Talks with Seventeen* (New York: Harper & Row, 1962), 81–93.
38. Halprin, *Cities*, 127.
39. Stephen Steinberg, Yvonne Rainer interview, Museum of Performance + Design, San Francisco, Janice Ross Papers, 3.
40. Halprin, *A Life Spent Changing Places*, 141.
41. Sue Heinemann, in email communication with Janice Ross, February 1, 2024.
42. Amanda Levey, "Anna Halprin Hits the Main Stage of the Art World," *Whitecliffe College of Arts and Design ANZATA* 12, no. 1 (2017): 17.
43. Halprin, *Changing Places*, 228.

Chapter 2

1. Jacob's Pillow dance campus, home to the oldest summer dance festival in the nation and site of one of the earliest indoor spaces tailored for dance, the Ted Shawn Theatre, did not add an exclusively outdoor platform for dance until 1981, when an outdoor platform was built for additional rehearsal space for The School at Jacob's Pillow. It wasn't until 2021 that it was reconfigured to expand capacity and present outdoor performances as the Henry J. Leir Outdoor Stage/The Marcia & Seymour Simon Performance Space.
2. Lawrence Halprin personal papers, Lawrence Halprin, 1916–2009, Architectural Records, c. 1933–2009, in The Architectural Archives, University of Pennsylvania, Philadelphia, Dance Deck folders, 15 Ravine Way, Kentfield, California. (Note: $75 in 1954 is the equivalent of about $850 in 2024.)
3. Catherine Osgood Foster, "The Function of Theatre Is to Show the Word," "Arch Lauterer -Poet in the Theatre," *Impulse* (San Francisco), 1959, 15.
4. Ibid.
5. Herta Schmid, "Samuel Beckett's Play, *QUAD*: An Abstract Synthesis of the Theatre," *Canadian American Slavic Studies* 22, nos. 1–4 (1988): 263–64.
6. Interview with Anna Halprin, conducted by Janice Ross, Kentfield, California, May 25, 2001.
7. Kristina Wilson, *Mid-Century Modernism and the American Body: Race, Gender, and the Politics of Power in Design* (Princeton, NJ: Princeton University Press, 2021), 65.
8. Ibid., 27.
9. Donnell House video interview with Laurie Olin, The Cultural Landscape Foundation, October 5, 2007, accessed February 20, 2024, https://www.youtube.com/watch?v=H6rMkpf_0kY.

NOTES 233

10. Marc Treib, "Donnell Garden," *Society of Architectural Historians Archipedia*, accessed February 11, 2024, https://sah-archipedia.org/buildings/CA-01-097-0001.
11. *Lawrence Halprin: Changing Places*, catalog for Retrospective Exhibition on the Work of Lawrence Halprin, San Francisco Museum of Modern Art, 1986, 141.
12. Ibid., 71.
13. Lawrence Halprin, *A Life Spent Changing Places* (Philadelphia: University of Pennsylvania Press, 2011), 71.
14. Interview with Marc Dollinger, conducted online by Janice Ross, July 17, 2023.
15. Halprin, *A Life Spent Changing Places*, 70.
16. Ibid.
17. Interview with Fred Rosenbaum, conducted online by Janice Ross, Brooklyn, New York, July 21, 2023.
18. Fred Rosenbaum, "Rabbi Saul White Pierced Armor of S.F.'s Assimilationist Mentality," *Jewish News of Northern California*, December 22, 2003.
19. Fred Rosenbaum, *Cosmopolitans: A Social and Cultural History of the Jews of the San Francisco Bay Area* (Berkeley: University of California Press, 2009), 3.
20. Interview with Fred Rosenbaum.
21. Hasia Diner speaking about the film *American Jerusalem*. Leo Baeck Institute, New York, November 7, 2023, accessed February 14, 2024, https://www.youtube.com/watch?v=vtl0 ISgs490.
22. Recent neo-Marxist critiques have challenged readings of this democratic ethos of postmodern dance works like Anna's as operating more in a dictatorial and appropriative rather than egalitarian mode. Subjecting Anna's work process on the dance deck to a Fordist lens, Olive Mckeon has tried to assert that this work process "reflects a tension between the unleashing of collective creativity and a single author standing in for a group collaboration, [and] *Parades and Changes* harnessed concert dance to access that which is denied in capitalist production, namely the wholeness of activity, while also embodying aspects of a hierarchical production process."Mckeon, "Rethinking Anna Halprin's *Parades and Changes*: Postmodern Dance, Racialized Urban Restructuring, and Mid-1960s San Francisco," *TDR: The Drama Review* 64, no. 2, T246 (2020): 124. Mckeon's subjecting the Halprins' work to a purity test (itself argued from a standpoint of elite academic privilege) would render the routine practice of contemporary dancemaking (i.e., a choreographer sourcing movement from dancers and other disciplines) authoritarian and appropriative. Yet the majority of dance that employs improvisation as a material-generating process is often felt by dancers to be highly satisfying and personalized.
23. Mckeon, writing from a neo-Marxist perspective, has read the dance deck at the Halprin home as embodying paradox with an inference of hypocrisy by being de facto a metaphor for how Anna "found material support through her husband's architectural commissions": "Lawrence Halprin designed the deck that physically supported Anna's work, all the while bringing in well-paying commissions such as the North Park Shopping Center in Dallas. . . . As Halprin attempted to liberate modern dance from its conventions, her white, bourgeois social location facilitated a large degree of flexibility to pursue her aesthetic vision," ibid., 125. Mckeon's critique is again reductive and elides important details, collapsing the role of the landscape architect for the North Park Shopping Center with that of the developer and architect and implying that shopping centers are all de facto "rooted in the interests of private capitalists [and] perpetuate the possessive investment in whiteness," ibid., 130. Larry's efforts pulled precisely in the opposite direction: as the leading landscape architecture advocacy and preservation organization, The Cultural Landscape Foundation, details (https://www.tclf.org/northpark-center), Larry's innovations for the center were about making the experience of being in the shopping center more humanizing and less alienating for anyone who visited or worked there. With stealth styling, he was infusing nature into an experience of consumerism. The mall's interior was conceived as a series of modular spaces utilizing natural light and included fountains, benches, planters, and tiling. Since its inception, North Park has been considered an "art museum inside a shopping center."
24. Halprin, *A Life Spent Changing Places*, 70–71.
25. *Lawrence Halprin: Changing Places*, 116.
26. Anon., "Landscaping a Small Plot," *Sunset Magazine*, December 1949 (author and issue missing from clipping).

234 NOTES

27. Thomas Church and Lawrence Halprin, *House Beautiful*, April 1948, 38–45 (issue number missing from clipping), Halprin Family Collection.
28. Lawrence Halprin, "Letter to the Editor," *House Beautiful*, May 1948 (clipping from Lawrence Halprin scrapbooks is unpaginated), Halprin Family Collection.
29. Stephen Steinberg, interview with Lawrence and Anna Halprin, Museum of Performance + Design, San Francisco, Halprin Papers, reel 16:50 of transcript.
30. Ibid.
31. Ibid., 16:47.
32. Ibid., 16:47–48.
33. Anon., "Backyard Revolution: House Now Part of Whole Garden," *Vancouver Sun*, February 18, 1954, 2C, from Lawrence Halprin scrapbook, Halprin Family Collection.
34. Marian van Tuyl, "Arch Lauterer—Poet in the Theatre," *Impulse* (San Francisco), 1959, 17.
35. Elizabeth McPherson, ed., *The Bennington School of the Dance: A History in Writings and Interviews* (Jefferson, NC: McFarland, 2013), 12.
36. Helen Douglas, "Arch Lauterer on Dance in the Theatre," comments based on a 1945 interview Lauterer gave to Helen Douglas, reprinted with permission in van Tuyl, "Arch Lauterer—Poet in the Theatre," 39.
37. Quoted by van Tuyl, "Arch Lauterer—Poet in the Theatre," 16.
38. Douglas, "Arch Lauterer on Dance in the Theatre," 39.
39. Interview with Anna Halprin, conducted by Janice Ross, Kentfield, California, January 7, 2022.
40. Foster, "The Function of Theatre Is to Show the Word," 15.
41. Douglas, "Arch Lauterer on Dance in the Theatre," 40.
42. Ibid.
43. Ibid.
44. Interview with Norton Owen (archivist for Jacob's Pillow), conducted by phone by Janice Ross, Beckett, Massachusetts, September 1, 2023.
45. M. D. Morris, "Tanglewood Music Shed," *Music Journal* 23, no. 5 (1965): 68.
46. Interview with Norton Owen.
47. Janice Ross, *Anna Halprin: Experience as Dance* (Berkeley: University of California Press, 2007), 106.
48. Ibid. Erin Brannigan has erroneously written that "Cage and Cunningham ran workshops and gave performances" on the Halprin dance deck, which is incorrect; see *Choreography, Visual Art, and Experimental Composition, 1950s–1970s* (Abingdon and New York: Routledge, 2022), 33.
49. Interview with Norton Owen.
50. The Henry J. Leir Outdoor Stage was originally constructed in 1981 to provide an additional rehearsal area for The School at Jacob's Pillow. In 2021, it was reconfigured to expand capacity and present outdoor performances.
51. McPherson, ed., *The Bennington School of the Dance*, 263.
52. William L. Crosten, Director of the Department of Music, Stanford University, taped interview about Lauterer and Stanford's Dinkelspiel Auditorium. Dinkelspiel was a theater that Lauterer designed specifically for music performances. He was working on when he died. It subsequently opened in 1959. Transcript of Crosten's interview published in van Tuyl, "Arch Lauterer—Poet in the Theatre," 59–60.
53. Lawrence Halprin Papers, The Architectural Archives, Stuart Weitzman School of Design, University of Pennsylvania, Philadelphia.
54. Lawrence Halprin, "Salute From Lawrence Halprin," *Impulse* (San Francisco), 1959, 33.
55. Ibid.
56. Steinberg, interview with Anna and Lawrence Halprin, reel 16:49 of transcript, Halprin Archives, Museum of Performance + Design, San Francisco.
57. Halprin, "Dance Deck in the Woods," (San Francisco), 1956, 23.
58. Letter from Kenneth W. Brooks, A.I.A., to Thomas Creighton, Editor, *Progressive Architecture*, September 24, 1957. From personal clipping scrapbooks of Lawrence Halprin, Lawrence Halprin Papers, The Architectural Archives, Stuart Weitzman School of Design, University of Pennsylvania, Philadelphia.
59. Lawrence Halprin, "Houses: The Space Factor," *Progressive Architecture*, May 1958, 95–103. From personal clipping album of Lawrence Halprin, no issue number included.
60. Ibid., 23.
61. Ibid., 24.

NOTES   235

62. Steinberg, interview with Anna and Lawrence Halprin, reel 16:48–49 of transcript, Halprin Archives, Museum of Performance + Design, San Francisco.
63. Ibid., 49.
64. Ibid., 54.
65. Ibid., 55.
66. Ibid.
67. Ibid., 16.
68. Wilson, *Mid-Century Modernism and the American Body*, 7.
69. Ibid., 39.
70. Kimberly Chrisman-Campbell, "The Curious History of Mommy-and-Me Fashion," *The Atlantic*, May 13, 2018, 3.
71. In the 1970s when the indoor dance studio was built adjacent to the dance deck after Anna's recovery from cancer (in the summer of 1972), it was the first time that mirrors were added and only on one wall of the interior studio.
72. Margaret H'Doubler's dance studio at the University of Wisconsin–Madison did have mirrors on one wall, but these were almost always covered with floor-to-ceiling curtains when she taught.
73. Anna Halprin, interview with Ann Murphy, *In Dance*, January 1, 2013, accessed February 14, 2024, https://dancersgroup.org/2013/01/parades-and-changes-over-the-past-43-years-an-interview-with-anna-halprin/.
74. Ross, *Anna Halprin: Experience as Dance*, 140.
75. Anna Halprin, quoted in "Yvonne Rainer Interviews Anna Halprin," *Tulane Drama Review* 10, no. 5 (1965): 77.
76. Interview with A. A. Leath, conducted by Janice Ross, Madison, Wisconsin, September 8, 1992.
77. Ross, *Anna Halprin: Experience as Dance*, 181.
78. Ibid., 122.
79. Notes on Viktor Sklovski, "Iskusstvo kak Priem" (Moscow, 1929). For the most recent English translation, see Viktor Shklovsky, "Art as Device," in *Theory of Prose*, trans. Benjamin Sher, introduction by Gerald L. Bruns (Elmwood Park, IL: Dalkey Archive Press, 1990).
80. Anne Anlin Cheng, *Second Skin: Josephine Baker and the Modern Surface* (Oxford: Oxford University Press, 2011), 35.
81. Ibid., 120.
82. Stephen Steinberg, interview with Anna Halprin, Anna Halprin interview 2:30, reel 16:50 of transcript, Museum of Performance + Design, San Francisco, Halprin Papers.
83. Cheng has theorized the making of the smooth, naked, modern surface as part of a modernist rejection of the nineteenth-century fetishization of ornamentation and relying on a fetishization of bareness in its place; see *Second Skin*, 25.
84. Interview with Meredith Monk, conducted via phone by Janice Ross, Palo Alto, California, March 1, 2000.
85. Ann Hollander has written about how clothes shape bodies through their points of emphasis and also their covering up of parts deemed risqué for a particular era; see *Seeing through Clothes* (Berkeley: University of California Press, 1993).
86. Lynda Nead has written about the female nude as both a cultural and a sexual category, part of a "culture industry." "The body is always already in representation. There is no recourse to a semiotically innocent or unmediated body," she insists. See *The Female Nude: Art, Obscenity and Sexuality* (Oxfordshire: Routledge, 1992), 16, 59.
87. Cheng, *Second Skin*, 120.
88. From Ross, *Anna Halprin: Experience as Dance*, 175–76.
89. Eeo Stubblefield is the visual artist who originated the concept, body paint, costumes, and nature settings of *Still Dance*.
90. Interview with Jo Landor, conducted by Janice Ross, San Francisco, August 14, 1991.
91. Anna's stated intent in using nudity in performance was to explore "intimacy, sensuality and trust as opposed to sexuality." This parsing of nudity conveying sensuality as separate from sexuality did not always play out as she intended in the presence of audiences and critics, who could bring their own more salacious expectations to the performance. Stephen Steinberg, interview with Anna Halprin, Anna Halprin interview 2:29–30, reel 16, Museum of Performance + Design, San Francisco, Halprin Papers.

236 NOTES

92. Taking off one's clothes as part of a theatrical performance, no matter how earnest the intent, reveals undress as a form of dress because a theatrical frame imparts to any performing body the idea of clothing as a costume.

93. "While *Parades and Changes* is no doubt a response to the conventionality and homogenization of Fordism and embraces the 1960s counterculture," Olive Mckeon, the author of one such critique, writes, "it also reveals an opposing set of dynamics: the unspoken retention of control over a creative process by a single director; and a disengagement with what was happening in San Francisco's marginalized neighborhoods. Evincing the tensions of the period, Halprin's dance is marked by both the explosion of social movements and the responding forces of social domination." Mckeon, "Rethinking Anna Halprin's *Parades and Changes*," 119.

94. Interview with Marc Dollinger, conducted online by Janice Ross, July 17, 2023.

95. Interview with Carla Blank, conducted by Janice Ross via phone, June 22, 2004.

96. Stephen Steinberg, interview with Anna Halprin, Anna Halprin interview 2:29–30, reel 16, Museum of Performance + Design, San Francisco, Halprin Papers.

97. Interview with Jo Landor, conducted by Janice Ross, San Francisco, August 14, 1991.

98. This final stripping of the living body, while a logical progression into increased abstraction for her, and successful in Sweden, encountered a very different reception when the dancers performed it in the United States. At the 1967 performance at Hunter College in New York, public anxieties about the nudity being sexualized and, therefore, obscene threatened the performance. Sensationalist headlines greeted the return of the Halprin dancers from their European tour: "No pants dancers return" was one Anna often referenced that she said had been in a San Francisco newspaper. Interview with Anna Halprin, conducted by Janice Ross, Kentfield, California, November 11, 1995.

99. Janice Ross, *Moving Lessons: Margaret H'Doubler and the Beginning of Dance in American Education* (Madison: University of Wisconsin Press, 2000), 19–20.

100. Sarah Schrank, *Free and Natural: Nudity and the American Cult of the Body* (Philadelphia: University of Pennsylvania Press, 2019), chap. 2.

101. Ibid.

102. John Kaffson, book review of *Free and Natural Nudity and the American Cult of the Body*, by Sarah Schrank, *American Historical Review* 126, no. 1 (2021): 356–57.

103. There were other political resonances that public nudity also triggered. The 1960s in the San Francisco Bay Area was an era of openly sexual explorations of love-ins in Golden Gate Park and commercialized nudity in the topless dancing of the city's night clubs in North Beach. This too shadowed Anna's pursuit of nudity in workshops and choreography on the dance deck.

104. Anna Halprin, "Bath," undated choreographic notes, I, in Anna Halprin's Archives, Museum of Performance + Design, San Francisco.

105. Interview with Anna Halprin, conducted by Janice Ross, Kentfield, California, April 8, 1999.

106. Wilson, *Mid-Century Modernism and the American Body*, 100.

107. Interview with Anna Halprin, conducted by Janice Ross via phone, February 13, 2002.

108. Interview with Anna Halprin, conducted by Janice Ross, Kentfield, California, April 8, 1999.

109. Interview with Irving Penn, conducted by Janice Ross via phone, November 30, 1995.

110. Lawrence Halprin, and Jim Burns, *Taking Part: A Workshop Approach to Collective Creativity* (Cambridge, MA: MIT Press, 1974), *Experiments in the Environment*, 199.

111. Interview with Anna Halprin, conducted by Janice Ross, Kentfield, California, December 19, 2019.

112. Daria Halprin, comments from "An Afternoon with Daria Halprin," Jens Wazel Photography video, Kentfield, California, April 2011, accessed February 14, 2024, https://www.youtube.com/watch?v=iF9y4pfyD7Q.

113. Adrian Heathfield, "Before Judson & Some Other Things," essay in catalog for the New York Museum of Modern Art show *Judson Dance Theatre: The Work Is Never Done*, ed. Ana Janevski and Thomas J. Lax, 39.

114. Pierre Bal-Blanc and Lou Forster, text excerpted from *documenta 14: Daybook*, accessed February 11, 2024, https://www.documenta14.de/en/artists/13511/anna-halprin.

115. Pierre Bal-Blanc, "Anna Halprin's Dance Deck," *Flash Art*, May 29, 2020, accessed February 11, 2024, https://flash---art.com/2020/05/anna-halprins-dance-deck/.

Chapter 3

1. Kristina Wilson, *Mid-Century Modernism and the American Body: Race, Gender, and the Politics of Power in Design* (Princeton, NJ, and Oxford: Princeton University Press, 2021), 119.

NOTES   237

2. John Beardsley, "Foreword," *Landscape Design: Planning and Management of the Land* 31, nos. 1–2 (2012): 22–23.
3. Interview with Rana Halprin, conducted by Janice Ross, Mill Valley, California, October 18, 2023.
4. Wilson, *Mid-Century Modernism and the American Body*, 119.
5. Ibid.
6. Interview with Rana Halprin, conducted by Janice Ross, Mill Valley, California, September 1, 2021.
7. Interview with Daria Halprin, conducted by Janice Ross, Kentfield, California, September 1, 2021.
8. Ibid.
9. Interview with Daria Halprin, conducted by Janice Ross, Kentfield, California, July 20, 2022.
10. Interview with Rana Halprin, conducted by Janice Ross, Mill Valley, California, September 1, 2022.
11. Alexandra Lang, "In California, a Marriage of Dance and Design," *The New York Times*, September 22, 2014, accessed February 12, 2024, https://www.nytimes.com/2014/09/25/gar den/in-california-a-marriage-of-dance-and-design.html. For the print version, see Lang, "An Alliance of Dance and Design," *The New York Times*, September 25, 2014, D:2.
12. Ibid.
13. George Nelson, *Chairs*, ed. and introduction by George Nelson (New York: Acanthas Press, 1994/1999 [1953]), 12.
14. Ibid., 6.
15. Ibid.
16. Wilson, *Mid-Century Modernism and the American Body*, 141.
17. Anna Halprin, *Dancers Workshop*, no. 5 (circa 1968): 5. This belongs to a self-published, limited edition of twenty handmade booklets about the Dancers' Workshop, private collection of the author.
18. Beardsley, "Foreword," *Landscape Design: Planning and Management of the Land*, 23.
19. Halprin, *Dancers Workshop*, 4.
20. Interview with Morton Subotnick, conducted by Janice Ross via phone, January 29, 1992.
21. Ann Halprin, "The Four-Legged Stool," unpublished production notes, 1961, Anna Halprin Archives, Museum of Performance + Design.
22. Lawrence Halprin, "A Discussion of *The Five-Legged Stool*," *San Francisco Chronicle*, April 29, 1962, 3, from Halprin Articles folder, Stuart Weitzman School of Architecture and Design Archives, The University of Pennsylvania, Philadelphia.
23. Ibid.
24. Ibid.
25. Anna Halprin, "Introduction to Movement Ritual One," in *Moving Toward Life: Five Decades of Transformational Dance*, ed. Rachel Kaplan (Middletown, CT: Wesleyan University Press/ University Press of New England, 1995), 37.
26. Anon., *Apartment 6*, undated program notes, from the Anna Halprin Archives, Museum of Performance + Design, San Francisco.
27. Anon., "The Play Will Be Real—That Is, There Will Be No Play," program notes for *Apartment 6*, Anna Halprin Archives, Museum of Performance + Design, San Francisco.
28. Ibid.
29. Beardsley, "Foreword," *Landscape Journal: Design Planning and Management of the Land*, 2.
30. Douglas Davis, "The Golden Voyage," in *Lawrence Halprin: Changing Places*, San Francisco Museum of Modern Art catalog, July 3–August 24, 1986, 60–69, 65.
31. Lawrence Halprin, *The Five-Legged Stool* (second draft), 3, in Halprin Articles folder, Stuart Weitzman School of Architecture and Design Archives, University of Pennsylvania, Philadelphia.
32. Ibid.
33. Postcard announcement for *Ten Myths*, September 1967, Collection of John Rockwell, Museum of Performance + Design, San Francisco.
34. Halprin, *Dancers Workshop*, 18.
35. Anna Halprin, "Mutual Creation," *Tulane Drama Review* 13, no. 1 (1968): 166, reproduced in Kaplan, ed., *Moving Toward Life*, 133.
36. Interview with Casey Sonnabend, conducted by Janice Ross, Santa Cruz, California, September 12, 2022.

238 NOTES

37. Interview with Anna Halprin, conducted by Janice Ross, Kentfield, California, February 19, 2001.
38. Interview with Rana Halprin, conducted by Janice Ross, Mill Valley, California, October 18, 2023.
39. Ibid.
40. Wilson, *Mid-Century Modernism and the American Body*, 125.
41. Ibid., 138.
42. Randolph T. Hester, "Scoring Collective Creativity and Legitimizing Participatory Design," *Landscape Journal: Design, Planning, and Management of the Land* 31, nos. 1–2 (2012): 136.
43. Ibid.
44. D'Amato, Alison, "Movement as Matter: A Practice-Based Inquiry into the Substance of Dancing," *Dance Reseaerch Journal* 53, no. 3 (December 2022): 69–86.
45. Interview with Anna Halprin, conducted by Janice Ross, Kentfield, California, May 17, 2000.
46. Hester, "Scoring Collective Creativity and Legitimizing Participatory Design," 135.
47. Lawrence Halprin and Anna Halprin quoted in Shelly Kale, "Stern Grove: 'Mystical' Gift to San Francisco," Experiments in Environment: The Halprin Workshops 1966–1971, accessed February 14, 2024, https://experiments.californiahistoricalsociety.org/53/.
48. Ibid.

Chapter 4

1. Caitlin Lempres Brostrom, *The Houses of William Wurster: Frames for Living* (Princeton, NJ: Princeton Architectural Press, 2011); Witold Rybcznski, "The Picture Frame, Not the Picture," *Canadian Architect*, February 1, 2014, https://www.canadianarchitect.com/the-pict ure-frame-not-the-picture/.
2. Lawrence Halprin, *A Life Spent Changing Places* (Philadelphia: University of Pennsylvania Press, 2011), 76.
3. Gordon Young, "William Wurster Was Arguably California's Most Significant Architect. So Why Hasn't Anyone Heard of Him?," *Metro: Silicon Valley's Weekly Newspaper*, January 18–24, 1996, accessed February 14, 2024, http://www.metroactive.com/papers/metro/01.18.96/wurs ter-9603.html; Sam Whiting, "Berkeley Architect Wraps Up William Wurster Book" [profile of Caitlin Lampres Brostom], *San Francisco Chronicle*, February 5, 2012, accessed February 14, 2024, https://www.sfgate.com/magazine/article/Berkeley-architect-wraps-up-William-Wurs ter-book-2969821.php.
4. In 1923, after a disastrous Berkeley Hills fire, the home was rebuilt using the still-standing original columns and the flagstone porches but closing in the walls; see Oral History with Sulgwynn and Charles Quitzow, Bancroft Library, University of California, Berkeley.
5. Interview with Lawrence Halprin, conducted by Stephen Steinberg, reel 17:4, Museum of Performance + Design, San Francisco.
6. Ibid., reel 17:5.
7. Young, "William Wurster Was Arguably California's Most Significant Architect."
8. Margaret Crawford, review of *An Everyday Modernism: The Houses of William Wurster*, by Marc Treib, *Journal of the Society of Architectural Historians* 55, no. 3 (1996): 328–30.
9. Ibid.
10. Interview with Rana Halprin, conducted by Janice Ross, Mill Valley, California, September 9, 2022.
11. Sonja Dümpelmann, "Let All Be Educated Alike Up to a Certain Point," *Places*, June 2022, accessed February 14, 2024, https://placesjournal.org/article/olmsted-booker-t-washing ton-landscape-architecture-education/?cn-reloaded=1. The profession continues to enforce divisions between the design of landscapes and the labor of their actual construction, valuing the one over the other.
12. Jenny Odell, *How to Do Nothing: Resisting the Attention Economy* (New York: Penguin Random House, 2019), 109.
13. Ibid., 8.
14. Interview with Rana Halprin, conducted by Janice Ross, Mill Valley, California, October 18, 2023.
15. Marc Treib, "From the Garden: Lawrence Halprin and the Modern Landscape," *Landscape Journal: The Design, Planning, and Management of the Land* 31, nos. 1–2 (2012): 6.
16. Sibyl Moholy-Nagy, *Native Genius in Anonymous Architecture* (New York: Horizon Press, 1957), 53.

NOTES 239

17. Ibid.
18. Interview with Simone Forti, conducted by Janice Ross, Los Angeles, California, August 5, 2001.
19. Anna Halprin, *San Francisco Dancers' Workshop*, ed. Hope Coffin, no. 5 (1970): 3, unpublished, private collection of Janice Ross. This is no. 5 out of an edition of 20.
20. Ibid., 7.
21. Ibid., 4.
22. Interview with Larry Reed, conducted by Janice Ross via phone, January 13, 2002; quoted in Janice Ross, *Anna Halprin: Experience as Dance* (Berkeley: University of California Press, 2007), 268.
23. Ticruit Hewell, "An Award for Multi-Racial Dance Research," *San Francisco Chronicle*, undated, from the Anna Halprin Collection, Museum of Performance + Design, San Francisco.
24. Anna Halprin, email to Janice Ross, June 23, 2004.
25. Quoted in Ross, *Anna Halprin*, 268.
26. George Nelson, *Chairs*, ed. and introduction by George Nelson (New York: Acanthas Press, 1994/1999 [1953]), 4.
27. Halprin, *A Life Spent Changing Places*, 134.
28. Ibid.
29. Alison Hirsch, "Facilitation and/or Manipulation: Lawrence Halprin and 'Taking Part,'" *Landscape Journal: Design, Planning, and Management of the Land* 31, nos. 1–2 (2012): 132.
30. Halprin, *A Life Spent Changing Places*, 152.
31. Lawrence Halprin, *Lawrence Halprin: Changing Places*, San Francisco Museum of Modern Art catalog, 1986, 137.
32. Lawrence Halprin, "Nature into Landscape into Art," notes for a paper, June 5, 1985, 12, Lawrence Halprin Collection, Stuart Weitzman School of Design, The Architectural Archives, University of Pennsylvania, Philadelphia.
33. Interview with Anna Halprin, conducted by Janice Ross, Kentfield, California, May 1, 2003.
34. Ibid.
35. Ibid.
36. Daria Halprin, email posting to six hundred Zoom attendees for the planetary dance tribute to Anna on the occasion of her one hundredth birthday.
37. Ibid.
38. Interview with Daria Halprin, conducted by Janice Ross, Kentfield, California, October 18, 2023.

Chapter 5

1. Paul Ryan, a photographer who was hired to document the workshop and who photographed Anna eating sand, said of this moment: "for me it was Anna taking it a step further—everyone was playing with sand and she wanted to take it a step further and eat sand." From interview with Paul Ryan, conducted by Janice Ross, Santa Monica, California, July 31, 2023.
2. Ibid.
3. Donlyn Lyndon interview, San Francisco Museum of Modern Art video, *The Sea Ranch: Architecture, Environment, and Idealism*, accessed February 14, 2024, https://www.yout ube.com/watch?v=hKUHfBfF-3c.
4. Anna Halprin and Rachel Kaplan, *Making Dances That Matter: Resources for Community Creativity* (Middletown, CT: Wesleyan University Press, 2019), 29.
5. Lawrence Halprin, *A Life Spent Changing Places* (Philadelphia: University of Pennsylvania Press, 2011), 130.
6. Ibid., 124.
7. Interview with Daria Halprin, conducted by Janice Ross, Kentfield, California, July 20, 2022.
8. Aldo Leopold, *A Sand Country Almanac: Essays on Conservation from Round River* (New York: Ballantine Books, 1970), 240.
9. Lawrence Halprin and Jim Burns, with Anna Halprin and Paul Baum, *Taking Part: A Workshop Approach to Collective Creativity* (Cambridge, MA: MIT Press, 1974), 187.
10. Scores for the Driftwood Village, The Sea Ranch, California, 1968, typescript 11. From the Lawrence Halprin Collection, Stuart Weitzman School of Design, The Architectural Archives, University of Pennsylvania, Philadelphia.
11. Anna Halprin, *Circle the Earth: Myth and Ritual through Dance and the Environment*, ed. Rachel Kaplan, 20. Unpublished workbook, private collection of Janice Ross.

240 NOTES

12. Halprin, *A Life Spent Changing Places*, 132.
13. Alison Bick Hirsch, *City Choreographer Lawrence Halprin in Urban Renewal America* (Minneapolis: University of Minnesota Press, 2014), 272.
14. Ibid., 63.
15. Interview with Lawrence Halprin, conducted by Stephen Steinberg, San Francisco, 1988, reel 18:16, private collection of Janice Ross.
16. "The Sea Ranch Is Ready," *San Francisco Examiner* advertisement, July 27, 1965, Environmental Design Archive, University of California, Berkeley.
17. Interview with Rana Halprin, conducted by Janice Ross, Mill Valley, California, October 18, 2023.
18. Jennifer Dunlop Fletcher and Joseph Becker, eds., Quote by Al Boeke as part of Acknowledgments, *The Sea Ranch: Architecture, Environment and Idealism* (Munich, London, New York: DelMonico Books, Prestel and San Francisco Museum of Modern Art, 2018), 14.
19. William Turnbull Jr., "Ecological Architecture," *Progressive Architecture*, May 1966. Moore Lyndon Turnbull Whitaker Collection, box 23, folder 418, from Environmental Design Archives, University of California, Berkeley.
20. Pamela Knight, "Design for Sport," *Sports Illustrated*, March 28, 1966, 46–52.
21. Ibid., 52.
22. Chip Lord and Curt Schreier, Ant Farm, "Building in Place," *The Sea Ranch: Architecture, Environment and Idealism*, ed. Jennifer Dunlop Fletcher and Joseph Becker (Munich, London, New York: DelMonico Books, Prestel and San Francisco Museum of Modern Art, 2018), 156.
23. Ibid., 156–57.
24. Ibid.
25. Ibid.
26. Curt Schreier and Chip Lord video interviews, as part of the SFMOMA exhibition, *The Sea Ranch: Architecture, Environment, and Idealism*, San Francisco Museum of Modern Art website, accessed February 10, 2024, https://www.youtube.com/watch?v=hKUHfBfF-3c.
27. Ibid.
28. Simon Sadler, "That Sea Ranch Feeling," in *The Sea Ranch: Architecture, Environment and Idealism*, ed. Jennifer Dunlop Fletcher and Joseph Becker (New York et al.: Del Monico Books and San Francisco Museum of Modern Art, 2018), 85–86.
29. Ibid.
30. Ibid.
31. Halprin et al., *Taking Part*, 178.
32. Ibid., 179.
33. Ibid., 195.
34. Donlyn Lyndon interview, San Francisco Museum of Modern Art video.
35. Patricia Leigh Brown, "Utopia by the Sea," *The New York Times*, December 12, 2008.
36. Interview with Anna Halprin, conducted by Janice Ross, Kentfield, California, August 3, 2016.
37. Sarah Williams Goldhagen, *Welcome to Your World: How the Built Environment Shapes Our Lives* (New York: Harper Collins Publishers, 2017), 196.
38. Kenneth L. Helphand, *Lawrence Halprin* (Athens: University of Georgia Press and Library of American Landscape History, 2017), 201.

Bibliography

Part I: Archival Materials, Interviews, and Unpublished Sources

Anon. *Apartment 6*. Program notes [undated]. Anna Halprin Archives, Museum of Performance + Design, San Francisco.

Anon. "Backyard Revolution: House Now Part of Whole Garden." *Vancouver Sun*, February 18, 1954, 2C. From Lawrence Halprin scrapbook. Halprin Family Collection.

Anon. "Cities Don't Have to Be Ugly." *Engineering News-Record*, November 7, 1968. Lawrence Halprin and Associates, Collected Articles and Photocopies.

Anon. "Landscaping a Small Plot." *Sunset Magazine*, December 1949. (Author and issue missing from clipping)

Anon. "*The Play Will Be Real—That Is, There Will Be No Play*." Program notes for *Apartment 6*, Anna Halprin Archives, Museum of Performance + Design, San Francisco.

Anon. Postcard announcement for *Ten Myths*. September 1967. Collection of John Rockwell, Museum of Performance + Design, San Francisco.

Anon. "The Sea Ranch Is Ready." *San Francisco Examiner* advertisement, July 27, 1965. Environmental Design Archive, University of California, Berkeley.

Blank, Carla. Interview with Carla Blank, conducted by Janice Ross via phone, June 22, 2004.

Brooks, Kenneth W. Letter from Kenneth W. Brooks, A.I.A., to Thomas Creighton, Editor. *Progressive Architecture*, September 24, 1957. From personal clipping scrapbooks of Lawrence Halprin. Lawrence Halprin Papers, The Architectural Archives, Stuart Weitzman School of Design, University of Pennsylvania, Philadelphia.

Church, Thomas, and Lawrence Halprin. *House Beautiful*, April 1948, 38–45. (Issue number missing from clipping). Lawrence Halprin clipping albums. Halprin Family Collection.

Diner, Hasia. "Hasia Diner Speaks about the Film *American Jerusalem*." Leo Baeck Institute, February 18, 2014. Accessed February 20, 2024. https://www.youtube.com/watch?v=vtl0 ISgs490.

Dollinger, Marc. Interview with Marc Dollinger, conducted online by Janice Ross, July 17, 2023.

Forti, Simone. Interview with Simone Forti, conducted by Janice Ross, Los Angeles, CA, August 5, 2001.

Halprin, Anna. "Bath." Undated choreographic notes, I. Anna Halprin Archives, Museum of Performance + Design, San Francisco.

Halprin, Anna. *Circle the Earth: Myth and Ritual Through Dance and the Environment*. Edited by Rachel Kaplan. Unpublished workbook. Private collection of Janice Ross.

Halprin, Anna. *Dancers Workshop*. 5 (circa 1968). [Self-published, limited edition of twenty handmade booklets about the Dancers' Workshop]. Private collection of Janice Ross.

Halprin, Anna. Email correspondence with Janice Ross, June 23, 2004.

Halprin, Anna. "The Four-Legged Stool." Unpublished production notes, 1961. Anna Halprin Archives, Museum of Performance + Design, San Francisco.

Halprin, Anna. Interview with Anna Halprin, conducted by Janice Ross, Kentfield, CA, November 11, 1995.

Halprin, Anna. Interview with Anna Halprin, conducted by Janice Ross, Kentfield, CA, April 8, 1999.

Halprin, Anna. Interview with Anna Halprin, conducted by Janice Ross, Kentfield, CA, May 17, 2000.

242   BIBLIOGRAPHY

Halprin, Anna. Interview with Anna Halprin, conducted by Janice Ross, Kentfield, CA, February 19, 2001.

Halprin, Anna. Interview with Anna Halprin, conducted by Janice Ross, Kentfield, CA, May 25, 2001.

Halprin, Anna. Interview with Anna Halprin, conducted by Janice Ross via phone, February 13, 2002.

Halprin, Anna. Interview with Anna Halprin, conducted by Janice Ross, Kentfield, CA, May 1, 2003.

Halprin, Anna. Interview with Anna Halprin, conducted by Ann Murphy. *In Dance*, January 1, 2013. Accessed February 20, 2024. https://dancersgroup.org/2013/01/parades-and-chan ges-over-the-past-43-years-an-interview-with-anna-halprin/.

Halprin, Anna. Interview with Anna Halprin, conducted by Janice Ross, Kentfield, CA, August 3, 2016.

Halprin, Anna. Interview with Anna Halprin, conducted by Janice Ross, Kentfield, CA, December 19, 2019.

Halprin, Anna. Interview with Anna Halprin, conducted by Janice Ross, Kentfield, CA, January 7, 2019.

Halprin, Anna. Personal conversation with Janice Ross, Kentfield, CA, December 3, 1993.

Halprin, Anna. *San Francisco Dancers' Workshop*. Edited by Hope Coffin. 5 (1970) [unpublished]. Private collection of Janice Ross.

Halprin, Anna, and Lawrence Halprin. Interview with Anna and Lawrence Halprin, conducted by Stephen Steinberg, 1991. Museum of Performance + Design, San Francisco. (For KQED documentary *Inner Landscapes*)

Halprin, Daria. Comments from *An Afternoon with Daria Halprin*. Video by Jens Wazel Photography. Kentfield, CA, April 2011. Accessed February 10, 2024. https://www.youtube.com/watch?v=iF9y4pfyD7Q.

Halprin, Daria. Email posting to 600 Zoom attendees for the Planetary Dance tribute to Anna, on the occasion of her one hundredth birthday, 2020.

Halprin, Daria. Interview with Daria Halprin, conducted by Janice Ross, Kentfield, CA, October 18, 2023.

Halprin, Daria. Interview with Daria Halprin, conducted by Janice Ross, Kentfield, CA, July 20, 2022.

Halprin, Lawrence. Architectural Records, c. 1933–2009. The Architectural Archives, University of Pennsylvania, Philadelphia.

Halprin, Lawrence. "A Discussion of *The Five-Legged Stool*." *San Francisco Chronicle*, April 29, 1962. Halprin Articles folder, Archives, University of Pennsylvania, Philadelphia.

Halprin, Lawrence. *The Five-Legged Stool* (Second draft). Halprin Articles folder, The Architecture Archives, University of Pennsylvania, Philadelphia.

Halprin, Lawrence. "Houses: The Space Factor." *Progressive Architecture*, May 1958, 95–103. From personal clipping album of Lawrence Halprin. (No issue number included)

Halprin, Lawrence. Interview with Lawrence Halprin, conducted by Stephen Steinberg, San Francisco, 1988. Private collection of Janice Ross.

Halprin, Lawrence. Interview with Lawrence Halprin, conducted by Janice Ross, San Francisco, October 16, 2000. Private collection of Janice Ross.

Halprin, Lawrence. Lawrence Halprin Papers, The Architectural Archives, University of Pennsylvania, Philadelphia.

Halprin, Lawrence. Lawrence Halprin Personal Papers, 1916–2009, The Architectural Archives, University of Pennsylvania, Philadelphia.

Halprin, Lawrence. "Letter to the Editor." *House Beautiful*, May 1948. Clipping from Lawrence Halprin scrapbooks. Halprin Family Collection (unpaginated).

Halprin, Lawrence. "Nature into Landscape into Art." Notes for a paper, June 5, 1985. Lawrence Halprin Collection, The Architectural Archives, University of Pennsylvania, Philadelphia.

BIBLIOGRAPHY 243

Halprin, Lawrence. Scores for the Driftwood Village, The Sea Ranch, California, 1968. Lawrence Halprin Collection, The Architectural Archives, University of Pennsylvania, Philadelphia.

Halprin, Rana. Interview with Rana Halprin, conducted by Janice Ross, Mill Valley, CA, September 1, 2021.

Halprin, Rana. Interview with Rana Halprin, conducted by Janice Ross, Mill Valley, CA, September 1, 2022.

Halprin, Rana. Interview with Rana Halprin, conducted by Janice Ross, Mill Valley, CA, September 9, 2022.

Halprin, Rana. Interview with Rana Halprin, conducted by Janice Ross, Mill Valley, CA, October 18, 2023.

Hewell, Ticruit. "An Award for Multi-Racial Dance Research." *San Francisco Chronicle*, undated. Anna Halprin Collection, Museum of Performance + Design, San Francisco.

Landor, Jo. Interview with Jo Landor, conducted by Janice Ross, San Francisco, August 14, 1991.

Leath, A. A. Interview with A. A. Leath, conducted by Janice Ross, Madison, WI, September 8, 1992.

Lyndon, Donlyn. Interview with Donlyn Lyndon, San Francisco Museum of Modern Art video, *The Sea Ranch: Architecture, Environment, and Idealism*. Accessed February 20, 2024. https://www.youtube.com/watch?v=hKUHfBfF-3c.

Monk, Meredith. Interview with Meredith Monk, conducted by Janice Ross, Palo Alto, CA, March 1, 2000.

Olin, Laurie. Donnell House video interview with Laurie Olin. The Cultural Landscape Foundation. October 5, 2007. Accessed February 10, 2024. https://www.youtube.com/watch?v=H6rMkpf_0kY.

Owen, Norton. Interview with Norton Owen, conducted by Janice Ross via phone, Beckett, MA, September 1, 2023.

Penn, Irving. Interview with Irving Penn, conducted by Janice Ross via phone, November 30, 1995.

Quitzow, Sulgwynn, and Charles Quitzow. Oral History. Bancroft Library, University of California, Berkeley.

Rainer, Yvonne. Interview with Yvonne Rainer, conducted by Stephen Steinberg. Janice Ross Papers, Museum of Performance + Design, San Francisco.

Rainer, Yvonne, and Anna Halprin. "Yvonne Rainer Interviews Anna Halprin." *Tulane Drama Review* 10, no. 2 (1965): 142–67.

Reed, Larry. Interview with Larry Reed, conducted by Janice Ross via phone, January 13, 2002.

Rosenbaum, Fred. Interview with Fred Rosenbaum, conducted by Janice Ross via phone, Brooklyn, NY, July 21, 2023.

Ryan, Paul. Interview with Paul Ryan, conducted by Janice Ross, Santa Monica, CA, July 31, 2023.

Schreier, Curt, and Chip Lord. San Francisco Museum of Modern Art interviews, *The Sea Ranch: Architecture, Environment, and Idealism*. Accessed February 10, 2024. https://www.youtube.com/watch?v=hKUHfBfF-3c.

Sonnabend, Casey. Interview with Casey Sonnabend, conducted by Janice Ross, Santa Cruz, CA, September 12, 2022.

Subotnick, Morton. Interview with Morton Subotnick, conducted by Janice Ross via phone, January 29, 1992.

Turnbull, William, Jr. "Ecological Architecture." *Progressive Architecture*, May 1966. Environmental Design Archives, University of California, Berkeley.

Additional archival materials, as noted in the image captions, come from the following collections: Lawrence Halprin Archives, Stuart Weitzman School of Design, The Architectural Archives, University of Pennsylvania; Graduate School of Design, Harvard University; The Cultural Landscape Foundation; Anna Halprin Archives and Janice Ross Papers, Museum of

244 BIBLIOGRAPHY

Performance + Design, San Francisco; Wharton Esherick Museum; F. W. Olin Library, Special Collections, Northeastern University (formerly Mills College, Oakland, California); and the private collection of Janice Ross.

Part II: Primary and Secondary Sources, Published

Anon. "Protests Then and Now: Keller Fountain at 50." Portland Parks Foundation. June 17, 2020. Accessed February 8, 2023. https://www.portlandpf.org/news/2020/6/17/cn5ny46k9yogw5npg1tkt1lubv36r9.

Bal-Blanc, Pierre. "Anna Halprin's Dance Deck." *Flash Art*, May 29, 2020. Accessed February 11, 2024. https://flash---art.com/2020/05/anna-halprins-dance-deck/.

Bal-Blanc, Pierre, and Lou Forster. "Anna Halprin." *Documenta 14: Daybook*. Kassel, Germany. Accessed February 14, 2024. https://www.documenta14.de/en/artists/13511/anna-halprin.

Beardsley, John. "Foreword." *Landscape Journal: Design, Planning, and Management of the Land* 31, nos. 1–2 (2012): 1–3.

Brannigan, Erin. *Choreography, Visual Art, and Experimental Composition, 1950s–1970s*. Abingdon and New York: Routledge, 2022. Brostrom, Caitlin Lempres. *The Houses of William Wurster: Frames for Living*. Princeton, NJ: Princeton Architectural Press, 2011.

Brown, Patricia Leigh. "Utopia by the Sea." *The New York Times*, December 12, 2008.

Cabanne, Pierre. *Dialogues with Marcel Duchamp*. Boston: Da Capo Press, 1987.

Certeau, Michel de. *The Practice of Everyday Life*. 3rd ed. Translated by Steven Rendall. Berkeley: University of California Press, 2011.

Cheng, Anne Anlin. *Second Skin: Josephine Baker and the Modern Surface*. Oxford: Oxford University Press, 2011.

Chrisman-Campbell, Kimberly. "The Curious History of Mommy-and-Me Fashion." *The Atlantic*, May 13, 2018.

Crawford, Margaret. Review of *An Everyday Modernism: The Houses of William Wurster*, by Marc Treib, *Journal of the Society of Architectural Historians* 55, no. 3 (1996): 328–30.

Davis, Douglas. "The Golden Voyage." In *Lawrence Halprin: Changing Places*. San Francisco Museum of Modern Art, 1986. Exhibition catalog.

Douglas, Helen. "Arch Lauterer on Dance in the Theatre." *Impulse* (1959): 39–42.

Dümpelmann, Sonja. "Let All Be Educated Alike Up to a Certain Point." *Places*, June 2022. Accessed February 14, 2024. https://placesjournal.org/article/olmsted-booker-t-washington-landscape-architecture-education/?cn-reloaded=1.

Foster, Catherine Osgood. "The Function of Theatre Is to Show the Word." *Impulse* (1959): 15–18.Halprin, Anna. *Moving toward Life: Five Decades of Transformational Dance*. Edited by Rachel Kaplan. Middletown, CT: Wesleyan University Press/University Press of New England, 1995.

Halprin, Anna. "Mutual Creation." *Tulane Drama Review* 13, no. 1 (1968): 163–74.

Halprin, Anna, and Rachel Kaplan. *Making Dances That Matter: Resources for Community Creativity*. Middletown, CT: Wesleyan University Press, 2019.

Halprin, Lawrence. *Cities*. New York: Reinhold Publishing Corporation, 1963.

Halprin, Lawrence. "Salute." *Impulse*. San Francisco (1959): 33.

Halprin, Lawrence. *A Life Spent Changing Places*. Philadelphia: University of Pennsylvania Press, 2011.

Halprin, Lawrence, Foreword by Henry T. Hopkins, Introduction by Helene Fried, Essays by Jim Burns, Douglas David, Dr. Joseph Henderson, Teddy Kollek, Robert F. Macguire III, Charles Moore and Phyllis Tuchman, *Lawrence Halprin: Changing Places*. San Francisco: Museum of Modern Art, 1986. Catalog for retrospective exhibition on the work of Lawrence Halprin.

BIBLIOGRAPHY 245

Halprin, Lawrence, Jim Burns, Anna Halprin, and Paul Baum. *Taking Part: A Workshop Approach to Collective Creativity*. Cambridge, MA: MIT Press, 1974.

Haraway, Donna. "Tentacular Thinking: Anthropocene, Capitalocene, Chthulucene." In *Staying with the Trouble: Making Kin in the Chthulucene*, 30–57. Durham, NC: Duke University Press, 2016.

Heathfield, Adrian. "Before Judson & Some Other Things." In *Judson Dance Theatre: The Work Is Never Done*, edited by Ana Janevski and Thomas J. Lax, 36–44. New York: Museum of Modern Art, 2018.

Helphand, Kenneth L. *Lawrence Halprin*. Athens: University of Georgia Press and Library of American Landscape History, 2017.

Hester, Randolph T. "Scoring Collective Creativity and Legitimizing Participatory Design." *Landscape Journal: Design, Planning, and Management of the Land* 31, nos. 1–2 (2012): 135–43.

Hirsch, Alison Bick. *City Choreographer: Lawrence Halprin in Urban Renewal America*. Minneapolis: University of Minnesota Press, 2014.

Hirsch, Alison Bick. "Facilitation and/or Manipulation: Lawrence Halprin and 'Taking Part.'" *Landscape Journal: Design, Planning, and Management of the Land* 31, nos. 1–2 (2012): 117–34.

Hollander, Ann. *Seeing through Clothes*. Berkeley: University of California Press, 1993.

Huxtable, Ada Louise. "Coast Fountain Melds Art and Environment." *The New York Times*, June 21, 1970.

Kale, Shelly. "Stern Grove: 'Mystical' Gift to San Francisco." California Historical Society. August 14, 2015. https://experiments.californiahistoricalsociety.org/53/

Kasson, John. Book review of *Free and Natural Nudity and the American Cult of the Body*, by Sarah Schrank. *American Historical Review* 126, no. 1 (2021): 356–57.

Knight, Pamela. "Design for Sport." *Sports Illustrated*, March 28, 1966, 46–52.

Kuh, Katherine, ed. *The Artist's Voice. Talks with Seventeen*. New York: Harper & Row, 1962.

Lang, Alexandra. "In California, a Marriage of Dance and Design." *The New York Times*, September 22, 2014. Accessed February 12, 2024. https://www.nytimes.com/2014/09/25/garden/in-california-a-marriage-of-dance-and-design.html. (For the print version, see Lang, "An Alliance of Dance and Design," *The New York Times*, September 25, 2014, D:2)

Leopold, Aldo. *A Sand Country Almanac: Essays on Conservation from Round River*. New York: Ballantine Books, 1970.

Levey, Amanda. "Anna Halprin Hits the Main Stage of the Art World." *Whitecliffe College of Arts and Design ANZATA* 12, no. 1 (2017): 17.

Lord, Chip, and Curt Schreier. *The Sea Ranch: Architecture, Environment and Idealism*. Edited by Jennifer Dunlop Fletcher and Joseph Becker. Munich, London, New York and San Francisco, DelMonico Books, Prestel and San Francisco Museum of Modern Art, 2018. Exhibition catalog.

Mckeon, Olive. "Rethinking Anna Halprin's *Parades and Changes*: Postmodern Dance, Racialized Urban Restructuring, and Mid-1960s San Francisco." *TDR: The Drama Review* 64, no. 2, T246 (2020): 117–37.

McPherson, Elizabeth, ed. *The Bennington School of the Dance: A History in Writings and Interviews*. Jefferson, NC: McFarland, 2013.

Moholy-Nagy, Sibyl. *Native Genius in Anonymous Architecture*. New York: Horizon Press, 1957.

Morris, M. D. "Tanglewood Music Shed." *Music Journal* 23, no. 5 (1965): 68.

Nead, Lynda. *The Female Nude: Art, Obscenity, and Sexuality*. Oxfordshire: Routledge, 1992.

Nelson, George. *Chairs*. Edited and introduction by George Nelson. New York: Acanthas Press, 1994/1999 [1953].

Odell, Jenny. *How to Do Nothing: Resisting the Attention Economy*. New York: Penguin Random House, 2019.

246 BIBLIOGRAPHY

Rainey, Reuben M. "The Choreography of Memory: Lawrence Halprin's Franklin Delano Roosevelt Memorial." *Landscape Journal: Design, Planning and Management of the Land* 31, nos. 1–2 (2012): 161–82.

Rosenbaum, Fred. *Cosmopolitans: A Social and Cultural History of the Jews of the San Francisco Bay Area.* Berkeley: University of California Press, 2009.

Rosenbaum, Fred. "Rabbi Saul White Pierced Armor of S.F.'s Assimilationist Mentality." *The Jewish News of Northern California*, December 22, 2003.

Ross, Janice. *Anna Halprin: Experience as Dance.* Berkeley: University of California Press, 2007.

Ross, Janice. *Moving Lessons: Margaret H'Doubler and the Beginning of Dance in American Education.* Madison: University of Wisconsin Press, 2000.

Rybcznski, Witold. "The Picture Frame, Not the Picture." *Canadian Architect*, February 1, 2014. Accessed February 10, 2024. https://www.canadianarchitect.com/the-picture-frame-not-the-picture/.

Sadler, Simon. "That Sea Ranch Feeling." In *The Sea Ranch: Architecture, Environment and Idealism.* Edited by Jennifer Dunlop Fletcher and Joseph Becker, 85–86. Munich, London, New York and San Francisco: DelMonico Books, Prestel and San Francisco Museum of Modern Art, 2018.

Schmid, Herta. "Samuel Beckett's Play, *QUAD*: An Abstract Synthesis of the Theatre." *Canadian American Slavic Studies* 22, nos. 1–4 (1988): 263–87.

Schrank, Sarah. *Free and Natural: Nudity and the American Cult of the Body.* Philadelphia: University of Pennsylvania Press, 2019.

Sklovski, Viktor. "Iskusstvo kak Priem" (Moscow, 1929). Translated by Benjamin Sher, "Art as Device," in *Theory of Prose*, introduction by Gerald L. Bruns. Elmwood Park, IL: Dalkey Archive Press, 1990.

Treib, Marc. "Donnell Garden." *Society of Architectural Historians Archipedia.* Accessed February 11, 2024. https://sah-archipedia.org/buildings/CA-01-097-0001.

Treib, Marc. "From the Garden Lawrence Halprin and the Modern Landscape." *Landscape Journal: The Design, Planning, and Management of the Land* 31, nos. 1–2 (2012): 5–28.

Tunnard, Christopher. *Gardens in the Modern Landscape.* London: Architectural Press, 1938.

Tuyl, Marian van. "Arch Lauterer—Poet in the Theatre." *Impulse* (1959): 3.

Whiting, Sam. "Berkeley Architect Wraps up William Wurster Book" [Profile of Caitlin Lampres Brostom]. *San Francisco Chronicle*, February 5, 2012. Accessed February 14, 2024. https://www.sfgate.com/magazine/article/Berkeley-architect-wraps-up-William-Wurster-book-2969821.php.

Wilson, Kristina. *Mid-Century Modernism and the American Body: Race, Gender, and the Politics of Power in Design.* Princeton, NJ: Princeton University Press, 2021.

Young, Gordon. "William Wurster Was Arguably California's Most Significant Architect. So Why Hasn't Anyone Heard of Him?" *Metro: Silicon Valley's Weekly Newspaper*, January 18–24, 1996. Accessed February 14, 2024. http://www.metroactive.com/papers/metro/01.18.96/wurster-9603.html.

Index

For the benefit of digital users, indexed terms that span two pages (e.g., 52–53) may, on occasion, appear on only one of those pages.

Figures are indicated by an italic *f* following the page number.

Abrahams, Andrew, 212–14, 215*f*
Alcatraz Island, 159–61
Ally: Janine Antoni, Anna Halprin, Stephen Petronio (exhibition), 229
Allyship and social justice, 112–13
Amerkanian, Charles, 122–25, 125*f*
Anna Halprin: At the Origin of Performance (exhibition), 229
Anna Halprin: Body Radical (exhibition), 229
Anna Halprin / Dancing at 96 (film), 229
Anna Halprin: Parades and Changes (exhibition), 229
   See also Parades and Changes
Ant Farm, The, 218–19
antisemitism, 76–77, 231n.13
Apartment 6, 150–51, 157–58, 157–58*f*, 159–61
Appia, Adolphe, 69–70
Aquatic Park, 159–61
Arab women, 60
Arts and Crafts movement, 5–6
Associated Council of the Arts, 107–8
Astaire, Fred, 42
Auditorium Forecourt. See Ira Keller Forecourt Fountain
Awaken, 222*f*, 225–26, 230
   film of, 229

Baker, Josephine, 108–10
Bal-Blanc, Pierre, 127–28
Barnes, Edward Larrabee, 16–17
Bath, The, 7–8, 34–35, 110, 119*f*, 120–21
Battery Street, 196–97
Bauhaus, 5, 16–29, 50–52, 61–63, 69–70, 148, 186
   Staatliches Bauhaus, 16–17
Bauhaus Staircase (*Bauhaustreppe*), 26–29, 28*f*, 52–54
Baum, Paul, 121–25, 125*f*, 220–21
Bay Regional Style, 179–80, 181–82, 217–18
Beardsley, John, 133–35

Beats, The, 76–77
Bennington College, 68, 69, 85–86, 88
   Armory, 82–84
   School of Dance, 82–84
Berkeley, 67–68
   See also University of California, Berkeley
Berkeley Hills, 238n.4
Berkshire Hills, 85–87, 88
Big Brother, 120–21
Birds of America, 102–5, 104*f*
Birth of Venus, The, 142–44, 146*f*
Black dancers and performers, 42, 189, 191–93
   See also race and racialization
Black Mountain College, 26–29
Blank, Carla, 113–14
Blank Placard Dance, 6, 56–57, 57*f*
Blum & Poe Gallery, 133–34*f*, 138*f*
Blunk, JB
   benches, 130–32, 142, 144–47, 167
   chairs, 8, 130–32, 137–39, 140, 142, 144*f*, 144–47, 183
   Cone bench, 132*f*, 134*f*
   designs by/style of, 8–9, 130–48
   discomfort of his furniture, 8–9, 130–48, 149–51, 153–54, 155–56, 170–71
   table, 137–39, 138*f*
   "Throne" chair, 8–9, 132*f*, 136–37, 142–44, 143*f*, 145*f*
   Thrones and Benches, 133*f*, 136–39, 142
Boeke, Al, 215–17, 217*f*
Bohemian (aesthetic), 212
Boland, Sunni, 106*f*
Boston, 16–17, 22–23
   Symphony Orchestra, 85–86
Botticelli, Sandro, 142–44, 146*f*
Bourdieu, Pierre, 12–14
Boynton, Florence Treadwell (and family), 180–81
Branch Dance, 126–27, 128*f*
Brannigan, Erin, 234n.48

248 INDEX

Breath Made Visible: Anna Halprin (film), 174*f*, 188*f*, 214*f*, 229
Breuer, Marcel, 16–17
Brooks, Kenneth W., 90–92
Brostom, Caitlin Lempres, 179–80
Brown, Patricia Leigh, 224
Brown, Trisha, 105–6, 106*f*, 168–70
Bust, The, 56–57

Cambridge, Massachusetts, 22–23
Cargo net, 52
Cascade Mountain Range (Western), 34–35, 37–38, 133–35
Cascading Stairs, 46–50, 47*f*
Castle & Cook, 215–17
Cave of the Heart, 140–41
Caygill Garden, 29–32, 31*f*
Centre Pompidou, 33*f*, 115*f*, 172*f*
de Certeau, Michel, 4, 18
Ceremony of Us, 9–10, 189–96, 191*f*, 220–21
Chairs. See Nelson, George
Cheng, Anne Anlin, 108–9, 111–12, 235n.83
Chicago, 76, 142
Chicago Art Institute, 26–29
Christian women, 60
Church and Associates, 75
Church, Thomas, 73, 74*f*, 75, 182
City of David, 60–61
Clytemnestra, 140–41
Cold War, 1–2, 4, 7–8, 76, 77
Coleman, Wanda, 192
Condominium One development, 219, 223–24
Congregation Beth Sholom, 77
   See also Jewish; Judaism
Conversations with Anna Halprin (film), 229
Copenhagen, 90–91
   Tivoli Gardens in, 90–91
Corbusier, Le, 127–28
Corinthian columns, 180
Counterculture, 111, 112–13, 120–21, 122, 208–9, 236n.93
Courtesan and the Crone, The, 230
COVID-19 pandemic, 199–200
Crawford, Margaret, 182–83
Crosten, William L., 234n.52
Cubist, 25
Cultural Landscape Foundation, The, 233n.23
Cunningham, Merce, 82, 87, 127–28, 168, 169*f*

Dallas, 233n.23
D'Amato, Alison, 170–71
Dance deck, 1, 2, 5–7, 8, 9, 19, 20*f*, 29, 33–34, 39, 41–42, 47*f*, 47–52, 58–59, 63–64, 65–85,

66–71*f*, 87, 88, 89–129, 90–96*f*, 100–2*f*, 106*f*, 159, 165, 166–69*f*, 166–67, 168–71, 173–75, 180–81, 208, 215–17, 218, 224–25, 233n.23, 234n.48, 235n.71, 236n.103
   See also Cunningham, Merce; Halprin, Anna; Kentfield; Lauterer, Arch
Dance Office, 127–28
Delphi, 175–76
Dessau, 16–17
Divisadero Street, 56–57, 113–14, 162, 165*f*, 189–90, 191*f*
Documenta 14, 127–28
Dollinger, Marc, 75–76, 112–13
Dome of the Rock, 60–61
Dom-Ino house, 127–28
Donnell, Dewey, 73
Donnell Gardens, 7–8, 73–75, 74*f*, 81–82
Driftwood Beach, 208–9
Driftwood Village, 202, 203–6*f*, 205, 210, 218–19, 221, 223–25
Druz women, 60
Duchamp, Marcel, 48
Duncan, Isadora, 180
Dutch door, 182–83

East Coast, 82–84, 87–88, 106–7
Eastern Europe, 19–22, 183–84
eco-consciousness, 5, 181–205
   See also Halprin, Lawrence
eco-literacy, 193–97
   See also Halprin, Lawrence
eco-modernism, 139–40
   See also Halprin, Lawrence
Ekman, June, 106*f*
Ellis Island, 19–22
Embodied cognition, 226–27
Emerging Ecologies: Architecture and the Rise of Environmentalism (exhibition), 224–25
Emerson, Ruth, 106*f*
Errand into the Maze, 140–41
Esalen Institute, The, 111–12
   See also Perls, Dr. Fritz
Esherick, Wharton, 5–6, 14–16, 15*f*
Esposizione, 52
Experiments in Environment: The Halprin Workshops (exhibition), 229
Experiments in Environment workshops, 10, 109–10, 110*f*, 121–22, 123–25*f*, 142–44, 180–202, 203–6*f*, 208–9, 210–11, 217–25, 222*f*, 226–27
   See also Halprin, Anna; Sea Ranch, The
Expressionist dance (*Ausdruckstanz*), 16–17

INDEX 249

FDR Memorial, 6, 9, 37–38, 42–43, 46f, 147–48, 196–97, 210–11
Fetzer, Caroline, 85–86
Five-Legged Stool, The, 9, 140, 150–51, 154–58, 155f, 156f, 159–61
Floating staircase, 5–7, 9, 11–14, 12–13f, 16, 38–39, 41–42, 49–50, 52–54, 130
  See also Kentfield
Florence, Italy, 146f
Flushing Meadows, 14–16
Fordism, 233n.22, 236n.93
Forecourt Fountain. See Ira Keller Forecourt Fountain
Forti, Simone, 105–6, 106f, 187–89
Foster, Catherine Osgood, 68–69
Four-Legged Stool, The, 140, 150–54, 152f, 155–58
Franz, Joseph, 85–87
Freeway Park, 9–10, 133–35, 135f, 159, 161, 194–96, 195f, 197–99
Funk art, 140

Gardens without Walls. See Birds of America
Gelman, Susie Goldman, 61f
Gerber, Ruedi, 174f, 188f, 214f, 222f
German modernism, 5, 16–17
Germany, 16–17, 26–29, 115–16, 127–28
Gestalt psychology/therapy, 111–12, 159, 161–62, 189–90, 192
Ghirardelli Square, 9, 140, 159–61, 160f
Glover, Jerrie, 106f
Golden Gate Bridge, 76
Golden Gate Park, 236n.103
Goldhagen, Sarah Williams, 226
Gold Rush (era), 77, 113, 196–97
Graham, John, 53f, 103–5, 104–6f, 151–52, 155, 157–59, 157f
Graham, Martha, 82, 140–41, 141f
Graham Foundation, The, 142
Grateful Dead, 120–21
Grecian, 175–76
Greek (culture), 35–36, 180
Greek theatre (aesthetic and design), 166–67, 168–70, 173–75
Groat, Jenny Hunter, 187
Gropius, Walter, 16–17, 24–26, 26–27f
  See also Bauhaus
Gualala River, 208–9
Gualala State Beach, 208–9

Haas Promenade, The, 60, 61f
Habitus, 12–14
Hahn, Kim, 53f, 113–14

Haight-Ashbury, 113–14, 162, 192
Halprin, Anna or Ann (née Hannah Dorothy Schuman)
  aging/aging body in dance, 60–61, 63–64, 111–12, 139–40, 142, 171–73, 199–200
  audience participation and active spectatorship, 131–36, 149–65, 167, 170, 175–76, 192–93, 194–96, 202–5, 225–26
  cancer, 171–72, 235n.71
  challenging hierarchy, 78
  community in dance, 77–78
  death of, 4
  family life and motherhood, 1–2, 3, 5, 16, 22, 97–101, 102–3, 106–7
  healing and therapeutic approach, 6–7, 189–90
  improvisation and spontaneity, 1–2, 77–78, 89–90, 101, 105–7, 118f, 189–90, 202, 225–26
  influences on, 5, 12–14, 16–17, 23, 24, 39, 47–48, 60–61, 84–85, 88, 93–94, 101, 132–33, 137–39, 159, 170–71, 175–76, 179–80
  interdisciplinarity of, 23–26, 128–29, 142, 220–21
  naturalist or holistic aesthetic of, 6, 80–81, 84–85, 100–1, 108–9, 197–201, 205–6, 209–10, 218–19, 221–23, 224–26, 227, 239n.1
  rituals of, 212, 214f, 221–23
  "trust walk" exercise, 54–56, 54f
  workshops of, 39–41, 50, 52–54, 54f, 105–8, 106–10f, 109–11, 113–14, 120–26, 123–25f, 142–44, 150–51, 162–63, 165f, 168–70, 189–90, 191f, 202–5, 206f, 210–11, 218, 219–20, 221–25, 222f, 226–27, 239n.1
  writings by, 92–93, 151, 153, 154, 158, 162–63, 189, 239n.17
  See also Dance deck; Experiments in Environment workshops; nudity
Halprin, Daria, 16, 19, 20f, 47–53f, 80f, 97–99, 98–100f, 102–6, 104f, 112, 119–23f, 122, 125–26, 136–39, 142–44, 145f, 166f, 199–201, 202, 208, 212, 214–15, 239n.36
Halprin, Lawrence or Larry
  death of, 4, 60, 142, 175–76, 225
  ecological approach, 5, 18, 133–35, 139–40, 159, 193–97, 181–205, 210–11, 215–19, 224–25, 226, 227
  education and training, 16–29, 148, 186
  failing eyesight, 63
  family life, 3, 5, 16, 22, 91–92, 97–100, 105–6, 231n.13

250   INDEX

Halprin, Lawrence or Larry (*cont.*)
  garden designer, 3–4, 19, 29–32, 40*f*, 42,
    47–48, 73–75, 79–80, 184
  influences on, 2, 5, 6, 12–14, 16–29, 39,
    42–43, 55–56, 63, 88, 89, 93–94, 137–39,
    144–46, 170–71, 173–75, 179–80, 186–
    87, 210–11
  military service of, 17–18, 42–43, 208
  participatory and kinesthetic quality of
    designs, 2–3, 38–39, 131–36, 142, 144–46,
    147–48, 150, 159–62, 165, 167, 170, 173–
    75, 193–96, 219–20, 223–24, 226
  philosophy of design, 8–9, 18, 49–50, 55–
    56, 75, 79–80, 81, 170, 194–96, 210–12,
    220, 223–24
  photography by, 20*f*, 100*f*, 106*f*, 166–69*f*,
    168, 207*f*
  processional quality of designs, 37–39, 43,
    55–56, 55*f*, 63, 196–97
  repurposing of public and urban space, 35–
    37, 77–78, 194–96
  use of waterfalls and fountains, 5–6, 29–35,
    31*f*, 34–35*f*, 36–37, 38–39, 42–47, 44–46*f*,
    61–63, 194–96, 197*f*
  writings by, 19, 38–39, 49, 92, 122, 154, 161,
    177–79, 186, 193–94, 220, 223–24
  See also eco-consciousness; eco-literacy; eco-
    modernism; urban renewal
Halprin, Rana, 16, 19, 29, 97–99, 98–100*f*, 102–
  3, 105–6, 112, 122, 123*f*, 125–26, 133–35,
  136–37, 166*f*, 166–67, 182–83, 184, 212
Hangar, 10, 187–89, 188*f*
Haraway, Donna, 4
Hardoy (butterfly) chair, 80*f*, 97–99, 148
Hartford, Connecticut, 117–20
Harvard University, 226–27
  Graduate School of Design (GSD), 16–29,
    26–27*f*, 50–52, 148
HBCUs (historical Black colleges and
  universities), 183–84
H'Doubler, Margaret, 7–8, 16–17, 24, 101–2,
  105–6, 115–16, 235n.72
Healing Power of Dance (television
  documentary), 229
Heathfield, Adrian, 126–27
Heick, William, 187–89, 188*f*
Heinemann, Sue, 50
Hell's Angels, 120–21
Henry J. Leir Outdoor Stage/The Marcia &
  Seymour Simon Performance Space, 88,
  232n.1, 234n.50
  See also Shawn, Ted
Herman Miller furniture company, 148–49

Hester, Randolph T., 170, 173–75
Hickey, Patric, 162–63
Hill, Martha, 88
Hille, R. Thomas, 181–82
Hilton Hotel, 107–8
Hirsch, Alison, 193–94, 210–11
Holding Company, 120–21
Hollander, Ann, 235n.84
Hollywood, 42
Holm, Hanya, 82
Holocaust, 76–77
House Beautiful magazine, 73, 116, 167
Howard, Laura, 83*f*
Hubbard, Henry, 17–18
Hubernack, Vladimir, 120
Hudnut, Joseph, 16–17
Human Potential Movement, 111–12, 159
Humphrey, Doris, 32, 82
Hunter College, 120, 236n.98
Hunters Point Naval Shipyard, 159–61
Hurva Synagogue, 60–61
Huxtable, Ada Louis, 36–37

Intensive Care: Reflections on Death and Dying,
  171–72, 172*f*
Interstate Five Freeway, 194–96, 195*f*, 230
interwar, 5
In the Kitchen with Anna (film), 229
In the Studio with Anna Halprin (film), 229
Inverness, California, 144–46
Ira Keller Forecourt Fountain, 6, 33–36, 35–37*f*,
  37–39, 56–57
Isamu Noguchi Foundation and Museum, The,
  141*f*
Israel, 60, 61*f*, 224
Italian, 35–36, 52, 168

Jacob's Pillow, 85–87, 88, 232n.1, 234n.50
  School at, 232n.1
Janine Antoni and Anna Halprin: Paper Dance
  (exhibition), 229
Japan, 55*f*
Japanese pavilion buildings, 186
Jaques-Dalcroze, Émile, 69–70
Jerusalem, 60–61, 61*f*
Jewish
  European Jewry, 76–77
  heritage, 60–61
  household, 3
  identity, 75–76, 112–13, 183
  immigrants, 19–22, 183–84, 231n.13
  Jewish American, 1, 72–73, 76–77, 112–13,
    173–75, 231n.13

neighborhood, 35–36 (*see also* Marin; San Francisco)
people, 75–76, 113
rituals and holidays, 139–40, 223
women, 60, 108–9
See also Judaism
Johnson, Philip, 17–18
Joseph Esherick & Associates, 215–17, 217*f*
See also Esherick, Joseph
Journey in Sensuality: Anna Halprin and Rodin (documentary film), 222*f*, 229
Judaism, 75–77, 223
Orthodox, 76
Judson Dance Theater, 126–27, 127–28*f*
Judson Memorial Church, 126–27
Jungian psychology, 140–41, 161–62, 210–11

Kansas, 144–46
Kassel, 127–28
Katz, Michael, 119*f*
Kent, Adaline, 73–75
Kentfield, 8–9, 12–14*f*, 21*f*, 30*f*, 33–34, 40*f*, 64*f*, 66*f*, 79–80, 93–96*f*, 106*f*, 119*f*, 125*f*, 128–29, 131–32*f*, 139*f*, 143–45*f*, 157–58, 166*f*, 173–75, 178–79*f*, 180–81, 183, 221
Halprin home in, 1, 4, 5–8, 9–10, 11–14, 12–14*f*, 19–22, 21*f*, 24–25, 29, 30*f*, 33–34, 40*f*, 64*f*, 66*f*, 71*f*, 79–80, 93–96*f*, 106*f*, 119*f*, 125*f*, 131–32*f*, 139*f*, 143–44*f*, 148, 166*f*, 173–75, 178–79*f*, 184, 200–1, 206–8, 212, 214–15, 224, 225–26, 227
Kent State University, 36
Kibbutz, 224
King Jr., Dr. Martin Luther, 189
Korean War, 144–46
KQED, 193
Kreutzberg, Harald, 16–17

Ladders. *See* scaffolds
Land ethic. *See* Leopold, Aldo
Landor, Jo, 114–15
Lanz of Salzberg Tyrolean dress, 97–99
Lathrop, Welland, 97
Lauterer, Arch, 6–7, 67–70, 81–86, 83*f*, 88–89, 91–92, 95, 127–28, 234n.52
Leath, A.A., 53*f*, 105–6, 106*f*, 126–27, 151–52, 155, 157–58, 157–58*f*, 187
Leistiko, Norma, 187–89
Leopold, Aldo, 209
Levey, Amanda, 59–60
Levi's Plaza, 9, 147*f*, 159, 161, 196–99, 197*f*
Levi Strauss Company, 196–97
Levi Strauss jeans, 196–97

loamy stairs, 50, 51*f*
Look Magazine, 120–21
Lord, Chip, 218, 219–20
Los Angeles, 133–34*f*, 138*f*, 189, 192, 193
South Central, 192
Lovejoy Fountain (Park), 33–35, 34*f*, 36–37, 38–39
Luening, Otto, 69
Lunch, 107–8
Lyndon, Donlyn, 223–24

Macel, Christine, 58–59
MacFadden, Bernarr, 115–16
Marathon Oil Company, 73
Marin, 29, 66–67, 75–76, 112–13, 212, 219–20
Civic Center, 173, 174*f*
County, 8–9, 19–22, 58*f*, 76, 77, 81–82, 112–13, 130–31, 173
Dance Children's Dance Cooperative, 102–3
Mark Taper Forum, 192
Market Street, 56–57
Massachusetts, 85–87
Maybeck, Bernard, 180
McKeon, Olive, 231n.13, 233n.22–233n.23, 236n.93
Mills College, 67–68, 82–84, 83*f*
Mill Valley, 57–58, 76, 79–80, 80*f*, 148
Moderna Museet, 53*f*
Moholy-Nagy, Lázló, 186
Moholy-Nagy, Sibyl, 186
"Mommy and me" fashion, 97–99, 98*f*
Monk, Meredith, 105–7, 111
Moore, Charles, 207*f*, 212
Moore, Lyndon, Turnbull & Whitaker, 215–17, 217*f*
See also Moore, Charles; Turnbull, William
Morning with Anna, A (film), 229
Morris, M.D., 86–87
Morris, Robert, 105–6, 113–14
"Motation," 8–9, 49–50, 147–48
Mount of Olives, 60–61
Mount Tamalpais, 2, 14–16, 19–22, 50, 57–58, 105–6, 181–82
State Park, 57–58
Munari, Bruno, 168
Museum of Modern Art (San Francisco), 159–61
Museum of Modern Art (New York), 126–27, 127–28*f*, 224–25
Muybridge, Eadweard, 48

Nachtkultur, 7–8, 115–16, 117
Nascita di Venere. See Birth of Venus, The

252 INDEX

National Park Service, 61–63
Native Genius in Anonymous Architecture. See
    Moholy-Nagy, Sibyl
Nazis, 16–17
Nead, Lynda, 235n.86
Nelson, George, 148–49, 167–68
Neo-Marxism, 233n.22–233n.23
New England, 87
New York, 48, 52–54, 105–7, 120, 126–27, 141*f*,
    180–81, 186–87, 193–94
New York, New York, 193–94
New York Times, The, 36–37, 142, 143*f*, 224
New York World's Fair (1940), 14–16, 15*f*
Nicholas Brothers, 42
Night Journey, 140–41, 141*f*
Nikolais, Alwin, 88–89
Noguchi, Isamu, 140–41, 141*f*
North Beach (San Francisco neighborhood),
    151, 236n.103
North Park Shopping Center, 233n.23
Novak, Yani, 53*f*
Nude Descending a Staircase, No. 2, 48
Nudism in Modern Life. See Parmelee, Maurice
nudity, or the nude body in dance, 1–2, 48, 78,
    103–5, 108–26, 110–15*f*, 123–24*f*, 142–44,
    197–99, 224–26, 235n.83, 235n.85–
    235n.86, 235n.88, 235n.91, 236n.98,
    236n.103
    See also Nachtkultur

Oakland, 82–84, 180
Odell, Jenny, 184
Odessa, 19–22
Ohio National Guard, 36
Olin, Laurie, 47–48, 73
Olmsted, Frederick Law, 183–84
Olympic Mountains, 194–96
On the Town, 193–94
Orinda, California, 29–32, 31*f*
Owen, Norton, 86–87

Pacific Ocean, 10, 117, 208–9
Palmer, Lynn, 151, 155
Parades and Changes, 6, 7–8, 32–33, 33*f*, 50–52,
    53*f*, 102–5, 110–14, 115*f*, 117–20, 142, 221,
    230, 233n.22, 236n.93
Paris, France, 33*f*, 115*f*, 172*f*
Parker, Terre, 222*f*, 225–26
Parmelee, Maurice, 116
Partch, Harry, 67–68
Partridge, Ron, 29–32, 31*f*
PBS, 193
Peace Walk, 60–61, 61*f*, 230

Penn, Irving, 120–21
People on a Slant, 187
Pera, Paul, 106*f*
Perls, Dr. Fritz, 111–12, 189–92, 235n.88
Pettygrove Park, 33–34
    place, 34–35
Planetary Dance, 50–52, 57–59, 58–59*f*, 230,
    239n.36
Planetary Dance for Ukraine (film), 229
Playhouse Repertory Theater (San Francisco),
    151, 152–55*f*, 153–54, 157*f*, 157–58
Portland, 32–33, 34*f*, 34–36, 35*f*
Portland Open Space Sequence, 32–39, 37*f*, 133–
    35, 151, 154, 159
postwar (post-World War II period), 1, 3, 4, 5,
    7–8, 26–29, 65–66, 72–73, 76–77, 97–99,
    116, 117–20, 144–46, 148, 149–50, 167
Practice of Everyday Life, The, See de
    Certeau, Michel
"Prelude" stairs, 29–42, 30*f*, 46–47
primitivism, 108–9
problem-solving, 23, 208–9, 220–21
Processions, 6, 50–52
Progressive Architecture, 90–92, 215–17

race and racialization, 5, 22–23, 72–73, 108–10,
    114, 117–20, 183–86, 189–93, 220
    See also Black dancers and performers;
    Jewish; White/Whiteness
*Radical Bodies: Anna Halprin, Simone Forti,
    and Yvonne Rainer in California and New
    York, 1955–1972* (exhibition), 229
Rainer, Yvonne, 52–54, 105–6
Ravine Way, 79–80, 103
Reed, Larry, 189–90
religion and spirituality, 75–76
    See also Jewish; Judaism
Remembering, 230
Remembering Lawrence, 230
Renaissance, 36–37, 142–44
Returning Home, 215*f*
Reynolds, Richard, 215–17
Richard and Rhoda Goldman Promenade, 61*f*
Richmond District, 77
Riley, Terry, 105–6
Ririe, Shirley, 106*f*
Robinson, Bill Bojangles, 42
Rodin, Auguste, 225–26
Rogers, Ginger, 42
Roma, 35–36
Romantic, 29–32
Roosevelt, President Franklin Delano, 42–43
Rosenbaum, Elana, 60

Rosenbaum, Fred, 76–77
Rosh Hashanah, 223
    See also Jewish; Judaism
Ross, Charles, 53*f*
Roth, William, 159–61
Rudolph, Paul, 17–18
Ryan, Paul G., 142–44, 202–5, 239n.1

Saarinen, Eero, 85–87
Sadler, Simon, 219–20
Sand County Almanac, A. See Leopold, Aldo
San Francisco, 56–57, 75–76, 97, 107–8, 113–
    14, 137–39, 151, 152*f*, 156*f*, 159–61, 160*f*,
    165*f*, 173–75, 175*f*, 180–81, 187, 189–92,
    191*f*, 196–97, 197*f*, 215–17, 218–19, 221,
    236n.93, 236n.98
    Airport, 187–89
    Bay, 2, 9–10, 19–22, 21*f*, 49, 66–67, 67*f*, 159–
        61, 184, 187–89, 188*f*, 206–8
    Bay Area, 29–32, 47–48, 75–77, 79–80, 87,
        113–14, 179–82, 202–5, 236n.103
    Civic Center, 56–57
    Playhouse (*see* San Francisco Repertory
        Theater)
    Police Department, 56–57
    suburb of, 1, 75–76, 211–12
San Francisco Chronicle, The, 142, 144*f*,
    154, 191–92
San Francisco Dancers' Workshop, 56–57,
    102–3, 120–21, 162–63, 165*f*, 189–90, 191*f*,
    237n.17
San Pablo Bay, 73–75
Santa Cruz, California, 182
Santos Meadow, 58*f*
Sarah Lawrence College, 82–84
Sausalito, 79–80, 120–21
scaffolds, 6, 52–54, 154
Schlemmer, Oskar, 23, 24–29, 28*f*, 52–54, 69–
    70, 232n.23
Schreier, Curt, 218–20
Schuman, Isadore, 19–22
Schuman, Jack (uncle to Anna Halprin),
    76, 79–80
Scores (Anna and Larry Halprin's method of
    written/verbal notation), 58–60, 59*f*, 103,
    121–22, 127–28, 142, 153–54, 162–65,
    209–10, 215–17, 239n.10
Sea Ranch, The (Halprin home), 4, 10, 117,
    118*f*, 139–40, 148, 173–75, 198–200*f*, 200–
    1, 202, 203–7*f*, 205–9, 211–27, 213–22*f*
Seattle, 133–35, 135*f*, 159, 161, 194–96, 195*f*
    Park Commission, 194–96
    Tacoma Airport, 194–96

Sender, Ramon, 113–14
Seniors Rocking, 9, 173–75, 174*f*, 230
    film of, 229
Serge Koussevitzky Music Shed, 86–87
Shawn, Ted, 85–86, 232n.1
    Theatre, 86–87, 232n.1
Shklovsky, Viktor, 107
Sierras or High Sierras (mountain range in
    California and Nevada), 33–34, 37–38,
    39–41, 42–43, 44–45*f*, 46–47, 63, 105–6,
    133–35, 196–97, 210–11
Sigmund Stern Grove, 9, 173–76, 175*f*
Skeleton (human) or skeletal, 6, 16–17, 101–
    2, 102*f*
Sling chairs, 137, 139*f*, 148
social class, 1, 3, 22–23, 71–72, 75, 79–80, 97–
    99, 112–13, 116, 202–5, 220, 224
Song of Songs, 230
Sonnabend, Casey, 163–65
Sonoma, 74*f*, 75
    Hills, 73
Source, The, 33–35, 36–37, 38–39
Spatial bricolage, 2–3
Spirit of Place, 175*f*, 175–76, 230
Spokane, Washington, 90–91
Sports Illustrated, 217–18
Stanford University, 234n.52
    Dinkelspiel Auditorium, 234n.52
Steep stairs, 50–60
Stern, Rosalie M., 173–75
Stern, Sigmund, 173–75
Still Dance, 9–10, 111–12, 197–200, 198*f*
    Tree Series section, 198*f*
Stockbridge, 85–87
Stockholm, 32–33, 53*f*, 111–12, 113–14
Stormy Weather, 42
Strauss, Lisa, 106*f*
Stubblefield, Eeo, 111–12, 197–99, 198*f*,
    235n.89
Studio Watts, 184–85, 189, 191*f*, 191–93
Subotnick, Morton, 113–14, 153
Sullivan, Andrew, 173–75
Sunset Magazine, 79–80
Sweden, 32–33, 52, 53*f*, 236n.98
    See also Stockholm
synagogues, 35–36

"Taking Part" summer workshops, 7–8
Tanglewood, 85–87
Tape Music Center, The, 113–14
Tashlich, 223
    See also Jewish; Judaism
Tayelet, 60

254 INDEX

Teatro la Fenice, 52
Temple, Shirley, 42
Ten Myths, The, 9, 161–65, 165*f*
    Myth One: Creation, 162–63
    Myth Seven: Carry, 163–65
    Myth Two: Atonement, 161–62, 165*f*
"Tentacular thinking," 4
"Throne" chair. *See* Blunk, JB
Treib, Marc, 73
Triadic Ballet (Triadisches Ballett), 24–25, 26–29, 69–70
Tulane University, 218
    School of Architecture, 218
Turnbull, William, 209*f*, 212
Tzvetin, Angelica Danadjieva, 194–96

Uffizi Gallery, 146*f*
Union Square, 206–8
Union Street, 187
University of California, Berkeley, 73, 170, 180
    College of Environmental Design, 73, 182
University of California, Los Angeles (UCLA), 50–52, 144–46
University of Wisconsin-Madison, 16–17, 22–23, 24, 105–6, 235n.72
Urban renewal, 5, 35–37, 159–61, 210–11
    See also Halprin, Lawrence or Larry; Hirsch, Alison

Venetian Arsenal, 58–59
Venice, 52, 59*f*
    St. Mark's Square (Piazza San Marco), 90–91
Venice Biennale, 52, 58–59, 59*f*
Vermont, 68, 85–86
Victorian windows, 193–94
Vietnam War, 36, 219–20
Visual empathy, 132–33, 135–36

Wadsworth Atheneum Museum of Art, 117–20
Ward, Willis, 106*f*
War Room, The. *See FDR Memorial*
Washington, D.C., 37–38, 42–43

West Coast, 18, 22, 73, 87, 117, 120–21, 159
White/Whiteness, 1, 71–73, 97–99, 108–9, 113, 116, 117–20, 183–84, 189–92, 193, 202–5, 224
    See also Jewish; race and racialization; social class
Wigman, Mary, 16–17
Williams, Paul, 72–73
Wilson, Kristina, 72–73, 97, 132–33
Windows of Halprin home, 9–10
    connection to nature, 177–79, 182, 184–85, 199–201, 200*f*
    expansive view of, 181–82, 185*f*
    mode of focusing/framing reflected in Anna Halprin's dances, 177–79, 181–82, 184, 186–93, 196–97
    modernist design of, 177–79, 178–79*f*, 184–85
    racial privilege of, 183
    welcoming quality of, 186, 208
    See also Wurster, William
Windsor (private girls' school), 22–23
Women's Peace Walk. See Peace Walk
Works Progress Administration, 173–75
World War II, 76–77, 82–84, 159–61, 208
Wright, Frank Lloyd, 72–73, 148–49
Wuppertal, 26–29, 232n.23
Wurster, Bernardi, and Emmons (architectural firm), 14–16, 19, 159–61
Wurster, Catherine Bauer, 182
Wurster, William, 3–4, 19, 177–80, 181–83, 184–87
    See also Windows of Halprin home

Yosemite Falls, 61–63, 131–32
    Lower Yosemite Fall, 61–63, 62*f*
    Upper Yosemite Fall, 61–63
Yosemite Falls Corridor, The, 61–64, 210–11
Yosemite National Park, 62*f*
Young, La Monte, 50–52, 105–6

Zionism, 75, 76–77

The manufacturer's authorised representative in the EU for product safety is Oxford
University Press España S.A. of El Parque Empresarial San Fernando de Henares,
Avenida de Castilla, 2 – 28830 Madrid (www.oup.es/en or product.safety@oup.com).
OUP España S.A. also acts as importer into Spain of products made by the manufacturer.

Printed in the USA/Agawam, MA
May 2, 2025

886845.014